"Finish it," some part of him said.

Kill myself, he thought. *God knows, no one else can.*

"No," that part of him said again. "Finish it."

Finish what? Lynan hunted down the thought.

Finish Silona. It was the only way he could be saved.

He slid out of the bed and dressed quickly. He found his weapons under his clothes and strapped them on. He stopped at the door. The Red Hands would follow him. They would never let him be. They would die for him.

"No one else will die for me," he said, and went to the window. He eased it open and lightly jumped outside. He was in the courtyard, and could see Red Hands posted at each corner. It was too dark for them to see him. Slowly, quietly, he made his way from the courtyard to the stables. He went behind the stables to the feeding yard and found a good Chett mare. The horse smelled him and started whinnying, but he held its head without hurting it and spoke to it and let it sniff the back of his hand and then his hair. He gathered a second mare the same way, and chose two bridles from some hanging from the yard fence, fitted them around the horses' heads, and led them out of the yard. He snuck back into the stable and took a saddle and blanket, returned to the horses, buckled one with the gear, and mounted. Holding tightly onto the reins of both horses, he kicked the one under him into a gallop, charging out of the palace before any of the guards could challenge him.

Through the dark Lynan Rosetheme rode, east and then south, across the Barda River and deep into enemy territory.

The Keys of Power

INHERITANCE

FIRE AND SWORD

SOVEREIGN

SOVEREIGN

Book Three of *The Keys of Power*

SIMON BROWN

DAW BOOKS, INC.

DONALD A. WOLLHEIM, FOUNDER
375 Hudson Street, New York, NY 10014

ELIZABETH R. WOLLHEIM
SHEILA E. GILBERT
PUBLISHERS
http://www.dawbooks.com

First Printing, October 2004
1 2 3 4 5 6 7 8 9 10

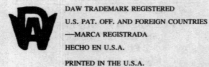

For the scattered band—Mark Connolly, Keith Dencio, Martin Hemsley, Peter Kramer, Peter Livingston, Paul Passant, and John Reid.

ACKNOWLEDGMENTS

As always, I owe a great debt to my first readers, Alison Tokley and Sean Williams, whose patience and perseverance are legendary.

My editors—Julia Stiles, Stephanie Smith, and Debra Euler—performed miracles with the text. Any remaining faults are due entirely to my own efforts.

My agents, Garth Nix and Russell Galen, have performed wonders on my behalf.

Thank you all.

IN the hour before first light, Lynan Rosetheme, outlaw prince of Grenda Lear, stood alone in the chill morning air. His white face was turned up to the sky, but his eyes were closed. He could smell the newly turned earth of many graves, and a little farther, the dryer, more pungent smell of horses. Some distance away he could smell humans, thousands and thousands of them—his own Chetts within a league or two, his enemy perhaps fifteen leagues south, and a large number unexpectedly north of his position.

He felt the softest of winds blowing around him, a cool westerly, and the wind brought the sound of something else he was not expecting. Cavalry. His eyes blinked open and for a moment he felt dizzy. The stars above wheeled in the sky and he had to spread his feet to remain steady. He brought his gaze down and saw the dark shape of Jenrosa sitting at the head of Kumul's grave. He heard someone behind him and turned quickly. It was Korigan, the tall, golden-skinned queen of the Chetts.

"You are mourning your friend," she said.

Lynan shook his head. "No." He looked back, then, at Kumul's grave and Jenrosa. It still seemed unbelievable to him that his friend's body was under that mound; mere earth—mere death, for that matter—could not vanquish the giant warrior, the most famous soldier in all of Grenda Lear and Lynan's teacher and guardian.

"I hear riders coming from the west," he told Korigan. "Many hundred."

"Areava's knights?" she hissed urgently. "Again? How did they get around us?"

"Not knights. Chetts." He handled the Key of the Sword that

hung around his neck, still dark with the blood of Sendarus. It felt absurdly light.

"Eynon?" Korigan asked, her eyes widening.

"Possibly. If so, he is still many hours away."

"I will rouse the banners—"

"No," Lynan told her.

"But Eynon—"

"If it is Eynon, he does not come to make war," Lynan said with certainty. "At least not against us."

Korigan shook her head, but did not voice the objection that rose in her throat. She had never trusted Eynon, her most determined opponent among the Chetts.

"But send out some scouts," Lynan added.

"Just to be sure," Korigan said, smiling.

"Send most south to check on the kingdom army and send the rest north," Lynan told her.

"North?"

"There is a third army hereabouts, and I want to know its strength, who it belongs to and in what direction they are traveling."

"The Haxus king? Salokan?"

"Probably, and still in retreat." Lynan smiled mirthlessly. "Like us."

Korigan nodded and turned to leave. She hesitated, feeling the need to say more, to let him know she understood the pain he was going through. *Not now,* she told herself. *Later, when he has had the time to accept the death of Kumul.* She left.

Alone again, Lynan once more closed his eyes and concentrated on his other senses. The wind from the west dissipated, and soon after a warmer, more vigorous wind started from the east, carrying with it the smells of farmland and rivers and towns and, deep underneath, the tang of the sea.

The memory of Kumul's death haunted Ager all through his sleep. He woke with a start at first light. He stood up, beating his arms around himself to get the blood going, then absently strapped on his sword. He glanced down at Morfast, still asleep under their combined horse blankets. She was breathing slowly and evenly, and for a moment some warmth crept back into his heart. He bent over to kiss her lips, and gently traced a finger over the long scar that ran down her left cheek. She had never told him how she got that, but she was a Chett warrior, and most of them saw combat as soon as they could wield a sword. Then, like a biting wound, memories of the battle three days before flooded back into his memory. It was the first time since that terrible day he really felt the death of Kumul Alarn. Ager had to stop himself from groaning. He wanted to sink back down and hide himself under his arms, not wanting to face a world without his huge friend striding through it.

He shook his head to clear it. Thinking like that was too much like a death wish, and Kumul would have scoffed at him for it. He looked eastward, saw that sunrise was still a while off, and then saw Lynan standing against the horizon, not far from the graves of the Chetts who had fallen in the battle against Queen Areava's army. *But, Lynan, there is no time to grieve,* he thought to himself. *We lost the battle and the enemy will be after us even though you killed their captain.*

With his single eye, Ager watched the young prince for a moment before approaching him, marveling at how much Lynan had changed over the last year. War, the death of Kumul, and the blood of the vampire Silona had all transformed him into . . . Ager shook his head. He was not sure what his friend had become. When he got close enough to see Lynan's expression, he saw he was not grieving; instead, the prince seemed absorbed in himself and deep in thought. Ager did not want to disturb him and turned to leave.

"Don't go," Lynan said quietly.

"Your Majesty?"

Lynan snorted. "You call me that now."

Ager nodded. "You will be king."

"Even after our defeat?"

Ager studied Lynan closely. The youth's scar, running raggedly from his right ear to his jaw, was even more prominent than Morfast's own mark, and together with his hard white skin made him look as menacing as a demon. "You don't look like someone who thinks they have suffered a defeat."

"Oh, we were defeated all right." He blinked. "And we lost Kumul. I think I would rather have lost my army than him."

And still, to Ager, it did not look as if Lynan truly was grieving the loss. He felt in his bones that something was not quite right, but he could not put his finger on it. Lynan was saying the right words, but there was little emotion behind them, as if the combination of losing Kumul and fighting an army loyal to his sister had completely submerged his feelings.

"Possibilities are presenting themselves," Lynan continued.

"So will the enemy soon enough. They must be organized by now and cannot be far behind."

Lynan closed his eyes for a moment, and when he opened them said: "Areava's army is still in camp."

"How can you possibly know—"

"But there is another force to our north. They are moving away from us."

"Salokan," Ager said without doubt.

"Korigan is sending out scouts to make sure."

"It must be Salokan," Ager said. "Areava sent her army up here to deal with Salokan, not us. And Jenrosa's magic showed they were defeated and in retreat."

"I want to be sure. I don't want to be trapped between two forces. Our mobility is our greatest advantage."

For a moment neither man said anything. Ager then noticed Jenrosa sitting by Kumul's grave. "Have you talked to her in the last three days?"

"No," Lynan said quietly, not needing to ask who he was talking about. "I'm not sure . . . perhaps it would be best if you . . ."

"I think you need to go to her," Ager said with more certainty than he felt. He was as worried by Lynan's seeming indifference as he was about Jenrosa being alone with her grief.

Lynan nodded abruptly and left. Ager watched, resisting the urge to go with him. *He's no longer a boy,* he told himself.

Jenrosa stared at her hands, unwashed since the day of the battle and still gory with Kumul's blood. It was all she had left of him, except unreliable memories. As the sky lightened, she started to see patterns in the tracery of the blood; at first nothing definable, just glimpses of landscapes, unknown faces, mythical animals. But then it formed something like a map, and in her imagination she watched armies marching to and fro across her hands, watched great battles and watched great dying. A single tear fell from her eye and splashed onto her palm. Blood turned red again and whorled before coalescing into a face she recognized.

"Lynan," she whispered and, even as she said the name, his shadow fell across her. She looked up at him, and for a moment thought his pale skin had turned the color of blood. She put her hands to her face and looked away, gasping.

Lynan gazed down on her with concern. "Jenrosa?"

She looked up at him and saw that his skin was pale again, as pale as dawn. She let out a deep sigh that made her whole body shudder. "I thought . . ." she started, but could not finish.

He squatted beside her and took her hands in his own. She could not believe how cold they were, colder even than hers. A hundred things to say passed through her mind, but she did not want to say any of them.

"What will you do now?" he asked. She could tell from his tone that he was trying to be gentle, but there was a dryness about it that made him sound uncaring.

"Carry on, of course," she said, surprised by the sound of her own voice. She had expected it to be filled with emotion, but there was something of Lynan's dispassion about it, and she understood then that inside he must be feeling as desolate as she. "I am a magicker. I am a Chett magicker. I will stay with you and Ager and Gudon and the rest." She drew a deep breath. "I will avenge Kumul's death. Somehow."

"Then, come," Lynan said. "We will have need of you before long." He stood up, bringing her with him.

Suddenly, Jenrosa felt cold and shivered. Lynan took off his poncho and draped it around her shoulders, then signaled to Ager who hurried toward them.

"Take her to Lasthear," he told Ager. "She should be with other magickers. They will know how to make sure she rests."

Ager nodded and left with Jenrosa, his arm around her shoulders. Lynan thought his two friends looked terribly small then, and quite frail, so different from the confidence and strength they had all seemed to share when Kumul was alive. For the first time in a long time he actually noticed Ager's crookback, realized he was half-cripple; and Jenrosa, snub-nosed, pugnacious, with gray eyes that always seemed to see straight to the heart, appeared frail as an old woman. Lynan wanted to shout out that he would protect them, that everything was all right, but remembered he was standing beside Kumul's grave and realized it was a lie. He could protect none of them, really, and did not truly believe for a moment that everything was going to be all right.

The scouting groups Korigan sent out before sunrise returned halfway through the morning. They reported directly to Korigan, who then went to find Lynan. She found him with her cousin, Gudon, commander of Lynan's personal bodyguard, the Red

Hands, already mounted as if he had only been waiting for word from her.

"Areava's army still has not moved," Korigan said. "They are waiting to see what we do first."

"And the force to our north?"

"Salokan," Korigan confirmed. "He is moving as quickly as he can, but he has a lot of infantry and a lot of wounded with him and his progress is slow. He is heading due north, for the Haxus border."

"Why is the kingdom army not pursuing us?" Gudon asked. He was short for a Chett and had to look up to both Lynan and Korigan, but his wiry body and laughing eyes hid great physical and mental strength and endurance.

"We hurt them badly," Korigan said. "They are licking their wounds."

"And with Sendarus dead, and the Key of the Sword taken from him, they may not have a commander," Lynan added.

"Squabbling between seconds-in-command?" Gudon asked.

Lynan glanced at his oldest friend among the Chetts. "Maybe. Or maybe they don't know how badly we were hurt. Or maybe just indecisiveness. Kumul told me that my father once said a general should always do something. Better the wrong thing than nothing at all." Both Korigan and Gudon looked at him keenly then. Lynan laughed ruefully. "Don't worry. We'll be doing *something*."

For a moment no one said anything. Lynan seemed content just to sit on his mare. Eventually Gudon prodded, "What *are* we waiting for?"

Lynan pointed west. Gudon could see a faint haze on the horizon and scurrying birds in the air above it. "Eynon," Lynan said. Gudon glanced at Korigan and saw her worried expression. "But we are not going to wait for him. I am going to meet him."

"I'll call the banners," Korigan said. "You will meet him with your army behind you."

"No. I will go with my Red Hands. Wait for me here."

"But your Majesty, this is Eynon!" Korigan pleaded. "He knows that destroying you will destroy me and open the way for him to become king of the Chetts—"

"Do you really think Eynon can kill me?"

Korigan remembered the way the enemy had struck at him in the last battle with no effect at all. After Jenrosa had given him the blood of the wood vampire Silona to save his life he had become something more than human; to the Chetts he was the White Wolf returned, the apotheosis of myth. She blushed and shook her head.

"This needs to be done," Lynan said to her gently. "Trust me. Wait here. I will return before evening. Send out more scouts to keep watch over the kingdom's and Salokan's armies. When I come back I will want to know exactly where both are."

Many years ago, when Eynon was still a boy, his father had sent him on a trading expedition to the east. Accompanying one of the midsummer caravans across the Algonka Pass, he saw with wide-eyed wonder the rich lands between the sea and the Ufero Mountains, lost count of the teeming thousands that lived there, and marveled at the wealth even the smallest landowners displayed. Now, decades later, he still had to resist the temptation to just sit on his horse and gawp, open-mouthed, at the verdant pastures and forests through which he was leading his Chetts. He also had to resist the temptation to think this plush land produced only plush soldiers. He knew the armies produced here had conquered most of the continent of Theare for the Rosethemes, and under General Elynd Chisal—Prince Lynan's father—had even chased the mercenaries out of the Oceans of Grass, something the Chetts themselves had been unable to do.

Until Korigan's father united us all under his banner. Eynon breathed deeply. He understood what the old king—also called Lynan—had done had been for the good of all the Chetts, but in the internecine wars Lynan had waged to forge that unity, Eynon's own father had been killed. And now Lynan's namesake, the son of the great general and ally of Korigan, was creating a new destiny for the Chetts.

Eynon retrieved the Key of Union from a pouch around his waist and felt its weight in his hands. It was heavier than it should have been, although to his surprise it grew lighter day by day. His followers had expected him to place the Key around his neck. After all, had not the White Wolf himself sent it to him as a bribe, to bring him and his Horse Clan and all the clans allied to him back into the fold? But he had not done that. The Key had not been sent to him as a bribe, but as a reminder of where his real loyalty should lie; it had been a gentle prod from a wise prince.

And it had come with a greater gift, Eynon reminded himself. The heads of the mercenaries Prado and Rendle, two of his peoples' greatest enemies.

He put away the Key and looked up. His riders were passing through a wood and its shadows crisscrossed over them like the fingers of giant hands. For all its beauty, this part of the world made Eynon feel trapped. The landscape seemed to settle in against him. Back on the Oceans of Grass everything was open and flat, but here even the sky seemed to close over him.

He studied the face of the rider next to him, saw that it showed no fear or anxiety. Rather it showed a kind of eagerness. He was as long as Eynon, which was tall for a Chett, but narrower and more supple, although some of that came from his youth. Except in stature, he looked very much like his brother, Gudon, and had the same ready laugh and good nature.

"You have enjoyed your stay with us, Makon?" Eynon asked.

The youth carefully regarded his host. "I will tell Lynan that you have been the most generous of hosts."

Eynon was surprised by the answer, and then realized Makon had misunderstood his question. Of course, Lynan was uppermost in the man's mind. It was something he and his people could not help noticing about Makon and all the Red Hands he had brought with him to deliver Lynan's gift: they were infatuated with the White Wolf. The eastern prince was already more myth than man, and that more than anything had convinced Eynon he had no choice but to support him in his struggle. After all, who could hold out against myth?

There was a shout up ahead from one of his van, and a moment later a rider was galloping toward them. She passed Eynon, wheeled and came along beside him. "Chetts. Many of them. Red Hands."

"How far?" Eynon asked.

"About an hour from here."

"And Lynan?"

"He leads them," she said, and looked as if she was about to say something else, but she nervously eyed Makon and obviously decided to say no more.

"Tell the van to continue," Eynon said. "We will join you presently."

The rider rushed away.

"I would like to go on ahead to greet Lynan," Makon said.

Eynon's first impulse was to ask Makon to stay with him—he wanted to make his own impression on Lynan without the prince being colored by any report his emissary might make—but letting

Makon go was a demonstration of his own confidence and authority.

"Give Prince Lynan my regards."

Makon grinned his thanks, spurred his horse to the gallop, and
was soon gone from sight.

The two forces met at noon where the road left the woods and
wound its way through a grassy field. Both leaders ordered their re-
spective forces to hang back, and rode to meet each other in the
center. When Eynon was close enough to Lynan to get his first
proper look at the prince, he could not help grunting in surprise at
the changes he saw. Where before Lynan had seemed uncomfortable in his pale skin, like a calf dressed in a wolf's hide, he had
since grown into it. Lynan was small and wiry and white as snow,
and his gaze—as cold as winter—never wavered from Eynon's
face. They stopped a few paces from each other, and made no move
to take each other's arms in greeting; they had no need for false ca-
maraderie between them. Each knew what was happening.

"I am glad you came," Lynan said.

"I believe you," Eynon replied without irony. Then he noticed
the Key of the Sword hanging from the prince's neck. He could not
help staring at it.

"Courtesy of Areava," Lynan said.

Eynon looked up in surprise. "You have slain the queen?" He
could not help sounding as shocked as he felt.

"No. She had given it to her lover. An Amanite called
Sendarus."

"Then you have defeated Grenda Lear?"

Lynan shook his head. "We were beaten."

Eynon blinked. For a moment he could think of nothing to say,
then: "You are in retreat?"

"No. Both sides were badly mauled. I think the kingdom army
was hurt the worst, but they held the field. Technically, that means
they had the victory."

"A Chett would not consider that a victory," Eynon said matter-
of-factly. "A blood-soaked field isn't worth the life of one warrior.
If they lost more warriors than you, then you won."

"I lost Kumul," Lynan said bluntly. "I did not win."

"God, lad, I did not expect to be greeted with a celebration, but
I was not expecting this feast of bad tidings."

The way Eynon had said "lad" made Lynan think of Kumul. In
a strange way—his speech and the manner in which he held him-

self—the chief reminded him of his dead guardian. He pushed the thought away. "It is best you know exactly how I stand before you commit yourself to my cause."

"You are so sure that is why I have come?"

"You brought the Key of Union," Lynan said with certainty.

Eynon could not help grinning. "And how do you stand?"

"My army is mostly intact. The kingdom army is not chasing us; they have little cavalry left to speak of, and most of that is made up of knights from the Twenty Houses who are not at all suited to pursuit. There is a third army to the north of us: Salokan's retreating invasion force."

"You met Kendra's heavy cavalry?"

"And destroyed most of it." Lynan closed his eyes for a moment. "That was Kumul's doing."

"You forgot to mention one thing in your appraisal."

Lynan thought for a moment. "I do not think so . . ."

"You defeated the mercenaries under Prado and Rendle."

"Ah."

"So, as I see it, you have at least one victory to your credit, and possibly a second." Eynon reached into the pouch around his waist and brought out the Key of Union. "This is yours, I believe," he said and handed it to Lynan.

"Thank you," Lynan responded simply, taking it and putting it around his neck. It clinked against the Key of the Sword and for the briefest of moments he felt a surge of power course through his veins. He was so surprised by it that he barely heard the cheering of the Red Hands behind him.

Gudon sat at the back of the circle that surrounded Lynan. He was both amused and a little frustrated by the gathering, but had expected that to be the way from the beginning. Closest to Lynan were Korigan and Eynon, old rivals now fighting for the same cause, but old rivals nonetheless. Backed up by their allied clan chiefs, each was arguing for a different strategy for the Chett army.

The discussion was heated, deadlocked and acrimonious. Gudon wondered how different it would have been had Kumul been present, and concluded that his presence would only have raised the temperature even higher. In the time he had known him, Gudon had learned that putting Kumul in a debate was like dropping a lit torch in a dry stable. He winced. *Would have been like,* he corrected himself.

His gaze wandered from Eynon to Korigan as each repeatedly argued for their particular plan. They were like desert and sea; their natures were so different, different as two Chetts could be, considering they were both natural leaders. Physically they shared the same golden skin, black hair, and brown eyes of their people, but while both had height, Korigan was as lean and lithe as a grass wolf and as beautiful as a clear night on the Oceans of Grass, while Eynon was thickset, with muscles like knotted ropes and a face that would terrify the hardiest warrior it was so ugly and battered. Occasionally, Gudon's gaze drifted to Jenrosa sitting among the other clan magickers, looking both foreign and Chett at the same time. Like most easterners she was fair-skinned, and freckles sprinkled her face, but there was something about her manner, forthright and honest, that seemed typically Chett to Gudon. He could tell Jenrosa was trying to concentrate on what was being said—or shouted—but her mind obviously was elsewhere.

And in between it all squatted Lynan, impassive, making no attempt whatsoever to adjudicate between his fractious followers. He waited until Korigan and Eynon had spent themselves, then stood up. All other conversations stopped. Lynan looked at Korigan.

"As I understand it, you want me to move against the kingdom army and finish what we were unable to finish in the battle three days ago."

Korigan nodded, and he looked at Eynon.

"And you want me to move directly on the provincial capital Daavis, taking it while the kingdom's only army in Hume is still recovering."

Eynon nodded. Lynan breathed deeply and then looked directly at Ager, sitting quietly beside Gudon. "And you, old Crookback, what is your advice?"

Ager blinked in surprise. All eyes rested on him, everyone aware that as one of Lynan's original companions he had more influence than the average chief.

Ager cleared his throat. "I say, what does the White Wolf want to do?"

Lynan smiled, and a sigh passed through the meeting. Both Korigan and Eynon looked abashed.

"The White Wolf says we will not attack the kingdom army, and nor will we attack Daavis."

"Surely we're not retreating back to the Oceans of Grass!" Eynon declared. Under Lynan's suddenly cool stare, he swallowed and said hurriedly: "I did not bring my followers all this way to go back again without striking some blow for your Majesty."

Oh, that was coolly said, Gudon thought, and he could see that Lynan was amused by it as well.

"You and your followers will strike a blow for me, Eynon," Lynan told him, speaking loud enough for all at the meeting to hear. "And for all Chetts."

"Then who are we going after?" Korigan asked. "I speak for all the Chetts when I say we would like a second chance to attack the kingdom, either against its army or against Daavis."

"So would I," Lynan said. "But not now."

"Why?"

"Two reasons. First, we don't know whether or not there are kingdom reinforcements on the way. Second, it is the expected thing to do."

"So we go after Salokan," Ager guessed aloud.

There was a shocked silence. Eventually, Korigan asked, "But why make a second enemy? He's running away from Grenda Lear, and as long as we don't interfere, he'll scamper all the way back to Haxus."

"Salokan is already an enemy. Haxus was always a base for mercenaries during the Slaver War, and was again for Rendle this winter. I should not have to remind any here how much pain and misery the slavers caused the Chetts; without Haxus as their main base, they would not have been able to operate as freely as they did."

"When do we go after him?" Ager asked.

"Is the army ready?" Lynan asked Korigan.

"Yes, your Majesty."

"Then we go after Salokan tonight."

2

FOR the third day in a row, Charion searched the eastern horizon for any sign of dust, puzzled and concerned she could not see any. She had been mentally preparing for an attack from Prince Lynan and his Chett army since the end of their first battle, but even her few remaining foot scouts had found no trace of the enemy within five leagues. True, some of the scouts had not come back, but Lynan's own pickets would be out whether or not he intended to attack. She was puzzled because she had expected Lynan to use his army's greater mobility to surround her and try to finish what they had started, and concerned because she was afraid that instead he had maneuvered around her to get to Daavis. Normally she would not have been worried; the Chetts were nomad warriors, and all their famed ferocity and courage would avail them nothing without a siege engine against the walls of Daavis. But after Salokan's siege, the poor city was in no state to resist a determined assault.

Galen appeared by her side. "If Lynan was going to attack us, surely he would have been here by now," he said.

Charion glanced at the tall Kendran noble and nodded. "We have to get back to Daavis." She looked at him warily then. "*I* have to get back to Daavis. I will not speak for you."

Galen did not answer right away. He knew she was offering him a gift, and was surprised by it. The surviving knights of Kendra's Twenty Houses would follow his command, and Charion was letting him decide just how far her command extended in her own kingdom. *These are extraordinary times,* he thought. He knew that half a year ago he could not have imagined that he would ever serve under an Amanite prince, let alone learn to respect him and mourn his passing. And now Queen Charion, perhaps the least respected of all the provincial rulers, was proving herself as much a diplomat as Sendarus. *Maybe Usharna and Areava have been right all along. Grenda Lear truly is more than just the city of Kendra.*

"You have command here," he said evenly. "Unless Areava commands otherwise, I am at your service."

Charion's face showed no expression, but he saw her body relax with the release of tension. "Did you send to her our messages about the battle and the death of her husband?" she asked after a moment.

"A pigeon went in the night."

"I must protect my capital. From there I can regroup."

"And the knights? They will fight behind the walls of Daavis if that is your wish, but they can be better employed."

He watched her carefully as she considered his question. When he first met her, he thought she looked like nothing more than an overgrown porcelain doll, beautiful but fragile, with a vile temper and an ingrained distrust of anyone from one of Kendra's noble families, the Twenty Houses. But she had proven herself to be as doughty a warrior as any he had ever met, and with a better grasp of tactics and strategy. Like Queen Areava Rosetheme back in Kendra, she was fiercely devoted to her people and her kingdom, something which sometimes blinded her to the wider world, and her distrust of Galen and his ilk had softened under the conflict and duress they had shared.

"For the moment I need a rearguard," she said eventually, "one strong enough to dissuade any enemy scouts from following us but mobile enough to avoid serious trouble. Once we get to Daavis, we'll have a better idea of our situation—and maybe news from Areava—and we can decide then how best to use your heavy cavalry."

"When do we leave?"

"Tomorrow. First light, in case Lynan changes his mind about attacking us."

"Your Majesty?"

The words echoed in the dark room. Orkid Gravespear, chancellor of the kingdom of Grenda Lear, felt foolish standing in the doorway of Queen Areava's private chambers. Behind him, Harnan Beresard fidgeted with his writing equipment, looking even more thin and reedy than usual next to the big Amanite. While Harnan was sandy-haired and wore a close-trimmed beard in the latest fashion, Orkid looked as dark and gloomy as a storm cloud, and with his thick patrician beard that left the upper lip bare, he reminded people of one of the ancient rock carvings of kings and warriors.

"Your Majesty? Your people have need of you—"

"Enough, old bear," Areava said, not even bothering to glance at them. She looked pallid, even consumptive, in her grief. Her gray eyes stared into the distance, unfocused, her yellow hair was splayed carelessly and unbrushed on her pillow.

Still, Orkid sighed with relief. At least she was talking to him.

"The kingdom needs its queen," he persisted.

"My brother needs his sister," she replied. "The Key of the Heart has taken his mind, leaving nothing but a child behind."

"I have correspondence," Harnan said from the background in a hopeful voice. "Urgent messages that need answers."

"Orkid, you take care of it," she said dismissively.

The two men looked at each other with something like resignation. "I told you," Harnan mouthed.

"Your Majesty, others can take care of his Highness," Orkid persisted. "But only you can run Grenda Lear."

"Olio needs me."

Orkid retreated from the doorway and a guard took his place. Harnan looked at him desperately. "What can we do?" the secretary pleaded.

The chancellor shook his head. "I'm not sure. If only there was some way to help her brother . . ." His voice drifted off for a moment, and then he said to Harnan: "Find Edaytor Fanhow."

"The prelate? All the magisters of the theurgia have said there is nothing they can do to help his Highness. They say the Key of the Heart has stolen his mind. If the magisters themselves can do nothing, what can that fat bureaucrat—"

"Just bring Fanhow to my office," Orkid insisted, and left before Harnan could argue any more.

Father Powl, Primate of the Church of the Righteous God, was leading the daily service for the soul of tiny, mutilated Usharna, the baby Areava had lost at the moment of birth at the same time she had lost her husband Sendarus at the hand of Lynan. The dead baby had been dressed and her body smeared with preserving lotions, the worst of her terrible wounds covered in scented wrapping. She would stay exposed on the altar of the royal chapel until Areava herself came to give her blessing for the child's cremation, and from all accounts Areava had not stirred from her rooms for over a day.

When the service was done, the other priests left to attend their duties, but Powl stayed behind, kneeling in front of the altar, his face contorted in concentration.

"Without your name the kingdom cannot be protected from evil, my Lord," he whispered fiercely. "Please have mercy on your people. Please have mercy on Queen Areava, who has suffered mightily. Please accept this child's soul into your keeping. And please, Lord, please let me know your name so that Grenda Lear may be saved from all that is wrong with this world."

He waited for God to answer him, hoping that he had been forgiven for murdering his predecessor—Giros Northam; without the name of God, Powl had nothing but the title of primate. But God, as always, remained silent.

His small, thin body shaking with the effort spent praying, Powl rose unsteadily to his feet. He turned and saw Father Rown waiting for him at the end of the chapel. Powl swallowed, and wondered if his second-in-command had heard any part of his prayer. There was nothing in the priest's expression that showed he did, and Powl let himself relax.

"Father? Is there something I can do for you?"

"I am concerned for her Majesty," Rown said.

"As we all are, my son."

"I thought she might see me, being her confessor, but . . ." the priest shrugged, and his usually round, pleasant face was drawn with concern, ". . . but she will see no one, not even the chancellor." He looked pleadingly at Powl. "Your Grace, you were her confessor for many years before me. You may know her better than any living man. Maybe you can get through to her?"

Powl lowered his gaze. He, the primate of the kingdom's church, could not even get through to God. What chance did he have with Areava? He sighed deeply, then nodded. "I will try."

"What exactly did you and Prince Olio do with the sick?" Orkid asked.

"Healed them," Magicker Prelate Edaytor Fanhow answered.

The two men were sitting opposite each other at Orkid's large, plain desk.

"Through the Key of the Heart?"

"Yes. At first his Highness needed a magicker to help channel the power of the Key, but the more he used it, the more attuned the Key became to Olio's own presence. In the end he could use it by himself."

"And what happened on the day of the fire?"

"He was being escorted back to the palace from the docks where he'd been helping those fleeing the fire in the old quarter of the city. On the way he came across the ruins of an inn where the worst injured were being cared for. He told his guards to wait outside. We're not sure what happened afterward. That he healed many people there is no doubt, but how long it took for the Key to completely use him up is not known. By the time I got there, he was as he is now."

"The Key damaged his brain?"

Edaytor shrugged. "No one knows. The theurgia know less about the Keys of Power than the Rosethemes themselves. I don't think any of the Keys have ever been used as extensively as Olio used his in the last year."

"The theurgia know no way to reach him," Orkid said; a statement, not a question.

"That's right."

"Do you?"

Edaytor looked up surprised. "What do you mean?"

"You were closest to the prince during this time. Is there anything you can think of that might help bring him back?"

The prelate shook his head. "No."

"Are you sure?"

"What do you think I've been doing the last three days!" Edaytor snapped. Orkid recoiled in surprise, and Edaytor gasped at what he had done. "Chancellor, I'm sorry—"

Orkid waved him quiet. "No, I am sorry. You answered my question the first time." *There is more to this man than Harnan knows; perhaps more than any of us know.* And then he understood that among all at court, only Olio himself had truly seen the prelate for the man he was, seen beneath the overweight, kind-faced fellow made prelate over all the theurgia by his fellow magickers because they thought him so indifferent in wit and ability he would not get in their way. Orkid realized that explained a great deal about the relationship between Olio and Edaytor: two men whose generosity and innate kindness was mistaken by most for fecklessness and weakness. "I need your help."

"*My* help?"

"More accurately, the queen and the kingdom need your help."

"Anything."

"Stay with Olio. Try and find a way to heal him. Use whatever resources you need."

"Me? But surely Dr. Trion, or one of the more powerful magickers, would be better suited. I can recommend a number—"

"No. I do not think any within the theurgia will be able to help, or maybe it's that they are afraid to dabble with any of the Keys; you yourself just told me their power lay beyond any magicker's ken. And this problem is certainly beyond Dr. Trion's experience. You were closest to Olio. You knew him better than anyone, except the queen herself."

"Then the queen, surely, should have the task."

"The queen has other duties. The kingdom needs her. Her responsibility to all her people outweighs her responsibility to her brother."

"But she has lost so much in the last three days," Edaytor said reasonably. "Her husband and child as well as Olio. Surely the kingdom can give her some time to herself."

"She might yet lose the kingdom," Orkid said somberly.

Edaytor stared at the chancellor in amazement. "Surely not!"

"Our army is still in the north, victorious—if we can believe what Queen Charion wrote us—but battered. The outlaw Prince Lynan has crossed from the Oceans of Grass to the east with a Chett army, and his next move will, no doubt, be to organize support against Areava." He pursed his lips. "And of course against Olio, as Areava's brother."

Edaytor was lost for words. He knew the situation in the north was troublesome, but the kingdom had been secure for so long under Usharna it was hard to believe anything could seriously threaten it, even her renegade son Lynan who had never been anyone of significance within the court while Usharna was alive. There were many things that mystified Edaytor, but one of the most troubling was why Usharna, on her deathbed, had given Lynan one of the Keys of Power.

"So, you see," Orkid continued, "it is vital that Areava's attention be diverted entirely to the welfare of the kingdom as a whole."

"Yes. Yes, I see."

"Shall we go, then?"

"Go?"

Orkid stood up. "To Areava's chambers. She is looking after Olio there."

Edaytor realized then he had surrendered already and there was no point in arguing any further. In something of a daze he followed the chancellor, feeling a mixture of dread and anticipation. *Maybe, just maybe,* a part of his mind was saying, *I can do something.* He wished he felt more convinced.

They reached the royal chambers the same time as Father Powl; Edaytor thought the priest looked on the edge of nervous exhaustion, and wondered if he looked the same way. Among the three of them, only Orkid—severe and determined—gave the impression he was still in control of something, even if it was his own destiny.

"I can come back later," Father Powl said, and seemed glad to have the excuse to leave. Orkid quickly reached out to hold him.

"Please, Father, stay. Perhaps all three of us together can turn the queen away from her grief."

Powl looked uncertain but nodded. Orkid signaled for the guard at Areava's door to leave them alone, and when he was gone called out: "Your Majesty, there is someone here to see Prince Olio."

"Who would want to see my poor imbecile brother?"

Orkid looked at Edaytor. The prelate took a deep breath. "Your Majesty, it is Prelate Fanhow. Your brother and I were close—"

He was interrupted by a low wail. "You! It is your fault my brother is lost!"

Edaytor visibly wilted, and his skin paled to the color of chalk. He opened his mouth, but no words came out. How could he answer such an accusation? Deep in his heart, he knew there was some truth in her charge. If he had not supported Olio's crusade to heal the sick and dying children of the city of Kendra, he would not have succumbed to the magic of Key of the Heart. When he and the prince had started their crusade to help the poor and the ill in Kendra, their hopes had been so high. And now all was brought low.

"He was your brother's closest friend!" Orkid said quickly. "If anyone can help him, it is the prelate."

"I can help him," the queen countered. "No one knew him as well as I."

"But, your Majesty, your kingdom has need of you!" Orkid pleaded.

"My kingdom can do without me—" Areava began.

"Enough!" Father Powl shouted, and both Orkid and Edaytor jumped.

For a shocked moment there was complete silence. The guard reappeared, but Orkid waved him off furiously.

"How dare you!" Areava returned, her voice round with anger. "I am your queen, *Primate!*" She made his title sound like an insult.

"And I was your confessor!" Powl said quickly. "As you know Olio, I know you. I know that the one thing that has remained constant in your whole life has been your sense of duty!"

"You know *nothing* about me!"

"I *know* that ever since you were a child your greatest wish has been to serve the kingdom as well as your mother did."

Orkid and Edaytor tensed, expecting another blistering reply, but there was only silence. Father Powl was making signs at Edaytor, and the prelate finally caught on; it was his turn to add to the pressure on her.

"Your Majesty, I know you blame me for your brother's illness, but as I love him as a friend I will strive all I can to marshal the combined theurgia to find a cure for whatever ails him."

Again silence reigned, and then, from the darkness, came the almost ghostly figure of Areava. She was dressed in nothing but an undershirt. Her hair was disheveled, her skin blotched, her eyes redrimmed. She stared at Edaytor for a long time, and the prelate made sure his own gaze did not waver from hers. Then she glanced at Orkid and Powl, but did not even try to match with them. Edaytor thought there was something of shame about her expression.

"If you can help Olio, I would be forever in your debt," she said.

"I will help Olio," Edaytor said simply.

Orkid stepped forward. "And you, your Majesty, will you now help your kingdom?"

She took a deep breath and said: "For all my life." Then she smiled wearily at him. "As you already knew."

The mountains around Pila were hidden behind a heavy, gray sky. Marin, king of Aman, stood alone in the watchtower that was the oldest part of his royal castle. Gusting wind lashed at his hair and blew away his tears. In his right hand he held the small slip of paper that had come by carrier pigeon only an hour before. The message was from his brother, Orkid, and told him of the events of three days ago. He read with disbelief of the terrible death of his granddaughter in miscarriage. And then he read of the death of

Sendarus, his only child. He had felt the whole universe hold still. He had tried to read the words a second time, but had been unable to make sense of them.

Then the universe had started again.

His courtiers, sensing that something was awry, asked him what the message contained. He told them, his voice low and cold, and they joined him in uncomprehending shock. Then he had left his throne, ordered no one to follow him, not even his bodyguard, and climbed the watchtower from where his grief poured from him like a torrent.

He cried for his son, for his unknown granddaughter, for his long-dead wife and the love they had shared for Sendarus, and finally he cried for himself, overwhelmed by self-pity. It was this that finally brought him back from the black sea he had fallen in. He hated himself for it, he hated himself for being alive when his beloved son was dead. And there was more. Where before he had never thought of Lynan as anything but another tool in his ambition to make Aman great, the outlaw prince was now the slayer of Sendarus, and he hated him with a white rage that settled in his chest like a second heart, pumping new life into him.

He descended the tower, dark and grim and terrible like one of the old gods come down to earth, already planning what he must do to destroy Lynan. He realized with grim satisfaction that part of it was already being put in place by Amemun. The thought stopped him in his tracks. Amemun loved Sendarus almost as much as he did, and he would have to be told. Grief suddenly rose in him again, but he held onto his new hate and his mind cleared like a dry forest swept with a summer fire.

The old Amanite gave his most polite smile and graciously accepted the small morsel of food in his left hand. He blessed it in the name of the god of the desert, placed it into his right hand and put the morsel in his mouth. He pretended to chew and enjoy the food, then swallowed it whole, forcing down the bile that surged up his gullet. The heat inside the tent was oppressive, and he was feeling nauseous.

"Good!" Amemun declared, and his host, the headman of the Southern Chett tribe he found himself with, smiled appreciatively.

"As our honored guest, you must by tradition have the best portion of the feast."

"It was delicious," Amemun said. *Please, Lord of the Mountain, let me hold down my heaving stomach.*

"As headman I would normally have it," the host said, his tone suggesting another meaning.

It was Amemun's turn to smile appreciatively; he was on firmer ground now. After spending grueling weeks on the hot, arid plains that filled the south of the continent of Theare he had finally found his way to this man, rumored by shepherds living on the border lands between Aman and the desert to be one of the grand chiefs of the Southern Chetts. His name was Dekelon, and he looked to be a hundred years old. His head was bald, his skin the color of sun-baked mud, and his eyes brown, rheumy circles. Amemun could not help feeling soft, hairy and fat in comparison, although he knew he was fit and strong for his sixty years.

"Your hospitality will have its rewards," Amemun said.

"That is the way of things," Dekelon said. He motioned for his son and whispered something in his ear. The son nodded and left the tent, taking with him the rest of his father's relations and re-tainers. "Now we can talk. You have come a long way to see me."

"Is that so strange? Your reputation as the strongest and wisest of all the Southern Chetts is known even as far as Pila."

"There are two things you should know, Amemun of Aman," Dekelon said, his voice changing from the singsong tone he had used in greeting to something colder and flatter. "The first is that when we are alone, there is no need for flattery; it does not help your cause, whatever that cause may be."

"Ah. And the second?"

"We do not call ourselves the Southern Chetts as if we were nothing but a twig off a nobler and greater tree."

"I understand. By what name should I call your people?"

"We call ourselves the Saranah."

"I have heard this word from time to time," Amemun confessed.

"It is from an ancient tongue, and is the name of a bird that soars above the oceans, rarely touching the ground," Dekelon said. "Just as my people touch the ground here very lightly. We live on an old country, and poor, so we protect it and nurture it where we can, and scratch what living we are able from our goats and sheep and scat-tered plots of land."

"What ancient tongue?" Amemun asked, suddenly curious.

"Very few of our people know it anymore, and none at all in the east."

"Is it a tongue we all spoke once?"

Dekelon shrugged. "Perhaps." His tone suggested they were here to discuss matters more weighty than a dead and largely forgotten language.

Amemun sighed deeply. His natural curiosity made him want to pursue the subject, but he had traveled long and far to deliver an important message from his master, King Marin, and did not want to anger his host. "As you say, the Saranah live on an old and poor land. Perhaps it is time you found richer pasture?"

Dekelon glanced sharply at him. "Are you suggesting we move east, into Aman?"

Amemun blinked. He had not expected discussions to be so direct. "No."

"Then what *are* you suggesting?"

"That you move north."

For a moment Dekelon did not understand, but when he realized what Amemun was in fact suggesting, he wheezed in laughter. "Oh, that is a fine joke. We Saranah are scattered all over this land in our small tribes, and you want us to march north and occupy the Oceans of Grass. Our distant cousins, the Chetts, live there in huge clans. What will they say about it, do you think?"

"They are currently occupied with another matter," Amemun said lightly. "And who knows what is possible for the Saranah if they have rich friends behind them?"

Dekelon's face broke into a wide grin. "How rich?"

Amemun grinned in return. "Very," he said.

3

SALOKAN, king of Haxus, rode low over the saddle, his thin, graying hair whipping around his face. His own panting was drowned out by the panting of his horse. He peered in the dark, searching for any sign of the enemy, but all he could see was a blur of single trees and low bushes that seemed to reach out for him. His face was scratched in a hundred places, and he could taste blood trickling between his lips. He heard an arrow whistle over him and he cried out, digging his heels even deeper into the horse's flanks. It whinnied and put on an extra burst of speed. A group of infantry loomed in front of him, and for a strange second he could not tell if they were standing or lying down; then he saw the barbed shafts sticking out of their bodies and he rode over them.

Up above, the moon kept pace with him and he prayed for it to go away, prayed for its revealing light to be shut off. He passed low under a tree. A branch snagged his cloak and tore it off, almost unhorsing him. The muscles in his thighs and back were aching so badly the pain became a single mass. Another group of infantry, spearmen, and this time alive. They called to him desperately as he thundered past, but he ignored them.

And then the moon started to blink. Salokan risked looking up and saw that his horse was following a trail through a grove of thorn trees. The canopy became more and more dense and eventually the moon disappeared altogether. Salokan reined in and looked around desperately for any sign of pursuit; when he did not see any, he dismounted and led the horse away from the trail until he was sure no one would see him unless they were virtually on top of him. As he caught his breath, he absently checked the horse's girth straps, then allowed himself a few mouthfuls of weak red wine from a leather bottle in one of his saddlebags. The horse fidgeted, and he calmed it down by stroking its muzzle.

He tried to figure out what to do next.

How long should he wait here—wherever here was? Should he try and marshal any survivors, or set out by himself in a desperate bid to reach the safety of his own kingdom? But he could not concentrate on the future. All he could do was remember that only a short time ago he, Salokan, king of Haxus, had been looking forward to his evening meal. Although defeated in his attempt to capture Hume from the grasp of Grenda Lear, he and his army had shared some victories and were returning to Haxus intact and determined to try again at some future date. He knew he would soon be on home ground, with all the advantages that entailed, including reinforcements and internal lines of supply. It was not far from sunset, and scouts had told him there was a perfect camping site not half an hour from their present position.

He closed his eyes, trying to get rid of the memory, but it was no good.

There had been a commotion on the left flank. At first Salokan had thought it was nothing more than a rowdy joke between some of the spearmen, but then the noise grew louder and he noticed some of the spearmen out of formation and crossing in front of him. He called out to them, but they ignored him. He reined in his horse and told one of his aides to go see what the trouble was; the rest of his retinue crowded around him, his bodyguard making sure no one got too close. He had to order them aside so he could see what was going on. Some of the infantry were still moving his way, but most were still in marching order and continuing north. It was difficult to tell exactly what was happening, though, because the sun was low to the horizon and at best he could only make out the silhouettes of his troops.

There was a distant scream, and the sound was picked up by other voices. To Salokan, it had sounded dreadfully like panic. The aide reappeared, breathless and flushed. "We're being attacked!" he said, his voice filled with disbelief.

"Who is attacking us?" Salokan demanded.

"Some of our pickets came back wounded, and then a hail of arrows fell among the infantry. We don't know who. Riders appeared out of the sun and shot at us, then disappeared."

"Chetts," Salokan said in disbelief. "It can only be Chetts."

"On this side of the Algonka Pass?" another aide asked.

It's my fault, Salokan told himself. *All my fault.* Sending Rendle into the Oceans of Grass had been like throwing a stone at a hornet's nest: Rendle had once been a slaver, and the Chetts hated slavers more than anything else. The magnitude of his mistake filled him with a terrible dread. *What have I done?*

"What are your orders?" the first aide asked.

"My orders?" Salokan looked at him in a daze.

"What do you want us to do? How do want us to deploy the army?"

"The army," Salokan mouthed. He shook his head to clear it; he knew what had to be done. "Post the archers on the left flank. Get the infantry and cavalry behind them. No one—absolutely no one!—is to pursue or harass the Chetts. Let them come to us."

The aide nodded and wheeled his horse around to give out the orders, but just then a hail of arrows fell among the king and his retinue. The aide fell from his horse, pierced through the throat. Others fell. There were cries of pain and surprise. Before Salokan could rally them, more arrows plummeted out of the sky. Riderless horses bolted. His own horse started throwing its head back. He kept a tight rein and spurred his mount into a canter, leaving the dreadful confusion behind him. He tried to find one of his generals—any officer—to pass on his commands, but it was already too late. Formations were breaking up, individual soldiers fleeing in all directions. He heard a wild call behind him and looked over his shoulder. He saw a troop of Chett horse archers galloping through a gap in the marching line, loosing arrows as they went, scattering all before them.

It was then Salokan realised he had lost his grand invasion force once and for all, and he let the panic touch his own heart. He kicked his horse into a gallop and rode north, away from the terrible Chetts, away from his own disintegrating army.

After dismounting, he sighed heavily and leaned his forehead against the saddle, ashamed of his own flight. How could he, King Salokan of Haxus, have allowed himself to behave like a common recruit?

There was a crashing sound behind him as something heavy started moving through the vegetation. Salokan placed both hands over his horse's muzzle and froze. Then he heard voices. Although he could not make out individual words, there was no mistaking the accent. The Chetts were searching the grove for survivors. He almost panicked again, but retained enough self-control to lead his horse as quietly as possible back to the trail. The Chetts were making so much noise they could not have heard him. Once out from under the closest trees he mounted, leaned over the saddle and urged his horse into a quick walk. The sound of the search dropped behind him and he kicked the horse into a canter. And then the moon flickered back into life. He was riding out of the grove. At that moment there was a great cry ahead and to his left. An arrow magically appeared in his saddle, just a finger's width from his knee, and another caught at his hair. He dug in his spurs and the horse broke into a gallop. Salokan held on for dear life, expecting to feel an arrow in his back at any moment. He wished to God he had never left Haxus, wished to God he had never besieged Daavis, wished to God he had never sent Rendle into the Oceans of Grass after Prince Lynan. Most of all, he wished to God there were no Chetts on the continent of Theare.

The horse stumbled, managed to right itself, but it slowed down. Salokan jabbed with his heels, whipped with his reins, but the bloody animal was determined to see him killed. It stumbled a second time, fell, and sent the king tumbling onto the hard ground. He lay there winded for a long moment. A strange sound, like thrashing, caused him to sit up. His horse was on its side, two of its legs kicking in the air, the other two—broken—stirring uselessly in the grass.

Without thinking he stood up and drew his sword, bringing it down hard on the horse's neck. The animal jerked and then was still. Ever since he was a boy he had been told to never let any animal suffer. *And what about me? What about all my soldiers?* One of the saddlebags had split open, and his war crown, a simple gold circlet, had tumbled onto the ground. His arms slumped by his side, his sword point rested on the ground. He did not want to run anymore. Or fight. Or be afraid.

He sensed rather than heard the enemy gather around him. He waited for the arrows to pierce his body. The night air was cooling now, evaporating the sweat that made his face and hands shine in the moonlight. When nothing happened, after what seemed a long while, he lifted his head. There were ten mounted Chetts forming a circle around him.

"Get it over with," he said haughtily, and lifted his arms so their arrows could pierce straight into his heart and lungs.

"You stayed to slay your horse," one of the Chetts said.

"If I'd tried to run away, you'd have ridden me down," Salokan answered, trying to hold onto his pride by putting a sneer into his voice.

"Truth," the Chett admitted. He nodded to the dead animal. "Was this your horse?"

"What do you think?"

Surprisingly the Chett grinned and dismounted. He drew a saber and Salokan took a step back, automatically raising his own weapon to counter any attack, but the Chett ignored the king and used the saber to pick up the crown. "And is this yours?"

Salokan refused to answer. He knew he was going to die, and had no intention of amusing these barbarians any farther.

"My friend asked you a question," said a new voice from behind him. Salokan turned around. He was not sure which of the Chetts now in front of him had spoken, but there was something about the posture of the shortest one that drew attention to him. The Chett had his wide-brimmed hat drawn low so Salokan could not see his face.

"I am King Salokan of Haxus. I don't talk with herders."

The short Chett slipped easily off his mount and approached Salokan, stopping no more than two paces away from him. He lifted his chin and slipped his hat off his head.

Salokan gasped. The face he saw belonged to no Chett. Indeed, there was something about the man's features that were not entirely human. The skin was as pale as moonlight and had a slight luster to it as if it was made from carved ivory. A dreadful scar ran from the right ear all the way to the jaw. And the cold brown eyes were like those of a wolf.

"My name is Lynan Rosetheme."

Salokan was too surprised to speak. How could this creature be the young prince of Grenda Lear?

"I wish to talk to you about a certain mercenary called Rendle," the man continued, and took a step forward.

What drove Salokan to act then was something he never completely understood, but a mixture of fear and loathing made him raise his sword arm and bring it down in a mighty stroke.

And in the next moment his sword was spinning away from his hand and into the night. Salokan gasped in pain and grabbed his hand. Blood pumped from the stumps of three fingers. The pale prince was holding a saber. Salokan had never seen anyone move so fast.

"My hand—!" he cried, then coughed as the point of the prince's sword jabbed into his throat.

"Do you want to die, Salokan of Haxus?" Lynan Rosetheme asked.

Salokan did not want to answer. He did not want to show this strange creature and his Chett warriors how afraid he was. But the pain in his hand was overwhelming, and he could feel his blood, hot and slick, running down his arm, and he could feel the point of a saber pricking his wind pipe.

"No," he said weakly.

Lynan Rosetheme dropped the point of his saber and smiled at him. "Good. I'll need a governor to look after my interests in my new province of Haxus."

4

IT was a cool dawn for this time of year. Ager, who thought he had gotten used to the cold, could not help shivering. He looked over the gentle rolling landscape of Hume and tried to see only the woods and brooks and scattered farms, but he could not avoid seeing the bodies. Where the Haxus infantry had stood their ground and been scythed down by wave after wave of arrows, they lay in neat piles; where a fleeing column had been slaughtered soldier by soldier, bodies appeared in long straggling strings. Crows hopped over bloody heads and limbs, pecking at eyes and fingers. As the day warmed, the flies would come, great hovering clouds of them.

Ager shivered again. *It's the cold,* he told himself.

He felt bewildered. This time yesterday he had expected Lynan, defeated by Areava's army and shattered by the blow of losing Kumul, to retreat perhaps as far as the Oceans of Grass. Instead the prince had gone on the offensive. The night had been a long and bloody one, ending with the complete destruction of Salokan's army. The Chetts had the victory they needed to restore their morale and confidence.

It would be called the Battle of the Night, he knew. Such battles were very rare, commanders afraid of losing control, of banners and regiments attacking their own side by mistake, but Lynan had taken advantage of two facts—whereas Salokan had few cavalry, all his warriors were mounted and so knew anyone on foot was an enemy, and a full moon had been up for many hours.

Ager could not help feeling some sympathy for his foe, but he reminded himself that Haxus had long been a traditional enemy of all those living in the south of the continent of Theare, as well as the main base for the slave trade that once had preyed on the Chetts, including the Ocean clan.

My clan, he reminded himself.

Morfast rode up beside him and gently grasped his arm. He squeezed back, sighing deeply. "How many did we lose?"

"No more than thirty," she said. "But that includes all the adult members of the Delen family. They were surprised by Haxus cavalry and were cut down before they could react."

"How many children?"

"Three. They will be taken in by uncles and aunts."

Ager nodded wearily. "A hard blow for a child to lose so much of its family."

Morfast grinned savagely. "Many more Haxus children were made orphans last night."

The crookback's conscience rebelled against such bloody joy, but he knew the Chetts reveled in combat as no other people he had ever encountered, and he had been a soldier for most of his life.

"Was it like this under the General?" she asked him.

"The General?"

"In the Slaver War," she prodded.

Ager snorted in surprise. Although he had spent many years remembering his part in the Slaver War, revering the memory of General Elynd Chisal, Lynan's father, Morfast's question made him realize he had not really thought of those times since the first night he had met Lynan.

"Yes, I suppose it was like this. There was more reason to hate then, perhaps, and more reason to fight . . ." His voice trailed off when he realized what he was saying.

Morfast looked at him strangely. "You think the White Wolf should not have crossed to the east with an army?"

He shook his head and said quietly, "No, I don't think that." He did not add that there was no time during the Slaver War when he doubted he was doing the right thing, but now that he was part of an army that hoped to overthrow the legitimate ruler of Grenda Lear, doubt seemed to fill him. He understood the political necessity for it, understood it was not Lynan's fault that he had been driven to take this action by Orkid and Dejanus murdering Berayma—Usharna's eldest son and successor—and laying the blame on him, but none of that made Ager feel any better about going to war against the kingdom which he had served for so long. Perhaps, just perhaps, Kumul—for whom serving the legitimate ruler of

Grenda Lear had been his life work—died when he did because
God had more mercy than Ager had ever believed.

And as for this slaughter of the army from Haxus, a traditional
enemy, he could not help wonder if Salokan could not have been allowed to run home with his tail between his legs. Haxus had never
been a serious threat to Grenda Lear itself, more a nuisance than
anything else. Ironically, this was a possibility Kumul himself
would never have considered; for him, the argument would run that
Haxus was an enemy and you killed your enemies.

*But I am not a general and I am not a king-in-waiting, and I am
not Kumul Alarn. I am Ager Crookback. I do not understand these
things.*

At midday Lynan called another council. The attitude of all the
clan chiefs was noticeably different from the day before. When
asked for their advice, all they would do is ask in turn what Lynan
would have them do. Ager thought Lynan looked satisfied with
that response, and it made him feel uneasy; yet when the prince
asked him for his opinion, he had little to offer.

"We have two choices," he said.

"And they are?" Lynan urged.

"To turn our attention again to the kingdom, either by attacking
the remnants of Areava's army or by attacking Daavis, or to retreat
over the Algonka Pass and reconsider our strategy."

Lynan nodded, as if in agreement. "Will no one else add their
thoughts?"

There were muffled denials. Even Korigan and Eynon seemed
content to let their feuding go and wait on Lynan's word. He had
given them a great victory, perhaps the greatest in Chett history. He
was the son of the General. He was the White Wolf returned. Who
were they to question him?

Lynan turned to Jenrosa. "And what do the magickers say?"

Jenrosa looked up in surprise. "They say nothing on this."

"Has the earth been asked?" he insisted.

"The earth had no words."

"Have the eagle and karak been asked?"

"The eagle and karak had nothing to show us."

Lynan glanced quickly at the woman sitting directly behind Jenrosa. Lasthear, Jenrosa's teacher, nodded in agreement. Ager saw
the exchange and was offended on Jenrosa's behalf, then guiltily realized Lynan knew Jenrosa would still be greatly affected by

Kumul's death and might not understand everything her magic showed her.

"We need a base on this side of the Ufero Mountains from which to operate," Lynan said.

"If we capture Daavis, we will have such a base," Gudon suggested lightheartedly, and many laughed.

"Our army is made up of cavalry," Lynan said. "We have not the troops nor the wherewithal to assault a city."

"Are you suggesting we build a base in Hume?" Ager asked, resisting the temptation to add that the Chetts did not have the wherewithal for that either.

"We need something more secure, more permanent, than that," Lynan answered.

"What exactly are you suggesting?" Ager prompted.

Lynan smiled at him. "You said we had two choices. We move south, or we move west. There is a third choice."

Ager looked blankly at Lynan for a second, then opened his mouth in surprise. The answer was so obvious he felt a fool for not realizing it. He could tell by the expression on Korigan's face that she had seen the truth at the same time.

"Haxus," Ager said.

"Yes. We have defeated its army. We have captured its king. Haxus is open to us . . . if we move quickly enough."

"We need only march in and take it!" Eynon declared, his rough face showing his eagerness for battle. "A whole kingdom will fall to us from one battle!"

Lynan shook his head. "A whole kingdom does not fall because it loses its king," he said severely. "Grenda Lear lost my mother Usharna and my brother Berayma in one season and survived easily enough. But our chances in Haxus are greater than our chances in south Hume. Another army could be marching north from Kendra right now to join the army already in the province. Grenda Lear has vast resources to draw on."

"But in comparison, Haxus does not," Ager finished.

"But Haxus does have the troops, the experience, and the sappers we will need to besiege Grenda Lear's great cities."

"Like Daavis," one chief said, grinning like an excited child.

"Like Daavis," Lynan agreed. "And Sparro and Pila and one day even Kendra itself."

*   *   *

"He has ambition, your prince," Lasthear said. She was a small, softly-spoken Chett magicker, quiet and reserved in any company other than Jenrosa's.

"You can't get much more ambitious than wanting the throne of Grenda Lear," Jenrosa replied. She was sitting next to a circle she had traced in the dark brown dirt of Hume. *Good soil,* she told herself. It reminded her of the soil in the village where she was born. In a pang of self-pity she wished she had never left the village, but almost immediately cursed herself for a fool. She had hated her childhood, her mother nothing but a drunken sot, her father long dead or run away, her prospects no better than ending up as some farmer's wife.

In some ways she thought that fate would have been preferable to the one handed her. She was exiled from Kendra, the city she truly regarded as her home, and had lost Kumul, the only man she had ever truly loved. On top of all that she was afraid the Chett magickers had started regarding her as a Truespeaker, a great magicker that only appeared once every two or three generations. All she had ever wanted was a quiet life where she could use what she had once considered to be her modest magickal abilities for an equally modest profit. She had wanted a quiet and comfortable life, unconcerned with and untroubled by the greater world.

And then there was Lynan. She had tied herself to his fortunes first through necessity and later through genuine affection. For a brief period there had been four of them—Lynan, Jenrosa, Kumul, and Ager—and although their lives had been dangerous, their simple aim to stay alive had created a strong bond between them. But now one of their number was slain, Ager had a whole clan to fill up his time, and Lynan . . .

Jenrosa shivered.

Lynan had become something more and perhaps something less than human, and that had been her fault. She had saved his life by giving him the blood of the vampire Silona, and in doing so had changed the fate of the whole continent. She wondered if she should feel proud for all that she, an apprentice and insignificant magicker from the Theurgia of Stars, had achieved, but instead could only feel a kind of numbing dread that combined with her grief over Kumul to make her feel lethargic and witless.

"I did not mean that," Lasthear said after a while. She was sitting on the opposite side of the circle in the dirt.

Jenrosa glanced up at her. "You are talking about this invasion of Haxus?"

Lasthear nodded. "If he gains both Haxus and his sister's throne, Lynan will be the first to control the whole of the continent of Theare, except the desert in the south."

"Is that important?"

Lasthear did not answer but started calling to the earth. Jenrosa joined her automatically. Their voices threaded together and seemed to weave a path through the air around them. A dust devil whirled between them for a moment and then was gone. Jenrosa blinked dirt from her eyes and looked down at the circle. The suggestion of words appeared, dissolved, reformed again.

"A ruler," Jenrosa said aloud.

"A tyrant," Lasthear added.

"A woman."

"She owns the Keys of Power."

"A dead city."

"The price."

The dust devil reappeared and destroyed the circle. The two women leaned back in sudden exhaustion, their eyes closed. When Jenrosa opened her eyes again, she saw Lasthear looking at her with great earnestness.

"You think the answer was there, don't you?" It was more of an accusation than a question.

"You are the Truespeaker," Lasthear said. "You tell me."

"I don't believe we see the future."

"Neither do I. Magic no more determines our fate than spying a distant land from the top of a mountain means you will one day visit that land. Magic gives us glimpses of history: past, present and future." Lasthear reached out and took Jenrosa's hand. "Only the Truespeaker can interpret those glimpses of history, draw real meaning from them."

"I don't believe we see the future," Jenrosa repeated, taking her hand from Lasthear's. "And I don't believe I am the Truespeaker. I am not a Chett."

"We are all Chetts," Lasthear said without irony.

It took Lynan's army five days to reach the border of Haxus. Scouts ranging far and wide quickly found the fort Salokan had established as a staging post for his invasion of Grenda Lear, and also where he kept his reinforcements, mainly heavy infantry with a few squadrons of light cavalry for picket and scouting duties. Chett outriders reported that the fort commander was overconfident and lazy; the gates were open and unlocked, and the few pickets were relieved like clockwork, making it easy to plan an assault around their movements.

Because it was a fort, Lynan's army had to take it quickly or be forced into a siege, something the Chetts were temperamentally unsuited for and Lynan could ill afford to waste time on. Nor could Lynan risk moving deeper into Haxus with such a large enemy force behind him, and he was unwilling to detach a whole banner to cover his rear. The fort had to be taken by a sudden assault, and Lynan planned for the attack to start well before first light. If things went well, his riders would occupy the fort by sunrise; if things went badly, his army had a whole day to retreat to a safe distance. He gave command of the main attack to his Red Hands under Gudon; they had been trained to fight on foot using the short sword, and once inside the fort their horses would be more hindrance than help. They would be followed up by Ager with his Ocean clan, warriors who were proving to be among the toughest and most fanatical of the Chetts; Ager also commanded the remnants of the lancers, the banner savaged so fiercely by the knights of the Twenty Houses. Korigan and Eynon would lead the rest of the banners, eliminating any forces outside of the fort and maintaining constant archery fire against the fort's walls.

Two hours before first light, scouts reported to Lynan that the enemy pickets had been eliminated and replaced by his own riders. Before ordering the banners and their commanders to take their places, the prince had Salokan brought to him. The king was thin and pale and looked old before his time; his right hand bandaged to the wrist. Under instruction from Lynan, no one had talked to him since his capture, nor had anyone mistreated him. At this stage he was baggage, and Lynan wanted him to understand that.

"Does this fort have a name?" Lynan asked him.

Salokan blinked sleep away from his eyes and peered at the walls of the fort, not much more than a distant white line in the night. "Typerta," he said.

"That was your father's name, wasn't it?"

Salokan nodded. "It is a strong fort," he said, some of his haughtiness returning. "You will not be able to take it."

Lynan arched his eyebrows. "Truly? What would you suggest?"

"You don't really believe I would help you, do you?"

"You could order the garrison to stand down and surrender."

Salokan did not reply, but stood more stiffly and jutted out his chin. He was regained some of his courage as well as his haughtiness.

Lynan seemed disappointed. "As I expected." He turned to his commanders. "We take no prisoners. Slaughter everyone." He met each commander's gaze; only Ager seemed unsettled by the order, but he said nothing. The prince turned back to Salokan. "You will stay here by my side and watch."

To lower their profile, Gudon, Ager and their troops covered the first two thirds of the distance to the fort dismounted. They walked double file through depressions and around hills until they came to a natural bowl just over a league from the fort, led there by scouts posing as Haxus pickets. There the Red Hands mounted and formed two long lines. On Ager's advice, in case their charge ran into Haxus cavalry and to boost their morale after losing their leader Kumul, Gudon placed the lancers in a single line in front of the Red Hands and put them under the command of his brother Makon; they would be first into the attack, and their task would be to disperse any enemy horse and then peel away, giving Gudon and the bodyguard access to the fort's gate. Behind the Red Hands, Ager organized his own warriors, the only Chetts in Lynan's army who fought together as a clan and, with the Red Hands, the only Chetts Ager had trained to fight on foot.

Gudon and Ager embraced quickly and mounted. It was thirty minutes from first light and the changing of the Haxus pickets when Gudon gave the order to attack.

The five long lines of cavalry climbed out of the bowl, losing some of their orderliness. As they walked over the lip and onto level ground the lancers broke into a canter. Gudon counted slowly to thirty then ordered the Red Hands to a canter as well. By now they were only a league from the fort and he could see guards rushing along the high walls in panic. He glanced left and right, saw his own sweeping lines, watched his riders holding back their horses from the charge. Farther afield he could see the great dark masses of the banners under the command of Korigan and Eynon as they surged forward. He saw Makon raise and then lower his sword; the lancers burst from a canter to the charge, their long spears held overhand, their line still tight. Gudon smiled as he saw it, and wondered at what Kumul had wrought. And then it was his turn. He raised and lowered his sword and kicked his horse into a gallop. The Red Hands matched him, and with one voice they screamed their war cry.

Ahead he could see the fort gate still open like a cavernous mouth. Some soldiers ran around in front of it, but none of them made an attempt to close it. Then someone seemed to organize them and they started pushing two huge wooden doors into place. Gudon felt a terrible knot in his stomach as he realized the Red Hands would not make it in time, then watched with elation as Makon led the lancers straight for the gate instead of peeling away. The Haxus infantry in front of him scattered and the lancers burst through into the fort; seconds later Gudon and his warriors followed them through. As soon as he was past the gate, Gudon sheathed his saber, dismounted, and drew his short sword. The few enemy armed were already fleeing in all directions, the rest were still in their tents or just now tottering out half dressed and wondering what all the noise was about. Gudon assigned one troop to guard the entrance while the others spread out and started the slaughter. At first he stood back, making sure that pressure was applied whenever it looked like the defenders were starting to organize, but when Lynan himself appeared, he surrendered command and joined in the fight, reveling in the bloody fury that filled him.

Lynan forced Salokan to watch. The massacre went on for most of the morning, the last few hours being nothing more than the final mopping-up where scattered enemy soldiers were rooted out of hiding places or found feigning death among all the bodies. When all was done and not a single enemy was left alive, Lynan escorted Salokan around the fort. So much blood had been spilled that the ground was covered in a red mud; it crept over the toes of the king's boots. He tried to hide his face away from the slaughter, but whichever way he looked, he saw thousands of his soldiers turned into carrion. He closed his eyes, but then he could smell the blood and the shit and hear the panting of the exhausted Chetts. In the end he was more afraid of the dark than the light. When Lynan had finished his tour, he leaned over and whispered in Salokan's ear: "I will do this to every fort and camp, every farm and village, every town and city in Haxus that you do not order to surrender to me. And every time I do it, you will bear witness."

Jenrosa refused to enter the fort. She could hear the buzzing of flies two hundred paces away. Her stomach heaved and she turned away, but something stopped her from leaving. She groaned.

"We must listen to the earth again," she said urgently to Lasthear.

The two of them knelt down and scratched a circle, but before they could begin the calling, a rivulet of blood from the fort met the circle and started to fill it. Lasthear cried out and tried to erase it, but Jenrosa grabbed her hand. "Let it finish," she ordered. In horror she watched as the circle became a swollen red disk. She called to the earth and the dust devil came and spat specks of blood against their faces. Words formed in the pool and Jenrosa recited: "A red monarch."

She waited for Lasthear to speak the words she saw, but the woman's mouth was clamped shut. To Jenrosa it looked like invisible fingers grasped her jaw.

"A red woman," Jenrosa continued uncertainly.

And still Lasthear would not—or could not—speak.

"A red city."

And then the dust devil returned, spitting more blood, and ended the spell. Lasthear cried out in pain and shock. Jenrosa tottered to her feet, her breathing ragged, and started to cry. She shouted in anger and furiously wiped the blood and tears from her face.

Lynan was in the grove where even sunlight seemed liquid and green. There was no sound of bird or insect, but all the trees and ferns seemed fit to burst with life. He was lying on his back. He could smell the grass, sweet and young, and beneath it the earth, dark and moist. Above him a wind rustled the canopy. He looked down the length of his body, admiring his hard white skin. He noticed he had three of the Keys of Power. He moved aside the Key of Union and the Key of the Sword, and there lay the Key of the Scepter, the Monarch's Key. He sat up, surprised. When did he get this? Who gave it to him?

He held it up to study it in better light and dropped it with a start. It was covered in blood. He tugged its chain over his head and threw it away with all his strength. It sailed through the air, slowed, and then stopped, suspended.

"This is mine," said a too-familiar voice.

Lynan searched the among the trees for her.

"I gave it to you to keep for me," she said.

"I will not win the throne for your sake," he said.

Silona laughed, and the sound came from every direction, from the very forest itself. "You do everything for my sake," she said.

5

QUEEN Charion paused in her striding to look out over her capital from the walls that surrounded it. Daavis had been turned into a city where the houses, cannibalized for their stone and wood, seemed like hollow skulls. Everywhere she looked, her people scurried like ants, repairing city walls, restocking depots with food and armaments, tending livestock, pushing carts and pulling wagons and, if too young or too old to help, keeping out of the way. Parks and gardens had been turned into fields and pens. Cattle had been slaughtered and their meat dried and salted; sheep and goats were kept alive for their fleece and milk and an emergency meat supply. New cisterns had been dug and plastered and whitewashed, then filled with water from the Barda River. Metal bowls, cups, eating utensils, the backs of mirrors and gardening tools had been collected and melted down and were being converted into spear- and arrow-heads and swords and daggers. New tunnels were being dug parallel to the walls so enemy mining could be countered swiftly, and wooden frames constructed to prop up threatened walls. Long lines of elderly matrons were tearing clothing into strips, bleaching them in vats of urine, drying them, and folding them for bandages.

Charion breathed deeply. She commanded all this activity and all the countless minutiae that went with it. She could not remember the last time she had managed to sleep for more than two hours at a time, and she knew it was starting to show. She was even more crabby and acid-tongued than usual; food tasted like sawdust and wine like brackish water. She had worn the same dress now for God knew how long, having donated most of her clothes to her city's cause, not to mention most of the cooking pots and utensils from her palace's kitchens. She had even ordered most of the good quality palace furniture sent to the sawyer so the wood could be used in wall construction or in the making of arrows and spear hafts.

But her people had sacrificed as much. This was the second time in as many months that her people had been called on to prepare the city for a siege, and she had heard no word of criticism, no sound of complaint. She was proud of them.

Charion glanced down and saw workers laboring in one of the counter-mine tunnels. "Farben!" she shouted, and everyone in a radius of forty paces suddenly froze. All except Farben, that is, a small, balding official with a permanently harried expression, who hurried to her from the back of her entourage.

"Your Majesty?"

"I thought I ordered the trenches to be at least two paces deep?"

"You certainly did, your Maj—"

"Then why is this trench decidedly *less* than two paces deep?"

The workers in the trench looked worriedly at each other. Farben wrung his hands. "I don't know, your Maj—"

"Then get down and find out!" she ordered, and Farben scuttled down the nearest stairs and to the local work foreman, a large hairy man who scowled at him. Charion watched the two men argue for a moment before the foreman angrily grabbed a measuring stick, stuck it into the trench, pulled it out, and waved it at Farben. The official made a placating sound and hurried back to Charion.

"Well?" she demanded.

Farben was sweating from a mixture of nerves and fright. "It *is* two paces deep, your Majesty."

Charion looked surprised. "Really?" she said mildly, leaning over to look at the trenches a second time.

Farben nodded eagerly.

Charion harrumphed and set off again around the walls, yelling out observations that were carefully recorded for future action, "We need more stone here . . . shift labor from the cisterns to trench construction . . . we need more canvas to shelter the people in this quarter . . ." until she had done a complete circuit of the walls, ending at the northern gate. She dismissed her officials and gazed around once more, noting with relief that the walls were almost completed. Her biggest worry had been that Lynan would attack before she could repair all the damage done by Salokan when he attacked Daavis, but now it looked as if the city would be even better prepared than that time. Maybe she would even allow herself four hours sleep that night.

Before descending from the walls she looked northward over gently rolling farmland, now deserted and starting to look rundown. The next winter would be a hard one for her people. But they would survive. Somehow, they would all survive.

Galen and his men filled their helmets with water from a stream and let their horses drink from them; when the horses had finished, and none of them showed any signs of illness, the knights themselves slaked their thirst from the stream. When Galen had drunk his fill, he wet a scarf and wiped his face, then placed the scarf around his neck; the cool water trickled down his chest and back, bringing some relief from the heat. It was a hot day and even though at most the only armor the knights were dressed in were their greaves and helmets, they were all soaked in sweat. They were not used to summers this far north, and it was telling on them as well as their mounts.

Magmed, looking nothing like the young and arrogant knight who had set out all those months ago from Kendra, joined Galen. "It is nearly summer, and this stream shows no sign of drying; the weeds are still green right to the top of the bank. What do you think?"

Galen looked around. He liked this spot. The land sloped gently from west to east, the stream eventually disappearing in a copse of trees not a hundred paces away. He nodded. "Aye. We'll place an outpost here. There is water and wood and a good view of the surrounding land."

In fact, Galen admitted to himself, he liked this land a lot. Although the heat was not to his favor, it was at least a dry heat, unlike the sultry summers citizens experienced back in Kendra. The grass was starting to yellow, but there were enough waterways and cool valleys to keep livestock going until autumn rains replenished the earth. *You could raise good horses here,* he thought. *Good stallions for the knights of Kendra.*

As well, he admitted to himself, a property here would give him an excuse to be away from Kendra . . . and closer to Charion. As a member of the kingdom's aristocracy—the Twenty Houses—he found that Areava had made Kendra a little too chilly for his liking; her dislike for his kind was well known.

He had seen a great deal of Hume over the last ten days. His mixed command of knights from the Twenty Houses and light infantry from Aman had early established that Lynan's Chett army was not yet moving on Daavis, and so had subsequently pushed back the perimeter of the area under kingdom control farther and farther north of the city. Now he was in the process of establishing a series of outposts in wide arcs twenty leagues apart, each outpost equipped with signal fires and a garrison. This spot would provide the last outpost necessary for the line some sixty leagues out from Daavis. That was five days' march for most armies, three for Galen's force, and still two even for the Chetts, unmatched in mobility. Galen would push out another twenty leagues and establish a final ring of outposts. After that he would return to Daavis and see what Queen Charion had planned for him.

Or even Areava. She may have sent new instructions while he had been away.

For a moment he pictured the two women together. Areava, he had long admired from afar. She was cold, aloof, as beautiful as winter; and she was ruler of all Grenda Lear. For a long time he had harbored the secret dream of wedding her; her marriage to Sendarus had temporarily sunk that, but now that the man was dead, for which Galen was genuinely sorry, the way was open again. But now there was Charion.

He shook his head in wonder. Until a short while ago he had convinced himself he did not even like Charion, but after leaving her behind in Daavis he found he missed her intelligence and her strange dark beauty, the opposite of Areava's.

Yes, he thought. It would be good to get back to Daavis.

It was bright day in Kendra, and a gentle breeze wafted through the south gallery of the palace. Olio stood at the entrance to the gallery watching a kestrel flying high, high above the harbor. It made great circles in the sky, dipping and soaring, patiently waiting for the right moment to strike. Olio was hypnotized by it.

"Your Highness?"

Olio sighed and turned. It was the fat man with the funny clothes again. Olio had wanted to see his sister, but everyone kept on telling him she was too busy to see him. He asked for his mother or Berayma then, but apparently they were *very* busy, too. "And what of Lynan?" he asked one official. "I suppose he's busy as well!" The official had not answered that one, which Olio found strange. Instead, the only one who could come and see him was . . . now what was his name again . . . ?

"Do you remember me, your Highness? I am Prelate Edaytor Fanhow."

Ah, yes, that's right. "Hello, Prelate. That's a strange name."

"My name is Edaytor Fanhow. Prelate is my title."

Olio blinked at him. He did not want to admit he was getting confused.

"You can call me Edaytor," the fat man continued.

"I can call you anything I like," Olio said haughtily.

"That is true."

"I am a prince."

"That is true, too."

"My mother is queen of Grenda Lear."

He heard Edaytor take in a deep breath. "Are you so sure of that?"

Olio raised his eyebrows. "Of course I'm sure. I'm her son, aren't I?"

"When is the last time you saw your mother?"

Olio's forehead creased in thought. "Oh, a long time ago. She is very busy. She is queen, after all."

"Would you like to step out onto the gallery?"

Olio shrugged.

Edaytor stepped out first. "It is a beautiful day."

"There is a kestrel flying over the harbor."

Edaytor searched the sky for a moment before finding it. "I see it."

"The kestrel is the badge of my family," Olio said. "See?" He pinched out the kestrel emblem sewn into his shirt.

"It is a wonderful badge. It is the most famous badge in all of Grenda Lear."

"It means I am a Rosetheme," Olio added.

"You are Olio Rosetheme, prince of Grenda Lear."

Olio frowned. "Yes. Yes, I am."

"And do you remember what the Rosetheme family has that no other family has?"

"The crown," he said immediately.

Edaytor laughed. It was a nice sound, and for the first time Olio decided that maybe he liked this man.

"I mean other than the crown. Even greater symbols of royal authority, filled with magic and power."

Olio creased his forehead in thought again. He was silent for a long time. "Can you give me a clue?"

"There are four of them."

Olio's eyes lit up. "Oh, I know! I know! The Keys of Power! Mother wears them on chains around her neck."

Edaytor nodded, and licked his lips. "Can you tell me what the four Keys are?"

"Whew," Olio gushed.

"I know it's a hard question."

"There's one for fighting. It's got a sword. That's my favorite. There's one with a scepter. That's the most important Key. There's one with a circle. That's the most boring one. And there's one with . . ."

"Yes?"

"It has . . ." Olio shook his head as if he could loosen the answer from his brain. His unruly brown hair flopped over his eyes. "It has . . ." He glared at his feet, mouthing a word that would not come. He started to blush with anger.

"That's very good," Edaytor said hurriedly. "Three out of four. Do you want me to tell you what is on the fourth Key?"

"No," Olio said, unconvincingly feigning disinterest.

"Well, I'll tell you anyway. The fourth Key has a heart on it."

Olio slumped then, as if his whole body had been under great tension. "Yes," he said weakly. "I remember now. The Key of the Heart." He looked up at Edaytor, and the prelate saw something of the old Olio flicker across his face, but it was gone as quickly as it had come. Olio looked past Edaytor. "The kestrel is gone," he said flatly. "I don't expect we'll see it again today."

A message had come from Aman for Orkid, carried by pigeon. He did not open it until his office was empty, his clerks and secretaries all gone. The small scroll of paper had only a dozen words on it.

> *Amemun convinced Southern Chetts.*
> *You love the queen; Aman can still reign.*

Orkid stood up heavily and let the message burn over a candle flame. The meaning behind the words of his brother, King Marin, were plain enough, and they both frightened and exulted him.

The first part of the message meant his friend Amemun had

made contact with the fierce Southern Chetts and somehow persuaded them to side with the kingdom against their northern cousins on the Oceans of Grass. Orkid had never doubted that Grenda Lear would defeat Lynan and his allies in the long run, but forcing the rebel Chetts to protect their southern border would hasten the inevitable.

The second part of the message was equally clear. The grand plan—to have Marin's son Sendarus wed Areava and produce heirs to the throne of Grenda Lear with Amanite blood—had collapsed tragically with the death of Sendarus and his daughter. Some other way must be found to ensure the blood of Aman shared the throne of Grenda Lear. Marin was saying that way must now be found through Orkid himself.

How did he know my feelings toward Areava? he wondered with something like alarm. *Were they that obvious?*

Then Orkid remembered those long conversations with Amemun when he had escorted Sendarus to Usharna's court for the first time. Amemun had plied him with questions about Areava, had helped Orkid finalize the last details of the grand plan.

And then reported everything back to Marin, of course. I did not have to say the words to Amemum; he always knew how to read my mind.

He sat down again. He could never marry Areava. The council would not allow it, and the Twenty Houses would pull even farther away from supporting the throne, and he would not do that to her. And yet . . .

His own thoughts flagged his divided loyalty, something else Amemun had probably guessed at. He remembered the old teacher telling him that although Orkid's years in Kendra had not blunted his love for Aman, they had given him time to learn to love its rulers. He had not denied it then, and would not deny it now. He would do almost anything to be able to express his feeling to Areava in the hope—the desperate hope—that she might return them. That was the problem with Marin's suggestion. Areava regarded Orkid as a friend, a trusted adviser, her mother's contemporary and confidante, and not as a potential lover. He was honest to himself about that much, at least.

Could he turn her around, make her fall in love with him? It was a question he had been secretly asking himself for several years, every since Areava had first blossomed into womanhood. At the time he wondered if his response to her had been more than a reflection of his love for her mother, the unattainable Usharna, but as Areava continued to grow and develop so had his feelings toward her. He had been ashamed of those feelings when she married his nephew, Sendarus, and now that shame had turned to guilt because Sendarus' death had given him the chance with Areava he so desperately wanted. And now he had Marin's sanction as well.

He realized that in a terrible way he did not want this chance, did not want to pursue the matter to the point where the queen might spurn him. He had never been afraid of the assassin's knife, but he was afraid of Areava's rejection. Yet now a combination of desire and duty urged him on, and he knew that even if he could resist desire, he had never in his life been able to resist duty.

Constable Dejanus finished the evening rounds of the palace. He stood in the great courtyard watching a single window high in the east wing. He could see the silhouette of a dark figure through the glass, fluttering with the candle light.

One arrow would do it, he said to himself. *Straight through the window and into the bastard's black heart.*

The thought sent a delicious thrill down his spine. To be rid of Chancellor Orkid Gravespear once and for all! It was his greatest wish.

His hands on his hips, Dejanus circled where he stood. He was a power here, a power in the greatest palace on Theare, maybe even in the world. His chest swelled with the thought of it, making him look even larger than he already was. *I have no need to be afraid of anything.* And then, as it always did, the familiar voice in his head said, *Except Orkid.*

The puff went out of him, and his gaze returned to that window. As he watched, the light went out and the wavering shadow of the chancellor disappeared. "If only it was that easy," Dejanus said aloud, then looked around to make sure no one heard him. The courtyard was deserted. It was very dark, and he suddenly felt very exposed. He hurried to his own quarters. The guard on duty snapped to attention as he passed, and that rejuvenated some of his confidence. He settled in his bed with a flask of good wine, and in his mind played out the many ways he could kill Orkid. Maybe an arrow, he thought. Hire an archer with some grudge against the chancellor.

And the voice said, *Or if you were brave enough, you could sim-*

ply use your own knife. Dejanus could find no answer to that voice.
He never had.

He finished the flask and fell asleep dreaming of the day, the one
blessed day, when he *would* be brave enough.

Galen led his knights in double file through the newly restored
gates of Daavis. A cheering crowd lined the main avenue leading
to the palace, and Galen noticed the surprised and gratified looks
on the young Kendran knights he led. Nor could he ignore that the
crowd's praise made him sit even straighter than usual in his saddle. If nothing else, this campaign had taught them that there was
more to the kingdom of Grenda Lear than the city of Kendra, and
more to concern it than the petty goings-on of the nobility.

At least it finally taught me *that,* he admitted to himself, and felt
proud of the fact he was young and smart enough to adapt. Areava
and her mother had been right all along. The provinces needed to
be—deserved to be!—brought into the everyday decisions that
were made on their behalf in the royal palace far away on Kestrel
Bay. Grenda Lear certainly could not afford to ignore people like
Charion.

Galen marveled at the work the people of Daavis had done in
preparing their city for a siege, and at the sacrifices they were prepared to make. He saw some streets where not one house remained
standing, their stone scavenged for the walls. In their place were
makeshift shelters of canvas and sheeting, old wood and blankets.

Acknowledging the crowd with a broad smile, he wished he had
earned all this gratitude. Setting up a series of outposts was not exactly the gallant work he and his knights had trained for and
dreamed about. His smile waned when he remembered the battle
against Lynan. They had earned something that day, he thought. But
at what a cost. Half his knights dead on the field. It would be another generation at least before the Twenty Houses could field a full
regiment of cavalry again.

Charion herself was waiting for them before the palace. She was
wearing the crown of Hume and mounted on her show horse, a
fine-boned white stallion that looked magnificent but was too deli-
cate to actually ride to war. Her clothes looked bedraggled, but
Galen thought she still managed to look regal, even imperious, with
her long black hair falling from the crown like a dark waterfall over
her shoulders. He dismounted and bowed slightly before her. The
cheering went up a notch.

"We were not expecting such a warm welcome," he admitted to Charion.

"They are encouraging you to stay," she said. She caught his gaze. "Are you going to?"

"Unless Queen Areava orders us elsewhere, we will stay." He returned her stare. "Have you received such a communication?"

Charion smiled thinly. "Not yet, although I've received one from her chancellor."

"Orkid Gravespear?" Galen could not help the distaste in his voice. He immediately felt ashamed: his newfound generosity to the provinces obviously did not extend to Orkid, even though he was Sendarus' uncle. "What did he have to say?"

Charion dismounted now and offered her arm to Galen, who took it. Charion nodded to Farben who indicated to the rest of the knights to follow him. Charion and Galen then walked into the palace.

"The chancellor says Areava lost her baby."

Galen gasped in surprise. "I did not even know she was pregnant."

"Does she usually reveal these intimate secrets to her nobles?" Charion asked innocently.

"What?" He was momentarily confused by the question. "No, of course not. I meant . . ." He shut his mouth. He was not sure what he meant. He was filled with sadness for Areava's sake, and for poor lost Sendarus.

Charion read something of his feelings in his expression and patted his hand. "Orkid says she is recovering, but that her brother Olio was injured in some way. Apparently, there was a great fire in the city the same day our army met Lynan's. That is why we have not heard from Areava."

"A black day for the whole kingdom," Galen said lowly.

They reached Charion's throne room, and she ordered her servants away. When they were alone, she said, "Orkid made no mention of you or your knights. I do not know what Areava intends for you. Under the circumstances, you might feel it best to go on to Kendra."

For the second time Charion was offering him a way out of his royal predicament. He knew that as one of the kingdom's leading nobles he could help Areava back in Kendra, but he was a member of the Twenty Houses and she did not trust him, and she had others to rely on for advice and assistance. On the other hand, he could make a decisive difference here if Lynan attacked into southern Hume. He glanced at Charion, who was doing her best to seem unconcerned.

"Her Majesty will send for me if she needs me," he said.

Charion smiled mysteriously. "Which majesty?" she asked.

Galen coughed politely in his hand. "The one farthest from me," he replied, and saw her eyes widen slightly.

"You must be tired after your expedition," she said quickly. "And dusty."

Galen looked down at his clothes, then behind him. He had left dirty footprints all the way into the throne room. "I have been looking forward to a bath," he admitted.

"Then you shall have one. I will give you and your lieutenants rooms in the palace. We can talk again after you have rested."

"Your Majesty is most generous," he said, bowing to her for the second time, and started to withdraw.

"You will have rested by tonight," she added lightly.

"Fully," he replied, and matched her smile.

6

THE harbor was burning. Thick plumes of greasy smoke pillowed into the air. Ships blazed at their moorings, their masts crumbled and collapsed, their sheets sparkled, torn remnants of their sails whipped like beacons in the wind before going out. Charcoaled bodies bobbed with the currents under the docks, washed up on Kolbee's beach with barrels and other flotsam, smelled like rotten crackling. Seabirds wheeled overhead before diving on carcasses to feast like they never had before. In the middle of the harbor a single warship, flames shooting along its whole length, started to roll, slowly at first, but as the water sluiced over its side and then into its hold it quickly keeled over, its bow pointing slightly in the air. For a moment it looked as if it might hold, but then it slid beneath the water, stern first, and disappeared. An explosion of bubbles broke the surface and then nothing was left of its passing, not even a corpse.

Lynan could not look away from the destruction around him. In a terrible way it was beautiful. The harbor glowed with color, the clouds of smoke above seemed to shine with it, the air itself shimmered. He could smell burning wood and tar and canvas, and underneath all that the sweet smell of burning bodies. The sound of it was a giant's sigh, like something great coming to rest.

A Red Hand galloped up to Lynan and bowed. "Your Majesty, Queen Korigan reports that the city is secure. The fighting in the palace has been quelled. There is no other resistance."

Lynan nodded, relieved. The massacre at Fort Typerta had changed Salokan's attitude and he had cooperated ever since, ordering the surrender of every town and hamlet in his kingdom.

Only here at the capital, where there were other noble families, had the first real resistance been met. As it turned out, there were two main rival forces to Salokan, each led by one of the king's cousins; one took the palace and the other the fortified harbor, each hoping their stand would rally resistance against Lynan and at the same time rally support for their claim to the throne. Neither occurred. Indeed, the remnants of the Haxus army had followed Salokan—who was still king, after all—and been used to root out the rebels in both locations. When some noble refugees had tried to escape by ship, Lynan ordered fire arrows to destroy it and every other vessel at dock. The ensuing firestorm had turned the harbor into a pyre for the kingdom of Haxus.

Ager came beside him. "There is nothing more to be done here. We can leave a detachment to make sure no one else tries escaping by water."

"All the ships are gone," Lynan said distantly, still staring at the flames. He felt something inside him recoil at the sight of fire, but he forced himself to watch.

"More ships can come," Ager pointed out.

Lynan nodded. "You take care of it, then. I will go to the palace."

"Your Majesty!" someone shouted near the water's edge. Lynan saw one of the Haxus soldiers who had helped destroy the harbor's fortifications holding a dripping, bedraggled looking man by the collar of a torn and scorched jerkin. The man's skin was cut and scalded.

"Who is he?" Lynan asked.

"I recognize him," said another Haxus soldier. "He is the son of Count Vasiliy."

"The nobleman who held the harbor against us?" Lynan asked.

"The same."

The prisoner lifted his face and looked around, obviously dazed. Lynan regarded him for a moment, then said to the soldier holding him: "Kill him." The soldier nodded, drew a short sword, and stabbed the son of Count Vasiliy through the back. The nobleman gasped once and slumped to the ground.

Lynan turned his horse and left.

Jenrosa watched him leave. For a long while she had observed him as the harbor was destroyed, saw the flames reflected in his hard white skin, saw the way his expression did not change the whole time his army wreaked ruin at his command. Her mind heard the screams of the dying and wounded in the background, heard the crash of buildings as they collapsed under the fire, smelled the fear and despair rising into the air with the smoke. And Lynan had hardly blinked.

When he was gone, she could not help slumping in the saddle, as if her watching of Lynan had been a casting of some kind and had exhausted her. Lasthear put a hand on her arm. "Are you all right?"

Jenrosa did not answer. Something in the corner of her eye caught her attention and she turned to find it. At first, she did not recognize what it was, and then her gaze settled on the harbor waters, gold and glistening. She dismounted and went to the water's edge.

"Jenrosa?" Lasthear asked.

"It's nothing," Jenrosa said. She blinked. *No, there is something, but what?* A memory stirred deep in her mind. She bent over and swirled a hand in the water, sending ripples out in a circle, each ripple carrying its own reflection of the burning harbor. Again something moved a deep memory and she searched for it. She moved deeper into the water until it reached her waist.

"Jenrosa!" Lasthear cried out, her voice worried.

Jenrosa glanced over her shoulder, was surprised at Lasthear's expression. "There's nothing wrong."

"But you are so deep," Lasthear said.

Jenrosa could not help smiling. "This is not . . ." she started to say, then remembered she was talking to a Chett, someone who lived in the middle of the continent where the shallow lake at the High Sooq was the deepest water she ever saw. "I'm all right," she said. "I was brought up near the sea. I am in no danger."

Lasthear seemed uncertain, but said no more.

Jenrosa waited until the disturbance caused by her moving had calmed and then stared into the water, letting her eyes lose their focus, clearing her mind for the memory that was proving so elusive. Tentatively, she used her hand to cause a new cycle of ripples. Again each ripple carried a reflection of the burning harbor. Even as she watched the wash run out from her like mirrored rings, she saw in her mind's eye the incantation she wanted. She whispered the words. Nothing happened. She whispered the words again, and this time saw the last ripple reflected a harbor that was not burning at all: she caught a glimpse of a perfectly blue sky, of high-prowed Haxus ships, of wooden cranes and bustling docks.

She gasped in surprise and involuntarily took a step back toward land.

"Jenrosa!" Lasthear cried again.

"Be quiet!" she ordered sharply. She tried calming down her own heart which seemed ready to burst from her, but even as she did, her mind was racing. Where had the incantation come from? It had not been a memory after all: she had never learned those words, either from Lasthear or from her training with the theurgia. She·had called up something much deeper within her than mere memory.

She took a long breath and repeated the words as she set off more ripples, and this time each wave carried a different reflection. The words faded from her lips as she watched a hundred different scenes recede from her.

"The past is the same," she said, "but the present has no boundary."

She heard splashing behind her. The water around her became confused and choppy. She turned, her anger changing to surprise when she saw Lasthear standing right behind her, oblivious to the water lapping around her waist. "What did you say?" Lasthear demanded fiercely.

"What?"

"Just then, when you were watching the water. What did you say?"

Jenrosa blinked. "I'm not sure. I don't think—"

Lasthear grabbed Jenrosa's arms. "The past is the same," she said, almost shouting the words.

And Jenrosa said automatically, "But the present has no boundary."

Lasthear's face blanched. "Who told you those words?"

"I . . . I don't know."

"What incantation were you using?"

"I don't know. It came from somewhere inside my head. I'd never heard it before."

Lasthear let her go suddenly. "I startled you. I'm sorry."

Jenrosa suddenly became conscious that she and Lasthear were the center of some attention. Chetts were looking on as if they had been witness to some important occasion; Haxus soldiers just looked at them strangely. At that moment she heard Lasthear breathe in sharply.

"What's wrong?" Jenrosa asked.

"I have never been in this much water before," she said.

Jenrosa took her arm and guided her back to the shore. Lasthear thanked her and quickly mounted her horse to put as much distance as possible between her and the water. When Jenrosa mounted, others took it as a signal to go back to whatever it was they were doing before she entered the harbor. A short while later she and Lasthear were alone. For a while neither spoke; eventually, Lasthear let out a gust of air, as if she had been holding her breath ever since being up to her waist in water.

"I knew there was something special about you since the first time we did magic together, but I had no idea . . ." Her voice trailed off.

"You're not going to go on about the Truespeaker again, are you? Because if you are—"

Lasthear shook her head. "No."

Jenrosa shut her mouth.

Lasthear looked at her with uncertainty, as if Jenrosa was no longer the person she thought she was. "We have a story about a great magicker—"

"Oh, no," Jenrosa said quickly, holding up her hands. She could feel in her bones this was going to be about her in some way. "I'm not going to listen to this."

"He died over a thousand years ago," Lasthear went on.

"Oh," Jenrosa said, suddenly feeling foolish.

"In his time there were no Chetts, or Kendrans or Amanites or Haxans. There was only one people, and they were new to Theare. This great magicker was a man who was so honored by his people that they made him their ruler. For a long time the people prospered under his rule, but as he got older, he started having visions, terrible visions. At first, he told no one about them, but wrote them down in great books. One day an acolyte read one of the books and died in horrendous pain. When the magicker king found the body of the acolyte, he knew immediately what had happened, and he realized his madness was so great that one day it could destroy everything he had helped build. He called to him the greatest among his people and told them what was happening, and what he intended to do about it. He created four great talismans and put into them the four aspects of his power: his generosity, his wisdom, his strength, and his hope."

"Four talismans?" Jenrosa asked suspiciously.

"Yes, you see already. Four talismans that became the four Keys of Power. When he finished making them, he died. Instead of ruling in his name, the great ones he had called together fought among themselves for the talismans. One of them eventually gained control over all four, but by then the one people had divided into all the tribes that exist today."

"What was the name of this magicker king?"

"Colane Oeser."

Jenrosa shook her head and laughed lightly. "Never heard of him." For some reason she could not explain, she felt relief at that.

Lasthear shrugged. "It is not important. What is important is that his passing marked the breakup of the one people. The legend goes on to say that the people will be united again when one like him reappears."

Jenrosa stiffened. "One like him?"

"It was said he could see all possibilities for any course of action at the same time. He often said that 'The past is the same, but the present has no boundary.'"

"No!" Jenrosa said loudly. "No, this I will not believe!"

Lasthear looked sadly at Jenrosa but said nothing.

"No!" Jenrosa cried. She pulled hard on her reins and galloped away from Lasthear and the glistening harbor.

It took longer to garrison the harbor than Ager thought it would. Besides organizing a mixture of troops—Chett and Haxan—to secure the foreshore and its precincts, he had to set work gangs to put out fires and then clear away wreckage. Over the next few weeks the docks and warehouses would have to be repaired before traders would be able to visit Kolbee and unload their goods. Trade was the lifeblood of cities like Kolbee. Without it, eventually, they withered and died. Ager reminded himself to explain this carefully to Lynan, then snorted at his own arrogance. Lynan had been raised in the court of Usharna, and she would have made sure all her children knew how the kingdom paid for itself.

By the time it was nightfall, the worst of the fires were out and most of the bodies collected and taken away. Ager started the rounds then, making sure the new guards were doing their job properly. By the time he finished, the stars were riding high overhead, and he found himself standing on one of the less damaged docks. There was a sunken ship on one side, its mast sticking out of the water like a grave marker. He sat on the edge of the dock, his legs dangling over the side, and said a silent prayer for the sailors inside the ship's belly. He looked out from the harbor, and down the Oino river that led eventually to the sea north of Theare. He had been on a few merchant ships that, in more peaceful times, had made the run down the Oino to Kolbee. He remembered it being a pretty city. It would be again, he told himself, mostly believing it.

He sensed rather than heard someone move behind him, and as he looked over his good shoulder he placed one hand over the hilt of his sword. When he saw Morfast, he relaxed and smiled ruefully. "You'll never do any good as an assassin."

"I wanted to watch you without you knowing I was there," she said, and came to sit beside him.

"I could think of more entertaining ways to spend my time."

"I like watching you," she said plainly. "I try to imagine what it is you're thinking."

"And what did you imagine I was thinking just now?"

"Something about the water. I know you used to work on merchanters." She studied his face carefully. "There is a glint in your one eye, Ager. Do you miss those times?"

"No, not really. Not the work, anyway. But the sea. Yes, I miss the sea sometimes." He laughed softly. "It wasn't something I missed on the Oceans of Grass. That was like being at sea. The plains are well named."

"I would like to go to sea one day," Morfast said. "I have always been curious to know what it is like."

"I will take you," Ager said. "When the war is over."

Morfast leaned over to kiss his cheek. "You will be too busy working for the king to take anyone out to sea."

For a moment Ager did not know who she was talking about, then understood that, by the king, she meant Lynan. It made him feel odd, as if he was out of his true time and place.

"Yes, I suppose that's true," he said vaguely.

"And when you're not doing the king's business, you'll be looking after your clan."

Ager smiled suddenly. It still amazed him that he was the chief of a Chett clan. The clan's previous head had tried to ambush him one night because Ager had bested him in single combat. Having slain the chief and his immediate family—also in on the ambush—Ager had inherited the clan. He had grown to be as proud of his Chetts as they seemed to be of him, and they had proven their worth as warriors in three great battles. In fact, members of the Ocean clan regarded themselves as the equals of the Red Hands, Lynan's personal bodyguard.

"That would be no duty," he said softly, then looked at Morfast. "Where are we camped?"

"We are billeted!" she said. "His Majesty has placed the two of us in the palace so we may be near him while we are here."

"Ah." He tried not to sound disappointed.

The palace was dark. No one was around to light braziers and fires. Some moonlight filtered through lancet windows set high in the outer wall, adding an eerie silvery sheen to marble columns and pavers. Lynan's footsteps clinked hollowly in the hallways as he explored. With his acute eyesight he recognized a painting done by a Kendran artist that Usharna had sent to Salokan years ago as part of some trade agreement. Now it belonged to Grenda Lear again.

For I have conquered it, he told himself, *and Grenda Lear will belong to me.*

He studied the painting more closely. A stream of blood whipped across the bottom like a decorative sash. His feet squelched and he looked down. There were still great puddles of blood on the floor. The bodies had been removed hours ago, but no one had yet bothered to clean up properly. He wiped his feet on a dry part of the floor and went on. He could hear voices ahead and followed them. Eventually, he found himself in a long and relatively narrow hall. Someone had lit the braziers; the room was crisscrossed with shadows. There was a large stone seat against the centre of one of the walls.

Lynan realized this was the throne room. It was smaller than he had imagined. But then, he was used to the throne room in Kendra, which by itself must have been a quarter the size of this whole palace.

Korigan, long and regal, was sitting on one of the arms of the throne and giving instructions to a banner leader.

"You should be sitting in that," Lynan told her. The banner leader bowed low to Lynan and Korigan and hurried from the room. "After all, your Chetts won it." Korigan smiled easily, and he expected her to come back by saying it was his throne.

"It is below me," she said simply.

"Below you?" He could not help the surprise in his voice.

"Haxus is now nothing more than a province. This is a governor's chair, not a throne. I would not deign it with my backside." She was still smiling. "Nor should you."

"I am tired," he countered. "Bone dead. I will sit on it until I find someone else to fill it."

"And who will you find?" she asked.

"You speak as if I'd already made up my mind."

"And haven't you?"

Now Lynan smiled. "Yes."

"Salokan?"

"It was his kingdom. He knows it better than anyone."

"How do you know he won't rebel against you once you leave Haxus?"

"Is he nearby?"

"As you requested, he was assigned one of the rooms in the palace."

"Not his original quarters, I trust."

"Something much less grand."

"Would you bring him to me?"

When Korigan had gone, Lynan walked up to the throne. He was about to sit in it when he changed his mind. He was not sure what it was, but he knew that this was not his to have. He would sit in a throne one day, but not this one and not this day. He ran his hand along its polished stone. It was beautifully crafted, with a battle scene carved on its three closed sides. He wondered absently if they depicted a battle during the Slaver War. Unlikely, he told himself. Haxus won no great battles in that war. Lost a few, though. He noticed there was blood on the floor here, too. Pools of it. He wondered how many died to defend this empty throne.

"You wanted to see me?" asked a voice behind him.

Lynan turned to face Salokan. The once king stood slung-shouldered, but there was something about the way he held his head and the way his arms set straight against his sides that spoke defiance, not submission. In a strange way, he reminded Lynan of an insect, coolly indifferent to everyone around him and sure of his own superiority.

Korigan and one of the Red Hands stood behind Salokan. Lynan asked them to leave. The Red Hand turned on his heel and left immediately; Korigan seemed reluctant but nodded to Lynan and left, too.

"Are you happy to be back in your palace?" Lynan asked Salokan lightheartedly, going to him.

Salokan blinked but did not answer. Lynan took him by the arm.

Salokan tried to resist, but gasped in pain as Lynan tightened his grip.

"Let me show you around," Lynan said. He pointed to the throne. "Here is where you used to lord it over Haxus. And here is where your cousin's soldiers died defending it." He forced Salokan to accompany him on a walk around the entire room, making sure they stepped in every pool of blood. When they returned to the throne, he forced Salokan to sit in it.

"Now you are back, ready to lord it again." Lynan smiled thinly. "As governor of my province of Haxus."

Still Salokan did not answer. Lynan sighed, then with one quick motion drew his dagger. Salokan flinched, but he did not cry out. Lynan flipped the dagger in the air, caught it by its blade, and offered the grip to him. Salokan looked up warily.

"Go on," Lynan urged. "Take it."

"You are going to kill me, aren't you?" Salokan said. "Now that you have my kingdom, you don't need me alive anymore."

Lynan seemed to consider the words. "There's a certain logic in that," he conceded.

"I will take the dagger and you will strike me down, claiming I attacked you."

"You forget one thing. I don't need an excuse to kill you. In the eyes of the world, you are nothing. A king without a throne is less than a peasant."

"Then what does that make you?" Salokan spat back.

"Your conqueror," Lynan said easily, and offered the dagger again. Salokan took it reluctantly. "Now strike me." Salokan gaped at him. "Go on."

Salokan shook his head and dropped the dagger to the floor. The hall echoed with a metallic clang. Lynan looked disappointed. He picked up the dagger, grabbed Salokan's right hand and forced his fingers around the grip. Then, the horrified Salokan powerless to stop him, Lynan drove the dagger through his left forearm. A spray of blood spurted between them. Salokan used all his strength to pull away, to release the weapon, but Lynan held him in place with extraordinary ease.

"More sacrifice for your throne," Lynan said, grinning now, and pulled out the dagger. He let go of Salokan and stepped back, watching his bleeding wound with keen interest. Salokan tried to stand up, but Lynan used his gory right hand to push him back. He thrust his forearm into Salokan's face. "Look at it!" he commanded, and Salokan had no choice but to look, and as he did so he saw the flow of blood ease to a trickle and then stop altogether.

"That's not possible," Salokan said hoarsely.

Lynan reached out and grabbed Salokan's shirt, used it to wipe his forearm clean and presented it again for inspection. There was no wound. Not even a scratch. Bile flooded up Salokan's throat, and he grabbed his mouth with his hands to stop vomiting. Lynan leaned forward and whispered in his ear, "You will rule Haxus in my name because I say you will. If you disobey me in anything, if you rebel or join cause with my enemies, I will come back to this palace and eat you alive in front of your people."

7

AMEMUN looked down from the dune to wide green plains and could not help breathing a sigh of relief. After traveling for so long in the deserts of the Saranah, he longed to walk in a land that actually had grass and trees instead of the stunted bushes and spiky weeds that passed for vegetation in the south of the continent. Dekelon raised himself on his elbows to get a better view of the land that spread northward.

"The Oceans of Grass," he said, and could not hide the excitement in his voice. He turned to Amemun. "My people have dreamed of returning here for generations to exact our revenge on the Chetts and take back our land. And now it is possible."

Amemun smiled sympathetically. *I would have the same dream had I come from your home, old man,* he thought. Although, he corrected himself, since starting the expedition, Dekelon had ceased looking as old as he did. There was a sprightliness about his step and a clarity in his eyes that had not been there before.

"What now?" he asked.

"We wait until night before moving. On these plains we would stick out like trees in the desert."

Amemun glanced behind him at the small army Dekelon had gathered. There were four thousand warriors, all young and all male, wearing sheepskin lapcloths tied around their waists with long strands of dyed and twisted wool, and all were armed with a simple bow, javelin, and hunting knife. He still found it hard to believe just how quickly the Saranah had organized once he and Dekelon had come to an agreement about the level of Grenda Lear support for their invasion. In the end it was the temptation of new land, especially the richer pasture on the Oceans of Grass, that convinced the Saranah to take up arms. Financial support was not as important as the news that the Chetts had mobilized as never before and gone east with their army, leaving their southern border more vulnerable than it had been in living memory.

"My great-great-grandfather grew up here," Dekelon said, now gazing out over the plains again. "We were once the strongest and biggest clan on all the Oceans of Grass."

Amemun had heard the story before, not only from Dekelon but from every other Saranah who had bothered talking to him. *You were also the most aggressive,* Amemun wanted to add, but there was no benefit in needling new friends.

"When this is over, we will again be a clan. All our tribes can come together for the first time in over a hundred years."

"First you have to win back your land," Amemun reminded him.

Dekelon grinned. His bald pate shone in the sun, and he patted it. "My skull will lie in this good earth, not the desert behind us."

The pair eased their way down the dune. The army was camped in a deep gully that hid a small creek of fresh water and afforded shade during most of the day. Dekelon stretched himself out on the ground and almost immediately fell asleep. Amemun, native to the cool mountain sides of Aman, found it almost impossible to sleep during the day: the heat and the flies made him more uncomfortable than he could ever remember being before. He reminded himself that from now on they would be marching at night, and so would not be able to sleep then either. Cursing under his breath, he closed his eyes and tried to rest.

Savero of the Horse clan, nephew of great Eynon, swelled his chest in pride as he watched his clan's mighty herd make its way along the narrow valley called the Solstice Way. Four thousand head. No larger among the Chetts, except for possibly the White Wolf herd, and everyone knew they got that by reaving cattle from other clans. Savero fidgeted with his sword belt. Every time he swelled his chest, the belt would slip a little. Well, he would grow into it. He was already tall for his thirteen years. Eynon—the great Eynon—had said so himself. And he was already working as one of the clan's outriders. He could not help it; his chest swelled with pride again.

True, if Eynon had not gone to help out poor Prince Lynan, that strange albino creature from the east, and with him taken a good portion of the clan's warriors, Savero might still be among the young riders assigned to guard the clan's wagons. Whatever the reason, here he was, outriding for the mighty Horse clan—

He smelled something in the wind. He reined in and looked around. He sniffed the air. There it was again. Not animal. Not vegetable. Nothing he knew. Curious, he kneed his horse away from the lip of the valley and started crisscrossing the high ground, homing in on the scent.

There was something vaguely odd about it. Something that did not belong to the Oceans of Grass. He reined in a second time and looked around him. He could see nothing unusual. He could hear the low calling of the cattle rising from the valley, but not much else. Maybe he should get old Colden; he would know what the smell was. Colden knew everything there was to know about the Oceans of Grass. At least, that's what he told everyone around the camp fires at night. According to him, he had even taught Eynon how to ride and fight. Savero snorted. No one had taught Eynon how to ride and fight; he was born with a saber in his hand and stirrups around his feet. Now Savero sniggered, thinking how uncomfortable that must have been for his mother.

A breeze whipped up around him, and it was full of the strange smell. Whatever it was, it was getting closer. For the first time Savero felt his spine twinge. Just the slightest twinge. He tried puffing out his chest again, but it did not seem to work.

Colden, he reminded himself. *Get Colden.*

As he pulled his horse around, he heard the grass suddenly rustling not twenty paces from him. He looked over his shoulder and saw the face of a man, and the eyes in that face were staring at him with hatred. As he opened his mouth to cry out a warning, an arrow suddenly sprouted from his neck with a soft thwack. Savero gargled blood and toppled sideways from his saddle, dead before his small body hit the hard earth.

Dekelon peeked over the lip of the valley. For a moment his gaze drifted over the huge herd that moved in the valley below; he savored the sight, then focused on the high ground on the other side. For a long while nothing happened, then he saw it. A figure standing, disappearing, then standing again. That was the signal.

"We are all in place," he told Amemun.

Amemun grunted in his beard.

"You should see this herd . . ."

"I have seen cattle before," Amemun said shortly. "How much longer?"

"We are ready. We wait for the night fires to be lit. That is when they expect their outriders to return, and new outriders to leave."

"And when no outriders return, they will start to worry."

"Oh, their outriders will return," Dekelon said softly.

Colden made sure all the fires were stoked up bright and high. He did not want any of his young charges getting lost this far south; they could end up in the desert, disoriented, especially at night.

He led his horse in a slow circle around the main camp, peering into the growing darkness and wondering why he was not seeing any of his outriders yet. Gods, some of them still had their child's voice and should be in their mothers' huts, not out on patrol with a sword strapped to their waists. He wished he could do all their work for them. He wished he could send only the few real warriors he had on patrol, but knew he needed their experience to help control the herd.

He looked south and saw one of the outriders in the middle distance returning at an easy walk. Relief flooded through him. Which one was that, then? Judging by his size it would be Savero, the smallest and the bravest of the lot. He would make his uncle proud one day; Colden knew the boy was a favorite of Eynon's.

He remembered then what it was like when he was not much older than Savero and on his first patrols. For the first time in his life he had felt like a man. Indeed, by the time Eynon returned from campaigning for the White Wolf, Savero would be eligible to become a full warrior. He sighed heavily, constantly surprised how fast time flew by him. It did not seem that long ago that Savero was nothing but a squalling, shitting squib interested in nothing but his mother's milk, and now look at him!

He dug his heels in and rode to meet the youth. Something about the boy's posture seemed odd; even in this light Colden could see he was riding too stiffly, and his balance was obviously all wrong. Too long in the saddle. It was a lengthy turn out on patrol for one so young. Well, he would recover. They all did at that age. And the boy's sword belt was riding too low. Colden would have to talk to him about that, or maybe all that was needed was an extra hole for the buckle.

"Savero, lad," Colden called out when they were only twenty paces apart. "I thought you weren't coming home at all."

The boy said nothing, but kneed his horse toward Colden.

"I don't suppose you've seen any of the other riders, have you? You're the first back . . ."

His voice faded away when he realized he was not talking to Savero at all. For the briefest of moments he wondered which outrider it was, his brain at first failing to realize the rider was someone he did not recognize at all, and by then it was too late. He saw the glint of the knife blade as it stabbed toward him, smelled the breath of the man who wielded it, and then he was overcome by a flash of pain so great it stopped his heart. Wheezing, dying, paralyzed by the blow, Colden fell forward into the arms of his murderer who gently let him off his horse and silently dropped him to the ground.

Though fit for his age, Amemun could not keep up with the young Saranah warriors as they jumped up from their hiding places and with terrible screams charged the enemy camp. By the time he reached the first Chett hut, the air was already filled with the moans and cries of the dying. Riderless horses skittered among the tents and camp fires. At first all he saw were dead enemy warriors caught in the act of readying their weapons, but as he strode deeper into the camp, he started coming across slaughtered children and old folk with nothing more dangerous in their hands than sticks or cooking pots, their pale faces like masks in the moonlight.

The Saranah had formed a circle around the entire valley and were now tightening it. Dekelon's orders had been to ensure no Chett escaped, and his warriors—releasing a century of pent-up hate—were making sure of their task. Amemun could even see Dekelon directing the battle, heading north with a band of his own tribesmen driving the defenders into the center. To his right he saw a few individual struggles, including one on the very fringe of the camp. He ran towards it, and as he got closer saw a young Chett woman using a metal pan to fend off a Saranah warrior who was playing games with her, dancing from foot to foot and feinting to the left and right with his javelin. Amemun, making sure no other Saranah were nearby, came up behind him and ran him through cleanly with his dagger. The Saranah grunted in surprise and dropped. The Chett looked at him with a mixture of surprise and fear.

"Who are you . . . ?"

"No time for that," Amemun said, looking around him. "Run for your life. Tell the other clans the Saranah are here!"

The woman's eyes opened even wider.

"Quick!" Amemun hissed.

She grabbed for the reins of a passing horse and Amemun stopped her.

"They'll shoot you down if they see you! Keep low, get away!"

She fell into a crouch and scampered off. In a few seconds Amemun lost track of her in the grass. If she was lucky, she would stumble across a horse in the morning and be able to reach the territory of another clan in a day or two. Once that happened, the Chetts would respond to this new threat instead of attacking Grenda Lear, giving the kingdom the time it needed to prepare properly for the war.

He licked his lips nervously and looked around again to make sure no Saranah had seen what he had done. If Dekelon had had his way, and there had been no survivors, it would be weeks before the Chetts heard of the invasion and responded to it.

Good for the Saranah, Amemun thought, *but bad for Grenda Lear.*

8

HIS name was Captain Waylong and he was a sapper and a soldier; a sapper and a soldier for whom, exactly, was beyond him at the moment. As his company marched south past the border tree, a wideoak that had marked for centuries the meeting point of Haxus and Hume on this road, he pondered the strange turns and twists of fate. Only three months before he and his company had swung past the same wideoak, part of a Haxan army on its way to invade Grenda Lear. Now he was part of a Chett army, nominally under the command of a prince of Grenda Lear, on its way to invade . . . well, Grenda Lear. Without understanding all the politics involved, he certainly understood the irony.

Nor was he sure he understood his own feelings on the matter. He had been quite proud of being a Haxan, and almost as proud of his haughty and clever king, Salokan. After all, he had spent his whole life being a Haxan and learning to despise the weak and effeminate enemy south of the border. Now, although Salokan was still his ruler in name, Haxus was no longer an independent kingdom; indeed it did not properly belong to any kingdom, since the real power behind Salokan, Lynan Rosetheme, was not much more than an outlaw in his own homeland and possessed nothing except two of the mythical Keys of Power.

Just then a detachment of Chett cavalry trotted past. Waylong spat dust out of his mouth. Well, he corrected himself, possessed of nothing except two Keys of Power, the orphan kingdom of Haxus and a bloody huge army. He could not help grinning. *That's a damn sight more than many other kings can claim, I suppose.*

Despite all the political and moral conundrums he now carried

as extra baggage, Waylong had one thing to be grateful for. Lynan
Rosetheme was leaving Haxus. Thinking about that pale creature
sent a shiver down his spine, and he was glad his soil was free of it.

Unlike many of the soldiers in his company, Waylong had actually seen Lynan Rosetheme up close. As a captain he had been present when the remnants of the old Haxus officer corps had been
summoned to the palace in Kolbee. Salokan was seated in the
throne, and to his right and slightly behind him stood the conqueror,
small and white. The throne room was lined with the terrifying Red
Hands, Lynan's personal bodyguard; he had seen too many of his
own people go down beneath the short swords of those bastards.

Waylong remembered that Salokan had looked ill and almost as
pale as Lynan, and that his right hand was heavily bandaged. He remembered, too, how both men had eyes that seemed dead to the
world around them. It was the Chett queen Korigan who spoke and
explained the situation to them all: most would be reconstituted as
the new Haxus army, but how some specialty units, such as the sappers, would be moving south with the Chetts to invade Hume once
again. The assembled officers gave a faint-hearted cheer, neither
keen to return to the place of their defeats nor to serve under such
a forbidding master. But Salokan stood then and told them they
would be serving the best interests of Haxus, and how the destiny
of Haxus to take Hume would finally be realized. The officers
cheered a second time, with more gusto, but Waylong would never
forget how Salokan had sounded like a slave and not a king; he,
like Korigan, nothing more than a mouthpiece for some darker
presence.

And now here they all were, tramping through a country that
only months before had known peace for over fifteen years. Not
only his own company of sappers, but also quite a few units of
heavy infantry, their spears carried nonchalantly over their shoulders as if they were out hunting bear cubs. The rest of the Haxus
army Lynan had left behind, but none of his Chetts. Waylong
looked on with respect whenever the famous horse archers rode by,
sitting in their saddles with greater ease than any Haxus rider was
capable of; and he looked on with something like awe at the Chett
lancers, a kind of cavalry no one in the east thought the Chetts capable of producing. And then there were the Red Hands and the
Ocean Clan riders under the command of the ugliest human being
Waylong had ever seen; they carried the short sword as well as the

saber and recurve bow, and he had seen first-hand how proficient they were at using all three.

He looked briefly over his shoulder and wondered if he would ever again see his homeland, and realized with a dim pain that he no longer truly had a homeland. For better or worse, the Haxus he grew up in was gone forever.

"Every day you come closer," she said.

"I'm not coming for your sake," Lynan told her. They were standing in a green grove filled with a heavy mist. Lynan felt soaked through. His hair stuck to his scalp and his face was like seaweed on an exposed rock. His skin was as cold as marble. She was half lost in a tangle of vines and creepers, and it was hard to tell where she ended and the forest began.

"Of course you're coming for my sake." She smiled at him, and he could feel himself becoming aroused. Her voice was like a summer breeze, and her skin looked as soft as a carpet of moss. "You want to be with me again. I can hear your dreams. You dream about me all the time."

"No," Lynan said between his teeth, but even as he said the word he knew he was lying. "No!" he repeated, more fiercely, but it sounded no more convincing.

She stepped toward him, her outline blurring with the leaves and branches that surrounded her. Her beautiful face flickered in the shadows. She stopped a few paces from him. "You can lie to your friends, Lynan, but you cannot lie to me. We are the same, you and I, and I can read you as easily as I read the twisting tree and the burrowing badger."

He tried turning his gaze away from her, but it was useless. Wherever he looked, she was there. "I want nothing to do with you! Leave me alone!"

"All life desires me," she said sweetly.

"All life despises you," he spat back.

"There is less difference between them than you imagine."

"You sound like a priest," he said scornfully.

"And there is less difference between me and a priest than you imagine." Suddenly she was right before him, and she stroked his cheek with one scratchy finger. "We both want your soul."

"You want it for yourself."

"And now we are back to desire." She retreated a step and frowned in thought. "I remember what it was like. Centuries ago, before your kind came to Theare. I remember what it was to make love, to desire the body of another and not his soul. In a way I am more innocent now that I was then: my desire is less base, more pure. I desire the best in you, not the worst."

"You will take *everything* from me, my soul and my life."

"They are the only things about Lynan Rosetheme worth having." She laughed, and the sound of it was like leaves falling. "Oh, I cannot forget your gifts. The Keys of Power will look fine against my breasts."

"You shall never have them." But even as he said the words, the two Keys around his neck melted away and appeared around her own, the two talismans resting between her pale green breasts with nipples the color of old wood.

"What is it you desire the most, Lynan Rosetheme?" she asked, coming close to him again. Her breath brushed against his face like a cold wind. "What do you want, my conquering prince?"

Lynan felt his sex stiffening. His desire for her was overwhelming. Without volition his hands stretched out to cup her breasts.

"What is it you want?" Silona asked again, smiling sweetly. She took one of his hands and placed it between her thighs. "Above all else, is it Silona you desire?"

Deep within him stirred a terrible anger, something that belonged to Silona as much as it belonged to him. He pushed her away with a furious shout. She flew back in a flurry of whirling leaves and disappeared.

Lynan breathed in deeply with relief, but the breath froze when he heard Silona's laugh. At first he thought it came from in front of him, but then the grove itself seemed to take it up and the laughter surrounded him. Every tree and hedge became a reflection of her shape, every branch an arm, every gust of wind a breath from her fetid lungs. Terror swelled in him and he screamed.

Korigan woke with a start and knew instantly what had taken away her sleep. *She* was here, and Korigan could feel her presence as if the vampire was standing over her. She leaped out of her bed and rushed to Lynan's tent. The Red Hands on duty stepped aside for her and she entered. There was not enough light to see by, and she could hear no sound. It occurred to her that Lynan might be outside, and the thought almost panicked her. How would she find him? How could she protect him from Silona? At that moment she heard, as if from a great distance, a woman's voice saying Lynan's name. The sound of it was like ice in her brain and her skin seemed to crawl in revulsion. Then she heard, close by, Lynan's voice answer.

"You shall never have them."

The words were desperate. Following the direction of his voice she could see his dim outline on a cot.

Again, from far away, she heard Silona. "What is it you desire the most, Lynan Rosetheme?" Korigan saw he was naked, and as she watched he became aroused. She surprised herself by being ashamed for his sake, and even as she went to him to wake him he pushed away with his arms at some invisible presence. Silona laughed, and the sound came from all around the tent. Korigan froze, more afraid than she had ever been before, and she struggled against it vainly until Lynan screamed. Suddenly she was afraid for herself no more, and she rushed to him.

"Lynan! Wake up!" She took him in her arms. He sat up, struggled against her, tried to push her way. The Red Hands came into the tent, confused and alarmed. They carried torches. "Go!" she ordered them. "Leave one of the torches, but go! He'll be all right!" They left without hesitation. They knew about Lynan's nightmares—seen by them as a great sickness that only someone great could suffer—and knew as well that Korigan often helped him.

She turned back to Lynan, trying to force him down. "It's all right, I'm here! You're safe!"

His whole body shuddered. In the flickering light she saw his skin was shiny with sweat. His eyes opened and stared, terrified, at Korigan.

"It's me," she said as soothingly as possible, fighting to keep her voice calm.

"Silona!" he whimpered, and scuttled backward out of her arms.

"No, it is me, Korigan—"

"Silona!" he said again, louder, and the fear in his voice tore at Korigan's heart. She grasped his hands and used all her strength to pull him back so she could wrap his arms around him and force his head against her breasts. "Listen! Do you hear my heart? Silona has no heart. I am no vampire." Still he struggled against her. "Lynan, listen to me! I am Korigan! I am *your* queen!" She said the words so quickly they came out before she could stop them, and in shock almost let go of the prince.

"It's true," she said, but to herself more than to Lynan. Determination filled her and she grasped Lynan's head in her hands and kissed him on the mouth. He stopped struggling against her. She opened her eyes and saw the terror in his eyes drain away to be replaced by recognition.

He pulled away from her, gently. "Korigan?" He looked around him, dazed. "It was her—"

She dropped her hands and did not know what to do with them. "I know," she said falteringly. "I heard her, and I saw you fight her off."

"What . . . ?" The question died on his lips, and he would not meet her gaze.

Korigan did not know what to say either. Since her father's death had left her queen at age thirteen she had had to make choices to secure her throne and advance her people's interests, and every time she had seen clearly the consequences of her action; but this time she was confronted by a choice that might be the most important in her life and she could not see which path would best serve either her throne or her people. All she knew, and this with utter certainty, was what *she* wanted, and realizing that she also realized she had left herself no choice.

"It is too late for regret," she said quietly, again more to herself than to Lynan.

"Korigan?"

She closed her eyes, leaned forward and kissed him a second time, but without holding him to her. *Too quick!* she told herself, knowing now he would reject her a second time. But then his lips parted slightly and he kissed her back. His arms moved, surrounded her, embracing and capturing her at the same time. For the first time in her life Korigan had no thought for her throne or her people. For the first time in her life she thought about nothing except how she wanted something for herself, and how glorious it felt.

It was not yet dawn when Jenrosa woke. She left her tent and made for the small creek she had seen the day before. It was no more than two paces wide and a hand's breadth deep, but it would do. She knelt in front of the creek and scooped a hole out of the dirt nearby, then used her cupped hands to fill the hole with water. She waited for dawn and for the water to settle, then gently broke the surface with the tip of one finger and watched as the ripples spread out, each catching the sun's light and turning into golden rings. She sighed deeply and said: "The past is the same, but the present has no boundary."

The moment she uttered the last word the rings of gold turned to rings of blood, and then all the water in the hole turned red as if from some dreadful infection. Jenrosa gasped and quickly stood up. She felt nauseous and bent over to vomit, but could only dry retch. She stood up again and wiped spittle away from her mouth, tears flowing from her eyes.

What is wrong with me? What have I become?

She could not believe—*would* not believe—that she was seeing the future. *Of course there would be blood,* she told herself, *we're in the middle of a war. You do not have to be a magicker to predict that.*

Then what was happening? Why was everything she did tainted with blood? She woke up every morning tasting it on the back of her throat. She had dreams of rivers of blood cascading down the streets of Kendra, so much blood it could fill an ocean.

Deep down in her mind she already half knew the answer, but refused to drag it up to full awareness. It had to do with Lynan and Silona, but she did not want to stare the truth in the face. Not yet. Not until she was sure.

All my fault, she thought. *Everything is my fault.*

She started sobbing, at first from self-pity, but then real sorrow as the memory of Kumul welled up inside her and so overwhelmed her that she fell to all fours in the dirt. Her tears flowed now, falling off her cheeks into the hole of bloody water, and as they did the water cleared, becoming like crystal. When Jenrosa saw this, she rested back on her heels and forced herself to control her grief. She told herself that Kumul would have been ashamed of her, and that finally brought her up.

She touched the water again with the tip of her finger. "The past is the same but the present has no boundary," she said. And this time the ripples carried neither gold nor blood. She watched intently, trying to gather meaning from the images that flashed in the expanding rings, one after the other, and realized they were telling her the same story. Thousands of Chetts lay dead in a long green valley somewhere in the Oceans of Grass. "The same story," she said aloud. "So this must be the past." The last image showed a pennant with a flying bird on it. At first she thought it was the kestrel of the Rosethemes, but then realized it was like no bird she had ever seen before.

We have a new enemy, she told herself. *And they are already among us.*

9

POWL was late for a meeting with some of the church's parish priests and took a short cut through the library. His path was intercepted by a novitiate with a vexing theological question that took so long to posit that Powl leaned one hand against a book rest to listen to it. When the novitiate finished, the prelate, who had neither the time nor the inclination to answer, put off the youth with a polite promise to talk to him at some later date. The novitiate bowed and scurried off. Powl sighed in a mixture of frustration at the delay and vague memories of his own time as a novitiate, and lifted his hand from the rest. That's when he saw the book. For a second he did not recognize it, and then he saw the handwriting.

"I pray for guidance," he read, "and for the souls of all my people; I pray for peace and a future for all my children; I pray for answers and I pray for more questions. I am one man, alone and yet not lonely. I am one man who knows too many secrets. I pray for salvation."

His last words, Powl thought. The reminder of his predecessor made his guilt rise in him like black bile, but he suppressed it with the force of his will. Still, the memory of Primate Northam would not disappear from his mind so easily, and Powl found it possible to remember how much he loved him once. Northam had been his teacher and father, his example and his spiritual guide. Lastly, Northam had been his betrayer and his victim. *It is so strange one of God's creatures can be all of these things.*

He read the passage again and realized he did not entirely understand the prayer. *I have no right to understand,* he told himself, but a part of him knew he should still be able to understand prayer, the most basic element—the very heart—of all faith. He tried reading the passage again but came no closer to its mystery. He noticed, too, that the rest of the page and its opposite were completely blank.

This was the Book of Days, he realized with surprise, and the pages were blank after Northam's last entry because it had been his duty as Northam's successor to write new entries. How could he have forgotten? How could he have so grievously neglected his duty? He looked up and saw the shelf that held all the black-bound Books of Days. Without knowing, he had broken the tradition, a tradition maintained since the earliest time of the Church of the Righteous God, and for a fleeting moment he felt despair. How could he have so seriously neglected his responsibility as primate? How could God have let him do this? How could his fellow priests have let him do this?

"Father?"

Powl looked around. Father Rown regarded him with a mixture of concern and curiosity.

"Yes?"

"The parish priests are waiting."

"Of course."

"Father, are you well? Would you like me to handle the meeting?"

Powl shook his head to clear it. Rown misinterpreted the gesture.

"Then shall I tell them you are coming?"

"Yes."

"Are you sure you are all right?"

Powl straightened. He frowned. "Thank you, I am fine." Rown turned to go but Powl called him back. "After this meeting, I would like to discuss something with you. Something important."

Rown nodded. "Of course, Father. In your office?"

"No. Here. Right here." He tapped the Book of Days lying on its rest. "Right here."

Orkid was busy rushing between his office and that of the queen's secretary, Harnan Beresard, organizing the first council meeting since the disasters that had visited Grenda Lear. He had been able to put it off for a while, but pressure from Kendra's great families and commercial interests to resume its regular meetings was growing daily: they wanted to know Areava was healthy and still able to rule the kingdom, and they wanted to see her for themselves. It had taken him a full week of cajoling and arguing to bring Areava around, but in the end she had agreed. He now had a workable agenda that Areava had approved and was on his way to instruct Harnan to send out the summonses to the council members. His way was blocked by the imposing figure of Dejanus. Orkid glanced up from his notes, nodded curtly, and made to move around him.

Dejanus held out a hand to block his way.

Orkid stopped. Dejanus was one of the few people in the palace he had to look up to, which made him feel uncomfortable. "What is the meaning of this, Constable?"

"I need a word," Dejanus said. Orkid could smell the wine on his breath. The constable's face was an even deeper red than usual. This was a bad sign, and something to worry about, Orkid decided.

"Of course, but can't it wait? I have to see Harnan Beresard about sending out the queen's summonses to a council meeting."

"About time," Dejanus said gruffly. "In part, that's what I want to talk to you about. The summonses can wait a short while."

"You want to talk here? In the hallway?"

Dejanus looked around him. "No one roundabout to overhear us. Safer here than in your office or mine, where secretaries and guards can interrupt at any moment."

Orkid breathed deeply. "Very well. What is it about?"

"Like I said, it's to do with the next council meeting."

"What about it?"

"We'll be discussing the raising of a new army to send north against Prince Lynan." It was a statement, not a question.

"Of course." Orkid frowned, guessing where Dejanus was heading.

"I want its command."

Orkid shrugged. "Such decisions, naturally, are the queen's prerogative—"

"It's only that I should have had command of the last one instead of that miserable Amanite husband of the queen's."

"Careful what you say about Sendarus, you oaf. He was my nephew as well as Areava's beloved—"

"Don't tell me what I can and cannot say!" Dejanus shouted.

"For God's sake!" Orkid hissed. "Keep your voice down!"

Dejanus looked as if he was going to shout again, but common sense seemed to calm him. "We have a pact, you and I, Orkid

Gravespear, a pact sealed in King Berayma's own blood. You held the king's hands when I drove my blade through his neck. I can say what I bloody well like about Sendarus, or the queen for that matter." He jabbed Orkid on the chest with one huge, blunt finger. "I want command of the next army. It's owed me."

Orkid did not answer, but his mind was racing. Dejanus was getting out of control. For the first time in a long time, Orkid was afraid for his own personal safety.

"When it comes up in council, I want your support."

Orkid nodded. "I will see what I can do."

Dejanus grunted. "You'll do it, Chancellor. You've more at stake here than me. If Areava learned what we did to her brother, we'd both lose our lives, but Aman would lose everything."

Again, Orkid said nothing, but Dejanus could see the color drain out of the chancellor's face. He smiled grimly. "Nice to have that little chat," he said, patting Orkid on the shoulder. He walked away, leaving Orkid still as a rock.

As had become the norm, Edaytor Fanhow visited Prince Olio on the south gallery with its magnificent views of Kendra and its harbor. Often they would just stand side by side, silent, aware of each other's company but not enforcing it. When they did talk, it could be about anything, but eventually Edaytor would bring the conversation around to the subject of the Key of the Heart. Olio sometimes got angry at this, but usually it seemed as if he was aware there was something important—something *very* important—about the subject, and he would try and answer any question Edaytor put to him, and try and think of some questions in return.

On this occasion Edaytor started the discussion by raising the matter of his mother, another of his favorite subjects.

"Have you seen her?"

Olio sighed. "Oh, no. She is far too busy. Grenda Lear is a very big kingdom, and she is in charge of everything." He looked at Edaytor sideways. "Did you know Mother has a navy?"

Edaytor feigned surprise. "With ships?"

"Of course with ships. That's what a navy is. Warships. Lots of them. You can see some of them from up here." He pointed down to the military quays in the harbor. "Well, when they're in dock, you can see them," he added a little flatly.

"I have not seen your mother for a long time either. A year or more."

"Why would she want to see you?"

"Because I am Prelate of the Theurgia."

"Ah, yes. I remember. You are an important official."

"Yes, I like to think so."

"Not as important as a prince, though."

"Oh, no. Only a queen is more important than a prince."

Olio nodded. "I'm going to ask Mother to make me admiral of the navy."

"Admiral?"

"Yes, then she will give me the Key of the Sword."

"Is that your favorite Key?"

Olio frowned in thought. "I think so." He rubbed his temples with the palms of his hands. "Sometimes . . ." His voice trailed off.

"Sometimes?"

"Sometimes I think it isn't my favorite. Sometimes I think . . ." Again, his voice faded.

"The Key of the Heart."

Olio looked up in surprise. "Yes. How did you know?"

"We have talked about it before."

Suddenly Olio looked very wise, and it seemed incongruous to Edaytor because the prince—short, slight, and with his mop of unruly hair—appeared so childlike in other ways. "And we are going to talk about it again, aren't we?"

"Only if you want to," Edaytor said gently.

"You like to talk about it."

"Yes."

"Do you talk to others about it?"

Edaytor almost said "constantly," but how would he explain to Olio that he had the finest minds in the theurgia trying to discover how the Key of the Heart had sent Olio back to his childhood, had apparently wiped clean the man Olio had once been? "Yes, now and then."

Instead of wise, Olio now looked shrewd. "Why are *you* so interested in the Key?"

Edaytor thought about how to answer, and eventually said, "For your sake."

"Oh," Olio said, accepting the answer. He was a prince, after all, and a lot of people did a lot of things for his sake. Except his mother. He wished she could do more for his sake. He had not seen her for so long he sometimes cried when he thought about it, but only when he was alone. He did not want anyone to know that he cried. Princes should not cry. Especially princes who wanted to be admiral of the navy. And then a question came to him, one that surprised him because he was not sure he understood its implications. "Why for my sake?" he said quickly before he forgot it.

"Because I care for you."

Olio waved his hands impatiently. "No, no, that is not what I mean." He put his hands over his temples again. Why was thinking so hard sometimes? "I meant . . . I meant . . ." The question was still there, but it was so hard to force it out. Slowly, emphasizing each word, he said: "Why—is—it—for—my—sake?"

Edaytor was taken unawares. In some ways it was the question he had been waiting for, the question that showed some glimmer of the old Olio. He licked his lips and said slowly: "Because the Key hurt you once."

Olio blinked in surprise and stepped back from the prelate. "Hurt me? One of the Keys? My mother used it to hurt me?" His voice started rising in panic.

"No!" Edaytor said quickly. "No! Your mother would never, never hurt you. You used it!"

Olio froze. "I used it?"

Edaytor could only nod. He felt—he *knew*—he was close to something important, close to reestablishing a connection with the old Olio, but at the same time knew he had lost control of the discussion and did not know what to say next.

"I used it," Olio said, and although he was still looking at Edaytor he was seeing something else entirely. "I used it," he repeated. He bowed his head as if overcome by exhaustion.

Edaytor rested a hand on his shoulder. "Your Highness?"

Olio shook his head. "How could I have used one of the Keys? I am not a magicker." He looked sharply up at Edaytor and grabbed his hand. "But I remember. I remember having it."

At that moment the old Olio was back. Edaytor could see it in the prince's expression, in the sudden strength in his voice. But just as quickly it was gone again, and it was a lost, confused boy holding his hand.

Olio blinked, stood straighter. He pointed out to the harbor. "See? There is a warship returning to harbor. Isn't she fine?"

Edaytor did not know whether to laugh or cry. Olio had come so close to throwing off his sickness, but in the end simply had not had the strength needed. And as time went on, he was increasingly convinced that there was nothing he nor anyone else could do too help Olio find that strength.

And then it was his turn to blink and stand straighter. *No human has the strength Olio needs,* he told himself. *Which means . . . .*

"Oh, God. Of course," he said aloud.

"Of course what?" Olio asked.

Edaytor shook his head. "Nothing, your Highness. I have to go now."

"Really? Now?"

Edaytor patted the prince on the arm. "But I will be back. Soon. I promise."

Olio shrugged. "Where are you going?"

"To see the queen," Edaytor said absently. He was already thinking of how to propose to Areava what he was sure she would be reluctant to do.

"The queen? She will see you? I think she should see me before she sees you."

Edaytor realized what he had said so casually and saw the hurt again in Olio's face. "Oh, no. I'm not important enough to ever see the queen. I meant I will speak to one of her officials."

"Ah," Olio said, mollified, and turned back to view the harbor.

Edaytor bowed and left the south gallery. He stopped for a moment to orient himself, then hurried toward Areava's chambers. When he got there, he was stopped by two guards. He demanded to see the queen and one of the guards left to pass on the message. When he returned, it was in the company of Harnan Beresard. The secretary reminded Edaytor of a particularly elegant crane.

"Prelate Fanhow? How can I help?"

"You can't, Harnan. I need to see the queen urgently."

"Her Majesty is very busy with important matters—"

"—of State," Edaytor finished for the secretary. "Yes, I'm sure. But I need to see her about Olio." He shook his head. "Umm, Prince Olio."

Harnan looked at him dubiously. "I see. Relating to what, specifically?"

"I think that should be between me and the queen."

Harnan noticeably stiffened. "I see," he said through a straight mouth. "I will pass on your message."

"I will wait here for her reply," Edaytor said, trying to look like someone who would not brook delay.

"Suit yourself," Harnan said and left.

The two guards blocking Edaytor's way looked at him as if he was an unnecessary and unpleasant distraction, and his natural timidity took over. He avoided their gaze and pretended to look at the ceiling, at his shoes, at his fingernails. As time went on, he became increasingly uncomfortable and was starting to wish he had never come. But then all doubts disappeared when Areava herself, with Harnan in tow, appeared behind the guards and ordered them to let the prelate through. The guards snapped to attention and Edaytor sidled past them. He bowed deeply to Areava and threw a smug look at Harnan. Areava looped her arm through his and drew him away from all other ears.

"What about my brother?" she demanded, her voice a strange mixture of hope and threat.

"I think I know a way we can help him—"

"How?" she interrupted.

"—but it is risky, and may possibly make worse his Highness's illness."

Areava caught his gaze. Edaytor thought her eyes were as cold as ice, and he could not help a shiver down his spine.

"What sort of risk? Is this some new kind of magic the Theurgia have dreamed up.?"

Edaytor shook his head. "No, your Majesty." He pointed to the Key of the Heart around her neck. "It is by using that."

"You should know I have already tried that."

"I guessed you would have. But you felt nothing at all when you tried?"

"How did you know that?" she asked sharply, and tugged painfully at his arm.

"Because the Key has become attuned to Olio. Only he can use it now, unless someone is prepared to sacrifice himself or herself as he has to gain control over it."

Areava went white. "I must do that to save him?"

Edaytor looked at Areava in horror. "You, your Majesty? No, never! That price would be too high, even for Olio's sake."

"Then you're suggesting someone else sacrifice themselves?" She regarded him with new respect. "You're suggesting yourself? You love my brother that much?"

"If it would make him better, then yes, I would," he said without thinking, then paused, surprised by the admission. "But I do not think the Key would let me."

"Then what exactly do you have in mind?" she asked impatiently.

"We let Olio use it," he said.

Areava stood back from Edaytor and looked at him like she might at an idiot. "It was the Key that caused this blight afflicting him!"

"There are moments when we are talking—your brother and I—when I see flashes of the old prince. It's as if he is a prisoner in his own mind, but no matter how hard he tries, he has not the strength to break free. The Key has the strength he needs."

"But you don't know that, Prelate Fanhow. It might just as easily make him worse, or even kill him."

"It may, your Majesty," he admitted. "But I think not. I believe because he is so attuned to the Key he will be able to use it to heal himself."

"Then why had he not done so when he first became ill?"

"Because he overused the Key. He became subservient to it. Now that he has been without it for a long while, he may be able to reassert his mastery over it."

Areava took Edaytor's arm again and drew him close. "But you are not sure, are you?"

"I said there was a risk."

For a long while Areava said nothing, and Edaytor held his breath.

"If I agree, when do we do this?" she asked eventually.

"We give him the Key at those moments when he is most like his old self. Hopefully, there will be enough of him there to use it."

Areava nodded. "I will think on it and let you know my decision. I wish fervently you had come up with some other solution."

"As do I, your Majesty," Edaytor conceded.

Father Rown followed Powl to the library after the meeting with the parish priests. Powl stopped in front of the Book of Days.

"You know what this is?" Powl asked.

"Of course, your Grace," Rown replied.

Powl rested his hand on the book and drummed with his fingers. Rown waited patiently, his round eyes gazing steadily at the primate. Eventually Powl said: "It is one of my duties to write in this book."

"Yes, your Grace."

"Daily."

Rown nodded.

"I have had a lot on my mind since my predecessor's death."

"A great many tragic things have occurred," Rown elaborated, starting to wonder what the point of the discussion was.

"It wasn't possible for me to keep up with all the responsibilities of primate. After all, the succession was unexpected."

Rown lifted an eyebrow. "Unexpected? But Primate Northam gave you the name of God—"

"Yes, yes," Powl said irritably. "I didn't mean my succession was unexpected. I meant . . ." he rubbed his eyes with a thumb and forefinger. ". . . God . . . I meant that Northam's *death* was unexpected."

"Ah, yes, of course."

"The point is, you see, that as secretary I think you should have reminded me of my duties where I neglected . . . no . . . unintentionally avoided . . . them."

"I see," Rown said, his voice falling.

"This is not a reprimand, you understand."

"Of course not," Rown said, but Powl could see the priest did not believe it. His usually happy face was crestfallen.

"It's just that I know you are devoted to your service and would desire to be shown where certain deficiencies . . ." Instead of finishing the sentence, Powl waved a hand vaguely in the air.

"I understand, and thank your Grace for showing me the error of my ways."

"I accept that I am a frail creature prone to make mistakes as easily as the next man—indeed we both are—and may find it necessary from time to time to be reminded when I fall short of expectations. Such as filling in the Book of Days."

"I understand, your Grace. I will try harder in future."

Powl tried to smile convivially, but it just made his expression look patronizing. "Good. Excellent. Can I ask why you did not remind me about the Book of Days?"

"Forgive me, but I thought you had so much to do already in the hard times following Primate Northam's death I was afraid of laboring you with unnecessary details. And I was not sure you had forgotten. There may have been some other reason for your not continuing the tradition."

"I see. Well, now we both know better where we stand, I think."

"Yes, your Grace."

"Right. Thank you."

Rown bowed and left. Powl watched him go, silently cursing himself for confronting his secretary like that; the priest had done nothing to deserve his ill favor—it had not been Rown's fault that he had unknowingly replaced Powl as his predecessor's favorite to become primate of the Church, the knowledge of which had driven Powl to murder Northam. Powl turned to the book and from a pocket in his frock retrieved a pen and small bottle of ink. He carefully unscrewed the bottle's lid, dipped the pen, then lifted it to write.

But he had no words. His mind was empty of any pious thought, any revelation. Powl, Primate of the Church of the Righteous God, had nothing righteous to add to the Book of Days.

10

SEREFA enjoyed the first hour of filling water casks and roping them to the back of the outpost's donkey. It had been a warm morning with a gentle mist lifting off the ground and birds singing in the gallery along the stream. He had taken off his clothes and bathed before starting his chores and felt refreshed and at peace with the world. However, by the time he had hoisted the sixth cask, he was feeling less sanguine about life in general, and outpost work in particular. His imagination started painting pictures for him of the other knights in Daavis, enjoying good company, good wine and a comfortable bed at night, perhaps with a comfortable companion to help warm the sheets. All he had was three other knights who stank worse than he did, fresh water, and a horse blanket. And the constant birdsong was starting to irritate him.

With the sixth cask in place, he dressed quickly in his stained leather breeches and jerkin. He started strapping on his greaves and breastplate, but the day was getting hot and he decided to leave them off. He tucked them between the casks and began the walk back to the outpost, only a league away but at the top of a steep hill. His stomach rumbled and he hoped one of the others had started the breakfast fire. He cursed himself then, for he had forgotten that one of his tasks that morning had been to gather more wood. He was about to turn back when he noticed smoke coming from the top of the hill.

Worat on the dawn guard must have been able to scrape together enough chips and twigs to start cooking. He decided he could get the firewood later and resumed the climb up the hill, but stopped again when he saw just how big a fire Worat had started.

He's burning the corned beef again, Serefa told himself, and cursed loudly. Thick white smoke puffed above the hill. *The idiot's using the green wood meant for the signal fire . . .*

"Oh, shit!" he cursed. He let go of the donkey's lead and ran up the hill as fast as his legs would carry him. When he got there, he found the other three knights already dressed and holding the leads of their mounts. His horse had been saddled for him.

"Where?" he asked.

Worat pointed northeast, and Serefa saw a long streaming line of enemy soldiers. Judging by the speed the line was moving, they must have been cavalry. They looked like ants from this high up.

"About a hundred riders?"

"About," agreed one of the others. "Scouting party."

"And coming this way," he said absently and to no one in particular. His stomach rumbled again. "They're at least an hour away."

Worat snorted. "You and your gut can wait until we get to Daavis," he said.

They started down the hill, meeting the donkey half way. They filled their water bottles from one of the casks and Serefa retrieved his armor.

"Do you think they were Chetts?" Serefa asked.

"We can wait and ask them if you like," Worat said, then yelped and turned round in his saddle. Serefa had time to see the short black arrow sticking out of the knight's eye before he toppled off his horse. Something hissed by his ear and he heard the man behind him gurgle blood. Without thinking, Serefa threw himself over his horse and kicked his heels in. The horse was too afraid of the slope to move, and Serefa cursed it as he threw himself off. Just as he did so an arrow thwacked into the saddle, and then another into the animal's chest. The horse screamed and dropped. The third knight was half-running, half-scrabbling down the slope. He had gotten almost to the bottom when a single Chett leaped up from behind a depression with his bow and used it like an ax, whacking it across the knight's face. The knight fell backward, jerked like a puppet, and then was still.

Serefa drew his sword and charged downhill, slipping and sliding, desperately trying to keep his balance and watching as the Chett righted his bow and fitted another arrow. His feet skidded out from under him when he was only two paces from the Chett, and a hastily fired arrow parted his hair. Serefa could not control his fall, and he barreled into the Chett, sending him pinwheeling back into the depression in which he had been hiding. When Serefa regained his footing, he looked over the edge and saw that the Chett had broken his neck. His sword drooped and his shoulders slumped. Then it occurred to him the Chett might not have been alone. He frantically looked around him, but saw no sign of any more enemies. Keeping his heart under control he checked on his fellows. All three were dead. Two horses had been killed as well and another was lame. The fourth horse—Worat's—was nowhere in sight. Serefa heard a noise and he looked up to see a horse he did not recognize galloping north around the hill. The Chett's mount, he reasoned. Now what could he do? The enemy column would catch up with him for sure if he tried to make it back to Daavis by foot.

The donkey brayed.

"Shut up," Serefa snapped. He blinked. The donkey. He sheathed his sword, quickly unloaded the water casks and led the donkey to level ground. Once there he carefully clambered onto its back. Without saddle or stirrups it took him some time to get it to go in the direction he wanted, but eventually they were moving at a pace that would have been something like a slow trot for a horse. With luck, he would keep just far enough ahead of the Chetts to survive until he made Daavis.

With luck, he repeated to himself.

It occurred to him then that being in Daavis might not put him in a more secure position. If there was a Chett scouting column heading south there was probably a Chett army not far behind it, and Serefa had no trouble guessing where that was heading.

Mally rolled the knucklebone. It landed with the number five uppermost. "That's it!" he cried. "That's what I need!" He moved his white stone five spaces along the polygonal playing area he had scratched in the walkway, landing on a red stone. "Your duke is gone!"

The old soldier grunted, then smiled at the small boy squatting opposite him. "Indeed. I think you have won the war."

Mally grinned from ear to ear. "Did you let me win, Brettin?"

"I would not cheat you like that, Mally," the soldier said. Not absolutely true. When his grandson was just learning the game, Brettin had let him win quite a few times, but not for over a year now. And Mally won more often than not. He was a smart boy. *Too smart to be a soldier,* Brettin thought. *Alas, it is all he's interested in. Well, his poor father had been one after me, so it's not surprising.*

"What were you keeping in your castle?" Mally asked.

"Let's see." Brettin flipped over the shells hiding his last few stones. "Two spearmen and an archer. What about you?"

Mally lifted his shells one by one. None of them had anything underneath.

"You little rascal," Brettin laughed. "I could have taken your castle anytime."

"But you didn't," Mally laughed back. "Another game?"

"I have to do my rounds soon, Mally . . ."

"Oh, Brettin, please? It won't take more than a few minutes."

"God, who's cocky all of a sudden?" He mussed Mally's hair. "All right. I'll set up first this time."

Mally agreed and stood up to stretch his legs. Brettin collected all the stones and shells and started deploying his troops, selecting a battering ram this time, together with the swordsmen to support it. Mally's father had been good with a sword, he remembered. But not good enough to beat off a Chett lancer. He forced himself to think about something else. His grandchildren. That would do. And his fine daughter-in-law, whom he loved as if she had been his blood daughter, and who loved him as dearly in return. Little Serven, only two, and sweet Mally, whom he loved above all else in the world. He would have to talk to Mally's mother about getting him real schooling and a real job, one that would not have him spilling his guts on a dusty, blasted battlefield. A tear came then. He wiped it away with a rough finger and concentrated on deploying his pieces.

Mally, meanwhile, was taking advantage of being allowed on the wall. It was not often his grandfather got patrol duty up here, and he loved to look out over the city and the wide, gentle Barda River to the south and the wide, gentle countryside to the north. One day he would go exploring. He would follow the river to its source in the Ufero Mountains and discover gold. And when he was rich, he would make an army for the great queen in Kendra and lead it north to defeat Haxus and then on to the Oceans of Grass to take his revenge on the Chetts for the death of his father.

North, across all those miles of farms and fields and rolling hills . . .

"Brettin."

"Yes, Mally."

"I see smoke."

"From a farm house?"

"No. White smoke. A whole tower of smoke. And there's another, south of the first."

Brettin stood up so quickly he dropped his spear. "Fuck," he said under his breath. "They're coming."

Mally, who knew when to pretend he did not hear Brettin swearing, said, "The Chetts?"

Brettin nodded. He picked up his spear and trotted to the nearest tower to give the alarm, Mally close on his heels.

Others watched the white smoke as well, and for them it meant something else.

"I'm sorry, Lynan," Korigan said. "The scouts failed. Daavis has been warned."

Lynan nodded wearily. "Well, it can't be helped. The enemy was better prepared this time. I had not counted on them establishing so many outposts so quickly."

"We can reach Daavis by nightfall if we push the army."

"No. We will arrive too tired and too late to do anything useful before it is too dark to fight. Truth, the city will be locked to us, and our cavalry will be of little use. We will wait until tomorrow."

"The Haxan sappers want us to cut wood for their machines."

"Fine. But not now. When we reach the city, there will be time to cut down whole forests if needs be. There's no reason for us to carry more than we have to on the way. This army moves slowly enough as it is."

Korigan grinned at him. "You are used to a purely Chett army. Now we have Salokan's infantry."

"And demoralized infantry at that. They have been beaten too many times this year to have much heart for the business of war."

"A victory will fix that."

Lynan harrumphed. "Then let's make sure we give them one."

Korigan studied Lynan's face. She could see the lines of worry creasing the corners of his mouth and eyes, the deep furrow that seemed permanently ploughed across his brow. The campaign in Haxus had been a fast, vicious one, but she had some idea how much it had taken out of him. She wanted to lean over and kiss him, but to do that in front of his army would embarrass him.

"You will have your victory, my love," she whispered.

"This time, yes. I will not let Grenda Lear defeat me twice." He turned to her and smiled slightly. "I have no doubt about that."

Korigan saw that it was true, and felt a twinge of fear. Since the night they had made love, she hoped she had learned something more about him, but in the clear light of day she knew the hope was fruitless. He was something new in her experience, a warrior and innocent at the same time, and she did not know how to make sense of that. In his rage, when he became more than a man, or maybe *less* than a man, he was terrifying, and yet for the rest he was small and almost childlike, and weighed down with worry. He did not want to fight, but only battle seemed to liberate him; the problem was, she did not think she could ever love the Lynan who swept all before him, the one who could not be wounded, the one who reveled in slaughter. And yet it was those very characteristics that had married his followers to him. The Chett warriors believed Lynan was almost godlike. They would follow him to their deaths if need be, and willingly. And Korigan knew that if it would advance his cause, to their deaths he would send them.

In that, we are different, she told herself, and prayed that it was true.

Farben pretended not to notice that Charion and Galen came out of her bedchamber together, both quickly strapping on sword belts and slipping mail hauberks over their heads. In fact, he hoped a lover might improve his queen's notorious temper. He even acknowledged to himself that the pair looked good together: tall, noble-looking Kendran knight with beautiful, proud, provincial queen.

"Two signal fires?" she demanded of him, snapping the question.

Well, perhaps her temper would improve over time. "Yes, your Majesty."

"Only two?"

Farben sighed. How many more ways could she ask the question? "Yes, your Majesty."

Charion and Galen exchanged glances. "That means the Chett scouts were well ahead of their army," Galen said. "It's the only way they could have surprised so many of the outposts."

"We may be lucky to have gotten any warning at all."

"I'll lead a detachment out right away. See if we can pin down the direction of their advance."

"No," Charion said.

Farben noticed the cross expression that flickered across Galen's face. Oh, good. Two of them with tempers like rutting bears. That's all the court needed.

"But we have to know what Lynan's intentions are," Galen insisted.

"You're thinking like a commander in the field, not in a city preparing for a siege. We know what Lynan's intentions are. He's heading straight for us. We know how fast his army can move. If they're not here tonight, they'll be here by tomorrow. What more can you learn by leading some of your knights north of the city? Other than what if feels like to be skewered by a Chett arrow, I mean."

Galen opened his mouth to reply, but his brain was working faster than his tongue and he closed it again. Farben noticed that, too, and decided the Kendran noble—just like Charion—might have some redeeming features after all.

"Get your knights together and keep them away from the walls. I don't want them tied down defending; I've got plenty of infantry to handle that. What I need is a sally force."

Galen smiled grimly. "It would suit us best," he admitted. "What about you?"

"My place is with my people. You can find me on the walls."

They stopped for a moment, shared a look that Farben could have translated had he wanted to, and went in different directions. Farben followed Charion, cleared his mind for the list of instructions that would follow.

"First, all my commanders are to meet me at the main gate. Second, all who can carry a weapon are to collect one from the armory, including any of the wounded who can walk. Third, send a carrier pigeon to Kendra. Tell them we will be under siege within a day. Ask them if they have an army on its way. Anything. What about Jes Prado and his mercenaries? Where are they?"

"Yes, your Majesty."

They had left the palace and were now striding up the city's central avenue to the main gate. Even though he had an advantage over her in height, he had to struggle to keep up with her. She waved confidently to anyone they passed. "Are you still following me, Farben?"

"In case you have more instructions," he said defensively.

"I have no more instructions," she said. "For now."

*   *   *

It was almost dark when the main part of Lynan's force arrived outside the walls of Daavis. Under explicit instructions not to assault the city, the Chett banners stayed out of bow range. When Lynan arrived soon after nightfall, he listened to the reports of his banner leaders and scouts, then decided to ride out and inspect the city walls himself.

"But it is dark," one of the officers pointed out.

Lynan smiled thinly. "I will see well enough."

The officer blushed. "I should not question—"

"Do not apologize," Lynan interrupted him. "It is not wrong to question."

His commanders bowed and left; Korigan, Ager, and Gudon stayed behind.

"Exactly how well do you see at night?" Ager asked.

"Almost as well as you might during the day."

Ager patted his empty eye socket. "That's not saying a great deal."

"I think my night vision is as good as Silona's."

The mention of the wood vampire's name made everyone fall silent. Lynan studied their faces, noticing they would not meet his eyes, not even Korigan. It made him feel lonely.

"I'd best get started," he said and went to his horse.

"Do you want company?" Korigan asked.

Lynan mounted, looked down at the small group of friends. He saw their love for him in their eyes and he felt a surge of love for all of them in turn, and a frustrating fear that he could not protect them all from harm. *I feel like a father to them,* he thought, forgetting he was the youngest of all.

"I will be fine," he told Korigan and tapped the horse into motion. Gudon mounted anyway and rode beside him. Lynan smiled at the Chett. "You do not believe I will be fine?"

"Truth, little master, I believe you would be fine swimming in the middle of the Barda River in the middle of a school of jaizru."

Lynan's smile turned into a grin. He too easily remembered the horror and the panic he had felt the first and last time he had encountered the flying eels. Invulnerable or not, it was not something he would care to experience again.

"Then you must be going to tell me something very important and very wise."

"You mock me," Gudon said insincerely, matching Lynan's grin.

"Indeed," Lynan admitted. "So get on with it."

Gudon's expression became more serious. "You cannot protect us by turning us away from you."

Lynan did not try to hide his surprise. "How did you know—?"

Gudon waved one hand. "We have gone through too much together for me not to understand how you sometimes think and sometimes feel, especially about those you care for. Losing Kumul has wounded you deeper than you will ever admit, even to yourself. But this is a war, Lynan, and we have attached ourselves to your fortunes for good or ill. We each of us made that decision for ourselves. Do not turn your back on us thinking that will save us from harm."

Lynan blushed. "I would never turn my back on you, Gudon, or any of the others."

"Not intentionally. We are your friends, Lynan, your companions-in-arms, not your children."

Lynan nodded. "I will not forget."

Gudon smiled again. "Then that is all the wisdom I have for you!" he declared and stopped his horse, letting Lynan pull ahead.

The prince had not gone more than fifty paces when another horse drew along side him. "Where do you go, Lynan?" asked the rider.

"Jenrosa. Are you keeping well?"

"There is something we must talk about."

"You, too? Can it wait? I want to see the walls of Daavis—"

"I will come with you," she said in a voice that meant "I will come with you whether you like it or not."

"You ignored my question," he observed.

And, as if to prove a point, she continued to ignore it. They rode together out of the main camp. The city walls rose white out of a dark plain. They looked formidable to Lynan, and he remembered they had proven themselves against Salokan. He counted the towers, and was even able to see the helms and lances of the city guards as they patrolled along the walls. He rode east first, then south to the Barda River. There he met patrols of Ager's Ocean clan waiting with bows to ambush any barge that attempted to leave the river downstream.

I should have thought of that, Lynan told himself. *What else have I missed? What would Kumul be telling me now?*

The thought of Kumul filled him with grief. He still had not had time to properly mourn the death of his friend. Ever since the death of his father when he was a small boy, Kumul had been his teacher and guardian, and had loved Lynan like a son. He glanced at Jenrosa and knew Kumul's death must be at least as hard on her.

"I miss Kumul," he said, surprised by the words. And then— with sudden certainty—he knew why he had said them: he and Jenrosa needed to talk about their loss and grief, had to help each other find a way to deal with it.

Jenrosa looked taken aback. Lynan could hear her breath quicken. "This isn't the time—"

"This is exactly the right time," he said quickly. "We haven't really talked since his death. We haven't sat down together and talked like friends; we haven't remembered him together like friends. I haven't even talked to Ager about any of this."

"I don't want to talk about it," she said flatly. "I don't want to remember the pain. We're in the middle of a war, and by the end of it Kumul's death will be . . ." Her voice trailed off. She was going to say "insignificant," but the lie stopped in her throat.

He reached out to touch her hand, but she retreated from him. Humiliated, not sure what to do, he withdrew. Jenrosa, too, seemed unsure what to do, or where to look.

Eventually Lynan said, "What is it you wanted to see me about?"

For a moment Jenrosa looked as if she did not understand the question.

"I'm sorry," she started, her tone apologetic, but he cut her off with a wave of his hand.

"What did you want to see me about?" he insisted, his voice hardening.

"The Chetts are being attacked on the Oceans of Grass."

"Who could possibly be attacking the Chetts?" he asked, his disbelief obvious.

"The enemy fight on foot, and they carry a pennant with a design of a bird I do not recognize."

"How do you know this? What magic . . ."

"Strong magic, Lasthear tells me." Jenrosa was about to say more, but changed her mind.

"Are you sure it is not something that has happened in the distant past? Or is still to be?"

She shook her head. "I used the magic two mornings ago. I'm sure I saw the attack as it was happening."

"Two mornings ago?" he demanded, suddenly in a rage. "God, woman, why didn't you tell me then?"

Suddenly nervous, Jenrosa said: "Because I wasn't sure of what I'd done, of what I'd seen."

"*Unsure?*" He almost bellowed the word. Jenrosa heard it ring out across the fields.

"Unsure about my magic," she said quickly, trying to keep her voice hushed. "I didn't want to believe I was doing it."

Lynan sat back in his saddle. The rage fell away from him, and he was left confused. He did not understand what she meant, but he could sense the fear in her. "But, Jenrosa, two days . . ."

"I'm here now," she said. "And I couldn't tell you in front of anyone else. I had to wait until you were alone."

"Why?"

"It was the Horse clan, Lynan. It was a massacre. I'm not sure, but I think there were no more than a handful of survivors."

"Eynon's clan?" He was aghast. "Wiped out?"

She nodded. "What was left of it on the Oceans of Grass."

"God."

"All he has now are the warriors he brought with him to serve you."

"It's my fault," he muttered, his voice distant.

"That's a stupid thing to say," she said abruptly. "You didn't know this would happen. And who's to say if Eynon had still been there the outcome would have been any different? But he'll want to go back."

"No," Lynan said emphatically.

"What do you mean? He has to go back."

"You said yourself there were probably no more than a handful of survivors. What will he go back to?"

"But the enemy, whoever it is, may still be there!" she said, her voice rising. "They have to be dealt with!"

"I need Eynon and his warriors here for the attack on Daavis. If he rushes off to the Oceans of Grass, I will have to call off the siege and we lose the initiative. I can't afford to let Areava dictate what happens in this war. Besides, we don't know that the attacker is still on the plains."

"But if they are, they could overrun the Oceans of Grass!"

"I won't let it be overrun!" he snapped. "There are still thousands of warriors on the plain—"

"The best are with you, Lynan. You know that."

"I will do what is best for all the Chetts," he said.

"You mean you'll do what's best for Lynan. The two aren't necessarily the same thing."

"I will do what's best for the Chetts," he repeated coldly. "Having them retreat back to the Oceans of Grass serves no one except Areava."

"Eynon will find out."

"I can't stop you from telling him—"

"Oh, stop it, Lynan! He won't find out from me! But even if there were no survivors, another clan's outriders will eventually come across the battle site. Or worse, whoever the attacker is will strike at another clan. How long do you think it will be before a rider comes with the news? A month? Less?"

He glanced at the walls of Daavis. "I only need a month."

"And what then? All of Haxus and Hume under your heel, what's next on your list?"

"What are you talking about? This isn't just about Lynan Rosetheme. It's about revealing Berayma's murderers. It's about Areava sending mercenaries against the Chetts. It's about keeping free the trade routes between east and west. It's about putting Ager back in his captain's uniform." He jabbed a finger at Jenrosa and his voice started rising. "And it's about getting you back in the Theurgia which is *all* you've cared about since we escaped from Kendra!"

Without thinking, Jenrosa slapped Lynan's face. He recoiled from her like a released spring. She looked at her hand and for a moment thought she could see blood on it. She screamed and rubbed it against her vest and looked at it again. There was nothing there, not even a smear. When she looked up again, Lynan was already gone, continuing north. For a long while she did not move. She was paralyzed by what she had done.

"I'm sorry," she said, too weakly for Lynan to hear.

11

NIGHT again. With a long sigh, Amemun dug his way out from underneath his cloak. There was food being cooked nearby and he was drawn to it the way fleas seem to be drawn to him of late. One of the Saranah offered him a large piece of beef which he accepted gratefully. He had not been starving on the expedition to the Oceans of Grass, but he found the usual Saranah fare of mutton jerky, dried yogurt, and seed bread about as appealing as parchment, although it had had the effect of making him almost as lean as his desert-born allies. As he chewed on the fresh meat, Dekelon appeared, giving instructions to a group of wounded warriors. They were being sent back to the Saranah homeland with the surviving cattle and other prizes looted from the Chett clan they had butchered two days before. They could have carried more if they were mounted or just used the Chett's own horses as pack animals, but as Dekelon had explained to him, no Saranah had ridden for over a hundred years, and the desert country could not support a large number of horses. Still, even the wounded were carrying what seemed to be a small mountain of loot. Amemun could imagine the glee with which the train would be received in that poor country.

Dekelon grabbed some food and joined Amemun.

"Where to next?" Amemun asked him.

"West. The plains get drier and the clans are more scattered."

"Less prizes for your people."

"Less chance of being discovered," Dekelon countered. "And for the moment that is more important."

"But, with most of the Chett warriors in the east with Lynan

Rosetheme, you should not worry about discovery. You could handle any single clan—"

"As long as Lynan Rosetheme's army stays in the east," Dekelon interrupted, his voice level.

Amemun eyed him warily, and not a little guiltily; if Lynan heard about what Dekelon and his raiders were doing on the Oceans of Grass, it would be due in no small part to Amemun. "What do you mean?"

"A messenger came last night from your king."

"Marin? What message?"

"An army from Grenda Lear defeated this Lynan in battle not far from the city of Daavis, and this occurred not long after the same army had forced the king of Haxus to retreat from besieging that same city."

"The Lord of the Mountain be blessed!" Amemun cried. This was better news than he had expected. And so soon! He had feared the war would drag on for months or even years. At this rate, Lynan and his Chett allies would be forced back to the Oceans of Grass before the end of summer.

"I can see what you are thinking," Dekelon said. "Does this mean the kingdom's support for the Saranah will dry up like one of our creeks in summer?"

Amemun thought quickly. "There is no reason to think one battle will end the war."

"That is exactly what *you* were thinking. And you did not answer my question."

"The money will come, as promised. My own life is surety for that."

"Exactly my thought," Dekelon said slowly.

Amemun decided it was time to change the subject. "Did Marin send any other news?"

Dekelon nodded. "But it was not good news. The queen lost her baby."

"Areava?"

"A daughter. Marin's granddaughter, as I understand it."

"And the queen?" Amemun asked, his voice subdued.

"Marin says nothing of that."

"Then she survived," he said with certainty, breathing out a sigh of relief. So much of Marin's plan—their plan!—depended on Areava and Sendarus having a child. If Areava survived, they could try again.

"The message had another part," Dekelon said carefully. "Your king says it will bring you great sorrow."

It was a moonless night. The Oceans of Grass ran away on either side of Amemun like a dark, waveless sea. The Saranah kept up a punishing pace, running at a strange half-lope that ate up the leagues. Up until tonight they had taken frequent breaks to allow Amemun to keep up, but tonight there were no breaks. Amemun, at the end of the line, was using all his energy keeping up with the dim shadow of the runner in front of him. He knew Dekelon was doing this to stop him from wallowing in his grief; in his own way, Dekelon was doing him a favor. But a kernel deep inside Amemun's heart knew the grief would wait. He was afraid it would be so great it might kill him.

Under the clear sky with its myriad stars, running in the great silent air of the great plains, Amemun found his mind drifting between memory and the present. There were times when he believed—knew as a fact—that Sendarus was still alive, and then the universe would wheel around and the weight of the truth would fill him with a pain he had never experienced before. The hardest part for Amemun—the wise counselor, the patient teacher, the guardian of princes—was that although he knew Sendarus' death was a great tragedy, he could not yet comprehend it. He had never believed that there could exist something in the world that was so beyond his experience, beyond his knowing, and in realizing that something like that *did* exist made a mockery of all that he had learned and believed in.

I have become a hollow man, he thought. And then: *No, not completely hollow.*

Deep within he could feel a bright, terrible canker. He would live long enough to bring about the fall and destruction of those who had slain his beloved Sendarus.

Marin sat alone at the great table in the great stone hall of his palace at Pila. Servants hovered nearby, but never within range of the candle light. They were like grey ghosts among the tapestries and doorways.

It was a cold night. Summer sometimes forgot to visit Pila high up in its mountainous roost. Marin thought cold lent a great clarity to the world: frost limned stone work and blade, snow revealed landscape, clouds of breath marked life. And cold suited sorrow, he thought; it matched the hard mind lost in grief.

He sneered at the invisible servants. They thought he was indulging himself. After a lifetime striving to improve the lot of his people and kingdom, they could not stand the thought of him doing something for himself, even it was self-pity.

He banged his goblet on the table. A servant scurried into view with a jug and poured him more wine, then scurried away again. Marin raised the goblet and silently toasted his dead son. He took a gulp, held up the goblet again, and toasted his brother, Orkid, who was so far away. Another gulp, and one more toast. To Amemun, wherever he may be.

The night was four hours old when the column halted. Amemun sunk to the ground in relief, but a warrior found him and told him Dekelon wanted to see him immediately. He followed the warrior back to the van where Dekelon waited with a scout who was panting with exertion.

"You should here this," Dekelon said, and nodded to the scout.

"Outriders," the scout gasped. "About three leagues distant."

"How can you see so far in the night?" Amemun asked skeptically.

"I can smell them," the scout replied in a tone that suggested the answer should have been obvious.

"Which direction are they heading?" Dekelon asked.

"Northwest."

"Any sign of a herd?"

"Droppings. It is not as large as the last clan's herd."

Dekelon glanced at Amemun. "It will be a hard run to catch up with them tonight. We follow them until daylight, rest up, then finish the pursuit tomorrow night."

Amemun shook his head. "We will run hard," he said urgently. "We will destroy this new clan tonight, and maybe tomorrow night we will find another one to take."

Dekelon gazed steadily at Amemun, but in the dark the Amanite could not read his expression. After a moment he grunted his agreement, and signed for the scout to lead them to their prey.

It was a wild run. Amemun, charged with a fierce anger, kept up with the Saranah column as it made its way across the Oceans of Grass. Their feet made a strange and muffled tattoo on the ground, a sound some of the enemy would hear but wonder at. Scouts ranging ahead located the nearest outriders and killed them, then ran on until they found the main encampment. When the column caught up with them, the scouts spread out to locate the remaining outriders while Dekelon deployed his force. By the time everyone was in position the eastern sky was just starting to lighten. Dekelon stood and waved his javelin. As one, the Saranah stood, screamed their war cry, and charged down on the camp.

Instead of waiting on the fringe of the group, this time Amemun charged with Dekelon. The first enemy he saw was a woman stumbling from the back of a wagon. He slashed at her midriff with his dagger and ran on. He stabbed a face that suddenly loomed before him, tripped over the body, smelled the blood that spurted over him. He scrabbled to his feet, ran around a whinnying horse with a dead rider slumped over its back and straight into a knot of men fighting with javelins and sabers; he drove the point of his dagger into the back of one of the fighters wearing a poncho and, as the Chett dropped, grasped the saber from his hand and used it to swipe at heads and limbs. In the darkness he could not be sure how many he injured, but the Chetts fell back in disorder from the sheer ferocity of his attack and were picked off one by one by pursuing Saranah.

All around him, shouts and screams rang out. He ran on, found himself in the middle of a corral formed by a circle of huts on wagons. In the middle was a large fire, its flames shooting into the sky from the fat it was eating off a body that had been thrown on it. He cut a square of hide from one of the huts and wrapped it around the saber, dipped it into the fire and used the flaming brand to light all the other huts. A mad Chett woman charged him, swinging a sword over her head. He barely deflected the blow, the force of it making him fall back. He stumbled and fell but managed to hold up his own blade, catching the woman in the flank. She shrieked and ran off.

Winded, Amemun used his saber as a prop to stand up. By the time he got his breath back, the entire ring of huts was ablaze, sparks spinning in the air, creamy smoke curling into the sky. Shielding his face from the heat, he broke through the ring. Shouts and screams were more distant now. He turned to follow them, but he had no more strength and his legs would not obey him. His arms slumped to his side and the sword slipped out of his grasp. The heat from the burning huts battered the skin on his face. He searched inside himself for the loss he felt at the death of Sendarus, and was dismayed to find it still there and just as strong.

When the sun rose, Dekelon found the Amanite in the same spot. "Are you all right?" he asked.

Amemun stared at him for a moment as if he did not know where he was. "Yes," he said eventually. "Do you think we will find another clan tonight?"

Dekelon shrugged. "I do not think so. They are rarely so close together."

"The night after?"

"It is possible."

"Good." He bent over to pick up the saber, admired its long, steel hardness. The body of a Chett warrior lay a few paces from him and he went over to it. An old man's face stared up into his own, blood caked around his eyes and mouth. For a second Amemun thought he was looking in a mirror. The thought seemed funny to him and he laughed as he undid the dead man's sword belt and sheath and strapped it around himself.

"I like this saber," he told Dekelon, sheathing it.

"You'll have a great need of it in the weeks to come."

"Did any of the enemy escape?"

"I don't think so."

Amemun nodded. He looked inside himself again. The pain was a little less, but it would need a great deal more blood before it went altogether.

12

AGER was dreaming about the sea. After the Slaver War and before meeting Lynan, he had worked on merchant ships as a supply clerk and purser. There was a great deal about ship life he did not miss—the food and drink, the storms and smell of bilge water—but there were some things he missed a great deal. In his dream he was lying on the aft deck of a small trader sailing a calm sea under a brilliant night sky. He could hear the sail flap gently with each caught breeze, the creak of the mast and yardarm, the tugging of the sheets. He could smell the ocean, the salty tang of life in the deep, and warm tar. He could see so many stars he knew he could not count them all in a lifetime. He felt each gust as it caressed his skin, stroking him to sleep, and his own breathing slowly timed itself with the gentle movement of the ship as it rocked with the swell. And then he opened his eyes and it was all changed. He was lying at the top of a small rise on the Oceans of Grass, and above him was the clearest blue sky he had ever seen. He could smell the musty earth, still damp with rain, and the clean scent of wild horses. He could see tall grass waving with each movement in the air, and high above a single eagle soaring and sliding, using its wing tips like rudders. He felt his body fold along the ground, and from deep in the earth the gentle rumble of a herd moving far away.

Part of him was wondering where he would be taken next when he was shaken awake. He sat up and turned to Morfast to ask what she thought she was doing, but she was still fast asleep. He looked the other way and saw Lynan's face staring at him in the darkness. It had a strange luminous quality, and in that place between dream and reality it seemed oddly appropriate.

"I'm sorry for waking you," Lynan said.

"What's wrong?"

"I need you to come with me. There is no need to disturb Morfast."

Ager dressed quickly and followed Lynan out of the tent. It was still dark. "What time is it?"

"It will be dawn soon. I want you to see something."

Lynan mounted his horse and held out to Ager the reins of his own mount, already saddled. Together they rode east, then south to the Barda River. "I was here earlier this evening," Lynan told him. "I thought I saw something in the walls, but I need you to tell me whether or not it is important."

"You need a sapper," Ager said.

"You were involved in sieges in the Slaver War."

"One or two, but you still need a sapper."

"You know how to set a siege?"

"I've taken part in sieges, Lynan, not directed them."

"But you know the basics," Lynan insisted. "You saw others do it."

"I suppose so."

"I need someone to direct the sappers and infantry we brought with us from Haxus."

Ager grinned. "I wondered when you'd be getting around to that. You don't trust the Haxan officers?"

"Not yet," Lynan admitted.

They were near the river now. They could hear water lap against the banks.

"And I will need to know how it is done," Lynan continued. "There may be many more cities to besiege."

A terrible vision flashed in Ager's mind of burning cities dotting the continent of Theare like the stars in the night sky in his dream of the sea. A shiver passed down his spine.

A tip of light showed on the eastern horizon.

"Now!" Lynan warned. "Watch the line of the north wall!"

Ager peered with his one eye along the wall, and as the sun rose it cast long shadows along its length. But not all the shadows were straight.

"God, it's uneven!" Ager cried.

"That's what I thought," Lynan said excitedly. "They must have hurried to repair damage done by Salokan. Part of the wall carries too much weight."

Ager looked crossly at Lynan. "If you know so much about it, why don't you personally command the engineers?"

"Last night, when I was here, I saw you had set archers along the bank to intercept any river traffic. I know I should have thought of that, but I did not. I don't have your experience. What I know about besieging walled cities I gleaned from books. What you know about besieging cities you've gained from experience. I know the difference."

Ager grunted but did not disagree. He felt foolish for questioning Lynan. He always seemed to have an answer ready these days. Once, of course, he did not, and he had relied on Kumul and Ager for advice; to Ager that time seemed an eon ago, now.

But that is what he is doing now, he reminded himself, and felt doubly foolish.

"Of course, the north wall is the one with the main gate in it," Ager said. "That means it will have the heaviest defenses."

"We will have to think of ways to weaken them."

"They will have to be very convincing ways to fool Charion, I think."

"You mean costly," Lynan said.

Ager nodded. "That's the problem with diversionary assaults. They have to have a genuine chance of breaking through to get an enemy to take them seriously."

Half the sun was over the horizon and the shadows along the north wall were beginning to distort.

"It is time we returned," Lynan said. They started riding back to camp. "Eynon feels he has a great deal to prove."

"Yes, he feels he missed out on . . ." Ager's voice dropped and he reined back, but Lynan let his horse walk on. "You're going to give him command of the diversionary attack, aren't you?"

"I have to show my trust in him," Lynan said over his shoulder.

Ager spurred his horse and caught up with the prince. "The fact that he is Korigan's main rival has nothing to do with it, of course."

"Of course," Lynan replied. Before Ager could say anything more, he added: "Someone has to command it. Someone's followers have to make the sacrifice."

"I understand," Ager said sarcastically.

"No, Ager, you do not understand," Lynan said, looking at him. Ager could not meet that gaze. "You do not understand at all."

*   *   *

Lasthear threw a handful of powder onto a small fire. Brightly colored sparks flew into the air. Jenrosa surprised herself by laughing.

"What magic is this?" she asked.

Lasthear laughed with her. "No magic." She opened her palm, and Jenrosa saw small particles of glittering powder caught between the folds of her skin. "These are metal scrapings. Copper, tin, that sort of thing. It amuses children." She produced a small pouch and tipped some of the contents into Jenrosa's hand. Jenrosa threw it onto the fire, and more sparks whooshed up between them.

Jenrosa laughed even harder. "The lesson being that I am a child?"

"In some ways," Lasthear said. "You have great courage. I have heard how you joined your companions when you could no longer flee from the mercenaries hunting you down at the Strangers' Sooq, and how you were wounded defending Lynan. But I also see how you are afraid of things which only children are truly afraid of—things inside yourself."

"I know many adults who are afraid of themselves."

"That does not mean it is not childish," Lasthear observed gently.

"You are beginning to sound like a priest," chided Jenrosa.

"You are afraid of being a Truespeaker."

Jenrosa bowed her head. "Yes."

"Why?"

"I don't know."

Lasthear shook her head in disappointment. "I think you do."

"Why did you ask me here?" Jenrosa asked irritably. She could hear how pugnacious she must have sounded, and was embarrassed by it. Lasthear was her teacher and friend, and deserved better from her.

Lasthear sighed and pointed to the fire. "I have shown you how to do magic with the earth and with the air. You showed yourself how to do magic with water. Now you must learn how to do magic with fire, the hardest of all elements to work with."

Jenrosa looked up excitedly. "I first met you when you were doing fire magic at the furnaces at the High Sooq."

"Yes, a kind of fire magic called shaping. I was helping the molten metal find its true shape and hold to it."

"Its true shape?"

"All people who possess special ability with a craft—weavers, potters, metal workers, tanners, cooks, story tellers—have the talent to take something raw and unused and give it a true shape, something it was always called to be. Metal workers take copper or iron or gold and let it become a shape, an object, true to its nature. The metal worker, the weaver, and potter and all who work a craft are magickers in their way. My job was to help the metal workers with the shaping; they can do it without me, but my singing made the job easier for them."

"This is what you are going to show me now?"

"No." Lasthear held out one hand and Jenrosa took it. "Now close your eyes and hear in your mind the incantation I make."

Jenrosa closed her eyes. At first, faintly, at the edge of her consciousness, Lasthear's words were nothing but a whisper, but as she listened with her mind, they became louder. She made out individual words that then flowed into sentences, and sentences that flowed into greater meanings. She understood and started adding her own power to the incantation. Suddenly Lasthear broke contact and Jenrosa opened her eyes.

"The fire is out!" she said, surprised.

"Not quite," Lasthear said, her voice subdued. She seemed tired.

Jenrosa looked again. Not only had the fire gone out, but none of the embers were aglow either. And yet . . . She put out her hand and yelped in surprise as she yanked it back. She blew on her palm.

"It's blazing hot!"

Lasthear said nothing but bent over the fireplace and studied the dark embers carefully. She said, "Show me not burn me" and picked out a piece of charcoaled wood. It sat in the middle of her palm without burning her.

"Souls are like flames," Lasthear told Jenrosa. "Let us see whose soul the flames wish to show us." She placed her other hand over the first and slowly raised it. As she did, a flame appeared from the ember and grew as it had more space. At first it seemed to Jenrosa to be just a flame, but soon she could start seeing more detail in its flickering existence—first the suggestion of a body, then definite limbs, and finally a head.

"Lynan," she whispered.

Lasthear nodded to the fireplace. "Now it is your turn."

Jenrosa bent over the fireplace. The invisible heat felt like it was scorching her skin. Then she noticed that the heat was coming from one particular part, and then one particular piece of half-burnt wood. "Show me not burn me," she said and picked it up, placing it in the palm of her left hand. Even though she could still feel the heat coming from it, the skin of her palm was undamaged. She cupped her hand with the other and slowly raised it. A flame appeared instantly. As with the first, she studied it intently, and as she did a figure started taking shape. When it was fully revealed she gasped and almost dropped the charcoal, but Lasthear shouted at her to hold steady.

"Who is it?" Lasthear asked.

The diminutive figure disappeared to be replaced by something that looked like a tree, then a moment later switched back again.

"*What* is it?" Lasthear asked.

"Silona," Jenrosa said hoarsely.

"Gods!" Lasthear cursed.

"Does the real Silona know we are doing this?"

Lasthear shook her head. "No, but it proves vampires still have souls." Jenrosa could hear the wonder in her voice. "That is something I would never have believed."

There was a scuffling noise behind her. She saw Lasthear look up in surprise and drop her own ember. In that moment the flaming figure in her own hand changed. She gasped a second time and this time did drop the ember. She glanced up to see if Lasthear had noticed the change, but her teacher was still looking at the intruder.

"Jenrosa," Lynan said. "I am sorry to interrupt your lessons."

Jenrosa stiffened.

"The lesson was over," she said and nodded to Lasthear who got up, bowed, and retreated. In her place stepped Lynan. His face was without emotion of any kind. Jenrosa thought he looked at her the way he might a perfect stranger.

"I want you to come with me," he said.

Jenrosa stood up and dusted soot from her hands. "Where are we going?"

"You're going to tell Eynon about your vision," he said.

She stared at him. "But last night you said—"

"You were right," Lynan said abruptly. "He needs to make a choice."

"What's happened?" she asked suspiciously. "What's changed?"

"As you so told me last night, Eynon will find out eventually. I want him to find out now." He turned and walked off without waiting to see whether or not she followed. Reluctantly, she did.

They found Eynon with the warriors of his Horse clan at the western edge of the Chett camp, busy sharpening thousands of sections of roughly hewn branches at both ends. When finished, the branches would be driven into the ground and linked with longer transverse sections to make a picket fence that would completely encircle Daavis.

"When do you want us to storm the city walls, your Majesty?" Eynon asked loudly so his men could hear. "You can send the other clans and banners home, you know. The Horse clan will take care of this for you."

His warriors cheered.

They really believe they can, Jenrosa thought.

Lynan smiled thinly. "We have some news," he told Eynon. "We need to talk."

"Oh?" Eynon gave the branch he had been working on to a warrior and led the way to his tent. It was too hot and stuffy inside and Jenrosa felt nauseous.

"Jenrosa has seen something using her magic," Lynan said. "You need to know about it."

Eynon looked at her curiously, and slowly, the words only coming from her reluctantly, she told the chief about her vision using the water magik.

Eynon's face went pale, his lips contracted into the thinnest of lines while his eyes widened in horror. "How . . . how sure are you?"

"Very," Lynan said for her.

Jenrosa glanced at him. She *was* certain about the accuracy of her vision, but she did not like Lynan speaking for her. Eynon saw her expression and looked doubtfully at her.

"But you can't be sure," he said, his voice almost pleading.

"I'm sorry, Eynon, but I think a great tragedy has befallen your clan."

Eynon opened his mouth to speak but no words came out. At last he managed to ask Jenrosa, "Their pennant. You mentioned the enemy had a strange pennant."

"It carried the device of a bird, but not one I recognized."

"Yes, it would be," he said.

"You know who the enemy was?" Lynan said.

"My clan's territory borders the great desert."

"The Southern Chetts! Of course!"

"You in the east call them that. We call them the Saranah. It was once the name of their clan."

"They were originally from the Oceans of Grass?" Lynan asked, astounded.

"Yes. Perhaps the largest of all the clans. They were butchers and raiders. Eventually all their neighboring clans combined to drive them away, into the desert. Occasionally, Saranah war bands will return to the Oceans of Grass to raid a lightly protected herd, but they've never invaded in the numbers necessary to take on a whole clan." He nodded to Jenrosa. "Your vision shows you true, magicker. I believe what you have told me."

"Then you have to make a choice," Lynan said.

"What choice?" Eynon asked. "I have to go back and find any survivors and hunt down the enemy—"

"You have to make a choice," Lynan said more loudly, speaking over him. "First, to go back immediately and look for survivors. Do that and I will have to retreat from Daavis. In fact, I'll have to retreat back to Haxus or even back to the Oceans of Grass."

"Your Majesty, I'm sorry, but I *must* go back—"

"Which means the Algonka Pass will fall under the kingdom's control. If the kingdom controls the pass, then they can send an army into the Oceans of Grass next summer and every Chett clan will meet the fate of your own. Your second choice is to stay here and help me take Daavis, after which you can go back to your home, search for survivors, and hunt down the enemy who did this to your people."

"But the delay would be too long!" Eynon declared. "How long do you think the siege can last? At least a month? Maybe until next winter!"

"The siege will be over in two weeks, with the help of you and your clan."

"How can you promise that?" Eynon demanded.

"There is a weakness in the walls surrounding the city. We can take advantage of that."

"That's a task for those clever wrights from Haxus you've brought with you, not my warriors."

Lynan nodded curtly. "I know. But to make sure Charion does not detect what we are planning her attention must be diverted entirely to some other threat."

"Ah," Eynon said and laughed softly. "Which is why you want me and my warriors."

Lynan did not reply.

"You know, it's funny, but my warriors really believe they *could* storm Daavis and win through." He came closer to Lynan and slowly, almost diffidently, put a finger against his chest. "But you know different, I'm bound. And I'm no fool."

"I would not be here if I thought you were a fool."

Eynon stepped back. "I will consider this."

"If we take Daavis, I will place under your command three troops of my Red Hands and three of the lancers to help you track down the Saranah who attacked your people. And I will make sure every head of cattle you lost is replaced from the herds of the other clans."

Eynon's eyes widened. "You would do this for me?"

"I will not allow the Horse clan to die under my reign."

Eynon looked at his hands as if searching for some sign there of his own fate. "I hope I live long enough to see you keep that promise."

"You used me," Jenrosa said to Lynan as they walked back.

Lynan did not answer.

"You used me to get your way with Eynon."

"You wanted to tell him what you saw in your vision."

"But not for this! Not to convince him to throw what's left of his clan against the walls of Daavis!"

"He is helping to guarantee his clan will survive into the future, and that there will be an Oceans of Grass under the control of the Chetts for them to live on."

"You are throwing away their lives."

Lynan stopped and grabbed her arms.

"You're hurting me!" she cried. She stared defiantly in to his eyes, but something there made her turn away.

"Listen to me, Jenrosa. I am at war with my sister for the throne of Grenda Lear, and the Chetts, for good or ill, have thrown their support behind me. They are my strongest weapon and I will use them, knowing that if I fail the cost for all of us, including the Chetts, will be terrible. I know that many of these warriors will die and that some clans may never recover from the war. I cannot help that any more. What I can do is ensure our side wins." He turned her around so she could see the entire Chett camp. "Look at them, Jenrosa. For the first time in their history, the fate of Grenda Lear depends on their courage and determination. Do you really think they will throw that away?"

He let her go and strode away from her.

"What choice do they have under you?" she called after him. "What choice do any of us have under you?"

Without stopping or turning, he said: "The same choice as Eynon: to leave."

An arrow missed Ager's ear by a finger's span. He cursed and ducked behind a wooden board placed in front of the shallow trench he was walking along. He found himself facing someone's bottom and he pushed it aside.

"Careful, you fool," the owner of the bottom said.

"Careful who you call a fool," Ager returned.

The other, a Haxan officer, turned around, saw who it was and paled. "Sorry."

An arrow thudded into the board. Both men winced with the sound of it.

"It's just that I have an aversion to arrows. I don't think I'd enjoy being struck by one."

"Take my word for it," Ager said, pointing to the empty socket where he used to have an eye. "You wouldn't."

The Haxan shuddered. "Forgive me for asking, but what are you doing here?"

"I was about to ask you the same question."

"Digging."

"Who gave you orders to dig?"

"I'm a sapper. What else would you have me do?"

Ager had no immediate answer to that. "What are you digging?"

The Haxan pointed farther down the trench where other sappers were huddling behind boards. "We're trying to find the entrances to the tunnels we started when we were last here."

"Isn't that a little risky? I thought the enemy would have found and collapsed them or set traps in them by now."

"Some, but not all. We hid them as best we could when King Salokan ordered our retreat. We knew it would save us a lot of work later on if he decided to return." Another arrow rattled the board. "And maybe some lives."

"Who are you?" Ager asked.

"Captain Waylong. I already know who you are."

"Prince Lynan has put me in charge of you and yours, Captain Waylong. I want a mine under the north wall, especially the section near the main gate."

"We tried that last time. Didn't work then."

"You wrought better than you know. There is a serious weakness there, and badly repaired in Charion's haste to prepare for a second siege."

Waylong showed surprise. "Really?"

"I have seen it for myself. If you can set off a mine underneath it, it will all come down. If we're lucky, the gatehouse will come down with it."

"You'd have to be bloody lucky," Waylong said, then remembered who he was talking to. "Excuse me, sir."

"Who's the senior officer here?"

"It was Yerman, sir, but earlier this morning he didn't duck fast enough. Under him, there were three of us captains."

"Well, you're senior officer from today. I give my orders to you, and you make sure they're carried out."

Waylong looked skeptically at the crookback. "Well and good, sir."

"You don't look too happy about the promotion."

"Depends, if you don't mind my being blunt."

"Depends on what?"

"On whether you're the kind to take advice."

Ager peered at him with his one eye and Waylong swallowed.

"What kind of advice?"

"That you let us dig more trenches before we start the mining."

"What do you need more trenches for?"

"We'll zigzag them toward the walls, sir, so your Chett archers can get close enough to shoot at their archers. That will make things go faster down here."

"How long do you need?"

"Two days."

"And then you start on the mining?"

"Yes. With your Chetts giving us cover, we can move out the dirt from tunneling twice as fast. We'll be under the walls in ten days."

Ager nodded. "I'll send you the Chetts you need." He turned to go back to the safety of the main camp, stopped and said: "By the way, Captain Waylong, the Chetts assigned to you will be under your command. Make sure they realize that."

Waylong swallowed again, so hard his throat bobbed. "Chetts under my command, sir?"

"That's what I said."

"Thank you, sir."

"Don't thank me. You're responsible for their safety as well as the safety of your own sappers. Understand?"

"Um, yes, sir."

"You'd better get started on your trenches."

On the second day of the siege of Daavis, Korigan rode up and down the stake fence that now surrounded the city. She talked to banner commanders and clan chiefs on the way, getting a feeling for the morale of the Chetts and their leaders. When she came to the Red Hands, Gudon joined her for the rest of the tour. By midday they had finished and the pair rode to a gentle hill near the center of the line that allowed them to look toward the north wall of the city.

Korigan dismounted, fidgeted with the girth straps on her saddle, remounted, and fidgeted with her sword belt and bow string and poncho. Gudon watched her for a while, then said: "What ails you, cousin. Did you sit on a branch from a thorn tree?"

"I don't know what you mean," she answered irritably, fiddling with the reins.

"You don't like being in the same place for too long."

"It's not that," she said, then shook her head. "Yes, it's that. I'm used to getting up in the morning and moving the whole clan to the next camp site. The only time a Chett is one place for more than a day is in winter at the High Sooq. But this is summer! We should be moving." She faced him. "Don't you feel it?"

"What ails you goes deeper than that."

"The Chetts have never carried out a siege before. Nor an assault. I don't know that we're ready for this."

"We have to be ready at some time. You have put us behind Lynan, and he intends to take the east, and the east is filled with cities, some of them with bigger walls than Daavis."

Korigan turned away from Gudon and her whole body tensed. "Gudon, did I do the right thing? Have I made a terrible mistake?"

"I remember having this conversation with Kayakun, your spy in the Strangers' Sooq," he said.

"What did you say to him?"

"That Lynan will make the Chetts the equal of any other people on the continent of Theare."

Korigan snorted. "We *already* knew that."

"No. We believed it. We told ourselves that. But we knew we had never been tested. During the Slaver War, it was the east and its armies that saved us from the mercenaries. Well, now we will know if we were right to believe it. We have defeated the mercenaries sent against us, in Haxus we have defeated Grenda Lear's oldest and most determined foe, and now we test ourselves against the kingdom itself."

"For the second time," she reminded him. "We lost the first battle, remember?"

"Did we?"

"We retreated from the field. We lost Kumul Alarn."

"And the enemy retreated to its burrow which we now encircle. We hurt them more than we knew, and we recovered the quickest."

"We still haven't met the full force of the kingdom," she said grimly. "They can raise an army so big it would take a week for it to pass though the Algonka Pass. My father told me of such an army."

"I know; it was created by Usharna and led by General Elynd Chisal. With it the General finally smashed Haxus and the mercenaries. Don't forget, Korigan, that Lynan is Elynd Chisal's son."

"How could I forget? He *is* the White Wolf, isn't he?"

"Who needs to know?" Gudon asked gently. "Queen Korigan of all the Chetts, or Korigan, Lynan's lover?"

She looked at him sharply. "Who else knows?"

"Everyone, of course."

Korigan blushed. "What do . . . what do my people say?"

"About time."

They both grinned then.

"Do you love him?" he asked.

Korigan nodded. "Yes. I have for many months, but was afraid to do anything about it. I had to make sure."

"That it was the right thing to do for your people?"

"Yes."

"Then trust your judgment now. Lynan is the king we have been waiting for."

Korigan laughed. "It's strange, isn't it? I am his consort. I have placed in his hands the fate of my people. I love him. And yet I must be the only one among us who doubts him."

Gudon grunted. "You are not the only one. Ager has his doubts, as does Jenrosa."

"His own companions? How can they doubt him after all they have been through together?"

"They have seen him change. They believe he is not the old Lynan they knew, and they are unsure of what he has become."

"And you, cousin? You have no doubts?"

Gudon shook his head. "Not since that night he almost died at the hands of Rendle's mercenaries. He returned to fight to the end with me and Ager and Kumul. He loved us more than he loved his own life."

"But that was before Jenrosa gave him the blood of Silona. He is not the same now as he was then."

"His heart is the same, and as long as his soul is still his own, what else matters?"

Jenrosa was pacing up and down outside her tent, Ager watching her anxiously. "I don't know what he has become, but I don't recognize him anymore."

Ager caught the eye of Lasthear, who had brought him to Jenrosa, and indicated she should leave. She bowed and departed, leaving no one else within earshot.

"Jenrosa, calm down," he said patiently.

"Calm down?" she cried, stopping to face him. "God, Ager! Do you know what he is planning to do?"

"I assume by 'he' you mean Lynan—"

"Who else?"

"—and what in particular has he done that has you so excited?"

She shook her hands in the air as if she was trying to beat some invisible enemy. "He's convinced Eynon to assault Daavis so he can try some deception or ploy against one of the city walls!"

Ager breathed heavily through his nose. So Lynan *had* gone ahead and done that. But he has his reasons. He must have his reasons. "Someone has to create a diversion for the main attack, Jenrosa," he said reasonably, trying to convince himself as much as her.

"But why the Horse clan?"

"Why not the Horse clan?"

"You mean Lynan didn't tell you?"

Ager looked at her blankly. "What are you talking about?"

She held her head between her hands. "I . . . I can't tell you. You should ask Lynan . . ."

Ager went to Jenrosa and took her hands in his own. He caught her gaze and held it. "What is it, Jenrosa? What has driven you to this state? Why are you so afraid of Lynan all of a sudden?"

She pulled herself out of his grip. "It isn't all of a sudden, Ager. And it's what he's doing that scares me. The old Lynan, the Lynan we knew before we met Silona, would never have done the things he's contemplating doing now."

"Like what?"

"The blood," she said hoarsely. Her gray eyes stared at her own hands. "All the blood. I see it every time I do magic. I see it on my hands, I see it in my dreams. And I see *her*, I see her together with Lynan."

Ager let her go, suddenly afraid, and retreated a step. "But you are unsure about the magic. You've said so yourself—"

"Call Lasthear back! She'll tell you. I'm their fucking True-speaker! Did you know that? They all think I'm like Gudon's mother. I'm the prize that only comes once every second generation! I can do things no one has been able to do for twenty years. I can make the water tell stories, I can conjure vampires in fire, I can make the earth run red with blood—"

"Stop it!" Ager shouted.

Jenrosa shut up and stared at Ager in shock. Her body started shaking like a leaf in a storm.

Pity overwhelmed Ager and he took her in his arms. At first she resisted, continuing to shake, but he held her tighter and she broke down, crying in great racking sobs. Ager said nothing, and when the sobbing started to ease, he led her inside her tent and laid her down on her cot.

She did not stop crying for a long time, and then only because she eased into a deep sleep. Ager pulled a blanket over her and stood up. He studied her face for a long time, trying—almost hoping—to find some sign of madness there. He could deal with that, he thought. He knew he could not deal with the other possibility: that Lynan had become something less than human.

Lynan told Ager the new trench work was to cover the west wall as well as the north. Ager made sure most of the visible activity was being spent on the extension in the hope it would convince those inside the city that the west wall was Lynan's principal objective. In four days the trenches were finished. As well, Captain Waylong informed Ager that two of the old Haxan tunnel entrances had not been found by the enemy and they could dig a mine under the north wall in four days. When Ager told Lynan the news, he knew what would happen next.

Lynan ordered the assault on the west wall to begin the following day.

13

CHARION woke, startled, staring into the dark. For a moment all she could think of were the shreds of a dream; fragments of a green forest, alluring and somehow threatening at the same time.

Then the sound of a trumpet, and she recognized the sound that had woken her. It had come from the west. She leaped out of her bed and rushed to the window. She could hear sounds of running soldiers, cries, the sound of fear, the low ringing of despair.

Someone banged on her door. Farben's voice. "Your Majesty! They attack the west wall! They attack the west wall!"

She hurried to the door and flung it open. Her small secretary was holding a torch, its flame exaggerating his drawn and worried features. "Get in!" she ordered, and used the light to slip on her hauberk and sword belt, then together they rushed out of the palace, her helmet under her arm, Farben pattering behind.

Around her sergeants and captains were shouting orders, making sure soldiers kept to their posts and did not automatically rush to the point of attack only to leave other sections of the wall vulnerable. Other inhabitants hovered near the doorways of their homes, hugging their children to them. Workers were busy lighting lamps spaced along the streets.

Galen joined her, looking dangerous and supremely martial in his armor. "The knights are ready," he told her. She nodded. As they drew closer to the west wall, she could hear the cries of the enemy, the wild whoops of the Chetts. She repressed the shiver starting up her spine. She had faced them once before and beaten them off. This time, in her own city, she would do it again.

The three of them reached stairs and ran up, went through a

guard tower and then they were there. She pulled a soldier aside to look over the parapet. She could see a scuttling tide of warriors gathering around the foot of the wall. Ladders were being raised. Ropes with hooks twirled in the air. Arrows flashed in the night, most clattering uselessly against the stone work, some found a mark.

"How many?" Galen asked.

Charion shrugged. "Too dark to be sure. Several hundred. A thousand."

"A diversion?"

Again she shrugged. How did he expect her to know so soon? Then she remembered he had never been though a siege, and although she had only gone through one, compared to Galen she was a veteran. The thought made her smile grimly. "Too early to tell."

An arrow whistled passed her ear.

"Put out that fucking torch!" a voice roared.

Farben whimpered and dropped the torch to the ground below, narrowly missing a worker stoking a fire under a cauldron of oil. More curses, and more whimpering from Farben.

"What are you doing here?" Charion asked the secretary.

"Waiting for orders," he said.

She looked at him then, a man almost as small as she and not suited for anything really except life at court; and yet he had never deserted her, had always been at her side if he could, in spite of any danger. A slight breeze made his wispy gray hair float around his scalp like smoke.

"Go back to the palace," she said gently. "I will ask for you if I need you."

Farben hesitated, did a little nervous dance with his feet.

"Go," she repeated.

He nodded, smiled thankfully, and left.

The top of a roughly made wooden ladder appeared over the wall. A soldier with a long, forked stick started pushing it away when Charion stopped him. She tested the ladder. "Wait until there is more weight against it." They waited a few seconds and Charion tested it again. "Now!" she ordered, and the soldier pushed with all his strength. Galen got behind and helped. The ladder seemed to balance in midair for a moment, then finally eased away from the wall. They heard no screams, but two very satisfying thumps. The soldier grinned at Charion, turned to thank Galen for his help. Something hit him in the head, flinging him off the walkway to land in a broken heap on the ground below.

Galen swore. "What was that?"

Something smacked hard into the tower behind them and dropped to the walkway. "They're throwing bloody rocks at us!" Galen said and scrunched down to present a smaller target.

Charion went over to the object and picked it up. "No," she said, surprised by its weight. "It's metal, not stone."

"Metal? That means . . ."

"Ballista!" Charion finished for him. She looked at Galen in alarm. "The Chetts don't have sappers!"

More guards were hit and everyone on the walkway hunkered down behind the parapets. A cluster of new ladders and rope hooks appeared; no one seemed to be in a hurry to expose themselves to the ballista to push them away.

"Come on!" Charion shouted to Galen, and together they stood up, grabbed one of the forked sticks, and forced a ladder far enough off balance for it to topple sideways. This time there were screams. Everyone else on the walkway, shamed into action, stood then and pushed at the ladders and severed the climbing ropes. A few of the defenders were hit by metal missiles, but no enemy made it to the top. When the last ladder was gone everyone ducked back down again.

"Who taught the Chetts to build artillery?" Galen asked, not expecting an answer.

Charion slapped the wall. "That's why Lynan didn't attack us right after the battle!"

Galen looked at her curiously. "What are you talking about?"

"He attacked Salokan! Don't you see? He had to rebuild his army's confidence, and Salokan's army was already defeated and in retreat. The Haxans had sappers. Lots of them."

"It wouldn't take him all this time to destroy an army and recruit its sappers," Galen said.

"No, but it might take him that long to conquer Haxus."

"God," Galen said as the implications of what Charion was suggesting sank in. "We're in trouble."

Charion nodded. All the hurried repair work they had done to Daavis had been in expectation of an assault by a Chett army unversed in the art of siege warfare and, even more importantly, without the expertise necessary to build artillery and siege engines. She had never expected Lynan's army to attempt anything more complex than scale the city walls or try and undermine them.

"We're going to lose Daavis," Galen said somberly.

"I'm not going to lose *my* city!" Charion said fiercely. "I beat off Salokan; I can beat off Lynan!"

Galen said nothing, but knew that Charion beat off Salokan because Sendarus and the force he commanded—which then had included Galen and the knights from the Twenty Houses—had arrived in time to break the siege. This time there would be no one marching to the rescue. It would take months for Grenda Lear to replace the army it lost when Lynan attacked Sendarus and effectively eliminated it as a fighting force.

"They're retreating!" someone called.

Charion and Galen risked glimpsing over the parapets. The Chetts were running back to their lines, taking their wounded with them.

"Do you have a sally port?" Galen asked suddenly.

"Yes. We call it the main gate."

"Oh."

"I'm not going to risk you and your knights yet, Galen," Charion told him.

"We're not much use where we are."

"I'll need you if the Chetts break through. A determined charge by your force should secure any breach long enough for us to reinforce from one of the other walls."

"Well, they're gone for the moment."

"They'll be back."

"How long?"

"Before evening," Charion said. "And they'll try here again, I'll warrant."

"How do you know that?"

"Because Lynan is trying to convince us this is where he'll be getting in."

As Eynon's warriors reached the safety of their lines, the first rays of a new day lit the eastern horizon. He had sent three hundred out, and most of them returned in good order and on their feet. When the count came back, he had lost thirty dead and that many again wounded. The reports of the survivors told him what he needed to know about the defenses, and he immediately started planning the next assault. Lynan, who had watched the attack with him, promised him more artillery.

"If any of our warriors can take that wall, yours can," Lynan told him.

Eynon knew Lynan was clumsily attempting to build up his confidence, but there was an element of truth in his words. His warriors had carried the attack without hesitation and had only pulled back because Eynon had given the command. Although the defenses would have been too much for that first assault, he was more confident the second would do better.

Maybe, just maybe. he allowed himself to think, *this exercise will end up being something more than a simple diversion.*

Eynon made sure his warriors were rested and well fed, keeping them behind barricades, out of sight of the city. Chett archers were peppering the walls in the north and east as well as the south, and he had heard Lynan was arranging for barges to be made or brought up from outlying villages so they could put pressure on the river wall as well. Meanwhile, the Haxan sappers were digging closer and closer to the city walls. One way or another, Eynon was sure, Lynan would find a way to keep his word and make the city fall within two weeks. Once Hume was in Chett hands and the Algonka Pass secured, he could hunt down the Saranah who had attacked his clan and wipe them out.

And then I will resurrect my clan, and we will become as strong and respected as we once were.

As the afternoon waned, Eynon gathered nearly five hundred of his warriors together. They brought with them scaling ladders and ropes and a fierce determination to succeed where their fellow clan warriors had failed in the morning. As well, this time Eynon had more of the devilish Haxan ballistae, and Lynan had allotted them more ammunition so they could give cover from the very start of the assault. Lynan had also sent the first constructed mangonels, pieces of artillery that awed the Chetts. Where the ballistae were machines based on the principle of the bow, the mangonels were something else altogether, in concept and scale something the Chetts had never seen before.

When it was two hours from sunset, Lynan joined Eynon again.

"Would you like to do something useful?" Eynon asked him.

Lynan looked at him with some amusement. "What did you have in mind?"

"Order the artillery. I want to go up with my warriors."

Lynan frowned. "I don't want to lose you, Eynon."

"Thank you for your concern," he said dryly. "But I want to

know what it is like out there for myself. I don't want my warriors to think I'm the kind of leader who will not share their danger."

Lynan seemed doubtful, and Eynon thought he was going to refuse him. "When you fought against the army of Grenda Lear, I understand *you* led the final attack against the knights from the Twenty Houses."

Lynan sighed. He had been outmaneuvered. "Very well."

"How quickly do those mangonels reload?"

"I'm assured by the Haxan crews they can send off a missile every three minutes."

"Too slow to be much use in the attack. Have them shoot as soon as we start the charge across the open ground. With any luck those huge stones will dislodge some of the enemy from behind the parapets. Then use the ballistae until you see my warriors are near the top."

Lynan nodded. "As you say. Good luck."

Eynon nodded and left to join his warriors. He waited until he judged the sun was shining directly in the eyes of any defenders behind the walls, stood up, and waved his sword in the air. As one, his Chetts broke cover and started running across the open ground toward the west wall. They had not gone twenty paces when he heard wood slam against wood followed by the whistle of stones hurled overhead by the Haxan mangonels. They hit the west wall with loud cracks; some of the stones disintegrated, others dropped to the ground. Pulverized dust swirled around the parapets, and Eynon could hear the screams of the wounded and dying even above the war cries of the Chetts.

Like a dark tide the attackers reached the wall and pooled under it to avoid the arrows of Hume archers. Eynon shouted orders and ladders were raised and climbing ropes with savage hooks whirled above heads. His warriors kept up their war cries and were answered by the defenders above. Missiles from the ballistae tattooed against the stone work, the sound softer if it hit a human target. The rope hooks whirled through the air, some finding purchase, others dropping. Warriors clambered up ladders, shinned up ropes. Eynon went to the nearest ladder and started climbing. From the corner of his eye, he saw liquid, creamy and steaming, pour down over three Chetts on the ladder next to his. They ignited before his eyes and fell to the ground where they writhed in pain but without sound. The warrior above him gave a victory cry as he reached the parapet, then screamed, toppled backward and over Eynon, an arrow in his eye. Then Eynon was there himself, facing a Hume archer desperately trying to nock another arrow. Eynon held on to the ladder with his sword hand and with the other unsheathed his dagger and flung it. The dagger clanged uselessly against the archer's helm, but he yelped in fright and took a step backward, disappearing over the walkway. Eynon scrabbled across the parapet and was over, his sword flashing in the golden sun as he sliced through archers and spearmen suddenly too crowded to fight back effectively.

Other Chetts made it to the walkway and soon they secured the central section of the wall, allowing even more warriors to clamber over.

"We've done it!" he cried. "We've done it! Get to the gate! Get to the gate!"

Their sabers whirling and cutting, the Chetts forced back the defenders. They reached a guard tower and killed all inside it, giving them possession of stairs leading down to the city itself. With wild whoops Eynon and his warriors poured down the stairs, scattering the defenders before them.

In the courtyard of the palace what was left of the knights of the Twenty Houses, about three hundred heavy cavalry, waited impatiently for the call to action. Among them was Serefa, still haunted by images of his companions left behind at the outpost from which he himself had barely escaped with his life. He wanted revenge against the Chetts, but for the moment all he could do was listen to the sounds of the assault on the west wall. He gripped his reins and prayed to God that he would let the Chetts win over the wall so the knights could be called into action, and at the same time felt terribly guilty that his wish might be granted.

After what seemed hours of listening to someone else's fight, the tone and pitch of the battle changed noticeably. It seemed closer, more desperate, and Serefa could feel in the sound the unmistakable current of panic. His heartbeat and breathing picked up, and he started sweating under his breastplate and helmet.

A messenger appeared at the courtyard entrance, looked around frantically until he found Galen and ran to him. The two exchanged terse words and the messenger left. Galen turned to his knights, raised his mailed fist, and waved it in the air. Serefa could not help grinning—God had granted him his wish.

They stayed at a walk until they had left the courtyard, then moved to a trot on the broad avenue leading directly west. The whole area was deserted. Ahead they could see small, antlike figures on the west wall and smoke starting to column into the air. Galen drew his sword, and the knights eased into a canter, the sound of their horses' hooves and their jangling armor echoing in the city, their formation easing into four lines to give the maximum frontage. Serefa found himself at the far right of the second line, and he could see the enemy on the ground, overwhelming desperate defenders trying to stop them getting to the main gate in the north wall. Galen lowered his sword and the knights went from canter to gallop. The sound they made turned into a pounding that could be heard above all other noise, and the Chetts looked up and saw with terror what was bearing down on them. Some tried to form a defensive line, but the knights were on them too quickly. Swords swung smashing through skull and limb; horses bit at faces and their hooves beat down on fallen bodies. The Chetts panicked and routed back to the stairs, but some of the knights, first among them Serefa, beat them to it and held them back while their fellows pressed in from the front.

One Chett, larger, more ferocious than the rest and incredibly ugly, made his way to the front and ducked under a slashing attack from Serefa before darting under his horse. Serefa heard his mount scream in pain and then it collapsed in a heap and he found himself standing, his feet aside the dead animal. Before he could react the Chett was behind him. A huge arm locked around his throat and pulled him back, and he felt a blade slide against his neck. He tried to struggle free, shouting for help, but the blade bit deep. He felt no pain, just a warm flood and a dark curtain falling over his eyes, and as he fell atop his slain horse the last thing he saw was the Chetts scrambling past and up the stairs in a desperate bid to escape destruction.

Galen cursed loudly as the last few Chetts managed to get down the other side of the wall before his knights could reach them, but as he watched the fleeing enemy he realized how few there were: a hundred perhaps, but not many more. Then he looked down on the other side at the Chett dead heaped against the stairs and the inside wall. They had fought with amazing ferocity and bravery, but in the end there was nothing they could do against his armored knights.

But it has not all gone our way, he reminded himself. After all, the Chetts had managed to get over the wall. There seemed to be as many slain defenders as there were Chetts, and a large number of them had been struck by those terrible Haxan missiles. He shouted for archers to shoot at the retreating Chetts, but even as he did so, the now familiar sound of more metal thwacking against the wall made him duck below the parapets. He made his way to the tower and then down the stairs where he was met by a frantic Farben.

"I thought you were sent back to the palace?" Galen said, admiring the little man's pluck.

"Have you seen the queen?" the secretary demanded.

Galen looked blankly at him for a moment. "No, I . . ." For a moment panic took him and he felt his muscles start to lock. "She must be here somewhere . . ."

"I haven't seen her!" Farben cried frantically. People were starting to look at them.

"Calm down!" Galen ordered, and saying it helped him calm himself. He grabbed a passing captain. "Have you seen the queen?"

The captain shook his head. "Not since the attack began. She was on the walkway—"

Galen did not let him finish. Despite his armor he sprinted back up to the walkway, Farben close behind. Keeping low, they turned over every dead defender, their hearts in their mouths, but found no sign of her.

"She must have made it back down," Galen said, breathing a sigh of relief.

"Unless she was knocked off the wall," Farben countered.

They returned to the ground and started searching among the heaps of dead and wounded. They had almost given up when Farben shouted and ran to a collection of three bodies. Galen could not see what had grabbed the secretary's attention until he drew closer and saw the glint of armor. He ran over and helped Farben pull off one dead guard and a headless Chett. And there was Charion, blood all over her breastplate and helmet, her face as pale as a winter sky, looking as frail and fragile as a porcelain doll.

"Oh, God . . ." Galen muttered and lifted her in his arms, Farben whimpering beside him. By now, other defenders had gathered around, recognizing who it was. Galen took off her helmet, but though there was a lot of dirt and blood matting her hair, there appeared to be no injury. He then took off her breastplate, and again there seemed to be no source for all the blood she was covered in.

It must all belong to the Chett, Galen told himself, hoping it was so.

Gingerly, Galen unlaced her jerkin and lifted her shirt. Half her chest was covered by a purple bruise that was rimmed with blood. He felt the skin tenderly. "Two broken ribs, at least," he said aloud. Charion moaned in pain, and Galen let out his breath. Farben looked ready to faint.

"She will be all right," Galen told the secretary, "as long as she is looked after. Get her to the palace. I will take over here."

Farben did not even question the knight, but ordered some of the guards to make a stretcher with spears and cloaks and ordered another to find a doctor.

When they were gone, Galen went about making sure there were enough guards put back on the west wall, using some of his own knights to make up the numbers. Then he visited all the wounded, determining whether or not they were fit for duty or needed to be withdrawn. Before he finished, he was joined by Magmed.

"We lost seventeen knights," the nobleman reported. "Most of them were trying to hold the stairs against the Chetts."

"I've put another fifty on the wall. That leaves us just over two hundred as reserve."

"The odds are getting worse all the time," Magmed said levelly.

Galen could only nod.

"As good a place as any to die, I suppose," Magmed continued. "I wish to God I could have a charge at Prince Lynan, though."

"You may yet get your wish," Galen returned. "Because I have no intention of going down with the city should it fall."

Magmed eyed him with surprise. "You're not going to—"

"Run?" Galen finished for him. "Of course not. But if the city is lost, we have to break out. I will not let my knights be slaughtered in the streets and in the buildings. If worse comes to worst, we still have Kendra to defend."

"Do you want us ready at the palace again?"

Galen nodded. As Magmed turned to leave, Galen held him back by the arm. "And tell Farben to ready the queen. I don't know how fit she is to travel, but if we leave her here, she will die at Lynan's hands."

Magmed looked shocked. "Even Lynan would not do that!"

Galen laughed bitterly. "Did you see what he did to Sendarus? Why would he stop at killing something as petty as a provincial ruler if he would not hesitate to slaughter his own sister's husband?"

Magmed nodded. "All right. Where will you be?"

"Here. With Charion gone, someone has to take charge of the defense."

"Do you think the Chetts will assault the west wall again?"

"Charion told me they would attack at this point at least twice, and the second time they almost made it to the main gate. They'll try again."

Ager was visiting the trenches opposite the north wall when he heard the war cries of Eynon's warriors as they started their third assault on the west wall. He sent a silent prayer for them, but forced himself to concentrate on his task. Captain Waylong had asked him to come and pointed out new work, mentioned the names of sappers who had performed exceptionally, detailed where they would go next.

"And the tunnels?" Ager asked. "How's the mining operation going?"

Waylong looked particularly well pleased. Keeping low behind barricades and mantlets he led the way to one of the tunnel entrances.

"We have four of these, three old ones and this new system."

"New system? How long will it take you to get to the wall from here? More time than we have, surely?"

Waylong shook his head. "We're not digging a completely new tunnel, only a new entrance. We've used this to intercept one of the old tunnels the enemy thought they had destroyed. They certainly caved in most of the early work, but they didn't finish the job. It takes us closer to the north wall than any other tunnel." Waylong licked his lips. "An hour ago we were no more than four paces from under the crooked section of the north wall."

"Already?" Ager's voice rose with excitement. "How long before you can set off the mine?"

"We're preparing the work as we go. By now they should be under the wall, but they're working as quietly as possible. The attacks your Chetts are carrying out against the west wall makes it hard for any counter-miners to hear the work, so that's when we do most of the close digging."

"How long before you can set off the mine?" Ager asked again, trying to keep the impatience out of his voice.

"Late this afternoon," Waylong answered. "You might want to wait until tomorrow morning—"

"This afternoon? God, why didn't you tell me this yesterday? We could have called off this morning's assault—"

"Because we didn't know yesterday!" Waylong interrupted. "We only intercepted the old tunnel last night. And I told you we need the noise of the assault to finish the dig without being detected."

Ager took a few deep breaths and nodded wearily. "I'm sorry. But we won't wait until tomorrow morning. Prince Lynan will want to try this afternoon. I need to know exactly when you can fire the mine."

"An hour before sunset. No earlier."

"Can you promise that?"

Waylong swallowed. There were so many things that could go wrong in a dig—counter-mining, a tunnel collapse, a miscalculation about tunnel length or an angle—but he knew Ager was not interested in hearing excuses. "We'll get it done," he said, hoping he sounded more confident than he felt. "I'll be there myself to fire it one hour before sunset."

Ager smiled grimly. "If you do this, I can promise you Lynan will be very grateful."

Waylong could not help swallowing again. He was not sure the pale prince's close attention would be a welcome thing. He felt more comfortable in his trenches and holes than being too close to someone that important. Or, he admitted to himself, someone so terrible.

"I'd better get back to it, then," he mumbled, half-bowed, half-saluted, and scrambled off.

A good officer, Ager thought to himself. *I'll have a word with Lynan about him.*

He found it strange to be thinking so highly of a captain from Haxus. He had spent most of his military career fighting men just like Waylong—had even been a captain himself once. When it came down to it, there was no difference between them really, except opportunity. It was ironic that he and Waylong were working together against a kingdom city.

He shook his head. Such thoughts did no one any good. There was a battle to be won, and enemies to kill. Thinking too deeply on it would send a man crazy.

Queen Charion had regained consciousness once since being brought back to the palace. She made some comment on being without a shirt in front of so many men, then passed out again. Doctors had spent hours with her making sure there were no serious internal injuries other than the three cracked ribs they had found. Unguents were placed on her bruising and her right arm put in a sling to stop it from moving. Galen had visited whenever he could. And all the time, never leaving her side, sat Farben. He amazed himself by not fretting. For the first time since the war had started, he found some kind of calm. His queen had been injured, and for Farben nothing else mattered. Charion was the center of his world, and when he found her wounded, he thought his world had collapsed. When he realized she was still alive, he understood how unimportant was everything else in his own life.

Charion moved in her sleep, moaning with the pain it caused her. Farben dipped a cloth in warm, scented water and used it to pat her forehead. Her features relaxed and she continued sleeping.

Outside, he heard the jangling of armor. Galen's armored squadron in the courtyard, ready for a last desperate battle. He knew Galen had effectively taken command of the city and was himself on the west wall where the greatest danger lay. Farben thought his queen had chosen well; that is, if she intended Galen to be more than simply her lover. He sighed heavily. She had had her fair share of lovers, none of them much good in Farben's eye: opportunists mostly, and one or two so stupid he thought Charion lucky to get anything at all from them. But Galen was noble born, and a natural commander, and Farben could tell he liked Charion.

Maybe, he thought, *Galen even loves her.*

He smiled. For many years, he had thought he was the only person in the kingdom who loved Charion. She was a short-tempered cow a lot of the time, but she was absolutely devoted to Hume and she always kept her word. It was easy being one of her secretaries, once you were used to the shouting and screaming.

The sound of fighting reached him. From the west again. How many more times would the Chetts throw themselves so bravely and bloodily against that wall? How long could Galen and the defenders resist?

Charion called out, crying in pain. Gently, Farben held her down, spoke soothing words to her.

Waylong lit the torch he had specially prepared with wood just turned from green and bound with dampened twine. He glanced one more time at the western horizon and entered the tunnel. For

the first few paces he could almost stand, but as it made its way
north and deeper into the ground he had to stoop lower and lower
until he was crouching. Finally, the tunnel widened enough for him
to stand again, and on all sides his workers had stacked dry brush
around the timber beams that kept the room from collapsing under
the weight of the north wall directly above. As well, the workers
had prepared two flimsy tables made from branches of dead trees,
and on each table rested a large round bowl filled with fine flour.
Two engineers were still there, slowly easing out the pegs that
joined roof beams to wall stays. When they were finished, he
waved them out, knelt down, and lit a special section of brush that
led to the timber frame.

He had done this twice before in his life, and always the temptation was to stay to ensure the cavity collapsed, but discretion
played a larger part in his makeup than curiosity and he moved as
quickly as he could back through the tunnel. He had gone not more
than forty paces when he heard the whooshing sound that meant the
brush around the timber and makeshift tables had caught light. He
tried to move even faster, knocking his head on the ceiling several
times.

Waylong was nearly halfway through the tunnel when the tables
collapsed, sending the flour into the air. The ensuing explosion sent
a wall of air through the tunnel that whipped his hair and clothes
around him, the heat burning against his exposed skin. He made
sure not to breathe for a few seconds, then took in great gulps of air.
He could see golden daylight ahead. Smoke now curled around
him. As the tunnel widened and he moved from a crouch to a stoop,
he started running, imagining he looked something like Ager in full
flight. The thought made him giggle hysterically and he almost
dropped his torch.

He leaped the last few paces out of the tunnel, followed by a
huge cloud of smoke that coughed into the air. Sappers gathered
around him, patting the soot and dirt off his clothes, but he ignored
them and peeked over the lip of the mantlet covering the trench to
see the north wall.

He groaned inside. It was still there, its stone surface turning
bronze in the late afternoon light.

Mally half-dragged, half-carried the water bucket up the stairs
to the north wall. He stopped every twenty paces and lolled out
three scoops of water for each guard until he finally came to the

gatehouse and there let the bucket be so he could stand next to his grandfather. Brettin was sergeant in charge of the gatehouse, and Mally could not have been prouder.

"They're attacking the west wall again," Mally told him.

Brettin nodded. "But they'll not get through."

"They did once," Mally pointed out.

"And were massacred for their efforts."

"Why do they keep on doing it?"

"Because they're barbarians, Mally, and know no better."

Mally thought about that for a moment before saying, cautiously, "I heard they had Haxans with them."

Brettin looked down at him and frowned. To his mind, little ones like Mally should not be told things that might make them afraid. "I've not seen any."

"They be digging the trenches and making the artillery." Mally leaned closer and whispered to Brettin. "And I heard they is mining, too."

Brettin took Mally's hand, took him out to the walkway and pointed down to where their own trenches had been dug. Inside the trenches three men lay flat on their stomachs with their ears to the ground. "See them?" Mally nodded. "They can hear enemy miners at work. We've got listeners like them scattered all around the land walls. No one will get through."

Mally said nothing, but even as he watched, he saw two of the listeners look at each other and shrug. He may only have been nine years old, but he knew what that signal meant. They could not hear a thing above the din of the assault on the west wall, and the crashing of enemy missiles against stone.

A bright flashing light in the corner of his eye caught his attention. He turned and saw a fireball arc over the west wall and land in an avenue. It scattered embers and sparks, but there was nothing there to catch fire. Then another fireball swung over the wall. It landed as far in as the first, but farther south. It disappeared through a warehouse roof. For a moment nothing happened, but even as Mally watched, flames started licking up from the roof. Workers in the streets gave the alarm, and soon there was a chain of men and women passing water buckets. After a short while they seemed to be making progress.

"They're beating the fire, Brettin!" Mally called proudly.

"This time," Brettin said in a low voice. He knew the enemy would shoot two or three fireballs at a time until they saw flames, telling them they had hit a good target. A moment later a cluster of fireballs followed the trajectory of the second, most of them hitting buildings of one kind or another. Even where he was, Mally could hear the screams of people caught in the sudden bombardment.

"They'll need more than buckets of water," Brettin said slowly. There heard a dull explosion and the wall seemed to shift.

"Was that from the warehouse?" Mally asked.

His grandfather's eyes widened. "Mally, I want you to take a message to your mumma for me." His voice was calm, but it sounded to Mally like Brettin was trying real hard to keep it that way. "I want you to tell her that I'll be home later than I thought. I'm on extra duty tonight."

Mally looked at Brettin curiously. "But you've been on duty since *last* night."

Brettin took Mally's hand and dragged him to the stairs. "In case you hadn't noticed, we're under attack!" he said angrily. "Now go home and tell your mumma what I said." He pushed Mally in the back to set him on his way. "Hurry!"

Mally, confused by the sudden change in his grandfather, hesitated for a second, but Brettin pushed him a second time, and he ran down the stairs as fast as he could. On the last two steps he thought he was going to fall because he swayed as though he would faint. Then his feet were on the ground and he was steady again. He looked back up at the wall to wave good-bye to Brettin, but he was not there. His feelings a little hurt he started to run, but stopped when he heard a sound like the grinding of giant teeth. He turned around and saw something he did not think was possible. The wall was moving. It was as if the stones had become as wobbly as fat. At first he thought it was amusing, not understanding what it meant, but when he saw some of the guards fall off the walkway and plummet to their death his heart froze with fear.

"Brettin!" he shouted and started running back, but even as he did so the wall leaned away from him and disappeared in a billowing cloud of dust and smoke, taking the guard tower with it. The cloud enveloped him, turning day into night. A stone ricocheted off the road and struck him in the head. He fell, bleeding, and knew no more.

Ager had not heard the mine explosion but had seen Waylong running out of the tunnel. He looked anxiously at the north wall; his heart sank when he saw nothing happen.

"Well?" Lynan demanded.

Ager could only shrug helplessly, but even as he did so a shout started among the sappers and his gaze shot back to the wall. For a moment he thought nothing had changed and was wondering what the commotion was about, then he saw that the top of the wall seemed to be waving slightly as if he was looking at it through a heat haze. Then it fell. His jaw dropped in amazement.

"That's it!" Lynan shouted. "Remove the barricade!"

Haxan sappers used ropes and pulleys to pull down a section of the picket fence about a hundred paces long. Lynan kicked his horse into action through the gap and, without being told, the warriors of the Red Hands and the Ocean clan streamed after him. The field between the Chett camp and Daavis was filled with charging cavalry, their riders screaming war cries, and in front was the terrible White Wolf.

Workers and civilians and soldiers who had rushed to the collapsed wall froze in place when they saw the tide rushing toward them, then with yelps of panic most of them scattered, trying to find some refuge. A small number of the soldiers tried to dress a line, but as the Chett charge drew closer, their courage failed them and they, too, ran for cover.

When the cavalry reached the collapsed wall, the charge, for all its elan, faltered as horses picked their way through rubble and broken bodies. Hume archers on those sections of the wall still standing picked off a few of the riders. Lynan dismounted and ran for the nearest stairs, followed by those Red Hands who saw what he was doing, and started clearing the walkway of any enemy. One archer managed to shoot an arrow through Lynan's leg, but it did not slow him down. Terrified, the archer threw himself off the wall before Lynan could reach him. In a few short moments the entire section of the north wall east of the break to the next guard tower was clear of the enemy.

Meanwhile the warriors from the Ocean clan had gotten through the rubble and were quickly organizing into troops, each troop directed by Ager down a different avenue or street to clear away any soldiers rushing to plug the gap caused by the fallen wall. Another group of Red Hands stormed what was left of the main gate, easily beating back the guards who were still in shock.

By now Korigan had brought up the rest of the banners; as the Red Hands cleared guard towers, they were ordered off their horses and up onto the walkways to hold the walls against any counterattack. Following Korigan were the Haxan sappers under the command of Captain Waylong, who immediately started clearing away rubble.

As his Red Hands cleared the last guard tower on the north wall, Lynan led them around to the west wall and slammed into the defenders still trying to beat off Eynon's fourth assault, unaware that the city had been breached from the north. The enemy soldiers panicked and, in their haste to escape the mad white prince, jammed the walkway so that their fellows could not even defend themselves against the Chetts climbing the wall on ladders and ropes. The next few moments saw the bloodiest fighting of the siege, and in the fore was Lynan, using a short sword he took from a fallen Red Hand, stabbing at anybody that was in front of him, using his strength to throw the enemy over the side. There was so much blood the walkway was slippery with it, and the smell of it filled Lynan's head. He did not want the slaughter to stop. Behind him came a wedge of his Red Hands, screaming and snarling, desperate to ensure Lynan was not isolated from them. The final blow for the defenders was the appearance of Eynon himself, filled with a rage that matched Lynan's. On the wall for the second time, the deaths of so many of his warriors fueling his anger, he fell on the Daavis soldiers like an avalanche. Together, the two leaders cut a swath to the first guard tower on the west wall, cleared it of enemies, and swept on to the next section of walkway, carrying all before them. More and more of Eynon's warriors clambered over the wall and down the stairs, slaying all who got in their way.

A moment came when Lynan was without an enemy to kill. He stood on the walkway, Chett warriors streaming around him, and looked out over the city. The sun was down and Daavis was dressed in a malevolent twilight filled with smoke and the cries of the dying. He could see his forces moving south from the north wall and east from the west wall, driving all before them. Houses, shops, and warehouses were on fire. Bodies clogged drains and doorways. In the middle of the city he could see the palace and wondered what was going on in the mind of Queen Charion. Did she know yet that her city had fallen?

As she left the darkness behind, the tails of her dreams slid against her consciousness. For a moment she remembered her misshapen tormenters with the kind voices of those she loved: her father scolding her, her first lover accusing her of betraying him,

Galen calling her a slut, Farben refusing to carry out her orders. And over all of them a voice she had not heard before, male and female, coming from a great distance and speaking of blood.

And then it was all gone, and in its place were new sounds no less terrifying but dramatically more immediate.

Her eyes blinked open and she saw Farben's face looking down at hers with great concern. "Your Majesty? How are you feeling?"

"I'm feeling fine," she wanted to say, but the words came out slurred. She tried to sit up, but pain rippled through her chest and her breath whooshed out of her.

"Don't move," Farben's voice pleaded. "You're hurt."

"What happened?"

"You fell defending the west wall."

"How long ago?"

"Yesterday." He looked out the room's only window.

"I don't remember . . ."

"You were unconscious, your Majesty. You are lucky to be alive. Galen and I brought you back here—"

"Galen! Where is he?"

"He took your place on the wall. He is a good soldier."

"Yes," Charion agreed vaguely. Her eyelids fluttered.

"You should get more sleep," Farben told her.

It was tempting. But something had woken her. Something was wrong. Then she heard the sounds again. "What's happening?"

"The Chetts are attacking again. Galen will beat them back."

"No. The sounds are closer than that—"

"Galen will beat them back," Farben repeated.

She tried sitting up again, but once more the pain defeated her. "What is wrong with me?"

"You have some broken ribs. You are bruised from shoulder to hip."

Charion caught his gaze and said with sudden sternness. "How would you know?"

Farben blushed. "When we found you, we did not know if you had been cut or stabbed. There was so much blood—"

"*We?*"

Farben sighed. He could not believe he was having this conversation. Why did Charion always find a way to make him feel so foolish?

"*We?*" she persisted.

"Galen and I," he snapped impatiently. Then he said something that surprised him even more than Charion. "And don't you pretend that he hasn't seen it all before."

She blinked in amazement. He went white as her bed sheet.

"What did you say?" she asked, more shocked than angry.

"I . . . I . . ."

He was saved by more cries from outside.

"What is happening, Farben?" Charion demanded. "And don't put me off this time?"

"All I know for sure is that there was a fourth attack on the west wall."

"A fourth attack?"

"The third was this morning. The fourth started not long ago."

"Help me up," she ordered.

"You must rest, your Majesty. You are in no fit state—"

"Help me up!"

There was no denying that voice. He shook his head, but put a hand behind the small of her back and helped her into a sitting position. She tried to put her hands down to help take the weight off him, but discovered her right arm was in a sling.

"What use is this?" she cried.

"It's to protect you. The doctors were afraid if you moved that side too much you might send the end of one of the broken ribs into a lung."

"Oh."

With Farben's help she did sit up. With some effort and not a little pain she was able to swing her legs over the side of the bed.

"Right. Now I want you to help me stand."

"No," Farben said. "You've been badly hurt—"

"A few cracked ribs do not make for a serious injury."

"I have explicit directions from the doctors—"

"And now you have explicit instructions from me."

Again, that tone of voice could not be disobeyed, least of all by Farben. He let her put an arm around his neck, and as he stood straight, he brought her with him. For a moment they stayed like that, misshapen twins, until Charion eased her arm away and stood up by herself.

"That's better," she said, but could not stop the pain from edging her voice.

A new voice, harried and exhausted, said: "Thank God you're on your feet. We have no time to lose."

"Galen?"

The Kendran, his armor streaked with smoke and blood and carrying a few new dents, stood before her, looking concerned at how pale she was. "I am sorry, but we have to go."

"Go? What are you talking about?" Charion looked at Farben, who could only shrug.

Galen licked his lips. "Daavis is lost."

"No."

"The north wall is taken. They undermined it."

"But it would take them weeks to reach the north wall—"

"Only if we found all the old tunnels," Farben interrupted. "Remember, your Majesty, they have Haxan sappers with them."

Charion swayed on her feet, and both Farben and Galen reached out for her.

"And the west wall has gone now," Galen continued. "I barely escaped with my own life. Lynan is like a demon. No one can stand before him."

Charion shook off their hands. "Then I will stay and fight for my city!"

"You will die for your city," Galen pointed out.

"So be it," Charion said simply, and then to Farben: "Get me my sword."

"If you wish so much to die, then why not do it retaking Daavis at a later date?" Galen asked.

"Sophistry," she said. And then to Farben again: "Did you not hear me? I said get my sword!"

"No, your Majesty," Farben said firmly. He turned to Galen. "You will take her with you and your knights?"

Galen nodded. "We will ride through what is left of the north gate and then head east."

"The Chetts will catch us," Charion said, looking sternly at Farben.

"The Chetts are too busy looting Daavis," Galen told her.

And then Farben saw something he never expected to witness. Tears came to Charion's eyes.

"They are looting my city?"

Galen nodded and dared to grip her arm again. "You are coming with me now."

Before she could respond, Farben took her other arm, disregarding the sling and her yelps of pain, and between them they helped her through the palace and to the courtyard. The knights were all mounted, their horses edgy from the smoke hanging in the air and the nervousness of their riders. Magmed appeared with two horses, and Galen and Farben carefully lifted Charion onto one of them.

"I am not dressed for riding," she said weakly.

"You will do," Galen told her. He looked at Farben. "You can ride with me, if you wish."

"No. You must ride swiftly. I will only hinder you."

"Farben, you cannot stay here," Charion said.

"Of course I can, your Majesty. Some one must make sure no one damages the palace."

Galen mounted. "We will return with an army."

Farben nodded. "I know. Look after my queen."

"I promise."

Charion leaned over to stroke Farben's cheek. "I'm sorry."

Farben quickly kissed the palm of her hand. "I look forward to your return. I will greet you here at this spot and you can shout at me all you like."

Charion laughed amid her tears.

"Now go," Farben told Galen.

Galen and Magmed flanked Charion, and the troop set off. Farben watched them go, then looked at his own hands, surprised they were not shaking. He was afraid of what would happen next, but his queen would be safe—he knew Galen would ride through hell to make it so—and he found that made everything else comparatively easy to bear. He sighed heavily and returned to the palace.

〈 14 〉

IT was called the Castle Tower by those without respect, for it was as tall as a castle tower and seemed as well built. Tomlin, who had been in his profession his whole working life and who had inherited his position from his father, called it simply the Pigeon House for that is what it was. Situated within the grounds of the palace in Kendra but built as a separate structure, it gave Tomlin the grandest views of the city bar none. On this particular day the sun was high and bright, and a fresh southerly wind kept the air perfectly cool. Anyone other than Tomlin would also have said the southerly swept away the worst of the smell from the Pigeon House, but he no longer noticed the smell. Indeed, its source—the huge white cake of bird droppings that settled at every level of the house—brought him the major portion of his income. Those who owned the city's market gardens loved the stuff, and he was more than happy to scrape it up and put it in small cloth bags and sell it to them.

But Tomlin's real love was the pigeons themselves. He knew them all by name, and could recount their pedigree back generation after generation. His father had made sure he learned to write so he could keep perfect records in case his memory failed him, and these he maintained scrupulously.

He had finished distributing the feed for the day, and was checking the water in each coop, when there was a commotion in the fourth level.

"Bloody One Leg!" he cursed, drew his long knife and rushed down the two flights of stairs to get to the level. But the terrible, one-legged crow who regularly tried to catch one of his pigeons was nowhere to be found. Tomlin had almost caught the bloody black bird once, which is why it only had one leg, but it was a clever beast and seemed to delight in tormenting him. His first thought was the crow was teasing him, perhaps to draw him away from one of the other levels, but then he heard the commotion again in several of the coops on the north wall.

That surprised him. He could have sworn they were empty earlier in the morning. Still holding onto his knife he opened the little wooden catch to one of the coops and saw that indeed one of his pigeons had returned. "White Wing!" he said in surprise, for there was no message on its leg. He opened another catch, and there was Chevron, also without a message. He peeked inside the twelve other coops on the north wall, and they were occupied as well.

"All from Daavis," he said aloud to himself, mystified. He sheathed his knife and went up to the sixth level to retrieve the feed bag and water flask and then back down to the fourth level to care for the returned birds. The routine helped to settle his mind, and slowly it unraveled the mystery. The answer gave him no comfort, however, for he knew what it meant for the kingdom of Grenda Lear.

Powl had stayed up most of the night composing a brief paragraph he hoped would do for the Book of Days. That morning, straight after prayers in the royal chapel, he went to the library with the piece of paper he had written on and copied the paragraph into the book in his best hand.

"We must always strive to find God inside of us," he read softly as he wrote. "To fill ourselves with nothing but our own life is to fall short of His expectation for us, and to fall short of all that we can achieve. To have God inside of us is to be complete."

He sealed his ink bottle and put it and the pen back in his pocket. The piece of paper he put over a candle, letting it go only when the flames burned the tips of his fingers. Black smoke curled to the roof of the library, and he watched it until it had completely dispersed.

I am like that, he thought, *striving to reach God but disappearing into air instead. How can one reach God without knowing his name?*

He read again his first contribution to the Book of Days and realized it read more like the beginning of a sermon than something that was in itself complete. He had failed this test, as well, and was embarrassed to think his priests would read it and wonder. Some would not understand the message and think it was their fault because they were not smart enough or holy enough. And yet Powl knew it would be his fault. His sin was multiplying, staining the innocent under his care.

Father Rown entered the library carrying an armful of papers. "It is almost time for the council meeting, your Grace. I took the liberty of bringing your papers." He held out half his load.

"Thank you, Father," Powl said, accepting them. "Have you studied the agenda?"

"Yes, your Grace. The most important item concerns the raising of a new army. It is the first on the list."

"Yes," Powl said vaguely. He wanted to say he had thought on the issue deeply. After all, the first army had come about largely because of his advice in council while still nothing but his predecessor's secretary. *And because of that Sendarus is dead,* he thought to himself, and then quickly, *No! I wanted Olio to command it. It was not I who sent Sendarus to his death.*

"Your Grace?"

"This will be the first council meeting since the death of the princess."

"Little Usharna?"

"And your first as my secretary."

"Yes, and I thank you for the honor. I was not expecting—"

"You must not be afraid to speak up," Powl interrupted him. "You are there to present your opinion."

"Thank you, your Grace, I will endeavor—"

"But never forget you are the queen's subject, not the council's. Follow my lead on any vote. If for some reason I am not at a council meeting, Orkid will guide you, and you will have my proxy."

"Yes, your Grace," Rown said, his expression perplexed. "*Orkid* is to guide me?"

"When I am not present. Only Orkid. Do you understand?"

"Yes, your Grace."

"Very well. Lead on. We mustn't be late."

Father Rown hurriedly left; Powl lingered for a moment, glancing once more at the Book of Days and wishing he had not written his little paragraph.

Orkid Gravespear had risked a great deal to rouse Areava out of her depression. He had worked hard to get her to call her council together, knowing that the work of the kingdom was the only thing that would occupy enough of her time to stop her falling into grief whenever she thought of her dead husband and child and her wounded Olio, or worse, falling into rage every time she thought of her outlawed brother, Prince Lynan. But now he knew Dejanus would put himself forward as commander of the new army Areava must create to defend the kingdom, he wished the council was not meeting at all. Orkid had to support Dejanus or risk the constable revealing to Areava how they had murdered her brother to set her on the throne. After the initial shock of their last meeting had worn off, he had believed Dejanus had been bluffing, but his spies reported the constable was drinking almost constantly, and a drunk Dejanus might do anything without fear of consequence.

Orkid thought Dejanus had trouble leading himself to the lavatory let alone leading a kingdom army into battle against Lynan and his Chetts, but he did not know what to do. The thought of getting one of his people to assassinate the constable crossed his mind constantly, but if the assassin should fail, Dejanus would not hesitate to take revenge or—in an act of suicidal rage—tell Areava the truth about her brother's death.

He had never consciously worked against the interests of the kingdom, believing even Berayma's murder had been for the long-term benefit of Grenda Lear, but Orkid knew supporting Dejanus in his bid for command would be a betrayal of everything he loved and strove for. Yet there was no choice.

He checked the sand clock on the windowsill and saw it was time for the council to convene. He stood up heavily and gathered his papers together. He was about to leave when there was a disturbance in his secretary's office.

"I must see him! It is urgent I see him! They won't let me see the queen!"

He did not recognize the voice, but the distress of the speaker was obvious.

"The chancellor is very busy," his secretary replied. "And he is late for a meeting—hi! Hold on there!"

A man strode into his office, followed by Orkid's harried-looking secretary. He was middle-aged, short, and smelled of something foul. Orkid was about to call for a guard, but the man grabbed Orkid by his coat and shook him.

"Your Eminence! You have to listen to me!"

"I'm not anyone's eminence!" Orkid put down his papers and wrenched at the man's hands. "And please remove—"

"It's Daavis, your Eminence! It's fallen!"

"—your hands . . ." Orkid stopped struggling.

"Daavis has fallen!" the man repeated. "But no one will let me see the queen to tell her! I don't know what to do—"

"Be quiet!" Orkid ordered.

The man could not refuse that voice. He released Orkid's coat and stepped back, struck dumb.

"Now tell me, who *are* you, exactly?"

The man could not open his mouth.

Orkid sighed and said more gently: "You must answer my question. Who are you?"

"Begging your Eminence's favor, your Eminence, I'm Tomlin."

"My title is chancellor, nothing else. And who is Tomlin?"

"I'm sorry, your . . . Chancellor. And I is Tomlin. Am Tomlin. Ah, I see what you mean. I am Tomlin the pigeon keeper."

Orkid rubbed his brow with one hand. "The pigeon keeper?"

"Yes. And I know that Daavis has fallen."

Keeping his anger under control, Orkid asked: "How can you possibly know this?"

"Because all of our pigeons have come home, Chancellor. All of them at the same time."

"Our pigeons? What do you mean *our* pigeons?"

"I mean all the palace's pigeons sent away to Daavis have come home at one time, but none with a message. And the only way that would happen is if their house was destroyed or they were let go urgent like."

Orkid understood then what Tomlin was trying to tell him. "This has never happened before?"

"Only once that I know of, and that in my father's time, when I was still apprenticed to him. The late queen's father had sent the nobleman Aftel Theso on a ship to explore the Sea Between and the story goes he was never heard of . . ."

"Yes, yes, I know the story," Orkid said impatiently.

"Well, sir Chancellor, we did hear from him in a sense. All the pigeons he took with him came back in one go, and my father said to me 'Oh, heck, he's gone,' and I said 'Who would that be, Da?' and he said 'Well, Duke Theso, of course, since all his pigeons have come to coop and not a one with a message.'"

"But it could have been an accident," Orkid pointed out, trying to reason the thing through. "Someone in Daavis could have let all the pigeons out at the same time by accident."

"Well, no. A pigeon house is a special place, you see. It's not like a chicken run with a single gate. Each pigeon has its own coop. Only way they could all come home is if the house was destroyed or they were let go like that. And seeing that Daavis is at the center of a war . . ." Tomlin's voice trailed off and he finished with a shrug. Then some thought activated him again: "Although Duke Theso, of course, did not have a house because he was just on a ship, so his pigeons could have been let go accidentally, although seeing as how he's never been seen or heard from since, it seems unlikely—"

"Yes, thank you," Orkid said quickly. He placed a firm hand on Tomlin's shoulder. "You must go back to your pigeon house. Speak no word of this to anyone, is that understood?"

Tomlin nodded vigorously. Orkid eyed his secretary. "And that includes you as well."

The secretary nodded in time with Tomlin.

"Or I will have both your gizzards cut out and fed to pigs," Orkid finished. "Now go."

Both Tomlin and the secretary disappeared. Orkid slumped on the edge of his desk. All he could think of was that, with Daavis gone, Hume itself must inevitably fall, which would open the way to the province of Chandra and then to Kendra itself.

He gathered his papers together hurriedly. The council must hear of this and a solution be found, or else everything he stood for, everything he believed in, would crumble away into dust. But first he had to see the queen.

Edaytor stopped when he realized his charge was no longer keeping up with him. He turned and saw Prince Olio watching with utmost concentration a game of castles being played by two young boys using nothing but scratched marks on the pavement and colored pebbles. The two boys themselves were concentrating so intently on their game that at first they did not notice either the prince or his escort of ten Royal Guards. Then one of the guards changed his stance and cast a shadow across the game.

One of the players looked up irritably and said: "Move out of the way you karak . . ." The boy gulped. "Fuck, sorry," he added quickly and in a more subdued voice.

The other boy looked up then and yelped in surprise.

"The blue pebbles are knights, I assume," Olio said interestedly.

"Yeah," the first boy muttered, his gaze drifting from one huge guard to the next.

"And the red ones?"

"Spearmen," the second boy said.

"Ah, I should have seen that." Olio bent over and turned up a gray pebble. "A sapper! Delightful!"

The first boy grabbed at the pebble, all thoughts of the guards fleeing from his mind. "Hey! Thanks for giving away my surprise!"

The second boy laughed.

"I'm sorry," Olio said quickly. "I wasn't thinking."

"Who do you think you are, anyway, interrupting a quiet game—"

"He thinks he is Prince Olio Rosetheme," Edaytor said in his most imperious tone. "And I am Edaytor Fanhow, Magicker Prelate."

"Oh," the boy said weakly, his gaze shifting again to the guards.

"My name's Elynd," the second boy said to Olio. "My mumma named me after your father."

Olio blinked in surprise at the boy. "I don't think so," he said, frowning in thought.

"I should know who I'm named after," the boy said.

"What his Highness means is that his father was not Elynd Chisal," Edaytor explained. "It was Duke Amptra—"

"Oh, that's right," the boy said quickly. "I was named after Prince Lynan's father." He closed his hand over his mouth and mumbled through his fingers. "Sorry."

Olio looked at him curiously. "Why?"

Edaytor took Olio by the arm and led him away from the boys.

"What's going on, Edaytor?" the prince asked, hanging back.

"We should let them get on with their game."

"Where are you taking me?"

"To the harbor. You always look at the ships from the palace, so I'm taking you to see them."

"Will there be warships?"

"Certainly."

"Can I go on one?"

"We will have to ask the captain for permission. I do not think you will be refused."

Olio ended his resistance and they left the two boys behind, the guards closing around them. Edaytor would rather have gone alone into the city with Olio, but in his present condition there was no chance Areava would have allowed that.

People stared at the group, not used to seeing royalty on their streets. Most did not know what to do, but some bowed and others smiled and waved. Olio would oblige by smiling and waving back at first, but after a while got bored and ignored them.

"How much farther do we have to walk?" he asked sullenly. "My feet are tired."

"Not far, your Highness. Just to the end of this street."

All around them was evidence of the great fire during which the old Olio had lost himself trying to heal the injured, and Edaytor slowed down the pace. They passed the skeletons of houses and shops, walked over blackened cobblestones, stepped over mangled pieces of metal that may once have been saucepans or ladles. Children carelessly played in the wreckage while around them workers were pulling down charred beams and posts or putting up new frames. Cats slunk around the ruins looking for rats and birds. The air in this old part of the city still smelled of burned wood and underneath, the faintest hint, of burned flesh.

"There was a fire," Olio said absently, surveying the damage.

"Yes, your Highness. A terrible fire. Do you remember it?"

"I don't think Queen Usharna would have let me see it. Fires are bad things."

"I think you saw this one," Edaytor persisted.

Olio said nothing, but the prelate could tell he was trying to remember. "No," he said, then cocked his head to one side. "Maybe. It was very hot."

He stopped suddenly and his entourage flowed around him. "What was this place?" he asked, pointing to a burned-out block that was three or four times larger than those around it.

Edaytor had to think about it for a while. There were no landmarks left standing to help him locate their position, but when he studied the shape of the block he realized where they were.

"It was a chapel, your Highness," he said roughly. It was where Olio first used the Key of the Heart to heal someone without the aid of a magicker, the prelude to his losing his mind to the same Key.

"Yes, of course it was," Olio said, his voice distant. He looked at Edaytor and his eyes focused. "I don't like it here."

"The harbor is close." He sniffed the air. "Can you smell the sea?"

Olio sniffed, too. "No. Only the burning. Take me away."

Edaytor held the prince's hand and led him down the street. A few minutes later they were in a part of the old city that had survived the great fire. All around them, people bustled at their work with no spare time to glance at the prince and his party. There were carters pushing loads between warehouses and shops, street hawkers and sellers, children rushing around and between the legs of adults, and priests, soldiers, magickers and sailors crowding the street. And then they were in the open, the narrow streets left behind as they entered the docks, a wide strip of land connecting quays to warehouses. There were dozens of ships tied to the quays, including many of the low-prowed and narrow-beamed warships of the Grenda Lear navy, their kestrel pennants fluttering from every mast. Olio headed for the nearest, Edaytor and the guards half-running to keep up. Someone on the ship must have seen the royal entourage on its way for, by the time Olio had reached the foot of the gangplank, an officer was standing to attention at the other end.

Olio waited for Edaytor to catch up and glanced at the officer nervously. "What do I do?" he pleaded in a low voice.

"Ask him for permission to come aboard," Edaytor whispered in his ear.

Olio cleared his throat. "Captain, may I come aboard? Please?"

The officer cleared his throat as well. "Your Highness!" he shouted, making Olio and Edaytor blink. "Captain Eblo is not aboard! I am watch officer! Ensign Pilburn at your service!"

"Can the watch officer give me permission?" Olio asked Edaytor.

The prelate shrugged. "Ask him."

"Can you give me permission to come aboard? Please?"

"Your Highness!" came the shout. "You have permission to come aboard!"

Olio breathed a sigh of relief. "Well, that's good," he said, and started up the gangplank. Before he took the second step, one of his guards stopped him and moved in front while another squeezed himself behind. They marched up the gangplank, the rhythm of their feet making it sway. Edaytor watched with curious pleasure as the sandwiched prince, so diminutive between the guards, was escorted on board the ship. The watch officer stepped back and stood to attention. When there was room, Edaytor followed with six of the remaining guards, two staying behind at the foot of the gangplank.

"So this is a warship," Olio said with self-satisfaction, and clicked his heels on the deck as if to prove the case.

"Your Highness!"

"You don't have to say it so loudly," Olio said. "Will you show me around? Have you any prisoners?"

"Prisoners?"

"Pirates," Olio continued, waving his hand in the air. "That sort of thing."

"No, your Highness. We have no pirates on board." Pilburn looked at Edaytor for guidance.

"Killed them all in action, I expect."

Pilburn's face contorted in confusion.

"Shall we start below?" Edaytor suggested.

"You can show me the brig," Olio said. "You do have a brig?"

"Yes, your Highness," the officer said, leading the way to the aft cabin.

"You don't have to keep on calling me 'your Highness.' It isn't etiquette. Just 'sir.'"

"Yes, sir," Pilburn said obediently.

Over the next ten minutes the royal entourage shuffled and crouched and squeezed through narrow ways and cabins below deck before emerging near the bow via a gangway.

"It's not a very big ship, really," Olio commented.

"It's built to be swift and sure, sir," the watch officer said. "That's why we are named the *Windsnapper*."

"That's certainly a wonderful name," Edaytor said.

"Have you seen any action?" Olio asked.

"Why yes, sir," Pilburn said, obviously offended at the question. "Three years ago we caught and destroyed a pirate sloop off the shores of Lurisia. Two years ago we were involved in an action against a smuggling port on the border of Hume and Haxus. We had two prisoners in the brig after that fight. And only last year, sir, we chased your outlaw brother out to sea—"

"We've probably taken up enough of your time, Ensign," Edaytor said quickly, talking over Pilburn. He gently pushed Olio toward the gangplank.

"My outlaw brother?" Olio asked. "What are you talking about, Ensign?"

"Your Highness?" Pilburn asked in turn, more confused now than ever before.

"We are due back at the palace," Edaytor said urgently to Olio. He caught the attention of one of the guards and nodded to Pilburn. The guard understood and immediately escorted the ensign back below decks. By now he had maneuvered the prince to the top of the gangplank, but Olio wedged his feet against it and would not be budged.

"What was that officer talking about, Edaytor?" Olio demanded.

"It was a slip of the tongue, your Highness," Edaytor answered, still gently trying to shove him down to the dock. "Nothing important—"

"I'm not a fool," Olio said, his voice deepening, and for the second time since Olio's accident Edaytor heard something of the old prince in that tone. He stepped back and Olio turned to face him. "You know something about my brother. Which one? Berayma or Lynan?"

Edaytor licked his lips. He did not know what was best: to continue to feign ignorance or tell the truth. Taking his courage in hand he decided on the latter. "Ensign Pilburn was talking about Prince Lynan."

Olio looked over Edaytor's shoulder, out over the harbor and toward the sea. "Lynan is made outlaw and fled overseas? Is that what all this is about? Is that why no one will talk to me anymore? Is that why my mother refuses to see me, or Berayma? Was it my fault?" His voice was rising, and he took hold of Edaytor's cloak. "Does my family want me outlawed as well?"

The guards were startled by this sudden outburst and did not know which way to look, afraid that if they caught the prince's eye he would ask them the same questions.

Edaytor rested his hands on Olio's fists and said as gently as he could: "You are loved by your family. No one thinks you have done anything wrong."

"But what happened to Lynan?" Olio demanded. "He is so young. How could he possibly be an outlaw?"

Edaytor could not meet Olio's questioning gaze. "There are some things you must know, but I am not the one to tell you."

"Then who is?"

"Your beloved sister. Areava will tell you." He took a deep, guilty breath. "It is time Areava told you everything."

"I am afraid," Olio said, his voice becoming small and childish again. "Edaytor, I don't know what to think."

Edaytor put an arm around Olio's shoulders. He tried to remember he was comforting a prince of the realm, not just a scared little boy. "Trust me, your Highness. You will be all right. There is no need for you to be afraid." He hoped the prince did not hear the lie in his voice.

*   *   *

Dejanus had not taken a drink for nearly a day. He was going to be cold sober for this all-important council meeting. He was finally going to get what he had wanted ever since he first took up soldiering—an army of his own. He got to the council room early and was irritated to find Harnan Beresard there already, setting up his small secretary's desk and carefully placing his various pens and papers upon it. But Harnan did not have a vote on the council, Dejanus reminded himself, and so was unimportant. He nodded to the secretary, hiding his disdain that someone who barely looked strong enough to support his own weight should have any influence at all on the queen, and then took his position near the entrance, standing as erectly as possible and giving full effect to his huge size. As each of the councillors arrived, he caught their attention, smiled grimly as befitted the times and nodded confidently at them. Some of the councillors—mainly members of the Twenty Houses—ignored him, some seemed surprised—and one or two even a little dismayed—by his attention, but many smiled back and seemed reassured that he was there. He did a quick count. He had more votes than he needed, as long as Orkid and the two priests backed him up. After their little chat, he was sure Orkid would not vote against him, at any rate, and the primate and his secretary would follow the chancellor's lead. The only obstacle remaining was the queen, who could veto any council decision if she so desired. Areava had exercised that prerogative very rarely, though, and never on major issues.

Satisfied, he took his seat. Areava, the chancellor, and the two priests had not yet arrived. He wondered what could be holding them up. Maybe they were already discussing giving Dejanus command of the new army? That would make sense; they would give the council a decision already made and with the throne's approval. There were two other vacant seats. Prince Olio's and the prelate's. He did not seriously expect Olio to appear, but the prelate had never missed a council meeting. Dejanus had no idea whatever which way Edaytor would vote on the matter, not that it would affect the outcome. Perhaps he was in the same meeting as the queen and Orkid.

Just then Orkid walked in by himself, his face dark and troubled like a bank of storm clouds, and the intricate story the constable had made up in his mind evaporated, leaving behind a great and hollow doubt. He could feel his heartbeat quicken. Perhaps he had been telling himself stories all the time. Maybe Orkid would call his bluff and refuse to support his bid for command of the army. Perhaps . . .

He bit his lip, the pain clearing his senses. This was no time to get carried away with fancies and illusion. Wait and see. Just wait and see.

Soon after Orkid came the primate with his new secretary. What was his name? Father Gown or something. He should know. He should know all these details. He dimly recalled approaching Powl on the night of the great fire and suggesting some kind of alliance, but could not recall how the idea was received. It did not bode well that Powl had avoided him ever since. Dejanus spared the prelate another glance, and could not help noticing that he seemed even smaller and thinner than usual, as if he had shrunk in on himself. Dejanus wondered if there may still be a possibility of swinging Powl to his side; he knew he had to increase his power base in the court, and winning over the church would go a long way to doing that.

He started drumming his fingers on the table. Where was the queen? She was becoming increasingly erratic, he was sure. A sign of trouble. Did she not have some ancestor known for his madness? Or was that some other noble family? He had trouble keeping history straight. A good thing, considering his own secret history. A king-slayer, an ex-mercenary who fought against Grenda Lear in the last war, and an ex-slaver to boot. No need to remember that history. Only the future really counted. Especially if the future included command of an army. *No!* he told himself. *Command of the army.*

Where was that bloody woman?

Areava was standing in the south gallery looking over her great city, the heart of great Grenda Lear, and feeling for the first time in her life that she might lose it all. She had wanted to see Olio, to hold him tightly—even the Olio who thought he was still ten years old and that their mother still ruled over a blessed kingdom—but when she had not been able to find him had remembered he was on an outing with Edaytor Fanhow. So she stood there looking out over Kendra and held herself instead.

"Your Majesty," Orkid had said as she was leaving to go to the council, "I have bad news."

She hated that phrase; in the last year it had heralded one brutal shock after another to everything she lived for. She had said nothing, but waited for the chancellor to continue. His skin was gray, his eyes deep sunk. She braced herself. It was going to be terrible.

But she had no idea how terrible.

Daavis fallen. Her hated half-brother Lynan was now a conqueror as well as a murderer. He was like a demon from the old myths, but she was no god to counter him. What could someone of flesh and blood do against something like Lynan?

The afternoon sun was always kind to Kendra, its yellow light making it golden. But today the sun made the city look wan, ephemeral, as if it might evaporate leaving nothing behind but Areava with her illusions and callow, impossible hopes for a peaceful future.

After Orkid had left she shouted, "God damn you, Lynan!" Startled pigeons fluttered into the air.

Oh, God damn, damn, damn you, she said to herself. *God damn Mother for ever marrying the General, God damn her for giving you a Key . . .*

She stopped herself, her expression startled. "No, I'm sorry!" she cried. She had not meant any of it. She just wanted things to be the way they were supposed to be, with Berayma on the throne and she and Olio helping him rule wisely and justly, and with little Lynan kept busy and out of the way.

But what God had given her was the nightmare opposite of everything she had ever wanted. It was Lynan who held power to rival that of the rightful monarch of Grenda Lear. Commoner blood or not, Lynan was fighting against his own, slaying his own, destroying his own. And she would never, never forgive him for it.

I will fight you, brother, she promised. *I will fight you until you are dead or I am slain. This kingdom will have one and only one ruler.*

She realized she had made an irrevocable decision. Her course was set, and there was no turning back. With some relief she realized also the decision meant her next action was clear.

She hurried out of the south gallery, swept down the great hall, and past her own chambers and burst into the council room, slamming shut the doors behind her. Everyone in the room jumped in their seat. She noted that all were present except Edaytor Fanhow and his charge, her brother. She nodded once to all of them as she sat down, ignored the tide of well-meant blandishments, and slapped her hand on the table.

"We have one overriding item to attend to," she told them. "The creation of a new army to combat Prince Lynan. The creation of a great army."

"Forgive me, your Majesty," the city mayor, Shant Tenor, said. "But since the terrible fire that has destroyed so much of the old city, many other issues of equal importance—"

"Daavis has fallen to Lynan and his army of Chetts," Areava said, cutting off the mayor.

Shant Tenor looked as if someone had told him his daughter had run off and married an Amanite sheep herder. His expression would have been comical if the situation had not been so grim.

"How . . . how can you be so certain?" her uncle Duke Holo Amptra asked.

"I do not have final confirmation," Areava said, "but the information we have received indicates the worst."

"What information?" asked Marshal Triam Lief, head of the kingdom's armed forces.

Areava glanced at Orkid. "I'm sorry, but that cannot be revealed at this point."

"Did your information say anything about the knights of the Twenty Houses?" the duke asked.

For the first time he could remember Areava looked at him with something like kindness. "I am sorry. I have no word on the knights, nor their commander, your son."

Holo nodded and looked down at his hands.

"But this is incredible!" the marshal continued. "How could Lynan take the city? He had been defeated by our army and was in retreat—"

"Obviously, he did not retreat far enough," Areava said harshly. "We have no other news at this moment. Which brings us back to my first point. The creation of a great army."

"A great army?" Shant Tenor said. Areava could tell from his tone he thought it sounded expensive. "What exactly makes an army great?"

"It will be the largest army ever seen on the continent of Theare. It will include soldiers from every province."

"How will we afford it?" the mayor asked querulously.

"How will you afford the Chetts running Kendra and the kingdom?" she countered.

The mayor blinked in confusion

"When will we have more details about the loss of Daavis?" asked Fleet Admiral Zoul Setchmar.

"I have sent messages to King Tomar," Orkid said. "He has military posts near the Hume border. Hopefully, he will be able to give us a more complete picture of the situation to our north. I would expect to hear from him within two or three days."

"Then perhaps we should reconvene at that point," the admiral said. There were murmurs of agreement from around the table.

"And waste that time?" Areava said. "No. I will not allow it to be said that this council dithered while an invading army ate away at the kingdom."

"Put like that . . ." the admiral said, letting his voice fade away.

"I want every ruler in our domain to be appraised of the situation," the queen continued. "I want their best units on their way within ten days."

"On their way to where?" Duke Amptra asked. "This city is the largest on the continent, but it could not house and feed a force as large as the one you suggest."

"I'm aware of that, Uncle," she countered. "They will congregate in southern Chandra. Orkid will let Tomar know our intentions."

The primate coughed into his hand. "Your Majesty, have you given any thought as to who will lead this force?"

"Not yet—" she began, but Orkid interrupted her.

"I believe the army will require an officer of proven experience," he said, his eyes resting on Marshal Lief.

Dejanus felt his skin tighten in shock and dismay. Orkid could not do this to him!

"But someone young enough to endure the rigors of a long and hard campaign," Orkid continued, and now his eyes rested on Dejanus.

The constable felt his stomach heave. It had happened! Orkid was going to give him his support!

"I suggest the Constable of the Royal Guard." Orkid ground the words out between his teeth.

There was a moment's silence as people absorbed what the chancellor had said. The expressions on most of the council showed confusion rather than anger or rejections. The first to speak was the primate. His voice seemed uncertain and distracted, but he supported Orkid's recommendation. Then so did the other priest, and quickly after the majority of the councillors. All eyes turned to Areava. But before she could speak the doors opened and Edaytor

Fanhow made an entrance. Everyone was now looking at him, except Dejanus who kept his gaze fixed on the queen.

You must agree! he screamed silently. *You must agree!*

"Prelate Fanhow?" she said instead. "Is everything all right? Where is my brother?"

"Yes. Everything is fine, and his Highness is safely returned to his chambers. I am sorry I am late. Have I missed much?"

Dejanus almost groaned aloud. He could not believe this was happening. As Fanhow took his seat, the queen and the chancellor appraised him of the situation in Hume. Its retelling seemed to make the news more real for most at the table, and everyone's face seemed to settle into the same despondent grimace.

"I see," Edaytor said. "And we were voting on the constable's appointment to lead the army?"

"Yes," Areava said. "Do you have an opinion on this?"

Fanhow glanced at Dejanus, but refused to meet his eyes. "As much as I admire Dejanus, I am not sure he would be the best man to lead this army you propose. He is undoubtedly a brave and skilful warrior, but what you need, surely, is someone with experience at leading such a force?"

"Whom would you propose?" Orkid asked testily. Areava looked at him in surprise.

Edaytor could only shrug. "I am not an expert on these matters, but surely someone like the marshal—"

"As you say," Orkid interrupted, "you are not an expert on these matters. Marshal Lief is a fine commander and administrator, but he has no more experience leading an army into combat than has Dejanus. Indeed, in the whole kingdom the only man who had such experience was the previous constable, the outlaw Kumul Alarn, now thankfully dead."

Edaytor blushed. "I bow to your greater knowledge," he said.

"How will you vote on this?" Orkid pushed.

"I will take your advice on this also," he conceded.

Orkid turned to Areava. "I believe the constable has the council's support, your Majesty. But as always, the final decision must be yours."

God's teeth! Dejanus thought. *Don't remind her!*

Areava regarded Dejanus coolly. His skin tightened again, which he took as a bad sign. For a long while she did not speak, and he could not guess what she was thinking.

Come on, you bitch, he silently urged, his teeth grinding together.

"I will accept the advice of my loyal councillors," she said, and not just Dejanus breathed out a sigh of relief. "Constable, you are now commander of the Great Army of Grenda Lear."

Olio had been left in his chambers by Edaytor and asked to stay there. He wanted to go to the south gallery. There he could see the kingdom. Here, all he could see was the royal bed and royal desk and royal night pot, and out his window all he could see were mountains. He was bored. Which got him thinking, mainly about Lynan. He could not understand how some one as young as Lynan could be made an outlaw. Whatever he had done must have been really bad. Olio thought about all the bad things he had done and wondered if he was next. It would explain why no one ever said anything to him about anything important. He sat on the edge of his window, his legs kicking against the wall, sucking between his teeth.

Bored.

He hoped Areava would come soon. God, he hoped anyone would come soon. There were two guards outside, but they would not talk to him. They would not even look at him. He must have been in a lot of trouble.

What had he done?

He tried to remember, but a part of his memory was blocked off from him. He could sense there was something there for him, but he did not know how to reach it, and every time he tried, it was like slipping on a wet stone—he just ended up somewhere else with a headache.

He heard footsteps outside his room and heard the guards snap to attention. That meant it was Areava. No one snapped to attention for Edaytor. The door opened and his sister came in, followed by the prelate. As she always did, she looked Olio up and down. He thought she looked as beautiful and imperious as a princess from one of the old stories.

"Get off the sash, Olio," she commanded, but her voice was gentle.

Olio obediently jumped off and stood before Areava. She leaned forward and kissed his cheek. Up close, he realized she was paler than usual, her face was drawn. She looked older than he remembered.

"You've come to tell me about Lynan, haven't you?"

His sister blanched, but nodded.

"Is Mother going to outlaw me, too? I've tried to remember what I've done wrong, but I can't think of anything that bad. Don't be angry with me."

He saw a tear in Areava's eye before she bowed her head so he could not see her face. She wiped away the tear with the back of her hand and looked up again. Olio thought she had the most beautiful eyes, like blue sapphires. The thought puzzled him. *What's a sapphire?*

She held up two amulets that hung from chains around her neck. "Do you know what these are?"

He studied them closely. "Pretty," he admitted.

"You don't recognize them?"

"I do," he said vaguely.

"Describe them for us," Edaytor said.

Olio glanced at Areava and she nodded encouragingly.

"There's one with a stick on it. And there's one with a heart."

"Do you know what the stick is?" Edaytor prompted.

"No."

"It's a scepter," Areava told him. "Only rulers have scepters."

"Then why do you have one?" he asked.

"Why do you think?"

Olio shrugged, blew air out of his mouth. "Can we play something else now?"

"Why do you think I'm wearing a scepter?" Areava persisted.

"Because you're a ruler, of course," he said, and laughed to show he knew it was a joke. But neither Areava nor Edaytor laughed, so he stopped, feeling a little foolish.

"That's right," Areava said solemnly.

"Does Mother know you've got a scepter?" His eyes widened suddenly. "That is Mother's scepter. She is queen and should have it."

"I am queen."

Olio looked at his sister. For the briefest of moments her words made absolute sense. He shook his head to clear it; he understood what a ridiculous thing she had said, but a part of him absolutely believed it.

"This is the Key of the Scepter, or the Ruler's Key," Areava continued. "It is one of the Keys of Power."

"No!" Olio cried. "Only Mother has the Keys of Power. No one else can wear them!"

"That was true while our mother was alive. Just before she died she gave each of us one of the Keys."

Olio blinked rapidly. "Mother's not dead. I don't believe you. She couldn't be . . ."

"She gave you this Key," Areava said, holding up the Key of the Heart.

"No," he said.

"Let him touch it," Edaytor told Areava.

She held it out to Olio, but he backed away from it. He ran into a wall and could go no farther. "Hold the Key," she said.

He shook his head.

Areava took off the chain holding the Key and held it out to him. "This is yours. I took it away from you. That was wrong. I am sorry. I want you to have it back now."

"It was mine?"

"Don't you remember?"

Olio groaned. "Sometimes. I think I've seen it before."

"Do you remember what it feels like to wear it?" Edaytor asked.

Olio shook his head again. "No." Then, in a much deeper voice. "Yes. My Key."

"Give it to him now!" Edaytor hissed to Areava.

She slipped the chain around her brother's neck and stepped back.

The first thing Olio felt was that the Key fell against his chest in the same way a proper key fitted the right lock. It was where it should be. But almost immediately the thought was squeezed out of him as if a giant hand had suddenly gripped his brain. He shouted out, not in pain but surprise. He closed his eyes, and burned in the back of his lids was the vision of a terrible blue river, startlingly bright, searingly hot. He heard a word repeated over and over and he chased it down with his mind until he heard it loud and clear. "No!"

And he screamed the word out loud and collapsed to the floor before either Areava or Edaytor could catch him.

15

THE Horse clan warriors gathered in front of Daavis' rebuilt main gate. Eynon, standing beneath the gate itself, gazed on them with immense pride, the sentiment matched only by his immense sadness there were so few. Except for another two hundred or so warriors too seriously wounded to ride back to the Oceans of Grass, the four troops before him were the entire strength of what had once been one of the Chett's largest and most powerful clans.

And will be again, Eynon told himself, as he had repeatedly during the terrible siege of Daavis. He heard the rumble of more horses behind him and turned to see Lynan and Makon riding ahead of several hundred more cavalry. The two men stopped by Eynon and let the force ride by. Eynon counted three troops of lancers and three of the Red Hands.

"I promised them to you," Lynan said. "You may keep them under your command for as long as you need them."

"Thank you, your Majesty," Eynon said gratefully. "It won't take long to hunt down the Saranah war band. You'll have your warriors back by winter."

"There is no hurry, Eynon," Lynan answered. "I was thinking you might want to do more than hunt down the war band." He and Makon shared a secret smile. Eynon was not sure he liked that.

"Meaning?"

"Meaning that if you feel the urge I see no reason for you to stop at the edge of the Oceans of Grass."

"You mean carry on to Saranah territory?" Lynan nodded, and Eynon already liked the idea. "To do as I wish?"

"Completely. I remember I also promised to replace every head of cattle you lost. I will, but I cannot do it before winter when the clans gather at the High Sooq. In the meantime, you might as well wreak a proper revenge."

"You are returning to the High Sooq this winter?" Eynon could not hide his surprise.

"No. There is the rest of the kingdom to win before I return to the Oceans of Grass."

"Then who will carry your authority at the High Sooq?" Eynon asked.

"You will."

"Your Majesty!" Eynon blurted.

Lynan and Makon laughed together. "I told you he would choke on it," Makon said.

"But what does Korigan say?"

"She is in agreement," Lynan told him. "She watched your clan four times assault the west wall of Daavis. She holds no doubts about you and your loyalty to my cause."

"She even agreed to let me go again," Makon added.

"Let you go?" Eynon asked.

"Makon knows the Red Hands," Lynan answered for him. "He has commanded them in his brother Gudon's absence and has proven himself in combat. Use him as one of your commanders. He can also vouch for your authority at the High Sooq. If those clans traditionally antagonistic to you doubt your word, Makon, being from Korigan's clan, will convince them quickly enough."

Eynon could not help grinning. "I would be happy to have Makon ride with me again." By now the extra six troops had lined up behind Eynon's own. One thousand experienced warriors. *With these,* Eynon thought, *I can carry the war far south indeed.*

"Remember, you can take whatever action against the Saranah you deem fit."

Eynon looked up sharply at Lynan. It was almost as if the prince had read his mind. "The Saranah will wish they had never left their desert," he said.

Jenrosa watched Eynon lead his combined force northwest from Daavis. They rode at an easy trot, confident and determined. Casually, almost absently, she licked the tip of one finger and used it to draw a line along the top of the stone parapet in front of her. She breathed softly over it. The only particles to move were made of red quartz. They scattered across the line, but almost immediately a soft breeze blew the other way sending the crystals back again. She was not surprised, but which of her imaginings did it fit? That was something no teacher could show you. One of her first instructors in the Theurgia of Stars had told her that the interpretation of magic was often no more than a test of someone's ability to fit the facts after the event; in other words, prescience was a matter for the gullible. She wanted to believe that, but she could not shake off what she had seen since joining the Chetts and since taking instruction under Lasthear.

What Jenrosa did not know, and was afraid to discover, was whether or not her understanding of what her magic showed her was the future, fixed and unchangeable, or *a* future, one that could be averted—or aimed for—through certain actions. The problem was that the latter seemed too much like prescience for the gullible.

She saw Lynan riding back to the palace. As he passed near her, he paused but did not look up. *He can feel me watching him,* she told herself. *We are connected so strongly.* A moment later he was on his way again. She observed Chetts bow to the pale prince as he rode by them. She observed the locals bow even lower to avert their eyes from his, the children scampering behind the nearest adult. Lynan, obviously deep in his own thoughts, ignored them all. After Daavis had been taken, there had been some looting, but Lynan had quickly stopped it and made sure only soldiers who resisted the occupation were killed. So far as conquerors went, Lynan seemed less cruel and more lenient than many others in history. Nonetheless, the citizens of Daavis avoided him when they could; Lynan's appearance and reputation were enough to scare people. He was so stiff and white on his horse that Jenrosa thought he looked like a marble statue.

"What are you now, my prince?" she wondered aloud. It occurred to her there was an even more important question. *What am I now?*

She knew she had no answers. For all her power at magic it was a hollow thing, nothing more than a conduit for more mystery and frustration than she would ever have believed possible as a bored student in Kendra all those years ago.

Wait, she told herself. *Not years ago. Only a year ago.*

"You are thinking of home," said Ager's voice.

She looked to her left. God, for a crookback he could move quietly when he wanted to.

"You think you are so wise," she jibed.

"I can tell," he said, ignoring her, "because of the look on your face. Whenever you think of home, your eyes lose focus and you face toward Kendra. I know a few merchants who would pay a small fortune to have you as navigator on one of their ships. They would always know which direction to travel to reach Kestrel Bay."

She smiled despite herself. "You still call Kendra home."

"Strange, isn't it? I wasn't born or raised there, and I've spent most of my life living somewhere else, but yes, Kendra is the place I've always thought of as my home. Maybe it is for anyone who thinks of themselves as belonging to Grenda Lear." Ager frowned then. "I don't know that I do anymore, not really."

"It's the Oceans of Grass for you?" Areava asked.

"Perhaps."

"Morfast loves you a great deal," Jenrosa observed. "And you her in return. It is obvious to anyone who sees you two together."

Ager grunted, smiled himself.

"And the Ocean clan is a noble one."

"That is my home now, I think."

"The clan?"

He nodded. "And what about Jenrosa Alucar? Where is her home these days? With the Chetts? Or do you still pine for the dusty halls of the theurgia?"

"I don't have a home anymore," she said shortly, trying to end the conversation.

"The Truespeaker will always have a home," Ager countered.

Jenrosa gritted her teeth. "I hoped you, of all people, would never call me that."

"Ah," Ager sighed. "So that's the problem."

"It's not a problem!" Jenrosa spat. "It's a delusion on the part of Lasthear and others who are so desperate for a new Truespeaker they are willing to see ability where there is none."

"That's a lie and you know it," Ager replied sharply. "Lasthear is no fool, and nor are the other Chett magickers who talk about you the same way the rest of the Chett people talk about Lynan."

"I don't have to listen to this—"

Ager grabbed her arm and swung her around to face him. "You are behaving like Lynan at the beginning of our exile. You have responsibilities you don't want to face, are afraid to shoulder. That's fine, I understand how you feel. But none of us has an excuse to behave like that anymore. Whether we like it or not the entire Chett nation has given itself into our hands. Lynan is their king—even

Korigan accepts that—and he has grown to recognize it. I am a clan chief, something I have grown to recognize. You are the True-speaker. It is time you grew to recognize that."

Jenrosa pulled out of his grip. "And Kumul? What was he meant to be before he was slaughtered?"

Ager shook his head. "That isn't fair. You were his lover, but Lynan and I loved him as well."

Jenrosa closed her eyes in shame. "I'm sorry . . ."

"Hasn't it occurred to you that we four were meant to leave Kendra together when we did? That fate or God or whatever it is that rules our lives had a purpose for us? Lynan will be king of Grenda Lear, of that I have no doubt now. I, who belong to the ocean, rule a clan named after it. You, a student magicker who never fitted in with the theurgia, discover you are perhaps the most powerful magicker of all. And Kumul . . . Kumul was our hero and sacrifice. He will be remembered by the Chetts for longer than you or I. Every time a Chett whispers the name of Lynan Rosetheme, the White Wolf, they will also whisper the name of the Giant, Kumul Alarn. His life was the price he paid for that destiny. He had no more say in it than we have in ours."

"And what will be our price?" she asked, her voice barely more than a whisper.

Ager looked away from her. "I do not know."

"I see only blood in my future, but whose blood I do not know."

"Don't be afraid now, Jenrosa. We have all gone too far to be afraid anymore."

"I don't believe in destiny, Ager," she said. "That would be a worse fate for us than you could imagine." And as she said the words, she realized she spoke the truth, and a great weight of doubt was lifted from her mind.

Lynan sat on Charion's throne. It was almost exactly the right size, he realized. *Then it is must be my destiny to possess it,* he told himself.

The man standing in front of him presented a peculiar mixture of fear and disdain. He was an ordinary looking fellow, someone Lynan would not have noticed in a crowd, but there was something about his character that he found very attractive, something he could not yet put his finger on.

"I am told your name is Farben," Lynan said.

"Yes." One of the Red Hands jabbed him in the back with the pommel of a sword. "Your Majesty," Farben finished.

Lynan hid a half-smile behind a finger. "And you were Charion's secretary?"

"*Queen* Charion's secretary. One of them."

"Do you know where she has gone?"

"For a ride," Farben said. "I expect her back shortly."

"With an army, no doubt."

"No doubt at all."

"And you stayed behind to protect home and hearth?" Farben did not answer. "That was very brave."

"I am attached to the many works of art in this building: statues, paintings, books. I wanted to make sure your barbarians did not use them for firewood or toilet paper."

That earned Farben another jab in the back. He broke out into a sweat, and nervously ran his fingers through his thinning hair.

"These so-called barbarians now rule your home, Farben," Lynan said matter-of-factly. "I would be careful what you say about them."

"My home is where my queen lives. The Chetts will never rule her."

That is what it is I like about him, Lynan thought. *His loyalty. He is petrified of me, and yet will not deny his fealty to Charion.*

"I want you to work for me," Lynan said. Farben stared at him, wide-eyed. "I need someone who knows this city to help me administer it."

"You cannot be serious."

"You will be serving Charion," Lynan added.

Farben laughed nervously at that. "A fine joke, your Majesty."

"If you truly believe she will return, then surely it is your duty to ensure her city is maintained for her?"

Farben's expression showed his confusion.

"I have already rebuilt the walls and city gate. Most of the rubble has been cleared away. My Haxan allies are rebuilding houses and shops. I want life here to return to normal as quickly as possible, but to best do that I need someone willing to take over the administration who knows the city and its people."

"You will use the city against your enemies," Farben said. He straightened himself before adding: "And they are my allies."

The Red Hand behind him raised the pommel of his sword again, but Lynan waved him down. "Undeniably. Nonetheless, a working Daavis best serves its own citizens, and those citizens may one day be Charion's once more."

"Not if you win," Farben pointed out.

"Don't be so sure. She is not my enemy. My sister is my enemy." Lynan could see Farben had no answer to that, but still he did not look convinced. "If she survives the war and is prepared to swear her allegiance to me, then I will happily return Hume to her, and Daavis as her capital. But what kind of city shall she receive if the conqueror is left alone to administer it?"

"If I accept your offer, people will think I am a traitor," Farben said feebly.

"Then you have my permission to let everyone in the city know you are working for Charion and not for me. You can put up notices to that effect if you like. I only ask you do no intentional harm to me or my cause."

"Your Majesty?" Farben could not believe his ears.

"There is a price to be paid," Lynan added.

Farben snickered. "I see."

"No, you do not see. The price is that when Charion swears her allegiance to me, so must you."

"You could force me to do that now."

Lynan shook his head. "You and I both know that is not true. No doubt I could force you to do a great many things. I might even get you to say the words, but they would be empty. I am prepared to wait for true loyalty."

Farben did not answer for a moment, then—ever so slightly— he bowed.

She was overwhelmingly desirable. Lynan could not help falling into her arms, embracing her as if she was and had always been his true love. They did not speak, their passion so powerful no words could express it. The forest surrounded and swallowed them. The world was rich and green and moist.

He entered her, moved easily in time with her body. His hands felt her skin as smooth as paper. He kissed the sweat off her face and it tasted like dew. Her hair smelled like the earth. In turn she kissed his chest, his cheek, his forehead, his neck and finally his lips. He felt her tongue slide over his own.

Then pain, sudden and sharp, in the back of his throat. He tried to scream, but he had no air left. He struggled against her, but she was far too strong. She pinned him to the ground, her lips still around his, the needlelike tip of her tongue still impaled in him, sucking out his blood.

But he did not surrender. He placed his hands over the Keys sandwiched between them and held them tight. Strength and warmth shot through his body. The vampire screeched, flew off him into the air. His own blood sprayed down on him. She flapped her giant wings and disappeared into the night sky. He gasped for breath and felt life-giving air fill his lungs, and his eyes opened wide . . . to see the roof of Charion's private chambers above him, its ornate paintings seeming to come to life in the flickering candlelight beside the bed.

He sat up, panting, and he could taste blood on his tongue. He felt inside his mouth with a finger. There was no wound, and when he withdrew the finger it was unstained. He swung his legs over the side and stood up. The room had windows on two walls. He went to the closest and opened the wooden shutters. Clean night air rushed in, cooling his sweat. An old moon hung low above the horizon. A few wispy clouds faintly patterned the sky.

He saw something eclipse the moon, the silhouette of a wing. He gasped in surprise and jerked away from the opening. He told his heart to slow down, and his mind to stop imagining things. He peeped out the window. The moon was unchanged. There were no giant wings against the sky. The breeze smelled clean and dry and of ripening grain. It was the smell of autumn.

"Time is running out," he said softly into the night. "Time is running out."

He gathered his clothes and dressed quickly. Two Red Hands looked at him in surprise when he left the room and immediately fell in behind him. Usually he found the close company of his bodyguards irksome, but not tonight.

He found the room he was looking for in a wing of the palace opposite the courtyard from the royal quarters. "Just like Kendra," he mumbled to himself. He went to a desk, found paper and pen and ink underneath its lid, and brought them out. The two bodyguards stayed at the door.

At first he wrote quickly, but as the minutes passed, he slowed down until he was struggling over every word. Nearly an hour later he put down the pen and read what he had written. Then he drew out a second piece of paper and started again, finishing in half the time; this, too, he read, then folded it carefully and tucked it inside his shirt.

When he returned to his room, he found Korigan waiting for him. She looked very beautiful on the bed, long and golden and sure of herself.

"You still awake?" he asked, closing the door behind him and leaving the guards outside.

"I've been thinking about things. I was surprised to find you not only awake but absent." She patted the bed.

Lynan sat down next to her and kissed her. "I had some work to do."

"In the scriptorium."

He frowned. "Now how did you know that?"

She held his right hand and opened it palm upward. "Ink stains," she said, and smudged some of it. "Fresh. Also there's this." Before he could react, her hand darted inside his shirt and took out the folded paper. He tried to snatch it back, but she was too quick for him, retreating from the bed and dangling it before him like a lure.

"Letter to some old lover?"

"I don't have any old lovers."

It was her turn to frown. "Are you serious?"

Lynan nodded.

"You mean you were a . . . you know . . ."

"I am only eighteen," he said defensively.

"And I was only fifteen," she retorted, then shrugged. "Well, maybe you're late developers in the city."

"I think it's that you Chetts are early starters. It has to do with all the sex you see. The cows do it. The horses do it."

"Our parents do it."

"Well, yes, but you don't see . . ." She was smiling at him with perfect innocence. "You're not serious."

"Our parents teach us everything. We don't have schools like in the east, or—private tutors like you had."

"This isn't something any school in the east teaches."

"And your private tutors?"

He shook his head. "Fortunately. You never met my private tutors."

"So I was your first?"

"Yes."

"I'm flattered."

"Good," he said levelly. "Now can I have my paper back?"

"Personal, is it?"

"Not from you," he admitted. "But I'd rather not have it damaged. It took me a long time to write it and I don't want to have to start all over again."

"I can read it?" she asked.

"Yes."

Korigan was about to open it, then changed her mind and handed it back to Lynan. "Not much point, really, if I'm not learning something I'm not supposed to know."

"Fun or not, it's something you *should* know. It's a letter to King Tomar."

"Saying what?"

"Setting out my side of the story about Berayma's murder and subsequent events."

"The aim being?"

"I conclude by asking him to join me, or at least to offer me no resistance when I move through his territory."

"So you have decided to move on Kendra through Chandra?"

"It is the obvious way."

"Something Areava would, no doubt, be considering."

"And since it is the obvious way there is no harm in Areava believing it is the way Tomar thinks I will come."

Korigan's eyes narrowed. "You are either very clever or very foolish. I cannot make up my mind."

"Let me put you at your ease, then. I am very clever. Either Tomar joins my cause, in which case the letter has been well worth the time spent on it, or he rejects my cause, in which case he will be duty bound to inform Areava of the letter's contents."

Korigan put a finger to her chin. "In which case the time was still well spent. But you don't expect Areava to believe that going through Chandra is your real intention?"

"As long as she is kept off balance, it doesn't matter which direction she believes I am coming from."

Korigan laughed lightly. "Ah, I understand. You yourself don't yet know which direction you'll take."

"You see through me too easily," he said.

She snorted. "Whenever you give in that easily, I know you're not telling me the truth."

"Aha. That could have been my very intention—"

"Oh, stop it," she said and leaned forward quickly to kiss him on the lips.

He wrapped his arms around her and kissed her back. Then a

memory of his dream returned, unbidden, and he pulled back. She saw the expression in his face and grimaced.

"You saw her again tonight?"

He nodded, not willing to say the words.

"She is getting stronger," she said, then held his head in her hands. "But I am not Silona. I am Korigan. I am queen of the Chetts and I am your lover." She took his ink-stained hand and placed it under her own shirt, between her breasts. "That's my heart. It is yours."

She kissed him again, and this time he held her close and did not let her go.

Ten days after leaving Daavis, Eynon led his column over the Algonka Pass. A cold wind running from the tops of the Ufero Mountains made him shiver as he paused at the highest point of the pass. He could just make out at the edge of the horizon the first pale green flush of the Oceans of Grass, then the first of his troops trotted past, kicking up dust and obscuring the view. He tapped his mount's flanks and caught up to the lead, resisting the temptation to pick up the pace.

He was joined by Makon. They rode together in silence for a long while, then Eynon asked, "What's your question?"

Makon smiled easily. The months they had spent together on the Oceans of Grass, first in an air of mutual suspicion and later in one of mutual suspicion mixed with respect, meant they read each other's minds more closely than either would like.

"I haven't figured out what answer I want yet."

"Let me ask it for you. Which way once we reach the plains?" He glanced at Makon, and Makon nodded. "And then should we first head for the Strangers' Sooq or for my clan's traditional summer territory."

"Yes," Makon admitted.

"Like you I'm probably inclined to get to my territory as quickly as possible, but—undoubtedly like you—I think it's possible any survivors from my clan would probably have reached the Sooq by now, or at least word of what happened."

"I am leaning more toward the latter."

"As we get closer to the time when I will have to make the decision, so am I."

"Your decision is final, of course."

"Naturally. I am Eynon, chief of the Horse clan. You are Makon, commander of sixth tenths of my little army."

"Three tenths," Makon corrected him. "I have responsibility for the Red Hands. The lancers come directly under your command."

Eynon laughed to show he appreciated the joke. "Let's not fool ourselves, Makon. I like you. You like me. That is why Lynan wanted you to come with me. But you are Lynan's man, not mine."

"Lynan gave me explicit instructions to follow your orders."

"Come what may?"

"Come what may," Makon said seriously.

Eynon found himself believing him. Nevertheless . . .

"Until?"

"Until your task is completed."

"And who decides when that may be?"

"We will decide it together," Makon said easily.

"In a council it is always good to have an odd number in case there is an equal division."

"I will bow to your greater experience in such a situation."

"Yes," Eynon said, now serious. "You will."

It was Makon's turn to laugh. Eynon had laid the rules by which their relationship would work, and he would abide by them. Both of them understood—without it needing to be said—that ultimately Makon's course would be decided by what best served Lynan's interests. As long as Eynon's own interests coincided, there would be no problem. When those interests diverged, new rules would have to be established. Until then, Eynon was chief and Makon his underling.

Before evening fell, they reached the end of the pass. In the setting sun the plains shone like gold, and the heart of every Chett felt lighter for seeing it. Behind them, the Ufero Mountains marked the boundary between their world and the new world they had set out to win for their new king and the glory of their people. Each Chett knew if they survived the coming war against the Saranah they would return to the east to complete the conquest, but even if every province in the east was to fall to the White Wolf's army so that he could claim every city, every town, and every farm, for the Chetts there was and always would be only one true home, and that was the Oceans of Grass.

With the sun shining on their eager faces, the column descended from the pass.

16

HE was rescued from drowning.

For a long time Olio had felt he was immersed in something like water: seeing the world through a refracted, shimmering light, hearing sounds that were distorted and ponderous, separated from reality by a different kind of space and time.

Then he was pulled out of it, the sea falling away from him. Light as hard as steel pierced his eyes and he blinked back tears. Sharp sounds, almost percussive, assailed his ears. And then he smelled bedclothes and herbs and stone walls and late summer.

How long had he been asleep? What a godawful nightmare. He must have been drinking again. He looked down at himself. The Key of the Heart lay heavy against his chest. He touched it and he heard a single tone, like the sound of a distant bell, and felt his hand tingle. Had this been responsible? He looked around. He was in his bedchamber. Nothing was different.

And yet.

He sniffed the air again. Yes, late summer. Maybe autumn. The smell of ripening fields. But yesterday it had been spring or early summer. He was sure of it. He swung out of bed and stood up. Then fell down, his legs giving way beneath him. Startled, he tried standing up more carefully. He became dizzy and stretched out his fingertips to steady himself against the end of his bed.

I won't ever touch another drop of wine, he promised himself, and almost immediately realized his condition had nothing to do with alcohol. In fact, he distinctly remembered having already given up wine. He made his way to the south window. Curtains fluttered as they caught the edge of a westerly.

We don't get westerlies in spring, he reminded himself. Something was wrong with his view, but he could not put his finger on it right away. There was the harbor, with its forest of masts. There was the old city, and above it the houses of the merchants, and above them . . . His gaze wandered back to the old city. He rubbed his eyes, thinking sleep was blurring them. But the smudge was still there, like charcoal smeared across a canvas.

Charcoal. Fire.

"Oh, God!" he gasped, suddenly smelling the smoke, feeling the heat of flames on his skin and hearing the cries of the dying and wounded. He automatically grasped the Key and fell backward, collapsing on the edge of his bed, his eyes squeezed shut.

"No!" he shouted, and as quickly as his senses had been assailed, he was free again. He opened his eyes and lay on his bed panting for breath, confused and frightened.

His door burst open and two guards rushed in. "Your Highness, are you all right?" one asked. They looked around the room as if expecting to find an intruder. The second guard loped to the window and peered out.

"Yes," Olio said, his fear disappearing. He wished the confusion would as well. "I think so."

The guards glanced at each other, obviously not convinced.

"Could you get Dr. Trion for me?" Olio asked. "I don't think I'm well."

The guards bowed and left, closing the door behind them. He heard the lock click, and rather than being angry or upset about it, all he could do was wonder why they had done it.

What had happened to him? What was it that had flashed in his memory? Something to do with fire and . . .

The old city had almost all been burned down. That explained the black smudge across the cityscape he saw from the window. But when had this happened? And what had he to do with it? He rubbed his temples with the palms of his hands, trying to remember, but it made no difference. Had he caused it, God forbid? Or been harmed in it?

The last felt more like it. He thought that if he had caused it, nothing would stop him from remembering.

He heard people coming, more than two, and he wondered who else the guard had brought beside the doctor. The door was unlocked, then opened, and there stood Areava.

"Good morning, sister," he said, pleasantly surprised. "I'm sorry they've disturbed you over this. I just wanted to see Dr. Trion. Did you bring him with you?"

She stood aside and another entered, but still not the doctor. "Edaytor? Did the guard bring anyone else? The cook, maybe? Or a stable groom?"

Areava and Edaytor stared at him. He, in turn, stared at them. They both seemed much, much older and careworn than he remembered. He could not decipher their expressions, which seemed to be a strange combination of awe, curiosity, relief, and some pleasure. "It's just that I seem to be feeling incredibly weak this morning. I don't know what I've done—"

"That would be because you have been asleep for nearly five days," Areava said.

"Asleep all summer and more," Edaytor corrected her.

Olio was not sure what to make out of that. "Well," he said slowly, "would one of you care to explain what you mean?" He stood up unsteadily and waited.

"I don't know where to begin," Areava replied after a while, and her voice started wavering. If Olio did not know her better, he would have sworn she was about to cry. The possibility disturbed him more than his own disorientation. Areava *never* cried.

She took a slow step toward him, then virtually leaped the remaining distance, gathered him in her arms, and hugged him so tightly the breath was squeezed out of his lungs. So startled was he that he did not embrace her in turn, but hung in her grip like a cloth doll. He glanced at the prelate for some kind of explanation, but almost went into shock when he saw that the *prelate* was crying.

When Areava eventually let him go, he took a deep breath. Ignoring the pain in his ribs, he took his sister's hand and patted it.

"Something has happened, hasn't it?" he ventured.

Dejanus sat at the head of the table. No one asked him to, or offered it to him, but he took the privilege for himself. Similarly, when Marshal Lief, Fleet Admiral Setchmar, Chancellor Gravespear, and Duke Holo Amptra finally arrived, without discussion he started the first meeting of the Great Army Committee by calling for order. The others looked at him with mild annoyance since no one actually had been speaking at the time. He nodded to the priest assigned as secretary to the committee, and the man distributed a written page to everyone present.

"What's this?" Orkid asked.

"The schedule of equipment and supplies necessary for the creation of the Great Army."

"This first meeting was supposed to be about discussing the creation of such a schedule," Lief said.

"In that case I've saved the committee a great deal of time," Dejanus answered. "Now we can move directly to discussions on how to achieve the schedule."

The other members exchanged wary glances, then read the paper in front of them, their eyes widening as they did so.

"You can't be serious," Orkid said. "This will bankrupt the kingdom."

"Then the queen can raise taxes," Dejanus countered. "Better a bankrupt kingdom than a razed kingdom."

"The provinces will never stand for it," Duke Amptra objected.

"How unexpected to hear a member of the Twenty Houses protest on behalf of the provinces," Dejanus said.

The duke blushed and started to rise from his seat. The marshal put a hand out to stop him.

"I don't believe the provinces will mind overly," Dejanus continued, "considering the fate of Daavis and its ruler."

"The fate of its ruler? What do we know about the fate of its ruler?"

Dejanus shrugged. "Well, if the city was destroyed, we can assume Charion died while defending it."

"We don't know that Daavis was destroyed," the marshal said, "let alone what happened to *Queen* Charion."

Orkid put up his hands to stop the discussion turning into an argument. "Whatever the condition of Hume's capital, I think the constable is right. The other provinces will provide what we ask of them to stop Prince Lynan from reaching Kendra." Holo and the marshal scowled at him. "However, I do think the demand on Aman in this instance is excessive."

Dejanus grinned at the chancellor. "No more than a fair contribution considering the province's favored position in court."

Orkid could not help noticing that Holo and the marshal now were smiling nastily at him. It occurred to him that Dejanus was playing them all with unexpected cunning. Animal cunning, he explained to himself, the way a grass wolf might exploit the weakness of a karak herd.

"Nonetheless, considering the substantial contribution Aman has already made to the first army, I ask the sum be reconsidered."

Dejanus turned to the secretary. "Make a note of that," he said. "The chancellor believes Aman's contribution is too high."

"That isn't exactly what I said—"

"And now that we've all seen the schedule," Dejanus said, speaking over Orkid, "we can set about finding ways to implement it."

Again the others exchanged glances, but no one complained or criticized. They were allowing themselves to be boxed in, but were so taken aback by Dejanus' assertiveness they were not sure how to counter it.

"As I understand it, Kendra is already on a war footing," Dejanus continued.

"It has been for half a year," Lief said. "Foundries must give over half their time to the production of war goods. Similarly with lumber mills, weavers, tool makers . . ."

"And farms, fisheries?"

Lief shook his head. "No. To now, we have produced enough—"

"It won't feed this proposed Great Army," Orkid said. "We will need to divert more of the kingdom's agricultural production."

"The kingdom has never done that," Holo objected. "Not even during the Slaver War."

"Grenda Lear itself was never seriously threatened during the Slaver War," Dejanus said. *I should know, I was on the other side.* "Now it is."

"To meet this schedule, we will have to raise the level for industry," Setchmar said. "Maybe to six tenths or even seven tenths of their production."

"That will cause inflation," Orkid pointed out. "The common people will suffer."

"For a short period at least," Setchmar agreed. "But it might lower the cost to the kingdom for buying war goods."

"Inflation?" Dejanus shook his head. "Why should it cause inflation?"

"Because there will be less domestic goods produced," Setchmar explained in a tone that suggested it was obvious.

Dejanus nodded, pretending to understand, something Orkid observed. "Of course," the chancellor said quickly, "we could mint more coins to provide the common people with the money they needed."

All on the committee stared at him, horrified. All except De-

janus. "A good idea," he said, trying to sound wiser than he felt.
After all, if goods were going to cost more, what could be simpler
than increasing the supply of money? He turned to the secretary.
"Make a note of that."

The secretary, who had already made a note of it, was not sure
what to write.

"Write that I suggest the kingdom mint more money to help the
common people," Dejanus said brusquely. The secretary duly noted
it. Those committee members who thought the idea a terrible one
now understood why Orkid had suggested it.

"These troop contributions you've listed here for the provinces
might necessitate conscription," the marshal said carefully. "Especially if you want the troops in Chandra by the date you've specified under Item Twelve."

There were mumbles of agreement from around the table.

Dejanus glanced at the secretary who now knew how the constable wanted the minutes to be recorded. He wrote down that Dejanus suggested conscription be introduced in the provinces to
ensure troop levels were met.

Orkid smiled easily. The constable may have possessed an animal cunning, but like a hungry grass wolf he was easily led out
from cover. He checked the schedule for any other items he might
profitably bring to Dejanus' attention.

Powl stood alone in the tower room. There was an empty bottle, covered in dust, on the floor. The wooden shutters to the only
window were open. The round stone walls had a deep inset at
about head height, and this was filled with ancient tomes. The
books of Colanus, Kendra's first great king. And, if the legends
were right, the first magicker.

Powl pulled out one of the books, waving away a cloud of dust,
and opened it. The writing was almost unrecognizable. One or two
of the signs he knew from the alphabet used all over Grenda Lear,
but most of them were unknown to him.

"He gathered the old knowledge before him," Powl murmured
to himself, remembering part of the legend of Colanus he had
read in the church library. *But what old knowledge? And how do
I read it?*

He put the book back and took out another. As far as he could
tell, it used the same script as the first book. He turned a few pages
experimentally, felt one of the leaves between his thumb and fore-

finger. Not paper exactly, but not parchment either. Nor brittle, nor
yellow with age. There were no illustrations or diagrams. Just
words in this strange writing, and probably in a strange language.

Powl sighed heavily. *I will not find what I seek among these volumes. It was stupid of me to think that I would.* He replaced the second book and ran his finger along the spines of the entire library,
walking a circuit of the room. *But where else can I look for the
name of God?*

He stopped. Something had caught his attention. For a long moment he looked around, trying to discover what it was. He had
given up and turned to leave the room when it happened again.

"The books," he said aloud. "Something about the books." He
studied the spines closely, but there was nothing about them that
seemed extraordinary. "Except that they are in this strange room
and completely unreadable."

Powl pulled another book out and held the spine up to the light.
That's when he saw it. His attention had not been caught by something visible but by something he had felt with the tip of his finger.
The spine had been embossed about a third of the way down. He
angled the book to see if he could cast a shadow, but the embossing
was too shallow to see more than a suggestion of a depression. He
ran his finger along all the spines again, this time at the same level.
They were all embossed.

"Is this the clue, dear God?" he asked. "Is your name hidden
somewhere in these volumes?"

His desperation made him want to believe it. Perhaps God had
forgiven him his terrible crime. Perhaps his prayers had not been
for nothing after all.

"And all because of this?" Olio asked, holding up the Key of
the Heart.

"And all because of that," Edaytor said, looking at it the way he
might a spider. "I wish you would not handle it so readily."

"It is harmless now."

"You must not use it."

"I have no intention of using it."

"You have not come across any sick."

"I will stay locked in the palace."

"Well and good," Edaytor said. "But remember that the common
people now know what you are capable of."

"They know what the Key is capable of. By all accounts I was nothing more than its conduit. Anyone could use it."

"I do not think so. The Keys were made by your ancestor for the rulers of Grenda Lear, not for any other mortal."

Olio slipped the Key under his shirt. "Well and good, then; it means no one else will be subjected to its power as I was."

"How are you feeling now?"

Olio shrugged. "I am not sure. How am I supposed to feel? How did I feel the day before I lost my mind? Is it the same as I feel now? I no longer know these things. I do not know if how I am now is how Olio was before the fire. I do not know myself anymore. I have the mind of an adult with the memory of an infant."

"You have not forgotten everything, surely? You remember Kendra, your sister, the death of your mother, and the murder of Berayma."

"And the outlawry of my brother," Olio said sadly. "Yes. Facts and places and names I remember, but not what I felt or knew about them. I have vague recollections of being fond of Lynam—"

"You were," Edaytor confirmed. "You talked of him frequently and with great sorrow."

"—and yet I feel nothing at all for him now. I could not care less that he is an outlaw if it was not for the fact that he is threatening the kingdom. For that I owe him my spite and not my love, brother or no."

"I see," Edaytor said quietly. "And what about Areava? How do you feel about her? Or any of your other friends?"

Olio smiled at him "You, you mean?"

Edaytor blushed.

"As soon as I saw you both, I knew I cared about you, and that *is* how I feel."

Edaytor's blush deepened. "Perhaps it would be the same with Lynam, then."

"Perhaps," Olio said shortly. "That is something I do not wish to ponder. I cannot imagine a time when we may see each other again."

"His army might reach Kendra."

"No army has ever reached Kendra."

That does not mean there won't be a first time, Edaytor thought, but kept it to himself.

*   *   *

Areava went white with fury as she read the minutes from the first meeting of the Great Army Committee. As she read each page, she screwed it up in her fist and threw it to the floor. Harnan Beresard picked up each ball and flattened it out again, softly tsking through his teeth. Was it only secretaries who realized the importance of every single copy of every document?

When she got to the last sheet, she waved it under Orkid Gravespear's nose. "And what were you doing while Dejanus was plotting to destroy my kingdom from the inside?" she demanded.

Orkid sighed, spread his hands. "I don't think the matter is helped by exaggerating—"

"Inflation!" she cried over him. "Conscription! Treason trials!"

"I know it sounds bad—"

"Bad!" She screwed up the last sheet and threw it over her shoulder. Harnan scrabbled quickly enough to catch it before it hit the floor. "It sounds disastrous! Who gave him leadership of the committee?"

"He took it upon himself. He is commander of the Great Army, after all."

"Commander, yes!" Areava said, jabbing Orkid in the chest with each syllable. "Dictator, no!"

"They are only recommendations," Orkid countered.

"Recommendations for the destruction of Grenda Lear. If I forced the provincial rulers to introduce conscription, they would be overthrown and their people would open the gates of their capitals for Lynan and his Chetts to just stroll in. There were five of you on the committee, not just Dejanus. Why didn't you take control?"

"He is hard to counter at the moment. After all, he *is* commander."

"If you remind me Dejanus is commander of the Great Army just one more time, I will punch you on the nose!"

Orkid retreated a step. Even Harnan Beresard retreated a step. Areava seemed surprised by her threat.

"I'm sorry," she said, shaking her head. "It's just that I can't believe you, of all people, let Dejanus get away with this."

Orkid could only spread his hands again. He could not say the words himself. Areava had to do it without his help.

"He cannot stay on the committee," she said. "There's nothing for it. He stays as commander, but the committee will be responsible for all logistical and administrative issues concerning the Great Army until it is ready to march to war."

"I cannot agree," Orkid said, making sure he spoke loudly enough for Harnan to hear and trying not to sound as relieved as he felt. "It was his first meeting. If he is allowed a second chance—"

"If he is allowed a second chance, I may end up receiving the committee's advice to execute everyone in the kingdom with Chett blood! No, Orkid, my mind is made up. There is no place for Dejanus on the committee."

"Who will you replace him with?"

"No one, for the moment. That's a decision I will make in council."

"Will you tell him?"

"Must I?"

"It would be better coming from you."

"God. All right." She turned to Harnan. "Ask the constable to come and see me right away."

Harnan bowed and hurried off.

"He's not going to like this," Orkid warned her.

Areava snorted through her nose.

"Do you want me to stay?"

"No. It will only make it worse for him if you are present. I don't want to humiliate him. Go on, get out."

"Thank you," he said sincerely, and quickly left.

Dejanus woke in the middle of the night, fully alert, eyes as wide and white as lamps, sweat prickling his skin. He barked in relief. He was still alive. Tendrils from his nightmare slowly evaporated and in a short while all he could remember was the face of his enemy, with skin as white as ivory. The face had been vaguely familiar, the way that such things often are in dreams, but he could not recall now who it belonged to.

His mouth felt as dry as sand. He reached down beside the bed and grabbed a bottle. He was not sure what was in it, but it ran fiery and smooth down his throat and made the rim of his eyes burn. There was a man beside him. He looked down at Ikanus, still sleeping the sex off. He grunted. Or the bruises. He laughed at his own joke. She moaned again.

"Shut up," he said, not loudly enough to wake her, but loudly enough to finish his own waking.

That's when he remembered, and the memory made him flush with anger.

"Bitch," he said hoarsely. "That yellow-haired bitch."

She had humiliated him in front of her pukey little secretary. He had wanted to take Harnan's neck in his two hands and crush it like a leather bag. Areava. He had wanted to kill her, too. Shove a dagger in her throat, just as he had done to her brother, Berayma. He had wanted to feel her warm blood splash over his hands. He wanted to scream his hate into her face as the air in her lungs whistled through the wound.

But, as always, he had done nothing.

Not cowardice, he told himself. Just common sense. The guards would cut me down without thinking. Him, their own constable. But it's that bitch they love.

"I am sorry, Dejanus," she had said. She even sounded apologetic.

"It was Orkid's idea, wasn't it?" he had said.

"No, he was against it."

Sure he was, he had thought. *Sure he was against it.*

She must have seen his doubt on his face. "Isn't that right, Harnan?"

The secretary had nodded. "I heard him say so."

"This is my decision, Dejanus. No one else's."

That was when he had wanted to kill them both. Rage filled him up and he could do nothing about it. He thought he was going to burst a blood vessel.

"Who will command the Great Army?" he had managed to ask.

Areava had looked surprised. "You are its commander, Dejanus. That will never change."

"But I am not good enough for the committee."

"That is not what I said," Areava blurted, and he could sense her growing anger then; his own seemed to diminish before it. "I said you were not temperamentally suited for the committee. That is a different thing altogether."

A cool night breeze brushed against his face and he was back in the inn room with a bottle of something or another and an aging whore. He felt the swelling in his lower lip. For an aging whore she could sure put up a fight. Why had she done that? Why did everyone want to get in his way? What had he done to any of them?

Ikanus moaned a third time, the sound almost a rattle.

She should not have hit him. That was a bad thing to do. It had made him angry all over again, as if he was right back in Areava's chambers and being humiliated.

"I am not temperamentally suited," he mumbled.

Dejanus got out of the bed and dressed, finished drinking the contents of the bottle. He leaned over and shook Ikanus to wake her. She did not move. He turned her over. Blood, sticky and black in the dark, covered her face.

"You shouldn't have hit me," he said, his voice almost gentle. He shook her again, but still she did not wake.

He put a hand under her jaw and felt for a pulse, then stood back in haste. For a fleeting moment he felt sorry for her, then angry.

What in God's name was he going to do with her body?

17

IT had been a long and exhausting ride for the knights of the Twenty Houses. They had charged through the remains of Daavis' north gate, losing many riders in the rubble and to Chett arrows, then east as fast and as far as their horses could carry them. It would not be long before Lynan or some other Chett commander sent a detachment after them, and they wanted to put as much distance as they could between them and the city. They rode through the night until the moon was high up, then dismounted and buried their armor to lighten their load. They rested for two hours and then continued on, eventually meeting again with the Barda River. Morning found them nearly fifteen leagues from Daavis, and Galen risked letting them rest again.

"But no fires," he told them. "No need to let the Chetts know our exact location."

While the others slept, he tended Charion. The ride had caused her constant pain, and he was worried one of her broken ribs may have damaged a lung or some other organ. He laid her down carefully on the ground and gave her some water. She sipped at it gratefully, then hovered between unconsciousness and a state of delirious half-sleep. He knew she needed to rest, but they could not afford to stay so close to the fallen city. At any moment he expected to hear the war cries of charging Chetts and a storm of their deadly arrows.

Before noon they were riding again, following the Barda east, pushing their mounts to the limit. In the late afternoon the Barda swung southeast. Galen ordered another, brief rest, then on again into the night. In the early hours of the third day of their flight he allowed several hours' rest, feeling safer now that they were approaching the province of Chandra—King Tomar's territory. Nonetheless, he kept a watch going, and sent scouts ahead to see if they could find a Chandra outpost or detachment.

The longer rest did Charion some good. She spoke a few words with Galen and ate a little dried meat. She was still vague enough not to worry about Galen showing Magmed the bruising and asking for his opinion.

"A good color," Magmed said. "It is going yellow, purple mainly on the edges. She is healing."

Galen agreed, and with that and the lack of any pursuit so far started to relax. As soon as he did, exhaustion felled him and he slumped, asleep, by Charion's side. Magmed undid his own cloak and put it across both of them.

For the next two days they continued to follow the Barda, stopping only long enough to rest the horses, then left the river behind as they moved directly east toward Sparro. Not long after they met their first patrol from Chandra. Ten light cavalry intercepted their course. There were some hurried explanations and the patrol galloped off for reinforcements in case the Chetts were not far behind. At least, that is what the patrol leader told Galen.

"There are no Chetts behind us," Magmed said to Galen. "If they had followed us that closely, we'd all be dead by now."

Galen agreed. "Perhaps the reinforcements are not for the Chetts but for us."

"Since when is King Tomar suspicious of knights from Kendra?"

"Maybe not Kendra," Galen replied, and nodded toward Charion, half-asleep in her saddle. "She is queen of Hume, Chandra's traditional enemy for centuries before union with the kingdom."

"But the whole kingdom is at war!" Magmed protested. "Surely these petty rivalries are put aside now?"

Galen shrugged. "Some hatreds are too old to put aside so easily."

"We must stop," Charion said weakly and reined in.

Galen copied immediately, letting the knights flow around them. "What are you doing?" he asked.

"This is Chandra."

"Yes. We're two, maybe three, days' ride from Sparro."

"I cannot go there."

"You must go there. Once safe in Sparro you can raise an army to take back your city."

Charion wobbled in the saddle. Galen took her arm to steady her.

"You don't understand," she said. "I cannot ask Chandra for help. The cost to Hume would be too high."

"Too high?" Galen sputtered. "You've lost Daavis! What higher price could you possibly pay?"

"I will win back my capital without the help of Tomar. I will rally my own people."

"You can't do that from Chandra—"

"Exactly. I must return to Hume. There are towns and villages north of the Barda where I can find refuge and start gathering an army together."

"But we are already in Chandra," he pleaded. "You can stay in Sparro long enough to recover, surely?"

She shook her head. "I said you didn't understand. I will go no farther with you."

Galen grimaced. For a fleeting moment he considered forcing Charion to come with him, but besides being fraught with political difficulties, he knew it could fatally damage their friendship.

Friendship? We love each other. At least, I love her.

Yet his own duty was clear. He had at his command the remnants of the knights of the Twenty Houses, and they would be needed to defend Kendra itself if Chandra should fall. Even now Areava might be calling together a new army, and she would need the knights to lead them. His cavalry was the single remaining unit in Grenda Lear with any experience of fighting Lynan and his army. He could not deprive Areava of all that was worth to the kingdom.

Magmed returned. "What is the holdup? Does the queen need someone to ride with her?"

"This queen will never share her saddle with another," Charion was able to mutter.

"She will not go to Chandra," Galen said shortly.

Magmed looked at Galen with an expression that said "Take care of it," but it was not as easy as that. Despite what Charion had said, he did understand why she should would go no farther, and knew enough about politics to see how winning back her kingdom with Tomar's help could be disastrous in the long term for her and her people. He opened his mouth to try and explain to Magmed, then snapped his jaw shut as he realized *he* did not have to be with the knights. Magmed could lead them until Galen was sure Charion was safe and rejoined the unit either at Sparro or farther south if necessary.

"I must take the queen back to her land," Galen said. "You are in command of the knights until I can return."

"I think this is foolishness," Magmed said bluntly.

"You always thought you could command the knights. I saw it in your face the first day we rode out of Kendra."

"I was a fool," Magmed admitted. "I was wrong about you and Sendarus. But I'm not wrong now. The knights need you to lead them."

Galen shook his head. "No. They need someone who has learned enough to take responsibility for decisions. That's you. I have a responsibility to Charion as well as the knights. Imagine what Areava would say if she learned we abandoned a fellow monarch to her fate after bringing her so far, or forced a fellow monarch to do something against her will?"

He watched Magmed struggle to come up with some refutation, but in the end the young duke could only growl in frustration. "Take a dozen knights with you."

"No. All the knights will be needed. Anyway, if we are attacked by the Chetts, a dozen knights will only give them more targets." He held out his hand.

Magmed took it hesitantly, but gripped it firmly. "I will command in your absence only," he said.

"I understand." He took the reins of Charion's horse and slowly eased it away from the column still riding around them. "We will meet again!" he cried out to Magmed, and started back west.

A few hours later a large body of Chandran cavalry met up with the knights. Their commander was a tall, thin man with long gray hair who rode a black horse that was one of the most formidable looking stallions Magmed had ever seen. Magmed halted the column and waited for the leader to pull up along side of him.

"You are not Galen Amptra," the man said, the voice not unfriendly. His eyes seemed as dark as jet. Magmed also noticed his short coat of mail was dented and scraped in good service, and the grip on the sword strapped to his back was well-worn.

"You know Galen?" Magmed inquired.

"I met him once," the man said, but did not elaborate further. He just waited.

Magmed cleared his throat. "I am Duke Magmed. I am in command of this column."

"You weren't earlier today."

"Galen has returned to Hume."

The man looked up and down the column. "Taking your guest with him, I see."

"My guest?"

The man scratched his chin with one gloved hand. "Are we going to run around like this all day?"

"Who *are* you?"

"My name is Barys Malayka."

Magmed could not hide his surprise. "*The* Barys Malayka?"

"If there is another, I know nothing about him."

"You are Tomar's champion! I listened to stories about you when I was only a small—"

Barys' hand shot out and gripped Magmed's arm. "Please, do not tell me you were only a small boy. I do not want to think about myself being so old that you heard stories about me when you were a small boy."

"But—"

Barys' grip tightened. "I really, really don't."

Magmed shut his mouth.

"Charion was with you." He made it a statement, not a question.

"She returned to her province in the company of Galen."

"She was hurt, I believe."

"Yes, but not seriously. She should fully recover."

If Barys was disappointed by this, he gave no sign of it. "As long as she and Galen Amptra are not captured or killed by the Chetts." He released his grip and sat back in his saddle. "Well, I had best accompany you back to Sparro."

"Thank you." Magmed surveyed Barys' force. He estimated it numbered around five hundred riders, about twice the number of knights. "You certainly brought a large escort with you."

"Better safe than sorry in these troublesome days. By the way, I see none of you is wearing armor."

"We had to bury it," Magmed said shamefully.

Barys scratched his chin again. "Well, maybe someday you can go back and get it."

Despite Charion's protestations, Galen did not head straight for a village or town. He found a deeply wooded area near one of the

Barda River's smaller tributaries where they and their horses could easily hide from any casual search. He refused to hear the queen's objections, letting her tire herself out. When she was asleep, he risked exploring the immediate area for nuts and berries, and used their helmets to bring fresh water from the stream. She slept for twelve hours, and when she woke just before dawn the next day she did not abuse him as he half-expected to happen.

"You should be with your knights," she sniffed.

"Yes, I should be."

"Do you think Areava will be angry with you?"

"Probably. If you were in her shoes, would you be angry with me?"

"Absolutely furious." She sat up with some effort, refusing help. "I would probably chop off your head."

"Well, she'll get her chance later."

She sniffed again. "I might intercede for you."

Galen nodded, accepting the compliment but not sure what to do with it. He handed her a handful of red berries. "These are very nice."

"Second baby berries," she said.

"I'm sorry?"

"Second babies are always early. Most berries ripen in autumn. These ripen in late summer."

"We don't have them in the south."

"Too cold there," she told him.

"It's not cold at all in Kendra," he said. "We haven't had snow for over ten years."

"It *is* cold," she said. "I visited Kendra when I was a child. Some formal gathering of all the provincial rulers during Usharna's reign."

"I was there. Perhaps we met."

"Oh, I don't think so. The Twenty Houses weren't keen on us provincials."

Galen blushed. "True."

"Anyway, I can tell you that Kendra is cold. Not only does it almost never snow in Hume, we don't even get frosts."

They fell silent for a while, then Charion said: "I think the Twenty Houses will look more kindly on us on the borders now."

"One of their members already does."

She smiled at him. "Yes, I know."

"In fact, I think you and your people have impressed every

member of the knights; the Twenty Houses will never look down on Hume again."

Charion sighed. "If there is a Hume," she reminded him.

"You will free your land," he said matter-of-factly.

She smiled at him a second time. He thought that was something of a record. "Yes," she said, "I will."

"Only a single rider?" King Tomar asked.

The soldier nodded.

"And all he did was give you this?" He held up the letter.

"Yes, your Majesty," the soldier said.

"All right, thank you. Make sure you are fed in the kitchen and given a bed for the night. You can return to your garrison tomorrow."

The soldier bowed and departed, leaving Tomar alone in his chamber. He looked at the letter, a folded piece of paper with his name written on it. He did not recognize the handwriting. Still, he was sure he knew from whom the letter came.

A single rider approaching unarmed, in the dark, one of his border posts with Hume. Oh, yes, he knew who this came from.

He put the letter down on a table next to the room's single lit lamp.

I do not want to read this, he thought. *It could lead to treason.*

He went to the west window, looking out over the dark lands between Sparro and Daavis. Somewhere out there lay the future.

Can a king truly commit treason? he asked himself. *If a king is devoted to his people and his nation, can it be possible?*

Something moved in the middle distance. As he watched it, he realized it was Barys returning with the knights, and his oldest and most determined foe, Charion of Hume. What should he do with her? Was it treason to think of anything but helping her to return to her kingdom?

In the dark the column looked like a snake sinuously weaving its way through grass.

He did not want these decisions forced on him now. Or any time. What was wrong with the way things were before?

He looked at the letter. Could he ignore it? Even before he tried to answer the question, he had picked it up and was turning it over in his hands.

Such a little thing with such terrible consequences. To read a few lines and set a whole nation on a new course.

He heard the distant clattering of hooves on stone. Barys had reached the outskirts of the city. He and his charges would be at the palace soon. He must make up his mind now. He could not honorably offer Charion sanctuary if later he must desert her.

He was startled by a knock on his door. He immediately thought of his champion, but Barys could not have reached the palace that quickly. "Who is it?"

A guard entered with another letter.

"Who is this from?" he asked, confused.

"Post rider from Kendra, your Majesty. Just arrived."

Tomar pocketed the first letter and received the second, viewing with alarm and some distaste the royal seal of the Rosetheme kestrel. He nodded to the guard to leave. He massaged his forehead with one hand and tried to ignore the headache he could feel was coming. He opened the letter from Areava and angled it near the lamp so he could read the cramped writing of her secretary. You'd think, when Usharna died, Areava would have taken the opportunity to retire her mother's staff.

The thought led to others and, without reading the letter, he lowered the hand holding it. Of course, she did not succeed her mother. He forgot sometimes. Poor, bloody Berayma, king for a day. All Areava could do was pick up the pieces.

He had never liked Areava; she was too aloof and too . . . well, Kendran. Berayma had been equally unbearable. Olio he liked, an affable stutterer. And Lynan. Lynan he liked a great deal. There was much of his late father in Lynan.

He retrieved the letter from his pocket, now holding one in each hand. Each represented a choice he must make, if not in the next few minutes or hours, then certainly before too much time had passed.

He heard horses enter the palace courtyard. He had, momentarily, forgotten about Charion. He may have to make a choice sooner than he wanted. When he heard footsteps clumping toward his chamber, he placed both letters underneath the lamp. There was another knock and the guard let Barys in, accompanied by a young man Tomar had never seen before.

"Your Majesty," Barys said. "May I present Duke Magmed of the Twenty Houses."

Magmed bowed his head. "Your Majesty, thank you for your hospitality. We have ridden long and hard after the fall of—"

"I was expecting Galen Amptra," Tomar said.

"Galen decided it best to accompany the wounded Queen Charion."

Tomar's eyes narrowed. "Accompany her where?"

"Back to Hume, apparently," Barys said.

"That's right, your Majesty. Queen Charion would not leave her province while it is under the heel of the outlaw Lynan—"

"Yes, yes," Tomar said, waving down the duke. He was almost overcome with relief. That decision, at least, could be delayed indefinitely. "Are you and your men well?"

Magmed's expression became sorrowful. "What is left of them. We number under three hundred."

"Three hundred! But you left Kendra numbering near enough a thousand!"

"Many of us were slain in the first battle against Lynan's army," Magmed said. "They are ferocious warriors, and they were led by Lynan himself."

"Did you see him?" Tomar asked, trying not to sound too interested.

Magmed visibly shuddered. "I saw him right enough. I saw him plough through my companions as if they were made of nothing but chaff. And I saw his face; he was so pale he looked as if he had come back from the dead. And I saw him being struck by broadsword and lance and mace and ax and not take a single injury."

Tomar and Barys exchanged a glance, one with the same meaning. Magmed caught it and understood what they were thinking. "This is no fancy on my part, your Majesty!" he said urgently. "Ask any of the others. I saw a lance enter Lynan's stomach and come out the other side. I saw him pull out the lance and use it to kill a knight. I saw a sword blade sink half a hand's breadth into his thigh, and when the blade was pulled out, there was no blood. I saw him kill four knights using nothing but his fist. With my own eyes I saw all of this."

King and champion looked aghast at Magmed, seeing in his eyes that he told the truth.

Lynan, what has happened to you? Tomar wondered silently.

"He was not slain, then?" Barys asked.

"Not by us."

The room fell quiet. Tomar returned to the window and gazed out into the night, out to the west.

"Your Majesty?" Barys said.

"Hmm?"

"Magmed and his men are our guests . . ."

"Yes, of course. Please, Barys, make sure they are housed and fed." He turned to face the knight. "You must stay as long as you think necessary. Tomorrow I will send a post rider to Kendra informing Areava of your arrival. I am sure she will communicate your next orders when she can."

Magmed bowed slightly. "Thank you, your Majesty."

Tomar nodded and Barys led Magmed out. Alone again, he made up his mind. He took out the first letter, carefully unfolded it, and read.

By the time Barys returned he had read it four times. It was in his pocket again when the champion knocked and entered.

"What do you think of the duke's story?" he asked.

Barys shrugged. "Whatever we think of it, he believes it."

"There is no doubt about that. Do you think this Magmed might be prone to exaggeration?"

"I cannot say for sure, but from what I have seen of him, he does not seem prone to excess of any kind."

"Unusual for a member of the Twenty Houses," Tomar said, more to himself than Barys.

"Unusual for a Kendran," Barys said, smiling slightly.

"And no sign of Charion?"

Barys shook his head. "I made sure Magmed or his people did not see it, but I sent scouts to locate them; they caught up with us before we reached Sparro. She is no longer in Chandra."

Tomar sighed deeply. "Well and good."

"It might have been useful to have the queen of Hume in your hands."

"Yes, but it is not a responsibility I would cherish. Areava would circumscribe any serious action on my part, anyway."

"I hear a post rider arrived from the capital tonight. A letter from the palace in Kendra?"

Tomar nodded, pulled out the second letter. Barys noticed the broken seal. "What does she want from us this time?"

"I don't know yet. You and Magmed interrupted me. Get some sleep. We will talk tomorrow."

Barys pursed his lips but took the hint and left as asked.

"Now your turn, Areava," Tomar said softly, and unfolded the letter from Kendra.

*   *   *

Galen found a small town early in the morning; although not much larger than a village it had its own chapel to the Church of the Righteous God and its own resident priest, Father Hern, a large, serious looking man. Together with the priest he returned to the woods to collect Charion and the horses. By noon, the queen was safely hidden away above the chapel, freshly bandaged and wrapped in a clean blanket to keep her warm. The horses were given to a local farmer to look after and their gear hidden in the priest's woodshed. Galen himself was given a priest's frock and cloak but warned by Father Hern to stay out of sight.

"You are far too martial in your bearing to fool anyone for long," the priest told him.

Galen grinned. "I was taught by priests. Some of them were damn martial."

"Ah, yes, that will be your city priest for you. Your average country priest is meek and mild and gentle as a newborn."

Galen looked the big man up and down. "Gentle like a great bear, maybe."

"How long will you stay?"

"Eager to see the back of us already?"

"You can stay as long as you wish, Galen Amptra," Hern replied. "But I can't keep you secret from the townspeople forever."

"You think they would betray us?"

"Most of them, no. But every community has one or two that prize coin above loyalty. More to the point, once Charion's presence is common knowledge, they will all talk about it. In twenty days a nearby town holds its annual fair, and the talk will spread there, mark my word. In another twenty days half of Hume will know Charion is hiding in my chapel. So I ask again: how long will you stay?"

"When Charion is on her feet, we will see. I know she had plans to organize resistance to Lynan. Is there a place nearby where we may find both sanctuary and solitude?"

Hern thought about it. "There are many woods hereabouts, of course, but they fringe the Barda, and it is a well-traveled river, or at least was before the war started."

"It may again if Lynan believes he holds Daavis safe. Trade has always been that city's lifeblood. Are there any outposts or forts nearby?"

Hern shook his head. "There were some watch stations along our borders with Chandra, and I daresay once with Haxus, but the former were stripped to deal with Salokan's invasion and the latter swept aside by the same. We have some ex-soldiers, but not enough to form a company, let alone an army, if that is Charion's wish."

"She may not be thinking of an army," Galen said, more to himself than Hern.

"There are the Marbles," Hern said.

"The Marbles?"

"There is a wooded group of hills overlooking the Barda River not far west of here. The hills are covered by giant round boulders. Where the boulders heap on top of each other, they form shallow caves. You could hide a small army there."

"That sounds as if it might be what we need. Does anyone go there?"

"Not regularly. The boulders stop farmers from using the hills for terracing. Occasionally a stonemason will send cutters to gather stone from there if there's a big order on; they provide a good sandstone, yellow and clean, if they're split properly, but they're too heavy to cart any distance."

"Well, I'll make no decision for Charion. This is her land, and you are all her people. We must wait and see what plans she has."

"How are Magmed and his knights?" Tomar asked Barys.

"Resting, your Majesty," Barys replied, studying his king closely. He was not sure what it was, but there was some change in Tomar's face, the way his sad eyes gazed at him, as if further troubles than he already bore had been laid on his shoulders. "They have had a hard campaign. Many are wounded, in spirit as well as body."

They were walking together from the king's private chambers to the throne room. Courtiers bowed to Tomar as they passed and he never neglected to acknowledge them. Barys felt some pride that he served such a conscientious king, and one so well loved by his people. Through all the tribulations of his life, including having his realm invaded by slavers and mercenaries and the early and tragic death of his wife, he had never wavered from his duty nor indulged in self-pity.

"You should know that the letter I received last night informed me of Areava's decision to create what she calls a Great Army."

"Grandiose."

"But in light of what has happened over the last few months, necessary if she has any hope of defeating Lynan."

"And what is our contribution to be?"

"She has not specified yet. However, the army will set its standard in Chandra."

Barys stopped in his tracks. "They are creating the army in Chandra?"

Tomar stopped, too, and nodded. "It makes sense, really. Kendra is too small for the purpose, and we are closest to the main threat."

"How great is this Great Army?"

"She says fifty thousand."

"God! We cannot afford to maintain such a large force—"

Tomar looped a hand around Barys's arm and started walking again. "I know, but let's not talk too loudly about it, eh?"

"You think this is Orkid's work?"

Tomar shrugged. "Possibly. Now that Sendarus is dead, the Amanites have lost influence in court. Orkid may be trying to recover lost ground."

"He had great influence over Usharna. How different will it be for the daughter?"

"You overestimate Orkid, Barys, and that is almost as dangerous as underestimating him. Usharna ruled Orkid, right enough, and he served her well. However, I do not know Areava well enough to tell you whether she is her own woman or not."

"What are you going to do about Magmed and the knights?"

"Nothing. They can stay here, unless Areava orders them back to Kendra. I suppose it depends on what Lynan does next. They are too few in number to influence the war now."

"You think he will invade Chandra?"

"No doubt about it. Without Chandra, he cannot reach Kendra. It's a matter of when he invades, not if."

"Do you think we can stop him?"

"Not by ourselves. Look what he and his Chetts did to Salokan and Charion." He smiled suddenly. "But don't worry; I'd be surprised if they crossed our border before winter." He absently patted his left pocket. "Plenty of time," he said more quietly.

18

LYNAN woke, wide-eyed, his mouth open in a silent scream, his muscles rigid with fear. For a moment he did not know where he was, and then he heard the even and gentle breathing of Korigan, asleep by his side.

Daavis. Night. Autumn.

Safe.

His muscles unlocked and he slumped back into the mattress. He closed his eyes in the vain hope he might find some more sleep, but after a few minutes knew it was useless and got out of bed. He dressed quickly and quietly, making sure not to disturb Korigan, and left the bedchamber. Two Red Hands saluted as he walked out and another two fell in behind him. He was not sure where he was going, but he felt the need to do something physically hard, something that would tire him out enough so that when he fell asleep there would be no nightmare to greet him.

He stopped in the courtyard. In the dim light of an early morning under a gray sky, the palace—the whole city—seemed suffocatingly close. He headed for the stables, chose a mare, and saddled it. His escorting Red Hands did likewise. When all three were done, they rode out of the palace then out of the city, heading north at a gallop until Lynan felt his horse struggling underneath him. He slowed to a walk and then dismounted. Leading their horses, Lynan and his bodyguard made their way back to Daavis. In the city people were on their way to work. Stalls were opening, carts carrying fresh produce from farms were rattling their way to markets, agile children carrying wooden platters laden with breads and cakes from bakeries wove their way through streets to shops and homes. The night cart was finishing its last run and leaving the city, making everyone who passed it wince with the smell. Cleaners were doing their morning course, picking up dead rodents and birds and any other animal that had died during the night and ended up on the street or in the gutters.

For the most part, the streets were so busy at this hour that no one had any time to pay attention to the short youth leading his horse toward the palace. His two companions elicited the occasional remark. Once or twice a passerby saw Lynan's face and gasped in sudden realization of who he was and paled in sudden fear, but before they could do or say anything he was past them and lost in the crowd.

When they reached the palace a Chett rushed forward to take his horse, but he waved her away and returned to the stables himself and, despite the protestations of the local hand, insisted on brushing down and feeding his own mare. When he was done, he felt hot and sweaty and relaxed. On the way back to his chambers, he saw Farben in the courtyard, busily and bossily giving instructions to several workers and at the same time directing clerks and secretaries. Farben stopped when he saw Lynan watching and approached him.

"Prince Lynan, was there something you wished to see me about?"

One of Farben's secretaries, a young, redheaded man, seemed surprised his master would presume to talk to Lynan at all.

"No. I am glad to see you about your duties."

"As we discussed, I must keep the city in order for the return of its rightful ruler." He said this without any hint of sarcasm.

Lynan smiled thinly, understanding Farben's need to remind everyone publicly and at every opportunity why he was working as administrator of an enemy-occupied city.

Korigan was awake and eating breakfast by the time Lynan arrived. She was still in bed with a big bowl of fruit nestled in her lap.

"Where did you go?"

"For a ride," he said, sitting down next to her and picking up a piece of fruit.

"You should have taken me with you."

"You were asleep. City life is softening you."

Korigan snorted in disgust. "We Chetts don't spurn luxury. Out on the Oceans of Grass we have no choice about when we sleep and what we sleep on. But when we have a chance to enjoy a soft bed and late morning, we indulge ourselves."

"So you don't miss the plains?"

Korigan looked serious. "Of course I do," she said, her voice distant, as if she was suddenly standing on the Oceans of Grass. "How much longer do we stay in Daavis?"

"Until reinforcements arrive from Haxus. We need to garrison this city, then stock supplies for our campaign into Chandra. Daavis will be our base until we capture Sparro."

"Reinforcements may not arrive until late autumn. Haxus is recovering from a defeat, remember. That means no campaign until next spring, and by then Areava will have organized a new army."

"Who says we have to wait for spring?"

"Will you fight in winter?"

"Winter in the east can be hard, but it is nothing compared to what the Chetts endure at the High Sooq. We can start our attack on Chandra when we're ready, even if it is in the middle of winter. Our Chetts will be fully rested by then."

"You are not going to ask for more warriors from the clans?"

Lynan shook his head. "No. We started with twenty thousand riders, and still have close to eighteen thousand. It is enough to take Chandra as long as Grenda Lear does not interfere with an army. Once we have Sparro, we can build an army to rival anything Areava can create, using troops from Chandra and Hume and Haxus."

"We Chetts aren't used to fighting with other forces. It will be hard to make us all work together."

"Nonetheless, with you and Ager and Gudon helping, we can do it." He looked downcast suddenly. He handled the fruit without eating it.

"It would have been a lot easier with Kumul," Korigan said for him.

"Yes. I think we will miss his presence the most in the coming months. When it was winter and everyone else wanted to stay indoors in front of a fire, drinking ale and telling stories, he would be exercising the guard or polishing swords or training recruits. He knew how to turn farm boys and fishermen and laborers into the kingdom's best soldiers. I don't have that knack."

"Ager might," Korigan observed.

Lynan smiled thinking about the crookback. "Yes, dear Ager. If anyone can do it now that Kumul is gone, it is he."

* * *

"Out of bed!"

Ager felt himself being rolled before he hit the cold stone floor with a thump. "Urgh," he mumbled.

Morfast stood over him, needled his back with her foot. All she got was another grunt. She shook her head in disbelief. He was getting too used to the comforts of so-called civilization. She went to the washstand and brought back a ewer, tipping its contents over his head.

"You didn't have to do that," Ager said, still on the ground. "I was already awake."

"Yes, like a tree is awake."

He turned suddenly, grasped her ankles, and yanked her legs out from underneath her. She fell on top of him. He kissed her.

"We are wasting time in Daavis," she said.

"There is much to be done here."

"Yes, but not for the Ocean clan. Lynan has his builders and carpenters and stonemasons to rebuild the city. We should be riding."

He kissed her again. There were some days he could not believe his good fortune. Since becoming chief of the Ocean clan he had found both a home and someone with whom he wanted to share the rest of his life, however long that may be.

"Don't tell me you don't feel it," she persisted.

He sighed and eased himself from underneath her. "Perhaps," he admitted, scrounging among the bed sheets for his breeches and jerkin. They were tangled in a clump at the bottom of the bed. Clothes always managed to do that. He wondered if there was a law involved.

"Hume itself has not been conquered yet," she said.

He laughed dryly. "The eastern provinces are not like the Oceans of Grass. If you take a capital city you take the heart out of a province. There is no capital city in the west."

"There are no cities at all," she pointed out.

"In the east the political and economic strength lies in cities and towns, and they are connected by trade and tradition with the capital. There is no Hume left to pacify because Hume became pacified the moment Daavis fell to us. And when we march on Chandra we will aim straight for Sparro. And when we take Kendra, the whole kingdom will fall into our hands like a ripe fruit."

Morfast shook her head. "How strange." She thumped her chest. "That is why the Chetts will never be conquered!"

Ager smiled grimly at her. "Wrong. Everyone can be conquered. You just have to know a people's weak points and go for them."

"We have no weak points," she said.

"Of course you have. Your sooqs and water holes. Your cattle. Your lack of organization. Your eagerness to bicker and argue among yourselves. All of these can be exploited. As they were by the mercenaries and the kings of Haxus during the Slaver War. Korigan's father had to go to war against his own people to unite them."

He went to the washstand, looked around for the water before remembering Morfast had disposed of it. "How am I supposed to clean myself now?"

"You are cleaned," she said, and ran her forgers through his soaked hair.

"But you are right. We must do something. I will talk to Lynan about it. Maybe he will release the Ocean clan to scout into Chandra."

Morfast's eyes lit up. "To battle?"

Ager shrugged, making his crookback rise in the air like a mountain. "Maybe. But to find where they are setting outposts so we may take or avoid them when our army finally moves."

"That could take weeks," she said excitedly.

Ager laughed. "Yes. It might take weeks."

"We would be together. Alone."

"Alone with a thousand Ocean Clan warriors."

It was her turn to shrug. "They are like family."

Ager groaned. "Nobody needs that big a family."

"You are our father, Ager, our chief."

He nodded and smiled. "Yes, and proud of it."

Morfast moistened her lips. "And we can always add to it."

Ager's smile turned into a grin. "That takes practice."

Morfast took his hand. "The more the better."

"I've just dressed," he protested, but weakly.

Galen thought it was a dry, scratchy, uncomfortable place with more than its fair share of spiders, scorpions, and centipedes. That's how he knew Charion would like it.

"Perfect," she said.

"It would be," he said under his breath, then louder, "The hills are higher than I thought they would be."

"Good defensive terrain," she mused, "and they run up close to the river." She stood on the highest point, a boulder about the size of a house, and looked west and northwest. "A good view."

"Can you see Daavis?"

"Not exactly. There is a smudge on the horizon which might be smoke from all the city's kitchens."

"Or it could just be a cloud."

"It probably is. But I do see the north road. It is far enough away to look like nothing but a little yellow string."

"Well, a hideaway with a view of a dusty road. Wonderful."

"Don't be sarcastic. It doesn't suit you. What this place gives me is a perfect lookout over Lynan's main route of reinforcement from Haxus."

Galen silently cursed himself; he should have realized the road's importance as soon as Charion mentioned it. He scrabbled to the top of the boulder and stood by her side. "How are your ribs?"

She slowly moved her right arm up and down. The arc of the swing she could take increased every day, and the bruising on her chest was now nothing more than a shrinking pinkish-yellow stain. "I'll be able to use a sword soon," she said.

"I wondered when you'd get around to that. Use a sword against whom?"

"Lynan, of course."

"I mean whom specifically?"

She pointed in the direction of the road. "Against them."

Galen squinted, barely able to make out a dark ripple on the northern road. "Troops?"

"Or supplies. Maybe even a small caravan. Whatever it is, destroying it will hurt Lynan." She continued to gaze northwestward. "Look there . . ."

Again, Galen squinted. "I can't even see the road that way—"

"Exactly. If I'm not mistaken—and," she said, turning to Galen, "I rarely am—that is the Elstra Gorge. It runs north-south for about a league."

This time Galen was keeping up with her. "A perfect site for an ambush."

"Exactly. Especially for a force of infantry."

"You're going to raise infantry?" This was the first he had heard about it.

"God's death, Galen," she said, shaking her head. "You nobles of the Twenty Houses really do think the world was made solely for your benefit."

"What did I do to deserve that slap in the face?" he asked testily.

"Where do you get your horses from?"

"Me, personally?"

"You and every other knight."

"Well, from our stables or farms outside of the city."

"And on these farms you grow what crops?"

"Not many. They're mainly horse ranges . . ." His voice dropped away.

"Exactly. You need to be rich to raise horses, especially war horses, since they need specialized training, feeding, and breeding. Look around you. This is farming and wood country. Not poor, by any standard, but not particularly rich. The land here is drier and has more clay than you get around Kendra or the green valleys you find everywhere in Chandra. The average farmer might own one horse, two at most, but they're likely to be old hacks with saggy backs and a tendency to bite. That's why I'm going to raise infantry. Besides, if we're going to use this hill as our hideaway, where would you suggest we put the horses?"

"I've never fought on foot," he said doubtfully.

"Yes, you have," she said, and patted his hand. "Defending my city, and by all accounts you fought well."

"How would you know?" he asked, but she could see he was flattered.

"Farben told me. I think he likes you." Her face grew solemn. "I hope he is all right."

Galen looked at the hill from Charion's point of view again and saw that she was right. It gave them an easily defended position, good views over the north road, access to the river, and lots of hidey-holes.

"Very well, you've convinced me," he told her. "What next?"

"We recruit."

"As soon as you do, word will spread about what you are doing. The Chetts will learn of it eventually and come looking."

"Let them. It's about time we gave them a bloody nose again."

"Do you seriously think we can win?"

Charion half-smiled and shook her head. "By ourselves? Of course not. I'm counting on your queen—sorry, *our* queen—coming to my rescue eventually. But everything I can do to help her cause I will do. We may only sting Lynan, but it might be enough. It might make all the difference in the world."

*   *   *

Lynan called his war council together. It was the first time he, Korigan, Gudon, Ager and Jenrosa had been alone together since the fall of Daavis. They met in a room Farben told them had been used by Charion for the same purpose, and sat around a square table. Lynan took a moment to study his companions, the people he cared more about than any others in the world. Korigan, his lover, tall and golden-skinned, the proudest of Chetts. Gudon, her cousin, and his first friend among the Chetts, with a mouth that always seemed ready to laugh and a way of the seeing the universe that always saw the light rather than the dark. Ager, humped and half-blind, one of the best soldiers and captains Kendra had ever produced, loyal and devoted to Lynan's cause. Jenrosa, sandy haired, gray-eyed, filled with grief for the lost Kumul.

Thinking of Kumul made Lynan heartsore. He realized he had always thought of Kumul as being invincible, incapable of dying. Kumul had been his father in all but name, his teacher and guide and protector. He shook his head and brought his mind back to the present.

"We have a few things to discuss. First, our reinforcements from Haxus have started to arrive."

"I've seen them," Ager said disdainfully. "Drips and drabs. Just recruits."

"We should expect little else after what Haxus has been through. But they can be trained up." He looked meaningfully at Ager, and the crookback sighed his understanding.

"We must also decide on a replacement for Kumul."

Jenrosa looked up sharply. "What do you mean by that?" she demanded.

"I mean we need someone to take over command of the banner of lancers," Lynan said, keeping his voice level. He glanced at Gudon. "I was thinking of your brother, Makon, but I had need of him elsewhere."

"Third, we must discuss the timing of our attack on Chandra."

"I've been giving that some thought myself," Ager said.

Lynan smiled. "I thought you might have. It wouldn't by any chance involve a long raiding party into Chandran territory?"

Ager looked abashed. "Possibly," he said, rather too meekly.

"Involving the Ocean clan?"

Ager shifted uncomfortably in his seat.

"First things first," Korigan said. "The reinforcements."

"Three hundred have arrived so far, in four groups," Lynan told them. "All spear."

"How many have you asked Salokan to send?"

"Just over three thousand, almost all of whom will be allotted to defend Daavis; a handful will be sappers, replacing those we lost assaulting this city."

"They are worth their weight in gold," Ager said. "Do you trust the Haxans to defend Daavis for you?"

"Only as much as I need to. If things go according to plan, we will have Sparro before next summer and Daavis will become less important in the scheme of things."

"Salokan won't make a grab for it?" Gudon asked.

Lynan remembered the last conversation he had with Salokan. "No. He will never betray us."

"That won't stop some Haxan defender with imagination trying to seize Daavis in his name."

"We will leave Chett officers to supervise any defense," Lynan said, "and with them a good contingent of Chett warriors."

"Three hundred reinforcements so far," Korigan said, shaking her head. "I hope the flow increases somewhat."

"Salokan sent those from among his own house troop as soon as he received my request. The remainder have since been conscripted and are being sent on their way south over the next few days. We should have them all halfway through autumn. Furthermore, they bring with them supplies—weapons, horses, some bullion."

"Bullion?" Korigan looked surprised. "We Chetts do not need coin for our services!"

"Not for us, cousin," Gudon said. "But for the city. Daavis must resume trade if it is to survive, and the Haxan troops will have to be paid."

"If you're wanting me to train up these drips and drabs, lad," Ager said, "you'll not be letting me dillydally around Chandra with my Ocean clan."

"I'm sorry, no," Lynan said.

"My people will be disappointed."

"I don't want that to happen, my friend. The Ocean clan can still carry out its long raid, but they'll do it under Morfast and not you."

Ager nodded. "Very well."

"The lancers," Jenrosa said, her voice flat. "Who will you have take them over? Who can replace Kumul in their hearts? And since you let three troops go with Eynon and Makon, you have not much more than that left here. The battle against the knights saw them lose nearly half their number."

Every word was aimed at Lynan, as if she was insulting him for so neglecting the lancers and in that way the memory of her beloved.

"I do not think anyone will replace Kumul in the hearts of the lancers," Lynan replied. "Nor for that matter in anyone else's heart. But I will not punish them for that by leaving them leaderless. We will increase their numbers when we reorganize some of the common banners." He turned to Korigan. "Arrange for two hundred more riders to be added to the lancers. Coordinate their training with Ager."

"I know nothing about heavy cavalry," Ager said.

"But you know about the discipline necessary to make heavy cavalry work."

"And its leader?" Jenrosa prodded.

Lynan met her gaze. "Terin of the Rain clan."

Jenrosa's expression was matched by the others'.

"He is too young!" Jenrosa declared.

"Truth, it is a great responsibility for Terin."

"He has his own clan, and has led one of our banners with skill and courage. As well, he deserves a reward for his part in our victory over the mercenaries. If not for him and his clan, Rendle would never have entered the trap we set for him."

"And who will take over his banner?"

Lynan shrugged. "It will have to be a clan chief. Many have shown initiative since we moved from the High Sooq in spring. Korigan can choose one she thinks most deserves promotion."

"Akota of the Moon clan."

Lynan looked at her in surprise. "She sided with Eynon against you."

Korigan nodded. "Truth. But she has fought valiantly for your cause since Eynon returned. As well, it will show those that originally sided with Eynon that there is no longer any enmity between the clans of the Chetts."

"She is old," Jenrosa mumbled.

"She is experienced," Korigan countered.

"Then it is settled," Lynan said firmly. "Now to the last issue: when do we resume the war?"

"As soon as Daavis is defended," Korigan said quickly.

"As soon as my clan has finished its raid," Ager said. "We cannot invade blindly. Chandra is a much tougher nut than Hume: richer, more populous, better roads, closer to Kendra—"

"We struck at Hume like a grass wolf strikes at karak," Gudon said. "Without warning."

"And we lost," Ager pointed out. "We did not know the size and composition of the enemy army."

Lynan sighed heavily. "Ager is right. We lost because having made the decision in my heart to strive for the throne of Grenda Lear I was too eager to come to grips with the kingdom army. I wanted it over and done with."

All eyes settled on him. None had genuinely felt Lynan was to blame for the loss, not even Jenrosa. Lynan saw what they were thinking.

"It was my decision, and that made it my responsibility. All we lost, including Kumul, we lost because I did not have the information I needed about the enemy to properly plan for the battle."

"Even Kumul would not lay that on you," Jenrosa said. Now all eyes turned to her. It was the gentlest thing any had heard her say for a long time.

"Thank you," Lynan said.

"So you will wait for the Ocean clan to finish their long raid before moving the whole army into Chandra?" Gudon asked.

Lynan nodded. "We will wait."

"Truth, little master, I understand your concerns," Gudon said, "but think of the advantage gained by striking quickly. You *are* the White Wolf."

"There are other reasons to hold off," Lynan told him, "reasons I do not want to go into right now. But you must trust me on this."

Gudon breathed out, looked perplexed, but nodded his agreement.

"Then we have finished," Lynan told them. They all stood to leave. Lynan went to Jenrosa and placed a hand on her arm. "Wait a while." He waited for the others to go and waved her back into her seat.

"I put off making a decision about the lancers for as long as I could," Lynan said.

"Thank you for telling me," she said a little stiffly, and then, more easily: "I knew it had to be done. I suppose I was afraid that replacing Kumul as the lancers' banner leader meant he was never coming back."

"It wasn't just that which delayed me," Lynan said, speaking slowly. "I don't know if I should tell you this, but I think you deserve to know. We have always been friends, but sometimes I cannot do things for my friends that I would like to."

Jenrosa looked at him with curiosity. She had no idea what he was talking about. "What do you mean? What else delayed your decision?"

"Many of the lancers expressed to me or Ager their wish that you take Kumul's place as their banner leader."

Jenrosa blinked. The idea seemed to her at once both absurd and desirable. She was no warrior, but to have carried on Kumul's work, and to do it in Kumul's name! "Why didn't you tell me?" she asked.

"I'm telling you now."

"But why didn't you consult with me on this?" Her voice became strident.

"The time when I had to consult with you or Ager or anyone else on how to lead this army is gone."

"That's what hurt Kumul the most!" she blurted out. She gasped even as she finished saying the words and turned away from Lynan.

Tears stung Lynan's eyes. "Yes, and knowing that hurt me as well. But understand, Jenrosa, my decision was made for everyone's good. You are a brave fighter, but you are no warrior, and I needed a warrior to lead the lancers. The lancers themselves—like both of us—wanted to keep Kumul any way they could, and having you as banner leader was a way for them to do that; but it would have been wrong. The last reason, the best reason, although you may not agree, is that you have a role to play in this army, a role no one else can fulfill. You are—"

"No!" she cried over him. "Don't say it, don't say that word!"

Lynan looked at her with sadness and bewilderment. He hated to see her so distressed, but did not completely understand where the distress came from. He recognized it stemmed from more than her grief over the death of Kumul, but that was all. If only he could ask her . . .

"All right," he said, and put a hand out to touch her, but she stood up suddenly and retreated from him.

"Are we finished?"

The tone in her voice told her they were, whether he wanted it to be or not. "Yes."

She nodded curtly and left.

*   *   *

Charion, crouching below the rocky outcrops that marked the lip of Elstra Gorge, gently slapped the shoulder of each of her new soldiers. They were a mixed bag but among the first to volunteer to fight for Hume and, even more importantly, were acquainted with the bow, even if it had been for hunting small game to supplement their diet as farmers or craft workers. She had sixty archers lined along the top of the gorge. Forty troops were armed with hand-to-hand weapons, spears mostly but a few with swords inherited from military service or from some ancestor who had done likewise; they were under the command of Galen and situated in a dry river gully that ran into the gorge near its southern end. She got to the end of the line and risked peeping over the outcrop to see Father Hern on the opposite side, responsible for half the archers. They gave each other a short wave, then both turned their attention to the column snaking its way through the gorge. Charion estimated there were about one hundred fifty enemy soldiers, marching two abreast, divided into two sections with a large baggage train in between. They were infantry, all armed with spear and sword and wearing a mass-produced helm as their only protection. Even from where she was situated, Charion could tell the enemy were as new to the military life as her own soldiers: they carried their weapons either too stiffly or without any care at all, and their helms did not always fit as well as they should. Furthermore, and most importantly, they had no scouts out front or on the flanks. They could not have given her an easier target.

The hard part was waiting for exactly the right moment to strike. She kept a keen eye on her own soldiers, ready to stop anyone from standing and shooting prematurely; with the enemy so close, it was a real temptation.

She risked peeping one more time, to check she had accurately estimated their rate of march. Close enough, she decided as she sank back down and started counting. When she reached two hundred, she checked one more time. The last soldiers in the column were lined up with her position. It was time.

"Now!" she cried, leaping up. The enemy, every one, looked her way just in time to greet the thirty arrows that whistled down to them from her side. Most missed their targets, but three struck mortal or crippling blows, and another ten stuck in arms or legs. Then, right after, Father Hern called out. Dazed and confused, the enemy obligingly looked the other way just in time to receive another thirty arrows, these—having been better aimed—hitting more targets.

The column collapsed into confusion as a second flight from both directions swept their line. Most fell in panic, some because they were hit. No one gave orders. Another flight of arrows. By now, half the rear section of the column had been hit. Soldiers were rolling on the ground moaning and shouting in pain.

"Move along!" Charion ordered, and her thirty archers half-ran fifty meters south and started shooting at the vanguard. Hern let his group fire two more times into the rear before marching them south as well. In just a few minutes the enemy bolted. They dropped their weapons and started running back the way they had come. Charion, waiting for just this moment, ordered her archers to concentrate their shooting against the animals drawing the carts and wagons in the baggage train. Many of the arrows hit their target, but only a few caused immediately fatal wounds, most of the animals rearing and twisting across the road, blocking it with their loads. The soldiers of the van scrambled over the animals and each other to get away. Charion now gave her final signal, two arrows fired at the mouth of the dry gully. An instant later, Galen and his forty warriors streamed out and slammed into the fleeing enemy. They showed no mercy, unhesitatingly striking the enemy down from behind and flinging corpses aside to get at new targets. As the infantry hacked their way north, the two groups of archers ran to their original position to pour more arrows into the still disorganized rearguard. Some of the enemy at the very end of the column managed to escape the slaughter, but few others.

The battle was over quickly, and the gorge was filled with the smell of blood and death. Crows and even hawks were already circling above, waiting for the feast to start.

Charion joined Galen at the baggage train. He held up a handful of gold coins. "Money!" he shouted at her. "Haxan gold and silver. Enough to raise a small army!" He rushed to a couple of spilled boxes; straw littered the roadway, soaking up blood, and amid the straw were swords. Nearby wagons held many boxes the same size. "And we have enough arms now to equip it!"

Charion nodded. "We have to move," she said levelly. "It's possible the Chetts have sent a troop to escort this column on the last stage of their journey."

Galen grinned at her. "If not, they will in the future."

"And that will slow down Lynan even further."

Galen patted her shoulder. "You could at least offer a small smile. This is a wonderful victory! Look what you have done with only one hundred raw recruits!"

"Against equally raw, totally surprised, and very tired recruits," she said. "But yes, the victory was important. It will help raise morale and improve enlistment."

Galen became more serious. "And ensure Lynan comes after us."

Now Charion smiled, but there was no humor in it. "With any luck."

Ager had been given permission to ride with his clan as far as the border with Chandra. It would take three days to get there from Daavis, three days he intended to enjoy to the full. For the first few hours he set up a hard pace, eager to get the cobwebs out of his mind and those of his warriors. City living had its advantages, but it limited how you looked at the world and your place in it. Mounted on a horse, the wind in your hair, the smell of trees and earth in your nostrils, the sound of birdsong in your ear, the feel of raw sunlight on your skin, life broadened by the moment; so did Ager's grin as the city fell farther and farther behind.

Just before noon, Ager became aware of a heavier, deeper sound in the ground, as if the surface he was riding on had changed, but then he sensed a change in his warriors, a ripple that moved up the column from the rear to the van. He looked over his shoulder and groaned, seeing with his one good eye the unmistakable figure of Lynan riding his way.

He's changed his mind and is going to ask me to come back to Daavis today, he thought. Then he noticed two other details. Lynan's pennant—the gold circle in a dark red field—fluttered behind him, and the column of riders was noticeably thicker that it should be, four horses abreast instead of two.

"He's brought his Red Hands with him," he said aloud.

Morfast looked at him. "Lynan?"

Instead of answering, Ager put his hand up to stop the column, put his hands in his lap, and waited, trying to ignore the hundred questions that rose in his mind.

A minute later Lynan had caught up. He reined in, and sitting beside him was Gudon, grinning like a genial idiot.

"Decided to join us in Chandra, your Majesty?" Morfast asked lightly.

Lynan smiled at her. "I wish it were so." He settled back in his saddle and breathed deeply. "I wish to God it were so."

"What's happened?" Ager asked, suddenly impatient.

"We lost a column," Lynan said flatly.

"Where?"

"In a gorge about a day's travel north of here. Over a hundred reinforcements from Haxus were cut down, and all the supplies and money they escorted were taken."

"When?"

"Three days ago. Some of the survivors came into Daavis just after you and your clan left."

"And who?"

Lynan shrugged. "None of the survivors could tell us. It was a well-laid ambush. Archers on either side of the gorge, a reserve of infantry hidden in a gully. They didn't stand a chance." He looked up at the sky for a moment, then back down at his hands. "Things were getting too simple, weren't they, old friend? I should have known something like this would happen. It's just that in all the histories I've read, taking the capital of a kingdom would end all resistance."

"This is a civil war," Ager pointed out. "We don't have any histories of civil wars, except legends from the earliest days." He avoided Morfast's gaze, having only recently expressed to her exactly the same belief as Lynan's. He could see from his friend's face that there was something more. "Go on."

"The only thing all the survivors agreed upon was that the ambush was set off by a dark-haired woman."

"Charion. We knew she had escaped."

"To Chandra, we thought, and then to Kendra."

"Out of the way," Gudon added.

Lynan leaned across and patted Ager's shoulder. "Well, at least you know now that I haven't come to drag you back to the city."

Ager looked up suddenly, startled. "You haven't got all the banners out searching, have you?"

Lynan looked disappointedly at Ager. "I realize it could be a diversion, to empty the city of defenders. Korigan is still there, with the rest of our army. We only need our two banners to hunt down Charion. If her force had been any larger than one or two hundred, there would not have been any survivors from the Haxan column."

Ager nodded meekly by way of apology. "So we ride north?"

"Until we get to the gorge. Then we search for spoor."

Ager brightened. "A hunt!"

Gudon's grinned widened. "Truth, my friend, a hunt!"

Father Hern finished counting out two gold Haxan pieces and four silver. He carefully retied the leather money pouch, put it in his cloak pocket, and pushed the coins across the kitchen table. A small, dark-eyed man sitting opposite him looked at the coins for a moment, then at the priest.

"This comes from our queen?"

"You have known me for many years, Kivilas, and you trust me. I tell you that Queen Charion led the attack at Elstra Gorge. Hume is fighting back against the demon Lynan."

"The demon Lynan?" Kivilas smiled quizzically at that. "You pushing politics or religion, Father?"

"I have heard first-hand from Charion what this Lynan Rosetheme is like," Father Hern said. "He is a demon." His hands shook a little and he had to place them flat on the table to stop them. "I tell you plainly, I did not want to get involved, but after hearing from Charion herself what this Lynan has become, I felt I had no choice but to assist in any way that I could."

Kivilas' smile disappeared and his face went dark. "I have heard stories about his sister as well. I heard at the last fair that her daughter was born vomiting blood and killed two of the midwives before it could be slain."

Hern paled. Even he, with his church connections, had not heard *that* story. But he did not doubt it. "All the Rosetheme brood are cursed, I think. There is even a tale told of Olio, whom everyone knows is as gentle as a babe . . ."

Kivilas nodded to show that he, too, had heard this.

". . . performing dark magic the night Kendra went up in flames."

"Kendra has been destroyed?" This Kivilas could not believe, and his expression showed it. Kendra was indestructible. Even Hume farmers like himself, common as muck and filled with far more common sense than imagination, believed there was something almost mystical about the capital of Grenda Lear—the capital of the world!

Hern shook his head. "Not entirely. But everywhere from the palace to the docks is burned down."

"Then Areava will not send an army north! She will use her money to rebuild her city!"

"Charion and her Kendran aide assure me that Areava will not fail us. We can expect an army soon, maybe even before winter."

"No," Kivilas said. "You are a priest and are used to believing in difficult things, but I am a farmer and depend on what I see with my own eyes. I fought in the Slaver War, and I can tell you that no army moves that fast." He grimaced then. "Except maybe one from the Oceans of Grass."

Hern pushed the coins even farther across the table. "I know of your service to Hume and the kingdom. That is why I asked you to come. Your village can raise seven soldiers for Charion's army, eight including you. There's the equal of twenty-four silver pieces, pay for a full month and in advance. Take it and join our cause."

"We don't need the money to prove our loyalty to Queen Charion." He said her name almost with reverence.

"Charion knows this. She is not buying your loyalty, but making sure your village does not lose out by sending its best and strongest to join her. This money will keep food on the tables of your families while you are away."

Kivilas grunted in approval. His hand hovered over the coins. "And after the first month?"

"More bullion, captured from Haxus convoys."

Kivilas grinned and scooped the coins into one hand. "You'll have your eight soldiers."

"Not me," Hern said seriously. "Queen Charion."

It took the Chett force over a day to reach the gorge. They found signs of the slaughter readily enough. The road was littered with the half-eaten corpses of over a hundred soldiers, many of them bloated from their time in the sun. Flies hung in the air as thick as a dust cloud, and birds called and wheeled overhead waiting for the living to get out of the way so they could resume their feasting. Before anything else, Lynan ordered the dead gathered together in a huge pyre. It was noon before the job was done, and the stinking air was almost unbreathable. Lynan himself set fire to the mound.

The Chetts spread out north and south, east and west of the gorge, looking for any and every sign of passing. It did not take them long to discover that the enemy had approached from the east and then returned that way, heavily laden with booty.

"What lies between here and Sparro?" Lynan asked Ager.

"Woods, some hills, a few towns," Gudon answered before Ager could open his mouth. "Remember, little master, that I used to pilot a barge up and down the Barda River. I got to know this part of the world quite well."

"How many towns?"

Gudon shrugged. "I don't know. They have regular fairs, so a reasonable number, and villages between them."

"I don't like this," Ager said. "The enemy could disperse among any of the towns or villages, making it almost impossible to track them all down, especially their leaders."

"Nonetheless, we'll try," Lynan said. "I don't want the enemy working behind my lines if I have to advance on Chandra."

"That could take us the rest of autumn," Ager pointed out.

"...move east until we come to the first settlement. There we ...ions of the local area and we split in four groups to ...y towns and villages as possible in the shortest time. ...orfast divide the Ocean clan; Gudon and I divide the ...ands."

The others had no better idea, so they continued east until they came to a place too small to be even described as a village. The inhabitants were small plot farmers, working land rented from an owner who spent most of his time in Daavis. Their knowledge of the local area extended no more than twenty leagues in any direction, but that did include a couple of villages and one town.

"What's the town called?" Ager asked.

"Was called Esquidion," one farmer told them.

"Was called?" Lynan asked.

The farmer took a step back. He did not mind talking to the ugly bastard with a misshapen back, but this short, pale, scarred man scared him. "Priest's Town, if you don't mind."

"I don't mind," Lynan repeated, puzzled by the expression. "But why Priest's Town?"

The farmer looked at him as if he was stupid.

"Because a priest lives there, I dare say," Ager suggested.

"That's right," the farmer agreed. "He came about ten years ago and built a chapel an' all, and does the rounds for the whole area. He could draw you a map, if you don't mind."

"I don't . . ." Lynan shook his head. What was the point? "We go to Priest's Town, then. Have you seen any soldiers come this way?"

"Only yerselves."

Following the farmer's rather vague directions, they finally found a large town around noon. Leaving most of their column behind under the command of Morfast, Lynan, Gudon, and Ager rode down the dusty avenue that passed for the main street. They asked a local if the place was indeed Priest's Town, and were told in no uncertain terms that it was still called Esquidion by those born and bred here.

"But there is a priest hereabouts?" Ager asked.

"In the chapel," the local said, and pointed to a long, low building made from recently cut sandstone at the edge of town.

The three companions rode to the chapel and dismounted. Lynan moved to enter first, but Ager put an arm out and stopped him. "Let Gudon go first. The priest will not be too surprised by a Chett." Gudon agreed and entered, followed by Ager and Lynan. It was dark inside, and the priest would probably not have made much of any of them. There were low bench seats on either side of the large room they found themselves in, with an aisle running between them. At the end of the aisle, and facing the seats, was a plain, strongly-made chair. Behind that was a wall with a doorway.

"The back entrance?" Gudon asked.

"No," Ager said. "The main room is not as long as the building. Probably the priest's quarters."

Gudon went up to the door and knocked. They heard a chair scraping and then footsteps. The door opened and they were confronted by a huge man who seemed to fill the doorway. He looked down at Gudon and blinked in surprise.

"Good Father," Gudon said in his sweetest tone, "I hope we did not disturb your mediation?"

"Not at all," the priest said, a little too quickly for Lynan's ears. "How may I help you?"

"I come seeking information. I was directed to you."

"Really? Information of a spiritual sort, I assume?"

Gudon shook his head. "Alas, no. We were looking for information about the area; such things as the number of towns and villages, and the number of their inhabitants."

"I am a priest, not a mapmaker."

"You are also learned and well-traveled," Ager said, stepping from behind Gudon.

The priest did a good job of trying to hide his shock, and Lynan was sure it was not at the sight of the crookback. Working in a farming area like this, he was sure to see many with permanent injury of one kind or another; it was Ager himself, and the priest recognized him.

"I recognize your accent," Ager continued quickly. "You come from one of the villages to the east of Kendra."

"You have been there?" the priest asked, trying to sound interested, and to divert the course of discussion.

"No," Ager admitted, "but I have a companion who comes from a village in that area."

"Do you know the name of the vill—"

"Her name is Jenrosa Alucar," Ager said over him. "And before you ask, my name is Ager Parmer."

"Truth, mine is Gudon," said the Chett.

"Ah, yes." Fine beads of sweat had appeared on the priest's forehead. "I am Father Hern." He tried to peer behind Ager. "And your other friend?"

"Friend?" Ager asked. "Yes, I suppose he is. And my lord. Your Majesty?"

Lynan now stepped aside so the priest could see him clearly. "You already know who I am, don't you, Father Hern?"

The priest looked as if he was about to faint. Gudon reached out and took one of his arms, then helped him retreat into the back room and into a seat. Lynan took the only other seat, on the other side of a narrow table, and nodded to Gudon and Ager. His two companions straightened the priest's chair so Hern was forced to look directly at Lynan.

"And I am?"

"You are Prince Lynan Rosetheme."

"Almost," Lynan said. "I am *King* Lynan Rosetheme."

"Ah," the priest said, and looked away from Lynan's gaze.

"We need a map of the region," Lynan went on. "I want every town and village marked on it. I also want any other features peculiar to the area that you know of."

"Peculiar features?"

"Well, there is a gorge, I believe, some leagues west of here. You could put that on, for example."

"Elstra Gorge," Father Hern said, his voice tight.

"Pretty place," Lynan said. "I believe."

"Yes."

"Have you any paper? Pens? I'm afraid I didn't travel with any."

The priest stood up, but Ager forced him back down with some force. Everyone heard the heavy jingling come from one of the priest's pockets.

"Don't get up, Father Hern. Gudon will get them for you."

"In the cupboard behind you."

Gudon went to the cupboard and scrabbled around before returning with some roughly cut square sheets of paper as well as pen and ink. He placed them before the priest.

"Leave out no detail," Lynan said. "Even if you think it is unimportant."

"May I ask what this is for?" Father Hern asked.

"No."

The priest unscrewed the ink bottle, dipped the pen, and started, quickly sketching in the Barda River, then the gorge and Esquidion, then filling the spaces in between with other names. He paused after a few minutes and considered his work, added a few other items, then slipped the paper across to Lynan.

Lynan blew on it to dry the ink and picked it up. He thought the scale was pretty right, judging by where he placed the gorge and Esquidion in relation to the river, but he did not know the area as well as Gudon and he handed the map to the Chett. Gudon scanned it and nodded.

"It is good work, Father," Lynan said. "You were well trained. Did you learn under Primate Giros Northam?"

"No. The Primate did not do a lot of teaching when I was a novice. It was the time of the Slaver War, and he was involved in other things."

"As were my friends here," Lynan said. "I was too young, of course."

"Your father served valiantly."

"You knew him?"

"Only by reputation. I saw him once with your mother . . . Queen Usharna."

"Did you admire him?"

"Very much," Father Hern said quickly, and Lynan believed him. "No one in our church could help admiring the man who destroyed the slavers."

Lynan nodded, pursed his lips. "For his sake, then, I may not kill you."

The priest froze, his hands gripping the arms of his chair so tightly his knuckles went white. "I'm sorry if I've done something to offend you, Pri—King Lynan—"

"Stand up!" Lynan ordered, and Father Hern stood up. "Empty your cloak pockets!"

"My cloak pockets?"

"Empty them."

He did; first the left, some chalk, dried fruit, flint and steel; then the right, a single leather bag.

"Open the bag and empty it."

Gold and silver coins spilled, rolled and clinked on to the table. Lynan picked one up and studied it. "Haxan."

Father Hern's face went white.

"Where is she?"

"She?"

"Queen Charion. Where is she?"

"I've never seen Queen Charion. I couldn't even tell you what she looks like."

"I see. How long have you lived in Esquidion?"

"Lived here? About ten years."

Lynan turned to Gudon. "Return to the column. Bring it in. Burn this town to the ground. If anyone resists, kill them."

Lasthear took Jenrosa to a smithy she discovered in the poorer section of Daavis which possessed a small furnace and produced iron household goods. Lasthear asked the blacksmith if she could demonstrate to Jenrosa her magic, while he worked.

"Magic?" the smithy asked nervously.

"To speed up your work and improve the quality of the iron."

The smithy grinned and readily agreed.

Lasthear said to Jenrosa, "If you try to do both—make the furnace work more efficiently and improve the quality of the iron—you will greatly increase the stress you place on yourself without necessarily succeeding. It is best to concentrate on getting the magic right for one or the other."

Lasthear stood as near to the furnace as possible and started a chant. Whether it was the magic or simply his belief in the chant's efficacy, the blacksmith began working more energetically. In a short period he made two ladles and a cooking pot. Lasthear withdrew from the smithy to cool off. Sweat poured off her.

"Why don't you take your shirt off?" Jenrosa asked.

"What, here?" Lasthear asked, widening her arms to include the city. "Amongst all these *strangers?*" She was astounded.

"But at the High Sooq—"

"At the High Sooq, I was working with my people. They have seen naked magickers working next to foundries all their lives. Here, everyone wears clothes all the time."

"Maybe you could start a new fashion," Jenrosa said, a smile tugging at the corners of her mouth.

"Or a riot," Lasthear countered.

Jenrosa's smile broadened. "Well, at least you wouldn't get so hot."

Lasthear harrumphed and led the way back to the furnace. The new ladles and cooking pot had been placed on a work bench for the blacksmith's son to finish off. The blacksmith looked eagerly at Lasthear. "What next, Madam Magicker?"

"Have you something especially difficult or expensive to make?"

The man scratched his head. "Begging your pardon, but everything's difficult in a small furnace like this. Inherited it from my da, o'course, like most in my line, and seeing as how I'm wedged between Orvin the baker with his oven and Milt the tanner with his vats, there's no room left to expand—"

"Or something expensive?" Lasthear prompted.

"Well, the last big job I did was a mirror base for some cheap lady near the palace. Cheap for her, I mean. It paid off nearly all my debts—"

"But you have nothing like that now?"

"No, except for a new pan for Orvin next door who wants to try out a flatter loaf."

"What's so expensive about that?"

"Not expensive so much as extra difficult. It can't have ribbing or beading on the bottom, and has to be the right size. I keep on putting it off until I have more time, but the time don't come and Orvin's getting impatient."

"He's not the only one," Lasthear said under her breath. "Let's do it now. I'll help you."

The blacksmith grinned and started preparing for the task.

"I'm going to be using the second kind of chant," Lasthear told Jenrosa. "Although it takes more concentration to get right, it's slower and more evenly paced and in the end doesn't make you as tired . . . or sweaty."

Lasthear started singing, and the blacksmith, instead of setting to with urgent energy, fell in with the pattern of the chant. He worked carefully, methodically, but never tiring, and Jenrosa wondered if the chant might have an effect on the blacksmith as much as the fire.

Jenrosa moved from the side to stand behind the blacksmith,

taking care not to get in the way of his swinging hammer, and stared into the furnace. The flames whipped around inside their cage, driven by nature and magic, the heat buffeting Jenrosa like an invisible sea. She found herself almost hypnotized and, without meaning to, started picking up the chant, her voice rising and falling with Lasthear's. After a while she noticed there was something in the furnace that was neither flame nor ingot, something that writhed with the fire but was apart from it, more substantial. She tried to focus on the shape and her voice changed without her meaning it to, becoming deeper, stronger, and Lasthear's own voice followed like a stream running into a river.

The shape inside the furnace and the flames around it started to merge into something altogether new. Jenrosa could see buildings now, and the flickering silhouettes of people fleeing, burning, tumbling in the dirt. She tried to look away, caught a glimpse of the blacksmith hauling out his iron and hammering it, sparks waterfalling in the air, and then found her gaze following the iron as it reentered the furnace, saw again the terrible scene of carnage and destruction. She tried to bring the chant back to Lasthear's original song, but it resisted her. She felt as if she was pushing herself into a windstorm, and the air smelled of burning flesh. The fire got brighter and brighter and the vision was swept away, replaced with a face made up of the whitest, hottest flames, the face of Lynan peering out at hers.

She screamed, then reeled back and out of the smithy. She heard a terrible oath, a hammer falling, Lasthear calling to her, and then she was out in the cool air, still screaming and falling to the ground. Rough hands caught her, let her down gently. There were more cries. Water hissing and steaming. Lasthear's voice, attenuated, whispery, in her ear.

She opened her eyes. The blacksmith hovered over her, looking frightened and angry. His son cowered behind him. The smithy was filled with smoke. Lasthear put an arm under her back and helped her to her feet.

"The pan's right ruined, Madam Magicker, and that was my most expensive piece of iron."

"I'll replace the iron," Lasthear said to him over her shoulder, "and make sure the pan is done right next time."

"I don't know what your friend did, but it sure as hell made things hot in there. I think even the furnace might be cracked."

"My clan will pay for a new furnace, blacksmith. A better one."

The man nodded dumbly, not having anything more to say, and shepherded his son away.

"What happened?" she asked Jenrosa.

"You don't know?"

Lasthear breathed deeply. "How could I know? What you are capable of is so far beyond my experience . . ."

"Don't say that. Don't ever say that."

Lasthear stared at Jenrosa with a perplexed expression and did not seem to know what to say. Eventually, she managed, "Can you stand by yourself?"

"I think so." Jenrosa took all her weight on her feet; she felt dizzy but did not reach out for Lasthear. "I'm sorry for what I did to the blacksmith. Was anyone hurt?"

"No. I remember feeling a change in the song, something deeper and more powerful than anything I'd ever experienced before, then you stumbled backward out of the smithy. At the same time the heat became too much for all of us. I heard a crack, saw the blacksmith throw something in the tub of water, and get out with his son."

People were starting to mill around, and the blacksmith was babbling something to them and pointing at the two magickers.

"Let's get away," Lasthear said. "We need to talk about this."

Slowly at first, but with quickened pace as Jenrosa regained her senses, they made their way back to the palace and Jenrosa's room, getting a ewer of cold beer and two mugs from the kitchen on the way.

Lasthear poured the beer and, as she passed the mug to Jenrosa, asked, "Can you tell me what you saw in the furnace?"

"How do you know I saw anything?"

"When the song changed, I watched you very carefully. I know you saw something in there."

"I saw a village or town burning, and people on fire. And then I *smelled* it all burning."

"No wonder you pulled away," Lasthear said.

Jenrosa nodded and did not mention seeing Lynan's face at the end. It was that, not the horror of what she had seen before, that frightened her so much she was able to end the chant.

Lasthear looked down into her own mug as if searching for some private vision. "You have a destiny, Jenrosa Alucar, whether you like it or not."

"Enough," Jenrosa said angrily.

"No, it is not enough. You keep on hiding away from it, but all you do is hurt yourself more by denying what you are capable of. You keep on stumbling on aspects of your power that are waking now you have been taught how to use magic properly. You cannot avoid what you are. You cannot avoid whatever destiny is laid before you."

"There is no such thing as destiny. We make our own choices, decide our own future."

"Undeniably," Lasthear agreed, and Jenrosa looked up, surprised. "You make the mistake of assuming destiny is set down as law, that destiny demands only one path."

"Doesn't it? Isn't that what destiny means?"

"Your destiny is where you arrive. How you get there is entirely up to you."

Jenrosa laughed bitterly. "So it is set down as law? There is no change to the ending, only the road I take to get there."

"Which ending? The ending you saw in the river at Kolbee? Or in the fire in our camp during the siege? Can you be sure they are endings, Jenrosa, or merely crossroads on your way there?"

Jenrosa looked up at Lasthear, desperation in her eyes. "I see blood. All the blood of the world. That is all."

Lasthear paled. "I thought it might be something like that."

"What does it mean?"

"Death."

"Of course, it means death," Jenrosa spat, unable to control her fear and anger anymore.

"A close death," Lasthear continued.

Jenrosa shuddered involuntarily. "I know. I'm sorry."

Lasthear's eyes widened with understanding. "And you know whose, don't you?"

Jenrosa nodded savagely. "Yes. I've known since Kolbee. And every time I get a vision, it is the same. I know whose death it is." She closed her eyes in pain and grief. "And I know I will be the cause of it."

The very woods that protected their hideaway from easy detection also allowed the enemy to get within arrow shot without being seen. The first sign of anything awry was the scream of a sentry followed by the whistling of several hundred arrows falling among the boulders and trees. Charion and Galen sprung from their cave near the summit of the hill, swords in hand, looking every which way to determine the main axis of the attack. Arrows clattered on the ground nearby. More screams. Soldiers scrabbling for gear, sliding for cover.

"How did they find us?" Galen cried.

Charion did not answer. It was suddenly very quiet. There were no more flights of arrows, no more cries of the dying. Even the wounded seemed to be holding on to their breath.

"What is happening?" Galen asked.

Charion waved him silent. She could hear movement coming from the south side of the hill, from where the river ran closest. She started moving downslope, but Galen grabbed her arm. "Don't be a fool."

Charion twisted out of his grip and glared at him, but she moved no farther.

"Get down, your Majesty!" cried a nearby soldier.

"I agree," Galen said, and squatted behind a low bush, pulling the reluctant Charion down beside him.

"That's twice you've grabbed at my royal person this morning," she hissed at him.

He looked at her amazed. She had not reacted like that when they first woke this morning. "What about—"

"There's a difference," she said coolly, and turned her attention downslope again. She could see nothing among the vegetation and rocks, but she knew from the sound that there were a lot of enemy troops coming their way. Another flight of arrows ricocheted off rocks, slapped into leaves and tree trunks, into hands and faces.

"We're in trouble," she said bitterly. "We didn't have enough warning to prepare any proper defense. Our people are scattered all over this hill."

"Do you think we're surrounded?"

"They'd need five thousand to encircle this place completely, and we'd have seen that many coming."

"Then we can retreat."

"We can, we have horses. Our recruits can get off the hill, but once on flat ground they'll be pursued and cut down by the Chetts."

"They could surrender."

"Would you accept a surrender after having one of your columns slaughtered."

Galen breathed out heavily. "No. But the recruits have a better chance than you say. They can get away in the woods—the Chetts have to go on foot there, too—and our people are locals."

Charion shook her head. "I don't know . . ."

"What will happen if we stay here?"

"We'll die," she admitted. "Like we should have died in Daavis."

"That's an incredibly stupid and callous thing to say," Galen said.

She touched his face. "Yes, I'm sorry. We have to save as many of these farmers and townspeople as possible. If only we'd had more time, I could have done something with them."

"You already have. We've tagged the grass wolf, and with luck we'll get away with it." He risked looking around the bush. "Still clear. You go right, spreading the word. I'll go left. We'll meet on the other side, then descend to the horses."

Charion nodded, leaned forward, and quickly kissed Galen on the lips. "I think I love you," she said breathlessly and then was gone.

"Thanks," Galen said to empty air, and went the opposite way.

Lynan gazed at the blood on his hands. It had gone dark and gathered in the creases in his palms until his hands looked like they had been crisscrossed by red spiderwebs.

"The arrows are having an effect," Ager, squatting next to him, said to no one in particular.

Gudon grunted in agreement, but Lynan ignored him. He was absorbed by the color of his hands. He noticed the blood had also crusted under his fingernails. He curiously sniffed the ends of his fingers.

"Priest's blood," he muttered to himself. It smelled no different to him than anyone else's, which was a disappointment. He had expected there to be something special about it, tinged with the sacred. He remembered the priest bleeding after he had stabbed him. At first he had been shocked, as much by his own action as by the amount of blood, but that had changed to a terrible, secret glee, and for a fraction of a moment he understood Silona's desire for warm blood.

"Lynan, it is almost time," Ager said to him.

Lynan looked at him, blinked. His friend was a little out of focus. He blinked again. "What?"

"To attack. Our arrows won't last forever."

"Of course," Lynan said, and then he shouted: "Enough!" The Chetts put their bows away. He turned to Ager. "Now we see if all your short sword training with the Red Hands and Ocean clan will pay off."

"It will," Ager said confidently, drawing his short sword and kissing its blade. He met Lynan's gaze. "Just give the word."

Lynan drew his own sword and stood. "Up the hill!" he roared, and his voice was met with the bloodthirsty wolf calls of nearly two thousand Chetts as they followed Lynan and Ager and Gudon up the slope. Arrows fell among them, some finding a target, but not enough to slow them down. They hit the first hastily organized ring of defenders like a flood water, running over it easily, stabbing any who stayed to fight, shouting curses at those running away.

Lynan paused to survey the summit, and saw that the defenders everywhere were fleeing, but there was some order to it. For a moment he feared an ambush, then realized they had had no time to set up one. They had been ordered to run. They were getting away from him, from his vengeance. Anger boiled up in him. He screamed and set off in pursuit, leaping over rocks, clambering over boulders that would stop anyone else. He fell on two or three running defenders at a time, stabbing with his sword in one hand and dagger in the other, then rushing on to the next group. Word spread ahead of him, cries of fear and despair, and he used the sound to track them down and kill them. He reached the summit before anyone else and looked down the other side.

Too many for him to catch up with them all, and his brave Chetts were too far behind to make any difference. He turned and shouted for his warriors to go back down the hill, get their horses and circle around the hill; that way at least they would trap some before they reached the relative safety of the woods along the river. The command was passed on. Then he resumed the chase, his skin tight across his face, his eyes yellow with wild fury, bounding down the opposite slope like a goat, from boulder to boulder, flying over the deserting enemy and landing in front of them, killing, tearing, paying them back for daring to attack *his* soldiers in *his* kingdom. As the sun went down, he made his way to the bottom of the hill, his arms and hair red with blood, his lips and cheeks flecked with gore.

Charion pulled hard on the reins and her horse wheeled around. Galen, behind her, took the reins from her.

"What do you think you are doing? The Chetts can't be more than half a league behind us!"

She looked wildly at him. "God's death, man, can't you hear him?"

Galen swallowed back his fear. "Of course I can hear him! The whole bloody world can hear him! He's more demon than man! What are you going to do?"

"Stop him! He's slaughtering my soldiers, hunting them down like karak!"

"Not all of them, Charion! Most will escape. It is almost dark and they are already reaching the woods. You will only die if you try and confront Lynan by yourself."

"What difference does it make?" she cried at him. "You told me what he did to your knights. Could I stop him if I had a huge army behind me?"

Galen shook his head. "I don't know—"

"Then let's just end it now! Why keep on running?"

"Because I'm not giving up hope, and I'm not going to let you give up hope either."

Charion stopped resisting him, and he pulled her horse around again and kicked his own into a trot. After a while, she took the reins and rode beside him. He could hear her crying softly in the night, then found himself doing the same.

Lynan met his army at the bottom of the hill. He did not know how many he had killed, but he was still filled with an uncontrollable rage. He stared wide-eyed at his Chetts, and they could not meet his gaze. Even Gudon had to look away from him. Only Ager One-Eye, who had seen more horrors in his time than any in that group, could match him.

"Are you all right?" he asked.

Lynan nodded stiffly. "Yes. No sign of Charion?"

"No."

Some of his Red Hands pushed a group of men toward him. They were wounded, exhausted, obviously terrified of Lynan.

"Who are they?"

"Prisoners, your Majesty," one of the Red Hands said.

"Did I say anything about taking prisoners?"

The Red Hands glanced at each other, then shook their heads.

"We should take them back to Daavis with us for interrogation," Ager said.

"For what purpose?" Lynan demanded. "Their little army is scattered, their leader fled. Why keep these traitors alive?"

"Traitors?" said one of the prisoners, then blanched when he realized what he had done.

Lynan took a step toward him, his hand outstretched to take him by the throat. A young, redheaded man. Lynan stopped in midstride.

"I know you," he said under his breath.

The man started shaking uncontrollably.

"I have seen you somewhere before," Lynan continued. His hand shot out, grasped the man around the jaw, and pulled his face right next to his own. "What is your name?"

The man could not help staring into those yellow eyes, could not help being aware of the enemy's hard, white skin, could not help soiling himself in fear and pain.

"Answer me!" Lynan cried.

Ager put a hand on his shoulder. "Lynan, he can't speak. You have broken his jaw."

Lynan threw the man to the ground and drew his sword. With one savage swipe he decapitated the prisoner. Hot blood hissed over him. He bent down to pick up the head by its red hair. He brought the face right up against his again. "I *damn* well do know you." He turned to Ager. "You have my horse?"

Ager made a signal and a Chett brought his mare up for him. He mounted easily, still holding the severed head in one fist. He glanced at his Red Hands. "We don't need any prisoners. Kill them all."

As the column turned and started its way back to Daavis, all could hear the screams of the prisoners being slaughtered behind them. Gudon rode next to Ager, and together the two of them watched Lynan in the van.

"What's he doing?" Gudon asked.

"Talking to the head," Ager said flatly.

"He called the prisoners 'traitors,' " Gudon said.

"And when he was interrogating the priest, he introduced himself as King Lynan. He's never done that before."

"Truth, my friend." Gudon licked his lips nervously. "Tell me, Ager Parmer, clan chief, do you recognize our Lynan any more?"

Ager felt a spasm pass along his deformed spine, a sensation he had not experienced for longer than he could remember. He knew what it meant. He was learning to be afraid again.

19

THE voices of one thousand Chetts in mourning rose into the air. Standing perfectly still by their mounts, their heads back, their mouths open, they cried the song of the dead in perfect unison. The ululating wail seemed to come from the very soil of the Oceans of Grass itself. Above them, no bird flew; around them, no animal moved.

On the ground surrounding the one thousand mourners were the bones of thousands of Chetts, the remains of Eynon's clan. The strong summer sun and scavengers had made the bones white as ivory; they could be seen shimmering in the grass from leagues away. When Eynon first saw the field, he knew in his heart what it was, although nothing in his experience could have prepared him. His whole body had become as heavy as iron, and yet he had still rode on, still made himself lead the survivors of his clan to this field of death.

When the song of the dead was finished, the Chetts mounted and gathered around Eynon. It seemed to him that in that moment that all of them, even the six hundred who belonged to Lynan's lancers and Red Hands, would follow him to the end of the earth to avenge what had been done here.

So be it, he thought. *Lynan gave me his boon to carry my revenge as far as I wanted, and I want to take it to its home.*

"We gather no bones," he told them. "There will be no funeral pyre. This field we call Solstice Way will forever more be the graveyard of our dead. No cattle will ever feed here, no other clan will ever call this its territory. From now until the end of the Oceans of Grass, this is where the Horse clan will come every summer to offer the song of the dead so the ghosts of our families and friends can rest knowing they have not been forgotten, and that their deaths did not go unavenged."

There was no cheering, no taking up of his cry. Eynon turned his mount west, and slowly so as not to disturb any of the remains, the whole column made its way out.

If Dekelon had not been with him the whole time the Saranah had been on the Oceans of Grass, he would not have recognized Amemun. The Amanite had lost so much weight he was now as trim as any of his desert warriors, he had shorn his beard back to nothing more than a stubble, and the saber he had taken from a dead Chett was now his closest friend—Dekelon was sure he talked to it at night.

The biggest change was in battle. Amemun was always among the first to charge the enemy, the one to kill the largest numbers, the one to show the least mercy.

Revenge was a wonderful thing, Dekelon thought. It had been the wind that over a century before blew his people off their rightful territory on the plains into the southern deserts, and now blew them right back again. It was the wind that drove so much of Saranah politics and society, and, as far as he could determine from the stories told by Amemun about the courts in Pila and Kendra, politics and society all over the continent. And it was the wind that blew new life into Amemun's old husk, giving him the strength and endurance of a man much younger and combining it with the hate that comes from losing not only someone you love, but someone around whom you had centered your life.

And Dekelon knew that revenge could also get in the way.

"I don't see why we can't continue," Amemun was arguing. "We can spare another hundred to take this booty back to your people. That will still give us—"

"Too few warriors," the Saranah said over him. "Every battle whittles away at our numbers. The last two attacks on Chett clans has resulted in scattering them farther west and north, not eliminating them. Word is spreading of our presence and, sooner rather than later, the clans in this part of the Oceans of Grass will combine and come after us."

"One more," Amemun pleaded. "One more attack. Your scouts have found spoor. We can catch the clan tonight, and by this time tomorrow we will all be on our way south."

Dekelon sighed heavily. He, too, wished to continue the slaughter and plunder—this had been a dream of his all his life—but he was leader of this war band, responsible for those under him and responsible for the booty they had gathered. In the season they had raged east and west across this part of the Oceans of Grass they had overrun six clans, and in the first four battles had slain every soul. But he felt in his bones that time was running out, and they were now not far from that part of the border where they had first crossed over. That was a sign, he was sure, that it was time to go back.

Still, he thought, *one more night. One more battle. If I return now, I might not see another season, might never fight another battle.*

He looked around him, at the expectant faces of his warriors. He could see it was what they wanted as well.

"Very well. One more. And then we go home."

He assigned eighty warriors, many wounded, to escort the booty from the last attack back to the southern desert, then gave orders to the scouts, who quickly ran north in the direction the spoor of the new clan had first been found. The rest of the war band gathered their weapons, fell into line, and followed behind at a far more leisurely trot.

It was a clear night with no moon. Eynon lay on his back and looked up at the sea of stars, but instead of the beauty he once saw, it now only reminded him of the field of bones he had left behind.

As many bones as there are stars, he thought.

A silhouette stood above him. He knew, without seeing the face, that it was Makon. For an instant he wondered if he had come to kill him, if that had been Lynan's plan all along, but something deep inside him told him that neither man would do a thing like that. Makon was too proud, and Lynan too confident.

"Can I talk to you?" Makon asked, sounding very young.

In fact, Eynon thought, *sounding his real age.* He sometimes forgot just how young Makon was.

"Of course, my friend," Eynon said, stressing the last word. Even as he said it, he realized it was true. He felt a little less alone.

"It's about Wennem."

"The woman we found at the Strangers' Sooq?"

Makon sat down heavily. "Yes. I can't stop thinking about her."

Eynon remembered the first time they saw her. Leaving the column outside the Sooq, he and Makon had ridden through the town asking for any information the locals might have had on the border raids. Most they talked to looked skeptically at them, not believing the Saranah would ever dare such a thing, especially now that the Chetts were united. It was not until they had nearly reached the end of the main street when an older man intercepted them.

"You are asking about the Saranah?" he said. Eynon nodded. "I have a woman in my care. You should see her."

Eynon and Makon dismounted and followed the man to his home. Inside he sat them down, gave them wine. "My name is Kayakun," he told them.

"I have heard of you," Makon said, suddenly excited. "Truth, my brother speaks of you with much praise."

"Your brother?"

"Gudon of the White Wolf clan."

"Ah, I should have recognized you." He looked at Eynon. "And I know you, chief of the Horse clan."

Eynon grunted. "You are one of Korigan's spies?"

Kayakun smiled, spread his hands. "If that's what you wish to call me, although I never spied on you."

Eynon lowered his gaze. It was true, he knew. He had learned over the last year that Korigan's spies had all operated on the fringe or completely outside the Oceans of Grass, protecting the interests of every clan. Truly, Korigan had acted as queen for all the Chetts. "You said something about a woman in your care?"

Kayakun nodded. "She came into the sooq about thirty days ago. She was on a sorry-looking mare, and so exhausted she was near death. She managed to mumble some words about a war band, but no one believed her. Those who found her brought her to me."

"They always bring you strangers?" Eynon asked.

"I am known for my interest in the world outside the sooq, even where trade is not concerned. Rare among the merchants that live here."

"Then they are not true Chetts," Eynon spat.

"Because they are concerned only with their own affairs? How long ago did that describe every clan on the plains?"

Eynon waved his hand. It was not an argument he had time for now. "The woman?" he urged.

"She is here, but she may not be able to tell you much. She was unconscious when I received her. Despite all that I could do, she did not wake for several days, and when she finally did, she could not—or would not—talk. She sits in the room I have given her, staring out the west window. She holds her hands in her lap so they do not shake."

Eynon and Makon exchanged glances. "Take me to her," Eynon said.

Kayakun led the way to a small, clean room with a low cot and a rough-made chair. Sitting on the chair was a woman who, at first impression, seemed to be very old; bent over herself, shoulders tucked in, her limbs thin and joints as angular as rocks. As they got closer, Eynon saw she was, in fact, quite young, with smooth skin and clear brown eyes that stared across the plains, searching.

He held his breath. He knew her. She was of his clan. Jenrosa Alucar had been right. His breath finally shuddered out of him. He did not realize how much he had still hoped against hope that she had been wrong.

"Wennem?"

The woman looked up at Eynon and she froze completely.

Eynon knelt down next to her and cupped her face in his hands. "Wennem? What has happened to you?"

For a long while nothing happened, and then a single tear tracked down her cheek. She opened her mouth to say something but could only make a croaking sound.

"What happened, Wennem?" Eynon gently asked again.

Kayakun left the room and returned with a cup of wine. He held the cup in front of the woman's mouth and slowly tipped some of the wine into her mouth. She sipped at it, swallowed, and lifted one hand to push the cup away. She opened her mouth again and uttered, "All dead."

"All dead?" Eynon heard his own voice crack.

She nodded slowly. "All dead," she repeated. "My husband. My baby." She grabbed Eynon's arms suddenly and shook him. "My baby! Dead!"

Eynon wrapped his arms around her and held her to him as tightly as he dared. Tears now flooded down her face, but she made no sound as the grief emptied from her and swallowed them all.

Under the stars again, Eynon said to Makon, "And what is it you are thinking about her?"

"That she should not be with us. She should have stayed at the Strangers' Sooq."

"I agree. But would you have tied her to her chair? It would have been the only way to stop her."

"No."

"I have seen you talk to her."

"I want to learn about our enemy."

"Does she tell you anything we don't already know?"

"No."

Eynon lifted himself on one elbow. "You like her."

"She has no one to look after her."

"She is a Chett. She can look after herself."

"She needs someone."

"What she needs is a strong mare and a strong sword and the opportunity to use them against the Saranah. That is what I am going to give her."

"You are her guardian."

Eynon opened his mouth to say "With all her family dead, of course I am her guardian," when he realized where Makon was trying to take the conversation. "Wennem is badly hurt," he said instead.

"I will protect her."

"What if you or she do not survive the campaign?"

"That is a risk whether or not we are together."

"How does she feel about you?"

Makon shrugged uselessly. "I am afraid to ask. It is so soon after she has lost everything she loved."

"I advise you to say nothing to her for the while. Wait."

"To see if we both survive," Makon said, nodding. "I thought you would say that."

"And you know it is what you would say if you were the clan chief and I the suitor."

Makon looked up sharply at the last word. "I am no suitor—" he started to say.

"You are Makon, commander of three troops of King Lynan's Red Hands, warrior of growing fame, son of a Truespeaker, brother of Gudon, friend of Eynon. And we are all in the middle of a war that may have no end in our lifetime, however long that may be for each of us."

Makon slumped on to his back. Eynon joined him and they both stared into the sky. After a while, Makon asked, "Did you have a wife?"

"Yes. A long time ago."

"Did you have children?"

"Two. One died in childbirth, together with his mother. The other died in the last battle against Korigan's father, taking a spear that was meant for me. She was thirteen, but already had slain three enemies."

Eynon blocked out the memories. Some pain never left, and it was best simply to ignore it, to make it a part of your life rather than the point of it. But he could shut his mind against it. He closed his eyes and saw again the faces of his wife and daughter, and even the strange cold, purple thing that had been, if only for a handful of moments, his son. He even heard again its last faint mewlings.

"Did you hear that?" Makon said, and quickly stood up.

Eynon blinked, looking up at Makon's dark shape. "What are you talking about?"

"Listen!" Makon said sharply, looking west.

Eynon stood up then and cupped his ears. For a long while there was nothing, and he was about to ask Makon what it was he had heard when a slight breeze came out of the west and he heard something faintly like crying.

"Yes. But I don't know—"

More sounds. Despair. Pain.

"God!" Eynon shouted. "It's them! It's the Saranah! They're attacking another clan!"

"So close?" Makon asked disbelievingly.

"Why not? They've obviously been ranging all along the border seeking out those clans that wander this far south in the summer and autumn. We had to come across them eventually, or their trail." He turned and shouted to the sleeping camp: "Arise! Arise! The enemy is near! The enemy is near!"

The response was almost immediate. Those still awake roused their companions, horses were saddled, gear thrown on, low fires stamped out. By the time the column was ready to ride, two scouts were galloping back from the west, breathless with their news. Eynon grabbed the first one and shouted in his face: "How far?"

The scout looked surprised that Eynon already seemed to know his news, but quickly gathered his wits. "An hour's ride, at least. I heard the fighting as soon as it started."

"An hour?" Makon cried. "We'll never make it in time."

"Gods, but we can try!" Eynon shouted, and kicked his horse into a fast trot that would eat up the leagues and still leave his mare some strength at the end for a charge. His column wheeled in behind him. Makon rode by Eynon's right-hand side, and soon after he saw a third figure sidle up beside them. He glanced around and saw the determined outline of Wennem's face; in her right hand she already gripped her sword.

Dekelon paused from the fighting and quickly looked around him. His warriors had hit from all sides, but because of the smaller size of their force now, some of the Chetts had inevitably escaped, most on horseback. Around him, some of the Saranah were starting to set alight the camp, the flames somehow making the dark night even more intense. He quickly searched for Amemun, and guessed he was in the midst of a clump of fighters that had encircled a staunch group of defenders and were gradually wearing them down. If Dekelon had his way, he would order his warriors back to send in flight after flight of arrows, but Amemun's enthusiasm for the kill was too keen and too contagious.

He should have been born one of us instead of one of those soft easterners.

He started walking among the bodies littering the ground, cutting the throats of the wounded, divesting them of any jewelry or fancy weapons. He did not have any idea how much booty his war band had gathered, but enough he was sure to set up his family for two or more generations. Already the uncrowned king of his people, he even thought about building something more permanent than the extended shack he now lived in. Something from stone imported from Aman, perhaps. Once he had a palace, no matter how small compared to the one in Pila or Kendra, it would not be long before he would be *called* king, and his family's dominance of the Saranah would be complete.

But only if he and his war band made it back to the desert.

He thought again about the escaping Chetts. Yes, it was time to go home. It would not be long before the clans in this part got together, and maybe even tried to hunt down his war band.

There were cries from the east. He looked up and grunted in surprise. Some of the Chetts had decided not to flee after all but make one last heroic charge. Amemun would be pleased.

Dekelon knelt down to pick up an interesting looking clasp, turned it this way and that to catch the light from a nearby burning wagon. Good work. Probably High Sooq made. His father had told him stories about the High Sooq, exaggerated over time, he was sure. One day he would like to see it; maybe he would when all this was over. King Dekelon, on a diplomatic mission from the Saranah to the Chetts, from the allies of victorious Queen Areava to the defeated supporters of the slain Prince Lynan. An offer of peace. He smiled to himself. For a price. He put the clasp in his belt pouch.

More cries from the east. He glanced up again and saw what was charging down on his war band.

Eynon surprised himself by staying so calm it almost felt as if he was floating above the Oceans of Grass and directing events like one of the gods. When they were still two leagues from the Chett camp, the first scattered groups of refugees flew past, wheeled, and joined the end of the column. He waited until there was only a league to go before allowing the lancers to take the van and straighten their line. Half a league to go, he gave the signal for his own clan's warriors to ride far out on the flanks, and they fanned out like the waters in a delta, streaming north and south. A quarter of a league to go, he nodded to Makon, who signaled the Red Hands to line up behind the lancers, sabers drawn. Only then, and when the enemy was less than two hundred paces away, did Eynon kick his mare into a gallop, take the lead, and lower his own sword. The lancers lowered their spears and charged, and suddenly earth and sky shook with the beating of their hooves. The Red Hands gave the cry of the White Wolf, and it echoed over the plains, freezing the blood of their enemies.

They rode through the camp like a wild wind; nothing opposing them could withstand the charge. The lancers skewered fleeing Saranah, who had never experienced anything like charging cavalry, piercing hearts and kidneys and lungs. Then the Red Hands hewed in, swinging their sabers in great arcs that lopped off heads as easily as limbs. Once through the camp the lancers wheeled and charged again, their line more ragged, their targets now diving closing close to the ground and coming up only to aim sword blow at the horses' bellies, but behind the lancers the Red Hands, now dismounted, caught and killed them. There seemed to be no escape east or west, so the Saranah with any wits left fled north and south, straight into the waiting arrows of the Horse clan archers.

Then, as quickly as it had started, the battle was over. Lancers rode through the camp looking for more enemy, the Red Hands sorted through the wounded to save what Chetts they could and killing anyone else, and the horse archers slowly closed the ring. At the end of it, Eynon and Makon were in the center of the camp, feeling as if there should have been more to it, more slaughter and blood, more to make up for all the death and destruction the

Saranah had caused their people. Some of their warriors wept that they had not themselves found an enemy to slay.

The whole time Eynon still sensed himself apart from it all, and he felt cheated. His burning hate had hid under his terrible calm and was not satiated. It filled him so completely he thought he would burst.

"Here," Makon said, moving one of the enemy corpses with his foot.

"What have you found?" Eynon asked tonelessly.

"This is no Saranah."

Eynon leaned over the body. "I know that dress. I have seen it at the Strangers' Sooq when I was a boy. This is an Amanite."

"Rich clothing," Makon said, sorting through it. "Some jewelry. A Chett . . . saber." He pulled something off a belt and held it up for Eynon. "And this little pretty."

Eynon handled the dagger, slipped it out of its sheath and touched the blade to his tongue. "This was a nobleman, or someone connected to a noble family. This is good steel, not forged. Rainbow steel. Gold-inlaid hilt."

Makon grunted. "Now we know who financed a war band this size."

Eynon felt his muscles suddenly relax. It was all right. There was more to come. "Now we know where to take our revenge," he said with something like joy.

In the morning, while Eynon was talking with the survivors of the Chett clan they had saved, Makon went to find Wennem. He found her squatting next to the corpse of the Amanite, and she was staring into his face as if trying to discover something there. Makon knelt next to her and hesitantly, gently, put a hand on her shoulder.

"Are you all right?"

"He saved my life," she said.

Makon blinked at her. "This man?"

"When they attacked the Horse clan, this man killed the Saranah who was going to slay me, then told me to run."

She gripped the stubble around the Amanite's jaw and moved it up and down to open and close his mouth. Dried blood cracked between his lips. "Why?" she asked the corpse. "Won't you tell me?" She started working the jaw more violently, and Makon heard the muscles click from rigor mortis.

"No, Wennem," Makon said. "Stop it."

Instead of stopping, she grabbed the man's white hair with her other hand and started pulling the face apart. "Why won't you tell me?" she screamed at it.

Makon grabbed her arms and tried dragging her away, but she stood suddenly and twisted out of his grip, drew her saber, and brought it down with one graceful, heavy blow against the Amanite's neck. The head rolled away, and dark, thick blood seeped onto the grass.

"I wanted to die with my husband and baby!" she cried, and fell to her knees, using both her hands to drive the saber point through the man's chest. She hung onto the grip and was suddenly overwhelmed by racking sobs. This time, when the tears came so did the wailing, and it tore at Makon's heart to hear it. He knelt beside her again and put his arms around her shoulders. She cried a while longer, then slumped against him, burying her head in his shoulder.

20

IN the throne room of Areava Rosetheme, surrounded by the pomp of the court and the most powerful and influential of Kendran citizenry dressed in all their finery, Orkid Gravespear found himself dwelling on his poor dead nephew.

Orkid felt guilty he was not able to grieve for him the way he wanted to. Sendarus had been in so many ways the son he had desired, and had been the linchpin in his brother's plan to raise Aman from vassal state to equal partner with Kendra in the kingdom of Grenda Lear. And yet, instead of grieving, he was wondering who could count all the possibilities in one life?

He watched Areava sitting on her throne, the chancellor in him admiring the manner in which she carried out her official duties, the bearing she maintained, her aloofness and majesty, and at the same time the man in him beholding the woman he knew he loved beyond almost all else.

Almost all else, he told himself, knowing that his work for Aman had been the reason behind everything he had done in his adult life.

Perhaps until now, he added, recognizing that the death of Sendarus had released the full strength of his feelings for Areava, feelings he had suspected for many years but always held at bay.

Well, now I can love in the name of duty.

If Amemun were here now, he would turn to him and ask him about the possibilities contained in one life, and he could almost hear the man's voice in his ear saying, "Many possibilities, but always one choice."

He thought he felt his friend's presence then, and he half-turned to check over his shoulder. A member of the Twenty Houses stood there, ignoring him, her attention fully on the queen. His eyes settled again on Areava, seeing beauty and strength and honor in her features, in her voice, in her actions. These days, even when she was nowhere near him, he found his thoughts settling on her, disturbing his peace and concentration. He recognized what he felt was passion, and smiled ruefully to think that Amemun would admire the elegance of duty and passion combining while still being confused by the latter; Amemun had never had any time for passion.

Orkid now made excuses to be with Areava. When once he would blithely take care of every little detail in his duty as chancellor, he would now store them up as items for discussion in his private meetings with the queen. When she held something, he imagined it was his hand; when she lightly touched something, he imagined it was his cheek; when she spoke, he imagined her words were just for him. When he saw the golden light of the sun reflect off glass or stone, he thought of Areava's yellow hair.

He was a child again, he knew. In so many ways helpless and exposed to feelings against which he no longer had the defense of duty. He found himself obsessed by all the possibilities now contained in his life and the knowledge that they were all meaningless without Areava herself making the single choice he so desperately wanted her to make: to love him in return.

Dejanus did not dare be at the funeral pyre himself; it had taken too many gold pieces to get the innkeeper of the Lost Sailor Tavern to keep quiet the fact he had been with Ikanus the night she had died. Or that her body had been covered in terrible bruises and her left cheekbone fractured. Still, when he found out from one of the tavern's waiters—and another of his informants—that Ikanus' ashes had been thrown over the sea near the harbor so that some of them might be blown by the wind or carried by the currents to her home province of Lurisia, he made sure he visited the spot and threw a last gold coin into the water to help her on her way. It soothed his conscience, and even helped him raise a tear.

But, he sighed to himself as he turned away from the sea and headed back to the palace, it had been her fault.

He was elemental, he thought. Wild and pure, his feelings as original as life itself, not bound by social constraints or self-deception or strange customs. He would pass through this world untainted, letting be when let be, but reacting without regret like a terrible storm to any threat.

In the warm autumn heat, with the city strong and proud around him, with the palace of Kendra rising over the world, he was afraid of nothing. He liked the day much more than the night; by day everything was plainly visible, deception could be exposed, he could stride through the streets sure and confident of his own power and his willingness to use it. On a day like this, he could even confront Orkid.

Except on this day there was no need. He was commander of the Great Army. He would be famous throughout the world. Dejanus the Conqueror. Even the name of the vaunted General Elynd Chisal would fade in comparison; it was ironic that this would happen at the expense of the General's own son. Who was also the son of that hag Usharna, he reminded himself, the great anti-slaver, the great anti-mercenary.

"The Great Bitch," he smirked to himself.

He raised his eyes to the palace where the new bitch lived, Usharna's whelp. When he had finished with Lynan and his rabble of Chett nomads she could not but help look to him for her security. He would be the most powerful man in the kingdom. Even Orkid Gravespear, chancellor, Amanite, enemy, would shrink in the shadow Dejanus would cast over the kingdom.

On that day, on that glorious day, he would never be frightened of anything ever again.

For the first time in his life Olio felt responsible for himself. It was a strange, partly unwelcome feeling. He had tasted responsibility before, toward his sister especially, and later toward the sick and dying he believed he could heal, but he saw now it had been a hollow thing because he had not understood the need to take charge of his own fate, that entry into true adulthood that came with a clear understanding of your own mortality and vulnerability to external events.

The moment of realization had come that morning when he was dressing. He had finished putting on his clothes and was replacing the Key of the Heart around his neck. He saw it reflected in the dress mirror and it caught his attention. Such a simple, beautiful amulet. It had stolen his mind and only reluctantly surrendered it back to him. It had been his fault. He had been a child playing with a thing of power, and had escaped by the thinnest of threads.

His eyes had moved up from the amulet to meet his own gaze, and for an instant he did not recognize the man standing before him. It was that surprise of meeting his own self—older, wiser, and wounded—that made him realize no one except he could be responsible for his own life. That part of him that was a prince of the realm would be spent in service to the kingdom, but that part that belonged to him and him alone he could now share or keep apart as he saw fit.

He went to his desk and sorted through the papers there. They were minutes from the council, left for him by Harnan Beresard. He had a lot to catch up with. He glanced outside. The sun was shining, the air was warm. He would rather go down to the harbor and stare at the sea, watch the ships leave with filled sails, listen to the seagulls and kestrels calling overhead.

No. Later perhaps, after the day's council meeting, and he could not faithfully attend that until he read up on the meeting he had missed. Still, that did not mean he could not enjoy the sun. He picked up the papers and left his chambers, heading for the courtyard in the church's wing of the palace. When he got there, he saw two novices in one corner speaking softly to one another, and a priest sitting under a tree, praying softly. Olio sat on a stone bench without shade across it and started reading. A short while later he stopped. While a part of his mind had been dealing with the dry recordings of the secretary, teasing out the most important details and subconsciously arranging them into some kind of overall picture, another part had been preoccupied with a question he had been asking himself ever since he had recovered, but which in light of his decision to accept all his responsibilities now took on greater urgency.

What was he to do with the Key of the Heart?

Powl studied the sheet in front of him. On it, he had carefully inscribed all the letters he had deciphered from the embossed spines of the volumes in Colanus' tower. It had taken many days of careful and secretive work, using the lightest paper he could find placed over each spine and gently rubbed with charcoal. He had checked inside the volumes themselves to make sure each symbol he copied actually existed somewhere in clear text, then arranged each group in rows according to their volume's place in the tower shelf. One hundred and twenty groups in all.

There were forty different symbols, seventeen of which he recognized from the common Theare alphabet. In thirty-one of the groups these symbols appeared together without any of the unrecognizable ones. At first, the discovery had excited him, but almost instantly realized the groups still made no sense to him. What did KELORA mean, for example, or KADRIAL? These were not words he knew, and there was no one in his experience with more knowledge of the world and everything in it.

He understood in an abstract way that he was giving himself this problem to solve because the most important problem in his life—discovering the name of God—was proving so elusive. He still held on to the faint possibility that these volumes with their secret and arcane knowledge might provide him with that name, but at the same time knew deep in his heart that the profane, no matter how extraordinary, would never reveal the sacred.

Nevertheless, there was a great mystery here, one never solved by all the prelates, magickers, and primates that had come before him. To be the first since Colanus himself to read the volumes, or even a portion of a single page, would be exhilarating.

Placing one slim hand on the one volume he had brought from the tower to his own room, he returned his attention to the sheet, his eye tracing each symbol and then scanning down each column of groups, looking for any clue that might open a window—just a crack—into this ancient language.

There was a knock on his door. He quickly folded the sheet and tucked it into the volume from the tower, then hid the volume itself under a stack of heavy books from the church library.

"Yes?"

Father Rown entered. "Here are Harnan's minutes to the last council meeting and the agenda for the meeting at noon. I've gone over them as you requested, and made some notations in the column for your attention."

Powl took the papers. "Thank you."

Rown nodded and started closing the door.

"Father?" Rown popped his head back into the room. "I am very grateful for your diligence and patience on my behalf."

"Thank you, your Grace," Rown said, smiling in surprise, and left.

Powl looked at the minutes, checked the notations made by

Rown, glanced at the agenda. Nothing unexpected. He scanned the pages quickly to make sure he had not missed anything. That's when he saw it. He stopped, looked up to clear his vision, and looked down again. It was still there. A pattern. In fact, two patterns. The first was Harnan's habit of adding a mark, which in and of itself had no meaning, to denote the start of each main point in the minutes. The second was the use of another mark, also without any meaning in and of itself, to separate items in the new agenda. Not all symbols represented letters, and perhaps not all groups of letters represented words. With sudden excitement he put the papers aside and dug out the sheet from the Colanus volume. What if it were the same here? What if, for example, two of the groups he could transcribe did not represent KELORA and KADRIEL but ELORA and ADRIEL, and the K symbol was nothing more than extra emphasis or even some kind of stylistic decoration? What if the K symbol represented an entire idea or thought and not a single sound?

God help me! He slumped back in his chair, his excitement evaporating as quickly as it had come. How could he possibly explore all the possible variants? He would need a dozen lifetimes. What had he been thinking?

He cursed himself. The problem was he had not been thinking. He had been avoiding those issues he most needed to confront because of his guilt at the way he had gained the primacy. With his own hands, the hands with which he wrote sermons and meaningless entries for the Book of Days, he had suffocated his predecessor. He had committed a murder in the name of God but for his own sake. His mind was occupying itself in inconsequential detail while his soul was lost altogether.

He picked up the sheet, ready to tear it in two, but stopped himself. He could not let this go. Profane or not, irrelevant or not, it was a mystery, and if he could not solve the mystery of God's name, then at least he could try and solve another. And it would not be just for himself. He was a priest and a learned man, the two occupations so closely related they were almost the same thing in his mind, so using his learning to increase knowledge for knowledge's sake was not simply a profane act but touched on something indefinably yet tangibly sacred.

The sun was slanting almost directly through his window. It was nearly noon. He hid the sheet again, covered the ancient volume.

He would come back to it later. He would find the window to this great secret and open it, and who knew hat he would learn?

Matters were almost under control again.

Areava sat at the head of the council table, aware her kingdom had been damaged but knowing it was still largely intact. She and the state had received terrible blows and survived. She had loyal councillors before her, drawn from the best her royal city had to offer. She had her trusted chancellor to her right, the selfless Orkid Gravespear. She had her mighty constable sitting opposite her, suitably chastised but eager to prove to himself anew, she was sure. Most importantly, by her left side once again, her brother Olio. She placed her left hand over his right; he curled his fingers around hers.

"This meeting of my executive council is now in session. You will see on your agenda that the first item for discussion is the creation and organization of the Great Army, and attached to the agenda is a schedule for recruitment and supply put together by the Great Army Committee for our consideration."

The councillors quickly scanned the document. Since the schedule had been produced hurriedly after Dejanus' dismissal from the committee, Areava closely watched his reaction for any sign of anger or rebuke, but she could not read his expression and he remained silent. Among the others there were muttered comments about the cost and some sharp intakes of breath at the scale of the operation, but no one fell off their seat or immediately raised any objections.

"I have communicated to King Tomar our intention to raise the Great Army's standard in southern Chandra."

"Has he replied?" Marshal Triam Lief asked.

"Not yet, but the message was only sent recently."

"He will not object, surely?" Mayor Shant Tenor piped up.

"We are asking a great deal of him," the marshal said.

"I do not expect any objection from his Majesty," Areava said firmly.

"Perhaps another letter stressing the urgency of the situation is in order?" the mayor suggested.

Areava opened her mouth to say she did not think that would be necessary, but before she could, Orkid said he would draft a letter for the queen's signature if that was the council's advice. Irritated by the compromise when in her view no compromise was necessary, she agreed in order to stop anyone thinking she and Orkid were dissenting.

"Are there any questions regarding the schedule?"

"How are we to meet the requirements for all this food?" asked Xella Povis, the head of the merchants' collective. "Can the kingdom's farmers produce enough, and if they can, how do we get it all to southern Chandra?"

"Getting it there will be no problem if we use the navy," Fleet Admiral Zoul Setchmar said quickly.

"We may be able to use merchant traders for the transport of most of the supplies," Orkid pointed out, saying what Xella Povis wanted to hear. "That would leave the navy free for other duties."

Areava let the conversation go and carefully observed her councillors at work. Most of them took their cue from self-interest, but she had expected that. Cleverly, the Great Army Committee had created a schedule that would pour at least some of the crown's money into the hands of every commercial interest, and distribute at least some of the political gain from the formation of the army to the constable, the marshal, and the fleet admiral. The result was that, to some extent, every one in the kingdom would feel that not only had they had made a contribution to the defense of the realm, but that they would also gain some benefit from it apart from defeating the outlaw Prince Lynan and his band of marauding Chetts. She wondered, almost wistfully, if any of them were capable of working for the kingdom's benefit without any expectation of reward. At that point, Olio removed his hand from hers to organize the papers in front of him. She glanced across and saw that he had actually written comments on his copy of the minutes. Surprised, she looked up at him, but he was concentrating on what was being discussed and did not notice.

Yes, she thought, at least one here is capable of that, and her heart filled with pride.

21

SOMEWHERE along the first day's ride back to Daavis from the battle on the hill, Lynan tucked his trophy into a saddlebag. Ager tried talking to him, but Lynan ignored him; Gudon tried as well, but with no more success.

The column camped not far from the gorge. The Chetts were tired, grimly thankful they had caught the enemy, but aware that something was wrong with their leader. Later, when almost all except the pickets had gone to sleep, Lynan stayed awake, squatting next to a slow-burning fire. Near him, as ever, were two Red Hands. Around midnight the pair was relieved, but Lynan had barely moved. On the ground before him, retrieved from the saddlebag, was the head of the red-haired prisoner, and his gaze never seemed to leave it.

In turn, Ager's gaze never left Lynan. He had waited until Morfast fell asleep and then slipped out from underneath their blanket to stand quietly by a clump of low and gnarly thorn trees just outside the range of the campfire's glare. He felt physically ill with fear. He had witnessed Lynan's battle rage before, but never had it possessed him for so long and with such strange effect, and he was afraid that Lynan was becoming not more than human but less, that Silona's blood had finally submerged his real self beneath something allied to and as horrible as her own nature. So intent was he on watching Lynan and so overtaken with his own anxiety, it was some time before he was aware that Gudon was standing behind him.

"Has there been any change?" the Chett asked.

Ager shook his head.

"This has not happened before, has it?"

Again, Ager shook his head.

"Perhaps it is because we are so much closer to Silona's forest. It is in Chandra, I believe, and we are near the border of that province."

"Yes," Ager said vaguely. "That might be it."

"Do you think he will be all right until we get to Daavis?"

"Possibly. But what difference will Daavis make?"

"Our magickers are there," Gudon said. "They may be able to help. Indeed, Jenrosa is there. Perhaps, if anyone can help, it is Jenrosa."

"So she is the next Truespeaker?"

"I don't know. But those who know about such things say she is very powerful indeed."

"Jenrosa may not want to help," Ager said.

"Truth. But I do not think she considers herself absolved from the changes in Lynan's behavior. She cannot forget that she was the one who gave him the vampire's blood."

"His changes in behavior? Maybe he was always like this, deep down, and Silona's blood has only made it worse. He has been through a great deal in his few years, seen and experienced too much."

"You make excuses for him," Gudon said.

"I am his friend."

"I am his friend as well, but he is our king, and that makes his behavior a concern for more than you and me."

Ager nodded wearily. "Truth," he said.

Gudon could not helping smiling at the use of the expression. "Every day you become more like a Chett."

"There are worse things to aspire to," Ager admitted. He turned to look at Gudon. "What can we do for Lynan?"

"*We* can do nothing except stand by him."

"I will watch over him tonight. You get some sleep."

"I will stay with you."

"Someone is going to have to keep an eye on him during the ride tomorrow, and you are a better horseman than me."

Gudon thought about it. "As you say."

"Go."

Gudon raised a hand in farewell and left. Ager missed the Chett's presence as soon as he was gone from sight. He sat down, made himself as comfortable as possible, and reluctantly returned his gaze to Lynan.

The column arrived in Daavis a day and a half after leaving the gorge. As far as Ager could tell, Lynan had not slept for a single moment the whole time; each day he rode at the head of the column, each night he squatted beside a fire and studied the head from his saddlebag. By the morning of the second day, the head was beginning to stink, but no one would say anything about it to him. Ager was exhausted, barely able to keep his eyes open despite catching snatches of sleep while mounted, but he had not the Chett ability to sleep properly in the saddle. Two long nights, together with all the anxiety and fears that accompanied them, had completely drained him. When he passed under the north gate of the city, he felt as if he had returned to some kind of sanctuary and his spirits lifted somewhat, making him sit more erect.

As soon as they entered the palace courtyard, they were met by a retinue of stable hands and servants. Their horses were taken away and linen towels soaked in warm sweet-scented water were handed to Lynan and his companions. When Ager looked up from washing his face, he saw that Lynan had kept the saddlebag from his horse, its lumpen shape slopped over his shoulder. A servant standing nearby was having difficulty breathing, and none of the servants would look directly at Lynan's face. Ager's spirits quickly sank again.

Korigan appeared and immediately ran to Lynan, but she stopped short when she saw what he was like, as if she had struck an invisible wall. Ager felt the cold flush he saw goosebump her skin.

"You are returned, my lord," she said hesitantly.

Lynan glanced at her. "Farben," he said.

Korigan frowned. "Farben?"

"Charion's secretary in charge of the city's administration."

"Yes, of course."

"Bring him to me in the throne room."

Korigan nodded. "All right. But don't you want to rest first? You look as if you have ridden long and hard—"

"Now," Lynan said. "And all the palace servants." He walked away from her and into the palace.

Ager flinched when he saw the pain on the queen's face. The realization that she did love Lynan came as something of a shock to him. She glanced at Ager, her expression asking the question she could not voice. He went to her and said: "Do as he asks, but bring Jenrosa as well, and any other powerful magickers you can find."

"How long—?"

"This is the third day."

"Oh, gods . . ."

"Get Jenrosa!" he urged and followed Lynan, catching up with him in the throne room where he had draped himself lengthways across Charion's stone chair, the saddlebag drooping from one hand, his heels kicking in the air. Two Red Hands stood on guard at the entrance, and Ager could tell they were on edge, not sure any more who—or what—it was they were protecting.

"Lynan? What is this?"

Lynan looked at him the way a large cat might look at a puppy. "I could hear you, you know."

"There was no reason for you not to hear me," Ager said, puzzled.

"Two nights ago. You and Gudon. I was talking with my friend here," he said, hitching the saddlebag, "but your voices kept on interrupting our conversation."

"I'm sorry."

"My hearing is very good, you know. 'Do as he asks, but bring Jenrosa as well.' "

Ager could not help blushing.

"There is nothing wrong with me. I am not ill. I have never felt better in my whole life."

"You have changed."

Lynan laughed lightly, but it was no sound Ager recognized. His fear returned in an icy rush, twice as strong as before.

"We all change, Ager." He frowned in thought for a moment. "Oh, sorry, I forgot. What was it you said to Gudon? 'His changes in behavior? Maybe he was always like this, deep down, and Silona's blood has only made it worse. He has been through a great deal in his few years, seen and experienced too much.' That was it, wasn't it?"

"I don't remember the exact words."

"That was it," Lynan said tightly. He breathed in heavily and closed his eyes, rubbing them with thumb and finger.

"You are tired."

"It is a very warm, very bright day," Lynan replied. Then his eyes snapped open and his gaze settled firmly on Ager's face. "Nothing I can't handle."

There were footsteps from the corridor outside. Both men turned to watch Korigan and Gudon enter with Farben, Jenrosa, and a retinue of servants and magickers. Ager thought they all looked as if they would rather be anywhere but in this throne room. Jenrosa, particularly, looked like a trapped animal.

"My lord," Korigan said, approaching him. "As you requested, I have brought Farben."

Lynan looked at all of the faces staring up at him. "Together with a small host, I see."

She threw a glance at Ager again, looking for guidance, but there was nothing he could do to help. They were all at sea together here, and only Lynan knew which direction they were sailing.

"You wanted to see me, your Majesty?" Farben said, and went to stand by Korigan. Ager could not help but admire the little man's bravery.

Lynan rolled his eyes. "I did? What could that have been about, I wonder?"

Farben said nothing. By now he could smell the thing in the saddlebag and his nose crinkled.

"Is something wrong?" Lynan asked solicitously.

"My lord?"

"Is something bothering you, Farben? You are doing something with your face."

"No, there is nothing wrong."

Lynan eased himself off the throne and went to Farben, put his free arm around the small man's shoulders and started walking him around the room, people edging out of their way. Farben seemed to shrink in that embrace, and Lynan held him even closer. "Good, because it would be terrible for the city of Daavis, and for your liege lady, if anything was to happen to you."

"I thank my lord for his concern."

"My concern is for the welfare of all my subjects," Lynan said breezily. He stopped, his brow creased in sudden thought. "Speaking of which, that is why I called for you."

Lynan stepped away from Farben and opened the saddlebag so that only the secretary could see inside it. The room filled quickly with the clinging, choking smell of decay.

"My lord, what is it you have?" Farben managed to force through his constricting throat.

Oh, God, Ager thought to himself. *Don't bring it out . . .*

But Lynan did. He put one hand in the bag and dragged out the head, holding it up so Farben could see the face.

Farben's reaction was immediate. He gasped, brought his hands over his mouth and stepped away. There were cries of dismay from the servants. Everyone else seemed caught in a terrible spell, unable to react at all.

"One of our subjects," Lynan said sadly. "One of our *loyal* subjects. Do you recognize him?"

Farben tried to speak but could only gag.

Lynan raised his eyebrows. "No?" Lynan considered the head. "Ah, I see what's wrong. He was taller in life." He held the head up higher. "How's that?"

"Coud . . . Coud . . ." Farben sputtered.

"Could I . . . ?" Lynan teased.

"Coudroun!"

"Coudroun?" Lynan twisted his hand so he could look on the dead man's face. Red hair stuck up between his fingers. "Hello, Coudroun."

Farben wiped his mouth and looked away from the dangling head. "He was one of my secretaries."

"A secretary with secretaries," Lynan mused. "Next you will be telling me you are a secretary with secrets."

"My lord, how . . . how did this happen? Where did you find poor Coudroun?"

"Where?" Lynan asked, his voice hardening like steel. It cut through the throne room. "Can you not tell me?"

"The last I saw of him, your Majesty, he was on his way to the region of Esquidion to order supplies of food and lumber and stone for the city. He was a good and faithful secretary. He was a good man with much promise . . ."

"On his way to Esquidion on whose orders?"

"Why, mine," Farben said quickly. "He would not have left without my explicit instruction. He would never do anything without consulting me." His voice was rising with distress. "My lord, I know his sister who lives in Daavis. She will be alone in the world now. Please tell me how you come to find him slain so brutally?"

"I didn't *find* him slain so brutally, Farben."

Farben looked up sharply, his face turning as white as Lynan's. "Your Majesty cannot mean . . ." His voice trailed off as he realised that was exactly what his majesty had meant.

Ager stepped forward. "Lynan—" Lynan whipped around to stare at Ager. The crookback felt his heart skip a beat. He swallowed and said, slowly and deliberately, "Your Majesty," and bowed.

"Yes?"

"It seems clear that Farben had no idea of this Coudroun's part in Charion's rebellion."

"Rebellion!" Farben cried, the word torn out of him.

Lynan wagged his head from side to side as if considering what Ager had said. "Well, that's one way to look at it," he conceded. Then his head straightened with a snap and he was again glaring at Farben. "But I cannot help wondering if one secretary can betray a master, then another might as easily."

"Your Majesty!" Farben squealed. "I have done nothing against you! I have taken your instructions to heart and worked only for the good of the city and its people in the expectation—" He stopped himself short.

"In the expectation of Charion's eventual return," Lynan finished for him.

"These were your conditions, my lord, set down by you," Farben pleaded. "You told me that when you won the throne of Grenda Lear, you would allow Charion to rule again in Hume."

"I also told you that I would not tolerate anyone working directly against my interests."

"I have not done so, I swear!"

"We have no reason to suspect Farben has played you foul, your Majesty," Korigan said, stepping forward next to Ager. "The walls are repaired, the streets cleared of all rubble, businesses are back to normal—"

"And traitors butcher my troops!" Lynan roared, swinging around to face her. Coudroun's head bumped into Farben's arm and the secretary involuntarily jumped out of the way. Lynan saw the motion and reacted immediately. His free hand shot out and grabbed Farben around the throat, lifting his feet off the ground and squeezing the air out of him.

"Your Majesty!" Ager and Korigan cried together. Other servants started to cry and back out of the throne room.

"No one leaves!" Lynan cried, and Red Hands moved to bar the door. "I trusted this man, my enemy! I gave him a chance to prove himself, to work for the common good of the people of Hume, but instead what I find is his own secretary raises a sword against my soldiers!"

As he shouted, Lynan turned slowly to face each group in the throne room, Farben swinging in the air, wheezing, kicking, trying to suck in a breath.

"Lynan!" Jenrosa yelled and stepped right before him. "You are killing him!"

Lynan looked at her as if she was stupid. "Well, of course I'm killing him!" he hissed at her. His forearm flexed, his fingers came together, and there was a sickening crack. Farben's body went instantly limp, and the smell of hot piss filled the room.

"Oh, God," Jenrosa said hoarsely.

Lynan moved around Jenrosa and started circling the throne room, his arms by his side, Farben's heels dragging on the floor, Coudroun's gory head swinging by its red hair. All but Ager, Gudon, Korigan, and Jenrosa huddled against the walls, terrified. His companions gathered together in the center of the room, turning to keep him in view, not knowing what to do, not even knowing who Lynan was anymore.

"Some changes," Lynan was saying, more to himself than anyone else. "That's what we need here. No more talk of Charion. No more talk of giving enemies a second chance. Daavis is an occupied enemy city. No more chances. I will hunt down all my enemies. I will have them. No more chances."

Ager wanted to close his single eye, to pretend none of this was happening, that the thing stalking around them was still, somehow, Prince Lynan Rosetheme, son of Elynd Chisal, his friend and liege lord. But he could not force his eyes shut and he could not keep out the rambling sentences, half-mad, half-incoherent, that spilled from Lynan's mouth. Korigan and Gudon were resolutely staring at the floor, gray-faced. Jenrosa, like Ager, stared at Lynan, her own eyes wide with something more than fear. Certainty, he thought. She was looking at Lynan with certainty.

"I will fill the streets with the heads of my enemies," Lynan was saying.

It was enough, Ager thought. It was all enough. He left his companions and barred Lynan's way.

"Ager. What are you still doing here?"

Ager put a hand on each of Lynan's. "Let them go," he said gently.

Lynan looked down at what he was holding as if he had not been aware he was carrying them. He released his grip. Farben's body slumped to the ground. Coudroun's head rolled until it bumped into one the servant's legs.

"Korigan?" Ager said, keeping his eyes on Lynan. "Would you help me get his Majesty to his chambers, please?"

Korigan moved quickly and, each taking an arm, they led Lynan out of the throne room. As they left, Ager looked over his shoulder to Jenrosa. He caught her eye, and saw that beside the certainty there was also resolution there, and once more the faint spark of hope flared in his heart.

22

TOMAR sat on his throne trying to stay awake as two land-owners argued a case before him. His secretaries had tried unsuccessfully to clarify their separate claims before the claimants entered, and now he was paying the price for it. He already knew what his decision would be, but tradition—if not justice—demanded that both claimants could put forward their case fully. He looked around, noticed that others in the court were also fighting off drooping eyelids and cavernous yawns. The law was a ponderous thing, he thought, made fat by centuries of bickering clerks and poor decisions. One day he would get around to codifying properly the statutes of Chandra, organizing them into some kind of hierarchy so that others besides himself could determine the outcomes of cases so important that grieves passed them onto the capital. And that's the other thing he would do, update the system of grieves. He had met a few during his reign, and a benighted lot they were, too.

No, he corrected himself, *not all of them.* There had been the brave little fellow in the Arran Valley who stood up to Jes Prado. Not a lot of common sense, maybe, but certainly more than his fair share of pluck. There was, after all, some good among the dross, even if you had to search hard for it. Reforming the system might increase the good and reduce the dross, and that would actually help reduce the problem of too many cases being passed on to the court.

He fidgeted uncomfortably on the throne; even with a cushion under his backside, it was an exercise in slow torture to sit through an open session in court, bedecked in his finery, holding the staff of judgment, desperately trying to look interested.

There was a commotion outside the throne room. Tomar held his hand up to stop the landowner who was droning on about ancient rights-of-way. The court sergeant was standing at the entrance, indicating that there was someone just out of sight waiting to see him. Then he noticed that the sergeant's lance of office was dressed over his right shoulder. The someone waiting was royalty.

Oh, God, not Areava, surely!

"My good sirs," he said to the claimants. "My apologies, but this case must be delayed to another time." He turned to one of his secretaries. "Arrange a special hearing for these two men. Their important matter must not be put off a moment longer than necessary."

The secretary nodded and gathered together the two landlords, who were indignant but given no time to object, and moved them aside. Tomar immediately signaled to the sergeant, who marched forward. Two figures—a man and a woman—fell in behind him. The man tall with the patrician bearing of his birthright and upbringing, every inch a nobleman, and she small but determined, battle-tested and regal. He recognized both, and the sight of the woman made him groan inside. He would rather it had been Areava.

"Queen Charion," he said.

Although every one in the room was already watching the approach of the unexpected guests, most had not seen the sergeant's lance and did not recognize them. When Tomar said the name, a murmur passed through the court like a breeze over a wheat field.

Their condition was pitiful. Their clothes were in tatters, their skin cut and bruised, their hair matted, their faces drawn with exhaustion. He was never sure what made him do it, but filled with a sudden and unexpected pity Tomar descended from the throne to greet them.

"King Tomar, forgive this intrusion," Charion said. "But we have ridden far and had nowhere else to go."

"Then you are welcome in my house," he said formally, knowing that with their arrival and with his words, events had been set in motion over which he would soon have no control.

Later that day Tomar called for his champion. When Barys arrived, he found the king sitting at a desk with three documents in front of him; two he recognized immediately as official letters from Kendra. The third was written neatly on a coarser paper, and he could see that Tomar had folded and unfolded it many times.

The king looked more weary than Barys could ever remember seeing him, and although a large man who had always carried his weight with ease, he now seemed distinctly unhealthy. A pale face accentuated the king's sad brown eyes, and Barys thought he saw a hint of despair in them.

"How long have you served me?" Tomar asked him, motioning for him to take the seat opposite his.

Barys had to think that one through. "Twenty years. Maybe more."

"Thirty-one," Tomar said.

"Really? I had no idea it had been that long. Are you going to retire me?"

"You will outlast me, old friend."

"We are the same age."

"You look older," Tomar quipped, trying unsuccessfully to smile.

Barys snorted. "Are you going to talk to me about these?" he asked, moving the documents around the table with a hand. He did not pretend not to be curious, but neither did he insult his king by trying to read them upside down.

Tomar picked up one of the Kendra letters. "This one you already know the contents of. It is from Areava informing us of her decision to plant the standard of her Great Army in southern Chandra."

"You know my thoughts on that."

"And this," Tomar continued, holding up the second letter from Kendra, "is from her chancellor." He gave it to Barys.

"It is her signature," Barys said.

"But his writing," Tomar replied. "I know it as well as I know my own. Read."

Barys did so. When he finished, he said, "This can hardly surprise you. They must be wondering why you have not formally agreed to their request."

"I think some in Kendra may have wondered. Areava was happy to let it go and let the army simply arrive, that way demonstrating to the people of Chandra that it was her decision to impose on this province and not mine. She is as wily as her mother, and in her own way as considerate of our sensibilities."

"Nevertheless, she did sign this second letter," Barys pointed out, "her consideration for our sensibilities notwithstanding."

"She was outmaneuvered," Tomar said. "Probably in council."

"By Orkid Gravespear?"

"Possibly, or maybe by someone from one of the Twenty Houses."

"You cannot actually know this."

Tomar shrugged. "I have no reason to find excuses for Areava. I do not like the woman. But I do think she is closer in style and intent to Usharna than any of her siblings, and this province lived quite well under Usharna's protective embrace."

"You have a soft spot for the old queen because she married Elynd."

With the mention of that name Tomar visibly stiffened, something Barys could not help noticing. Then it all clicked into place for him. He pointed to the third document. "That's from the General's son, isn't it?"

Tomar closed his eyes and nodded.

"I hope you have been keeping that on your person," Barys said. "If Areava or the chancellor—or, for God's sake, Charion—were to find out you had it, they would cut off your head."

"You would protect me," Tomar said, trying to keep his voice light.

"They would happily cut off mine first to get to you."

Tomar did not argue the point.

"Well, my lord, are you going to tell me what it says?"

Tomar picked up the letter, but hesitated in handing it over. "How well do you remember Elynd?" he asked suddenly.

"Very well," Barys said seriously. "I fought by his side in three great battles—"

"Yes, I know all that," Tomar said impatiently. "Did you like him?"

"Yes."

"And I," the king admitted. "I know he liked both of us. He thought we were . . ." Tomar struggled to find the word.

"As straight as a wind across the Oceans of Grass," Barys said.

Tomar smiled. "Yes, that's it. How clever of you to remember."

"The General had a way with words."

"Not all of them meant for polite society."

"What's the point of all this remembering?"

"He was as straight with us as we were with him. It was part of his nature, I think."

"He was half-Chett, after all," Barys said. "It is said they value honesty above almost all other virtues."

Tomar leaned forward urgently and grasped one of Barys' wrists, bringing his face within a finger's span of his champion's. "I believe the same of his son."

Barys, refusing to show he was surprised by the king's sudden actions, said as mundanely as possible: "So?"

Tomar let go of Barys and sat back. "For the thirty-one years you have served me as my champion, I have, in turn, served the throne of Grenda Lear as its governor of Chandra."

Barys took umbrage at that and was not afraid to show it. "Long before there was a palace in Kendra, your family ruled here."

"The point is my grandfather accepted the overrule of the Rosethemes, and Chandra has benefited from it. Our borders became stronger, our trade flourished, our people grew in numbers."

Barys leaned forward now, sensing that Tomar was about to cross a river and that its consequences would be irrevocable. "You are talking still about loyalty?"

"God, yes," Tomar breathed. "As king, my loyalty must ultimately reside with my own people."

"Agreed."

"But is loyalty best served by politics or truth?" Tomar caught Barys' gaze, and the champion realized the moment had arrived. This is what Tomar had been debating within himself since . . . he thought back . . . since the day he had escorted Magmed and the knights into Sparro. That was when he had received the first of the letters from Kendra. And, obvious now, when he had also received the letter from Lynan. But Tomar could no longer put off a decision because Charion had arrived, unannounced and unexpected, in his lap. If it had been any other refugee, a conundrum would not exist, but Chandra and Hume were rivals within Grenda Lear, and before that had been actual enemies with a history of countless border wars. Indeed, it had been the constant threat of incursions from Hume that had convinced Tomar's grandfather to accede to union with the kingdom. The fact that both countries were now provinces within that kingdom eliminated open conflict between them but did nothing to reduce the ancient enmity.

"This is a question you have had time to consider," Barys said carefully. "What is it you need of me?"

Tomar handed over the letter and Barys read it twice. When he finished, he asked, "Do you believe this? That the chancellor and this Dejanus actually murdered Berayma?"

"He is the General's son," Tomar said.

"And it makes sense," Barys conceded. "It fits in with your fears about Aman's growing power in court, something Lynan himself may not have been aware of at the time he was forced into exile."

"Usharna made sure Lynan was kept out of politics and the court. For what reason I do no know, perhaps for his protection because of his half-commoner heritage, but it made him the perfect figure of blame for Berayma's murder. Orkid and Dejanus would have killed him outright and left Areava—who had no love for Lynan—with no choice and no doubt."

"She still has no doubt," Barys pointed out. "Remember the Great Army, which she is gathering on your lands."

"Should I go to Areava with this letter?"

"She would execute you outright!" Barys said, astounded at the thought. "Lynan has led an invasion into her territory, slain her husband, taken one of her great cities . . . the original cause of all of this no longer matters!"

Tomar slapped the table with one hand. "It matters to me, Barys!" He stood up abruptly and walked around the room, his hands behind his back. Barys watched him patiently, without saying anything. Eventually the king stopped, turning back to his champion.

"The immediate issue is whether I accept Areava's request to allow the standard of the Great Army on my territory, or whether I accede to Lynan's request."

"To give his army free passage across Chandra to Kendra itself."

"Exactly. Do I side with my queen, and thereby side with Orkid and Dejanus and all that that means? Or do I side with Lynan, rebel and invader of this kingdom of Grenda Lear, and all that that means? Which is the greater betrayal?"

"What is best for Chandra?" Barys prompted.

Tomar's shoulders sagged and he shook his head in frustration. "I do not know, old friend."

23

FROM a hill near the end of the Oceans of Grass, Makon looked over a great camp. First light was returning color to the sky, and the curling, gray smoke of last night's fires were dispersing in a morning breeze.

Makon had never thought to see again anything like the gathering of Lynan's army at the High Sooq the previous winter, but now he was witnessing something similar in the homeland of the Horse clan. From the north, from the west, from the east, clans that had already sent so many of their own to war under Lynan's pennant now sent more to help Eynon and his people exact their revenge against the Saranah and Amanites. The original plan had been to call for reinforcements under Lynan's name at the next High Sooq, but word of what had happened to the Horse clan and others in the south of the Oceans of Grass traveled quickly, and soon individual clans were sending detachments to join Eynon without being asked.

Makon was old enough and wise enough to recognize what Lynan had done to the Chetts was unite them properly for the first time, despite the previous efforts of Korigan and her father, something perhaps only someone from outside the clan system could have done. Makon also recognized that what Lynan had created would not be destroyed easily, whether or not the White Wolf won the throne of Grenda Lear. Now, watching the warriors gather to fight for a single purpose without quibbling about command or payment, Makon understood what unification meant for his people. The Chetts had become a power, not just on the Oceans of Grass and its margins, but throughout the continent of Theare.

What was less certain for Makon was whether or not it was entirely a good thing. His instinct told him it was, that it was *always* a good thing to be stronger, but the Chetts had broken through the wall of their isolation in a way that would make it difficult for the rest of Theare to regard them in any way but as invaders. There would be a cost for that, maybe not due for a generation or ten generations, but it would come, and he was smart enough to see that it would be paid for by losing what it was that made them Chetts and by being absorbed into the general stream of civilization.

Lynan had given the Chetts a new future, but he had also ended forever their old way of life. By bursting onto the world in the way they had, they were ensuring that eventually they would diminish as a distinct people.

Wennem came up beside him. "Is it not terrible to see?" she said, looking over the gathering as it stirred in the morning. There was an excitement in her voice he had not heard before. As a Chett, he should have shared that excitement, coming as it did from the anticipation of making war against their enemies, but he could not help wishing that something other than the prospect of revenge had stirred her. Since leaving the Strangers' Sooq, Wennem had regained both weight and sanity, but to Makon's eyes she still looked too thin even for a Chett, and her single-minded obsession with revenge made him think that her mental health was still a fragile thing.

Tents were being lowered, fires put out, horses saddled. Riders joined their troops and then their troops collected into clans. Eynon had neither the time nor the inclination to reorganize them into banners independent of the clan system as Lynan had done with his force. In some ways, that would have been counterproductive—after all, this army had come together to revenge what had happened to their own and other clans. By the time the sun was actually over the horizon, seven thousand warriors were ready to ride south from the Oceans of Grass.

"Eynon will be expecting you," Wennem said. Together, they rode down to the head of the gathering, where the remnants of the Horse clan, together with the lancers and the Red Hands, were ready to lead the way.

Eynon greeted them and nodded to the rise they had been on. "Get a good view?"

"Thank you," Makon said.

"Are we impressive?"

"Very."

Eynon grunted, but Makon could see he was pleased.

"I had a new pennant made up last night."

Makon glanced up at the Horse clan pennant Eynon's force had been using. It was a narrow, fluttering cloth, nothing like the grand pennant the main clan would have flown before they were massacred by the Saranah.

"I cannot see it."

Eynon gave an order and a rider behind him unwound a large, rectangular flag from the staff he was holding. It caught the morning breeze and spanked in the air, and when Makon saw the gold circle on the blood-red field he could not help laughing in surprise.

"It is Lynan's pennant!" he called.

Eynon shook his head. "It is the standard for the Chetts now, however go Lynan's fortunes in the east."

Baterus had almost figured it out. Wrapped inside the ornate Chandran rug strapped to his back, right on top of the small brass ewer he would give to his wife, were fourteen brooches, seven pins, and two ornately carved daggers. Although a heavy load, it was still lighter than the food and extra arrows he had carried into the Oceans of Grass as part of Dekelon's war band. The only problem was the wound in his calf muscle—nothing dangerous, but it slowed him down enough to be useless in Dekelon's fast-moving campaign, so he had been ordered back home with a pile of booty.

The calf muscle twinged and he cursed under his breath. He had gutted the Chett brat who had sliced him there, and that gave him some satisfaction as he pushed the pain to the back of his mind.

Yes, he had almost figured it out now. He owed the Saranah three quarters of his booty. Say eleven of the brooches, five of the pins, one of the daggers and he would keep the rug. He chewed his lower lip. No, no, the tribe would not think that entirely fair. Say twelve of the brooches. They would not spite him one of the daggers, especially since he had lost his own fighting on behalf of the Saranah; admittedly that had been a rusty old iron blade with a cracked bone handle. Still, he could not go without a dagger. He knew which one he wanted, too: the one with a grip carved from ironwood into the shape of an eastern courtesan. Lovely. Good blade. Lovely.

So, he thought, give the tribe twelve of the brooches and all the pins—he did not need pins—and one of the daggers. That would leave him two of the brooches, and he would give the shell one to his wife and another to sweet Madro (and who knew what might come of that?), the dagger for himself and the rug.

Ah, the rug. That was the real problem. It was worth more than all the other pieces put together. The tribe might not look favorably on Baterus taking it for himself. But the tribe could not use it communally. And it would be a shame to sell it on for nothing but gold coins. Gold coins were not of themselves things of beauty, and this rug was the most beautiful thing Baterus had ever seen. Woven from fine wool, dyed in colors he had never imagined before, showing pictures of a great cavalry charge from some ancient myth of story. He would have it in his home, and all his neighbors would think him the finest among them because of it. In winter, it would help him keep his feet off the hard, cold floor. In summer, it would help him keep his feet off the hard, hot floor.

It was so fine, in fact, that even Dekelon himself might take it as part of his share of the booty. The idea made Baterus instantly feel glum. It would be fair, he admitted to himself. Dekelon had done more for the tribe with his war band than any previous chief since the exile from the Oceans of Grass. Every Saranah would be immeasurably wealthier because of Dekelon's initiative and daring.

He hefted the rug higher on his shoulders. *We will see. Dekelon may already have another rug in mind. Or two.*

A rumble. It was a feeling rather than a sound, like the most distant thunder on a suddenly cold summer night when the stars seem to drag across the sky. He looked up at the horizon. The other Saranah in the file, all laden down with loot, stopped and looked up as well. The sky was clear.

It was something deeper even than thunder. Something not from the sky but from . . .

Baterus glanced down at his feet. Earthquake? No, his body was not shaking, his feet not slipping away from under him. He stamped the earth with a foot as if answering some subterranean call. A fragment of a story popped into his mind then, a story about the old days when the Saranah were riders on the plains with so many horse that when the clan moved it sounded like . . .

"No," he said slowly under his breath. He dropped to all fours and put his ear to the ground. "Yes."

He did not cry out a warning, did not bother to unstrap the rug to arm himself with the lovely dagger, did not turn to see the doom falling on him and all the other Saranah. He just waited, the thunder swelling around him like the beginnings of a storm.

                                    *   *   *

The Chett army found their first enemy within hours of leaving the plains, a small band of returning Saranah warriors, all of whom had already been wounded in previous battles. They were shown no mercy, and two of them were set aside for torture so the location of their settlements could be learned. With that information, Eynon divided his force into four columns.

"This is a dry land, and if we stayed together we would strip it of all its grass and drink all of its water before we are through," Eynon told his commanders. "There are seven Saranah settlements within four days' ride of us. Three columns will take two settlements each; my column will take the last settlement, the one farthest from the plains. We will wait for the rest of you to catch up with us there. Take no prisoners, no booty, leave behind no living animal, foul every water source after you have used it. Use whatever means necessary to find out where other settlements are located so that we may destroy them as well."

The commanders looked uncomfortable.

"What is it?" Eynon demanded.

"What do we drink on the way back?" one of them asked.

"We don't come back this way," Eynon said flatly. "Once we have finished here, we hit Aman, and from Aman we can join up with King Lynan's forces in Chandra or Kendra."

"Aman is full of mountains," another commander said. "How will we conquer it? We are people of the grass, not the rock."

"We are not going to conquer it. We are going to gut it. By the time we have finished, they will have no more farms or towns or villages within ten leagues anywhere along our route. We are going to pay them back a hundredfold for sending the Saranah against us. We will teach the people in the east such a lesson that they will never again send an army into the Oceans of Grass to kill our people, steal our riches, and destroy our herds!"

Eynon spoke with such passion that most of the commanders gave him their support immediately, the wisdom of which they would later ponder. They also realized he was expressing the exact sentiments of most of their own warriors: what the Saranah and their Amanite masters had done to them could not go unpunished.

Makon's first impression of the lands to the south were that they were different than anything he had experienced before. The plains of his home and the rolling, gentle landscape of Hume were both covered in grass, a pale green and coarse on the plains, richer and gentler in the east, but the ground made the same sound under his horse's hoofs. The hard arid land of the south, however, made all sounds sharper, like stone hitting stone or bone on bone; there was not enough soil to protect the world from itself. Too, while Makon was used to the heat of summer back on the Oceans of Grass, here the light bounced off the ground so it surrounded you. The column moved through a shimmering heat haze even though it was now well into autumn, and horse and rider suffered.

Then, on the third day of their ride south, when either the heat was less or he simply was growing accustomed to it, he realized he was starting to feel at home. This was so unexpected it took him a time to figure out it was the horizon. Just like on the Oceans of Grass, the sky and land met at the most distant point, and all around was nothing but air. In Hume, Makon found it difficult not to feel penned in by the geography; the east was a world of small land-scapes, different stories, but the west, whether north on the plains or south in the desert, was the same story.

"Just a different rhythm," he said aloud to himself.

"What?" Wennem asked.

Makon shook his head.

"You are very quiet," Wennem said. "You used to speak a lot more."

"That's because you never spoke at all," Makon said lightly. "I had to make up for both of us."

"I wanted to speak," she said with a surprising urgency.

Makon nodded, pretending to understand. He wanted to touch her face, see her clear brown eyes settle on him with the same love he now knew he held for her.

"I wanted to tell everyone what had happened, but every time I started, I saw my family being killed and my mouth wouldn't make the words. It was like screaming without making any sound."

"And now?"

"It is still terrible, but far away, like it happened years ago. I try to remember what the faces of my husband and child looked like, but I can't anymore. It's only when I'm thinking of something else that a word or smell strikes me like lightning hitting a tree and for a heartbeat I see my husband clearly as if he were standing before me, or I'm holding my baby in my arms again. It is dreadful and wonderful at the same time."

"I hope you never forget," Makon said gently.

Wennem smiled uneasily. "I was hoping you would understand."

Makon had to resist the urge to turn to her. He was sure the words meant what he *thought* they meant, but was afraid of breaking contact with the lick of joy it kindled inside him.

So they rode together in silence, words suddenly too frail.

24

POWL had been seeking an answer to a conundrum, and felt that at last a resolution had been found. It was a turning point, he realized, in the way he regarded his faith and his work as primate for the Church of the Righteous God. As a priest he detested turning points—the path to salvation should always be straight—but as a scholar he delighted in the twists and turns that experience and knowledge introduced to life.

He carefully opened the new book he had started, filled with the strange letters from the ancient alphabet used in the volumes of Colanus. He reviewed what he had already written on its first few pages, then lifted his pen to continue the work. And hesitated.

He put the pen down.

Was he sure? Was he moving too fast? After all, it had only been a few nights ago that he gained his first real success—understanding that the symbols on the backs of the volumes, though not ideograms, were still in essence ideogrammatic. Each letter actually represented a sound and each group of letters a word, but the words themselves were not describing precisely the contents of the volumes but their part in the whole. He had been in the church library where he spent most of his time desperately trying to find some clue to the name of God. He was meticulously checking each theological tract on each shelf, when one book stood out—not because of its content, but because it was on the wrong shelf. The small red stamp on its spine indicated it belonged in the section on natural philosophy and not in the section on inductive reasoning. Struck by the idea that this might conceivably be the case with the words on the spines of the ancient volumes, the next day he visited the central library of the theurgia, carefully noting each of the major headings under which they catalogued their books. As with the church library, the headings reflected principle rather than subject, the essence of something rather than the thing itself. Later, he matched all transliterations he could make from the volumes and compared them to the headings. It was with a feeling of wonder and elation that he noticed some either matched perfectly or came too close just to be coincidence. The second group fired the real breakthrough, for it showed Powl what ancient, previously unknown letters he could substitute for letters from the modern alphabet used everywhere in Theare.

From there he was able to decipher most of the words and groups on the spines of the volumes from the tower. Any new word he wrote down carefully and tried to find in the main text of the volumes and guess at its meaning through context. If he found the same word appearing in a similar context, he assumed he was close to finding its real meaning. This did not always work, but what it did do was allow Powl to start compiling a simple and primitive dictionary.

By the night after his visit to the library of the theurgia, he knew he had the tools necessary to decipher all the volumes. For two days that is where he stopped.

The ancient magickers themselves had conspired against Colanus to get their hands on the volumes, realizing that they might be the source of all of Colanus' power, secular and magical. Colanus surprised the conspirators by giving them access to the volumes. Of course, they could not read them. And what right did Powl have to read them, or even attempt to decipher them for someone else? The primate was not interested in power as such, he told himself, and was not tempted for the same reasons as the ancient magickers. But he *was* interested in knowledge. It was his greatest strength and weakness as a priest. Knowledge was both the foundation and enemy of faith; without knowledge, there was no possibility of understanding God, but with it, God could be questioned.

Even from his earliest days as a novice, Powl had thought knowledge was a tool used by God to bring his people closer to him and he had pursued it with all his ability, and in those days after his breakthrough with the alphabet and language of the volumes, he came to believe he was in some way fulfilling God's purpose for him.

And for that there will be a reward, he told himself, wanting to believe it.

The name of God.

He picked up his pen again.

Olio and Edaytor walked together along the harbor front, a group of Royal Guards trailing behind. The naval docks were busy with ships being caulked and tarred, their sails mended, their wood sanded and polished, the sheets checked and stowed. The merchant docks were similarly busy, but with supplies being sorted and loaded. The workers were all grim-faced and serious. No one sang shanties or shouted a joke. There was no laughter. This was preparation for war.

Edaytor wrapped his cloak tighter around his round frame as a cool southerly breeze swept up from the sea.

"Another summer gone," he said.

Olio stopped suddenly. "It has been over a year since my mother died." He turned around slowly to view the docks and foreshore. "We're not far from where her pyre was lit." He shook his head. "Who could ever have imagined so much would change in so little a time?" He absently fingered the Key of the Heart, and when he looked up, it was to see the destroyed section of the old city. Some of it had been rebuilt, some was still in various stages of being cleaned out, but the charred skeletons of houses and shops still filled most of the space. On rainy days the smell of burned wood infused the city's air, making those with the strongest memories gag over their food.

"Have you decided what you are going to do with that?" Edaytor asked, pointing to the Key.

"Wear it," Olio answered lightly and tucked it back under his shirt.

"That's no answer, your Highness."

Olio laughed. "Whenever you say 'your Highness' like that, it's a kind of rebuke."

Edaytor looked horrified. "Your Highness!" he burst out before he could stop himself.

"See?"

Edaytor could only harrumph. He put his hands behind his back and bowed his head in embarrassment.

Olio put an arm around the prelate's broad shoulders. "Your

question is one I have been asking myself now since my recovery," he told him, resuming their walk.

"Have you come up with an answer?"

"Of a kind. It is my task in life, I think, to work as a healer." The prince felt Edaytor stiffen under his arm. "But not by using the Key of the Heart directly," he added quickly.

"Then it will involve the Key in some part?" Edaytor pushed.

"Do you know why they are called the Keys of Power?"

Edaytor glanced at the prince. "You are asking questions sidewise," he said. "Is this going to be a lecture?"

"No. You may already know the answer. I did not until I gave the subject a great deal of thought."

"Then to answer as best I can, the obvious reason they are called the Keys of Power is that they contain great magic and are capable of performing great magic."

"You are speaking like a magicker, as you should. But I think you are wrong. I think they are called the Keys of Power because of what they represent, not what they contain. For most people living in Grenda Lear, the Keys belong to the monarch and her family. The Keys represent sovereignty, majesty, stability. That is their true power."

Edaytor considered Olio's words, then asked: "And you derive from that?"

"That we can continue our work to heal the sick and injured, but this time in the open and with the full cooperation of both the church and the queen."

"Your part in this?"

"Purely symbolic. I am the possessor of the Key of Healing. It will be enough."

"Many believe you performed miracles the night of the fire. The common people will be looking for miracles again."

"By providing proper care for those who need it and cannot afford it for themselves, Edaytor, we will supply a flood of miracles. In time, the stories of that terrible night will become like ancient myths; the common people will pretend to believe in them while all the time being the level-headed laborers, cobblers, cooks, and sailors they have always been."

"You underestimate the power of myth," Edaytor said absently, for they had left the harbor behind and were strolling through the crowded foreshore markets. People bustled out of the way of the royal entourage. Edaytor noticed that some faces were scowling at the party. For getting in their way, he presumed. But then he noticed that those few who scowled were directing their attention toward the prince. That could not be, he told himself. No one dislikes Olio.

"I underestimate nothing of the sort," Olio said. There was a heavy tramping ahead. Even the royal entourage moved aside this time as a company of infantry marched past them on their way to the harbor. They carried backpacks as well as weapons.

"On their way to Chandra," Olio told Edaytor. "The Great Army gathers."

Edaytor repressed a shudder. He could not help thinking that great armies invited great disasters. Suddenly, he was overwhelmed with a fierce and burning love for Kendra, for this great city where he had lived all his life, yet at the same time he was afraid for it. Everyone assumed that Lynan would never reach this far, that Kendra was protected by armies, the Rosethemes, and the Keys of Power. He wanted to shout at them that Lynan had an army and was a Rosetheme and possessed two of the four Keys of Power. He wanted to go back to the harbor again and see once more the sun on the water and the ship's pennants in the breeze and the sea birds catching updrafts. He knew there would be other days when he could do it, but he could not escape the feeling that there would come a day—and sooner rather than later—when it would be the last time.

He trembled with the thought that Kendra might be mortal.

It was a meeting neither man looked forward to, but it was the third such and there would be at least one more. Orkid and Dejanus met in the constable's office, at Dejanus' insistence, and sat on opposite sides of a table and passed documents between each other.

"This is the meat requisition order," Orkid said. "The committee approved the cost at its last meeting."

Dejanus scanned it, signed it and passed it back.

"And this is the charcoal requisition order."

"What do I need charcoal for?" Dejanus demanded.

"Your blacksmiths need it."

Dejanus should have realized what the charcoal was for, and both men knew it. "And how much hold space will that take up?" he asked, using anger to cover his embarrassment.

Without any expression Orkid checked a black register that always seemed to be by his left hand. "One ship. We've assigned the *Rutherway*, single mast skip belonging to merchant Ogday Tyke of

Lurisia, to take the charcoal outbound and bring back any sick or wounded—"

"I don't need to know the name of the bloody ship!" Dejanus shouted. He signed the charcoal requisition form and threw it back at Orkid.

"You asked—"

"How many other bloody pieces of paper do I have to sign?"

"Some."

Dejanus leaned across the table. "And why do you need my signature on them anyway?" he hissed. "After all, I'm not on the bloody committee."

"Because you're the commander of the army, of course," Orkid replied. He breathed in heavily and put his hands down on his papers. "We've gone over this before. This is what you've always wanted, Dejanus, and now you have it. All the honor and glory that will go with being in charge of the largest army ever created by Grenda Lear. However, with the honor and glory comes all the detail and boredom. That you now have, too."

Dejanus sat back and sneered. "You enjoy ticking me off, don't you?"

Orkid turned his attention back to his papers. He picked one out and held it up for Dejanus. "Promotion list for officers from local regiments and one or two from Storia."

"Don't pretend you didn't hear me, you Amanite leech."

Orkid held up a second document. "And its opposite, a charge sheet for an incident down on the dock three days ago which resulted in the injury of two workers and necessitated the payment from the army's budget of—" he turned the document so he could read the figure at the bottom "—quite a considerable sum."

For a moment their eyes met. Orkid, impassive as a mountain, did not even blink. Dejanus took the documents, scribbled his signature, and gave them back.

"I can't wait to get out of this city," Dejanus said, his voice filling with self-pity. "Why am I stuck here when my army's already gathering in south Chandra?"

"Most of the army is yet to arrive in Chandra, and for now there is much that needs your attention here in Kendra."

Dejanus stood up, the legs of his chair screeching on the stone floor. "Nothing here needs my attention! It needs my signature. If it needed my attention, I would still be on the committee."

"If you were still on the committee," Orkid said levelly, "the whole kingdom would now be in revolt against the queen and you would be commanding nothing larger than a burial detail."

The chancellor watched with fascination as the constable's normally red face went white as snow and his eyebrows bristled like wire brushes.

"I should kill you for that," Dejanus said, his usual bellow now barely more than a strangled whisper.

"You always assume that I am against you, that when I tell you things I am trying to insult you. Because of our shared . . . past . . . you should know I cannot afford to do that. Why you insist on believing I would cut my own throat to hinder your career is beyond me."

"You didn't want me to be army commander. You didn't even want me to be constable."

"Yes and no. I did not want you to be army commander because I do not think it is a task you have the ability to perform. I did want you to be constable after Areava's ascension to the throne because I believed it was a task you did have the ability to perform."

Dejanus blinked, stumped by the chancellor's candor. It did not bleed away much of his anger, but he found himself without any cause for it other than his indignation at Orkid's opinion of his ability to command the Great Army, that and the suddenly terrifying thought Orkid might be right.

I will not be afraid again! he told himself fiercely. *I will not be afraid again!*

"I'll leave these papers here, shall I?" Orkid asked, patting the pile. "You can study them at your leisure and get them back to me after you've signed them."

"You know I won't read them."

"Yes, I know. But for the sake of the kingdom, Dejanus, at least pretend you know how to be a commander. That way I can pretend along with you."

Before Dejanus could think of an answer, Orkid was gone.

Areava found the loneliness hardest at night, and now that the weather was getting colder, it seemed to hover over her like a ghost. She bastioned herself with cushions and quilts, and still the bed felt as empty as if she was a leaf on a wide sea. Some nights it would be hours before she fell asleep, and she would wake at first light in a shock as if surprised she had found sleep at all. During the day she could hold off the loneliness through sheer hard work, but when she was alone, when she was too tired to read Harnan's notes or Orkid's reports or the royal correspondence, it would rise again and surround her. In a way, the loneliness was worse than the terrible grief she had experienced right after the deaths of Sendarus and her baby; the grief had been swamped by the magnitude of the disasters she and her kingdom had suffered, and in suffering together Areava found strength she had not expected.

But now Grenda Lear was getting on with its existence and Areava must at last face the solitary truth of her own life. As queen she was separated already from the mainstream of life, but as a widow her isolation was complete. At her worst she easily imagined she was unloved, unwanted, cast away, but it was against her nature to feel sorry for herself for long, and she would remember the love and support of Olio, and the devotion of Orkid Gravespear and Harnan Beresard. Ironically, she understood how it was possible to be alone because she was queen, and yet as queen she had more companionship than she did as a woman.

On top of all of that, her head was filled with the details of the war against Lynan. She knew by heart the size of each detachment of troops going to the Great Army and where it came from; she knew the number of ships, naval and merchant, involved in transporting and supplying that army, and she knew how much the whole affair was going to cost her kingdom. It would take a decade for the economy to recover. The crown itself would be in debt for most of her reign.

But Grenda Lear would survive, she told herself. Indeed, it would be stronger and more united because of Lynan's rebellion. In a way he had done her a favor by reducing Haxus—Grenda Lear's oldest enemy—to nothing more than a province ready for annexation once hostilities were over. The whole continent of Theare would come under the sway of her house. The Rosetheme kestrel would fly above every city, every port, every ship that plied the continent's seas.

She was slowly aware of a heavy weight growing between her breasts. For a moment she thought with dread it might be her heart, but realised almost right away it was the Key of the Scepter. In wonder, she lifted the quilt over her. The Key looked no different. She touched it gingerly and gasped when a spark flew between the Key and her finger. This had happened before to her, when she had first touched it after Berayma's murder.

What was happening?

Incredibly, even as her breathing and heartbeat increased in excitement and fear, she felt unconsciousness, heavy and dark, slip over her mind.

"No!" she cried out, but her voice was small and weak.

The Key was now so heavy it pressed down on her like a great stone weight.

And then she was no longer in Kendra.

A face flashed across her mind's eye, female, ancient and beautiful at the same time, alluring and terrible. Then a Chett's face, not a girl but not much older, strong, powerful and determined. *Like me,* Areava thought. Then Ager Parmer, one-eyed and serious. Another woman's face, also young, but unmistakably Kendran, and around her a great aura of power. The magicker who had escaped with Lynan, but a student no longer.

And then Lynan's face, but changed dramatically, cruelly; pale and scarred, his eyes too old for his eighteen years. He was naked, aroused, fevered, muttering obscenities.

Areava tried to look away.

Lynan still, and then another presence over him, speaking to him but in no tongue Areava understood. A glimpse of a face, the first one Areava had seen, with deep yellow eyes and irises without striation. Terrible eyes. The face turned away and dark wings wrapped around Lynan.

Areava felt an overwhelming need to flee. Again, she tried to look away, to send herself somewhere else, but whatever power had brought her here would not let her escape.

The thing with a woman's face smiled at her brother. Her lips parted and blood seeped from the corners of her mouth.

Areava screamed, and everything went dark.

25

LYNAN'S madness lasted four nights.

On the first night, the night Lynan had slain Farben, Jenrosa left the city by herself and made an incantation in the air. A ring of fire as red as the setting sun spread out in the sky, its moon shadow rippling along the ground like a bloody tide.

On the second night she left the city by herself and made an incantation on the earth. The ground beneath her feet coughed up the rotting body of a dead soldier, the flesh still hanging from its bones.

On the third night she left the city by herself and made an incantation in the water of the Barda River. The water broke in waves that spread out from her in a great circle. Fish fled the river and suffocated on the banks, twisting and flopping in pain.

On the fourth night, the night when she would make her greatest magic, she first walked slowly from her room to Lynan's private chambers. When she got there, the two Red Hands on duty immediately let her through; no one stopped a companion of the White Wolf.

Lynan was in his bed, his eyes open but his mind somewhere else. His lips constantly muttered strange sentences that no one understood. He took neither food nor drink, but he did not diminish. His skin shone in the candlelight like marble.

On his left side sat Korigan. On his right side sat Ager. They looked at Jenrosa when she entered. Korigan tried to smile. Ager's expression was asking questions she could not answer; not yet, anyway.

Ager made way for her. She leaned over Lynan and whispered in his ear, "The past is the same, but the present has no boundary."

Instantly, he stopped his muttering, and his head turned so he could look at her.

"What did you say?" Korigan asked urgently.

Jenrosa waved her quiet. Lynan was saying something, but she could not hear it.

"The past is the same," she repeated, "but the present has no boundary." She put her ear next to his mouth.

"The past is the present," said a voice that was not Lynan's.

Jenrosa shot up straight and stepped away from Lynan. He smiled at her, something sickly and depraved, and for an instant his eyes focused on her face. Then he turned his head back, his eyes glazed over once more, and he returned to his muttering.

"What happened?" Korigan demanded.

"What did you do?" Ager added.

Jenrosa shuddered. She felt dirty, infected. She wanted to run to the Barda River and throw herself in, sink like a stone to the bottom and drown.

Ager grasped her arm and she flinched from the contact.

"God's death, Jenrosa!" he called. "What's wrong?" Instinctively, he took a step toward her.

Jenrosa put her hands out to ward him away.

"Tell me what just happened," Korigan ordered, coming around to their side of the bed.

"I cannot tell you," Jenrosa said breathlessly. She shook her head to ward off any more questions. "Not yet. I will tell you later." She ran for the door.

"Jenrosa!" Korigan cried after her.

"Trust me!" she called back but did not stop. She ran until she reached her room. A single candle burned on a washstand. She splashed her face and throat with water. Shadows danced around her. She knew what they meant. She had not much time. She took some materials from one of her saddlebags at the foot of her bed and left. She intended to walk out of the palace, out of the city and into the country to perform the last of the four magics, but when she got outside was stopped by the sheer menace in the air and the realization she might not have enough time. Panic rose in her and she pushed it down with a great effort of will. Where could she go? She needed fire . . .

Almost at once she thought of the smithy. But would the blacksmith let her use it? She shouted an order to a passing patrol of Red Hands to follow her, and she made her way out of the palace and through the streets. When they arrived, the blacksmith was still at work, adding the finishing touches to one of the blades for a pair of shears. He saw them approach out of the corner of his eye and angrily barred their way, holding out his tongs like a sword with the red hot piece still in them.

"You lot have just put in my new furnace and now you want to destroy that one, too? I won't have it—"

Jenrosa nodded to the Red Hands. A short sword flashed in the air and the tongs clattered to the ground, broken in two. None too gently they evicted the shocked blacksmith from his own shop and set up guard outside.

Jenrosa made sure no one else was inside and closed the doors. Warm air blossomed inside the smithy. Sweat prickled her face. She gazed into the center of the furnace, steadied her heart, and began the incantation, her voice starting as barely a whisper and rising as the magic gained strength. The fire grew hotter as the chant continued, changing from orange to yellow to white, and its core seemed to pulse with a life of its own. Tendrils of flame licked out from the furnace, reaching for Jenrosa like grasping fingers. The tendrils merged together, created writhing patterns that suggested shapes Jenrosa thought she recognized but could put no name to; then she saw a face, indistinct, unrecognizable as any individual, but a face nonetheless with eyes and mouth and ears. The flames retreated. The heat in the smithy was almost unbearable; she felt as if she were standing in the middle of the sun. Sweat saturated her clothes, plastered her hair to her scalp.

More tendrils, sinuous, tinged with blue and green. Forests. Wings. A woman.

There, Jenrosa thought. *Now.*

The core changed color. A bright ruby point that swelled until it seemed to fill the whole furnace. A face, and this one she knew. She screamed at it in fear and hate, and the face screamed back at her.

A wall of air moved out from the furnace, picked up Jenrosa like a leaf in a storm and threw her against the smithy door. The door flew open and she tumbled outside among the startled Red Hands. Hands scrabbled to pick her up. She remembered to breathe. The cool night air touched her skin, made her shiver. She looked up and saw a cloud of black, greasy smoke pillow into the sky until a fresh breeze above the city walls caught it and whipped it away.

"Truespeaker, are you all right?" one of the Red Hands asked.

Jenrosa hardly noticed the title. "We have to get back to the palace. Quickly."

She tried to take a step but was too weak. Hands grabbed at her again.

"Best wait a while," another Red Hand said.

"Quickly!" she cried. "For Lynan's sake!"

That did it. They set off at a brisk trot, supporting Jenrosa between them.

"Hurry!" she called desperately, afraid she would be too late, and clutching at the dagger under her shirt.

The whole time Lynan was in the forest—and time behaved very strangely when he was there—she was never very far from him. Even when he could not see her, he could hear her song.

"I do not understand the words," he told her once.

"It is a song of desire," she replied. "A song of deep and great want."

"You are singing to me?"

"I am singing for you," she laughed.

The sun never rose in the forest, although the moon was so bright there was no need for it anyway. His eyes could tell colors and shapes apart as easily as they could in the day, and everything possessed a beautiful sheen, as if gilt in silver. When she was close, the color became more like jade or emerald.

When she was not singing for him, she was asking him questions.

One time she said to him, "Tell me about the queen."

"Which one?"

"The one you sleep with."

"The one I love."

"The one you sleep with," she insisted, the laugh never far from her voice.

"She is wild and beautiful."

"And she loves you."

"Yes."

"Tell me about the other one."

"The other queen?"

"The other woman. The one you love."

"No."

"You will not tell me about her?"

"I do not love her."

With one long, sharp nail she traced the shape of a heart on his chest. "Tell me about her."

"She is in pain all the time. I do not know how to reach her."

"But you do not love her," she said, pretending to pout.

"No."

"Tell me about her."

"The queen or the one I love?"

"The queen who hates you."

"She is my sister."

"She is half of you."

"No."

"She has half the Keys." She used her finger to lift the Keys and study them closely. "Is she beautiful?"

"I do not know."

"Is she as beautiful as you?"

"I do not know."

"I need all the Keys. Without them, we cannot be together forever."

"I know. I will kill her for you and take her Keys."

"Soon," she said, and then again, drawing out the word, rubbing her thigh against his. "Soon, my love."

"You can have my Keys now," he said.

She seemed to consider it, but let them drop from her finger. They clinked together. "No."

"But—"

She placed her hand over his mouth. "No." She lifted her hand and kissed him deeply. His head was filled with the great smell of her, of ancient earth and ancient sex. "I will not be half-complete." After a long while she pulled back from him. "I am half of you, too."

"If I am half my sister and half Silona, what is there of Lynan?"

"Nothing at all," she said, her voice mocking. "There never was."

Another time she said to him, "I will teach you to fly."

"You will make me like you. I will be like Silona."

"No one is like Silona," she said. "I am the last of my kind. I was here before your people came to Theare. We were hundreds then, each with our own great forest. At night we would fly over the continent and sing to one another. We would take each other on the wing. We had such beauty, such power."

"Why are you the last?"

"All the others were slain by iron and fire, their forests butchered for farms, their wings turned into cloaks for petty, horse-riding chieftains."

"The Chetts killed your people?"

"You are all Chetts, dear Lynan."

"Why are you still here?"

"Someone has to sing the song. Someone has to desire more than life."

Another time she said to him, "I will teach you pain."

She held his head in her clawed hands and her nails bit deep into his scalp. His blood ran down her wrists and she licked them clean. She scraped her clawed hands down his chest and thighs until the blood ran down his legs and pooled at his feet and she devoured it all.

The pain was all the ecstasy he had ever known.

"Do you know pain?" he asked her.

"I know only desire," she said, and he tasted the lie but was afraid to say so.

She saw the doubt in his face and it made her angry. She drew away from him.

"I am sorry," he said.

She ignored him.

"Come back. I am sorry."

She was smiling at him now, her face appearing behind branches and leaves. Teasing him.

"I will do anything," he said.

She drifted toward him, carried on a breeze, her great black wings rippling in the sky. Behind her head the moon gave her a halo.

But there was the moon, above him.

The light behind her flared suddenly. He heard her scream, and the sound of it was like a dagger thrust into his own body.

Night. A single candle flickered on the washstand. Ager seated on his right, his head bowed in sleep, his crookback moving up and down with his steady breathing. Korigan on his left, her long body slumped over the bed, her black hair spread out over the white sheets.

And himself.

It took a moment, then he remembered who he was. And he remembered her.

"How long?" he asked.

He felt his chest and scalp. There was no bleeding, no scars.

"God."

The light. Its echo still made him blink. What had it been?

He remembered it all. Tears sprang down his cheeks. His stomach roiled.

He wanted to vomit. He wanted to flay off his skin and throw it away. He wanted to cut off his sex. He wanted to dig out his own eyes, slice off his ears, lop off his own hands. He had been so fouled he would never be human again.

He glanced at his friends again. Ager stirred.

"No," he said firmly. They must not see him or touch him. He would be the cause of their death. He was becoming like her, like Silona, and everything close to him would corrupt. He would be a charnel house.

He wanted to close his eyes but was afraid of what he would see.

"Finish it," some part of him said.

Kill myself, he thought. *God knows, no one else can.*

"No," that part of him said again. "Finish it."

Finish what? He hunted down the thought.

Finish Silona. It was the only way he could be saved.

He slid out of the bed and dressed quickly. He found his weapons under his clothes and strapped them on. He stopped at the door. The Red Hands would follow him. They would never let him be. They would die for him.

"No one else will die for me," he said, and went to the window. He eased it open and lightly jumped outside. He was in the courtyard. He could see Red Hands posted at each corner. It was too dark for them to see him. Slowly, quietly, he made his way from the courtyard to the stables. There were two hands there playing a game under a lantern. They did not hear him. He went behind the stables to the feeding yard and found a good Chett mare. The horse smelled him and started whinnying, but he held its head without hurting it and spoke to it and let it sniff the back of his hand and then his hair. He gathered a second mare the same way. He chose two bridles from some hanging from the yard fence, fitted them around the horses' heads, and led them out of the yard. He snuck back into the stable and took a saddle and blanket, returned to the horses, buckled one with the gear, and mounted. Holding tightly onto the reins of both horses, he kicked the one under him into a gallop, charging out of the palace before any of the guards could challenge him.

Through the dark he rode, east and then south, across the Barda River and deep into enemy territory.

"Where is he?" Jenrosa shouted.

Ager and Korigan leaped into the air, both reaching for their weapons. Jenrosa ignored them and rushed to the bed, desperately whipping aside the sheets even though it was obvious even a child could not have been hiding under them.

Jenrosa grabbed Ager by his poncho. The Red Hands looked on in shock and surprise. Surely even the White Wolf would be more careful around the crookback?

"God's death, Ager," she shouted in his face, shaking him, "where is Lynan?"

"I . . ." He looked around confused. "I fell asleep . . ."

Jenrosa turned on Korigan. "You must have seen him! You must know where he is!"

Korigan looked blankly at her. "No. He was here." She looked up hopefully. "The Red Hands on guard . . ."

Jenrosa nodded to two of the Red Hands, who looked shamefacedly down at the ground. "Lynan did not go past them." She saw the open window and ran across to it. She leaned out, called Lynan's name, anger and panic in her voice. Red Hands gathered from around the courtyard.

Jenrosa turned around and slumped against the sill. "He's gone. I'm too late."

Now it was Ager's turn to grab Jenrosa. "What are you talking about? What's happened?"

She would not answer. To Ager, she seemed to fall in on herself, become at once diminished. He exchanged glances with Korigan.

"Get Gudon," he commanded one of the Red Hands, then ordered everyone except Korigan and Jenrosa to leave the room. When they were alone, Ager and Korigan guided Jenrosa to the empty bed. Ager got a cup of water and forced some of it down her throat. She gasped and coughed, tried to push him away.

"Now, tell me what's happened," Ager demanded.

"I tried to break the nexus between Lynan and Silona," she said wearily.

"And?"

"And I don't know. Something happened tonight. Maybe the nexus was broken." She rubbed her face with her hands. "Maybe."

"Then where is he?"

Jenrosa shrugged. "I don't know."

Ager threw away the cup. It shattered on the floor. He held her head in his hands and forced her to look at him. "You do know."

She pulled away from him, slapped at his hands, kicked at his legs. "I don't know!" she screamed. Ager retreated, surprised.

"I don't understand," Korigan said, looking between the two.

"Jenrosa used her magic to try and free Lynan from the vampire's grip."

"But something went wrong?" Neither answered her. "Is he Lynan again?"

Gudon came in, his usual cheery expression turned grim.

"Lynan is miss—" Ager started to explain.

"I know," Gudon interrupted. "Red Hands told me he rode out of the palace."

All eyes turned to him.

"When?" Jenrosa demanded, getting to her feet. *Maybe there is still time,* she thought. *Maybe if we can find him . . .*

"They came to me as soon as it happened."

"Then we have to go after him," Korigan said grimly, making for the door.

Ager stopped her.

"What are you doing?"

"Jenrosa?" Ager said. "You know where he is going."

How much can I tell them? Jenrosa thought. I can't finish this task without their help. She searched their faces as if she might find the answer there.

"Jenrosa?" Korigan urged. Jenrosa tried to close out the suffering she heard in that voice.

There's only one way to help Lynan now, she thought, *and all of us.* She said, "He must be going to her."

"What?"

"To Silona. I destroyed whatever direct control she established over him after the battle against Charion's rebels. But her hold over him is still strong. She must have called to him as the connection between them was cut. I think he is riding for the forest where she lives."

"Then we have to go after him," Korigan repeated, looking at Ager as if daring him to challenge her again.

"We cannot," Ager said tightly. "To do so is to risk losing everything he has fought for."

"We can't let him face Silona by himself!"

"That is not what I said. But you must stay here. You are the ruler of the Chetts, and in Lynan's absence the commander of all his forces. No one must know that Lynan has left Daavis."

"But he was seen by the Red Hands—"

"They will not talk about it," Gudon said over her. "I will make sure of that."

"Better, those who were on guard tonight can come with me to bring back Lynan," Ager said.

"You?" Gudon said. "Truth, better if I go. You will be missed."

Jenrosa saw her chance. "You will all be missed," she said. "Only I need go. He needs a magicker, not a warrior."

"You cannot go by yourself," Ager said.

"I will bring with me the Red Hands you would have taken."

"You will need more than a handful of guards to ride through Chandra."

"I am not going to war, Ager Parmer," she said. "As it is, we will not catch up with him before he reaches the forest. He is a lone rider, and a good one. Give me an escort of those Red Hands who were on duty tonight, no more. The rest of you must stay here and carry on as if Lynan is still here. By now everyone in the city knows he is ill, so they will not be surprised that he is not seen around the palace. Leave the rest to me."

The expression on all the faces of the other three showed their apprehension.

"You don't have a choice," Jenrosa said. "None of us has a choice anymore."

26

"YOU are twisting yourself apart, my lord," Barys told his master. King Tomar did not reply. He could not deny it, after all.

"You have, I think, already made a decision," Barys continued.

"Meaning?"

"That you are afraid to implement it."

Tomar was not offended. Coming from anyone else, he would have been. With Barys, however, it was an observation, not a criticism. Barys knew the king too well to question his courage, and was not himself ashamed of fear, having proven in countless battles that he could overcome it.

"There is something inherently unlikable about irrevocable decisions," Tomar said.

"You've made those before."

"Never easily, and never with so much at stake."

"The future of Chandra," Barys said heavily, and his shoulders seemed to bow a little as if they were taking some of the weight from Tomar's own.

"The future of all of Grenda Lear," Tomar corrected him.

They were riding side by side outside the walls of Sparro. Up ahead was a large, level plain called the Field of Spears where Chandra's army traditionally mustered before marching off to war. Gathered there at the moment were the remaining knights of the Twenty Houses. Without their armor they looked like nothing more than well-trained medium cavalry, but they moved with dash and elan. Many from the court had come to watch and admire their exercises and horsemanship.

"They do sit prettily," Barys said.

"They fight well, too. I saw them in action once. I think their charge is the most frightening thing I have ever witnessed. I would hate to be at the receiving end of one."

"They charged Lynan's lancers in their last major action."

"And won."

"Barely."

The pair exchanged glances and half-smiles. It occurred to the king then that being charged by his own province's cavalry when led by the tall, lean, gray-haired Barys might be as frightening as confronting Kendra's massed knights.

"The really interesting thing, of course," Tomar said, "is the fact that the Chetts have lancers at all."

Barys nodded. "Kumul Alarn's doing, I'd say. He was involved in a similar unit under the General before being promoted captain of the Red Shields."

"I wonder what else Lynan and his friends have introduced to the Chetts."

"A great cause. Lynan's."

They arrived at the field. The knights were practicing the charge, starting at one end of the field and making to the other at full gallop. There were three lines. At first the lines stayed straight, but as the charge progressed they became more ragged. Nevertheless, all the riders would have delivered their spear points against the enemy within one or two seconds of each other. That kind of shock was almost impossible to recover from, save for the best trained and sturdiest infantry. The knights were battle winners, the final reserve; theoretically that meant they were not used until the final deciding blow was needed. If practice was not so tidy, it was often the fault of the knights themselves, who were ever eager to demonstrate their prowess and bugger the tactics. Tomar remembered that the General refused to use the knights because they were so unreliable.

The two riders edged along the border of the field, leaving behind most of the spectators. There was a solitary mounted figure ahead, sitting well despite her diminutive size, and Tomar recognized Charion. His first impulse was to turn around and go back, but he forced himself to continue. She was his guest after all—a *royal* guest—and that bestowed obligations above and beyond making sure she had a roof over her head and food on her plate. As he got closer, he could not fail to see how miserable she was.

She has lost a kingdom, you fool, he rebuked himself. *Of course she's miserable. She has seen her city taken, her people killed, her inheritance ripped from her hands.*

But what to do with you, your Majesty? What in God's name to do with you?

"They are wonderful to watch!" he called out.

Her head turned in surprise. "King Tomar!"

"I am sorry for disturbing your reverie."

She smiled shyly, and for the first time Tomar realised how beautiful she was. If she had not been so young, and he not filled with so many memories of his first wife, he might have considered doing something about it. That would have merited a new chapter in the kingdom's history books, he thought; a merger between Chandra and Hume.

"You have not disturbed me, your Majesty," she said. "Or rather, I am glad to be disturbed from my thoughts."

He stopped next to her. Barys rode on a little to give them some privacy.

"You have survived a great deal these last few months," Tomar said consolingly. "It cannot be easy for you, especially here in exile."

"I will survive," she said, without hubris. "What is it you called out?"

He motioned to the knights. "I said they are wonderful to watch."

"They are magnificent. I have never seen such warriors. I had heard of them, of course, but thought they were just for show; Queen Usharna's parade leaders. When I win back Hume, I will create such a band."

They watched the knights in silence for a while, then Charion asked: "What will you do with us, your Majesty?"

The question hung in the air, like an echo of his own thoughts.

"We are yours to use," she said. "Prince Lynan and his army cannot be far off invading Chandra."

"We?"

"The knights and I. For now our fortunes are tied together."

"Areava is gathering an army in my south. I believe the first contingents have already arrived."

"As you say, the army is gathering in the south. Lynan can only attack your north. He must do it before winter, you know that."

Oh, yes, I know it. "So you would not go south? Your experience in fighting Lynan would be invaluable to the new army."

"My experience in *losing* to Lynan will benefit no one."

"My own army is a tight-knit one, Queen Charion," he said. "It would not be easy to incorporate you and the knights." He nodded to Barys. "And I already have a commander who would feel uncomfortable having a queen and three hundred Kendran nobleman running under his banner."

"There must be something we can do besides running away again."

The bitterness in her voice surprised him. This was not the time to argue with her. "I will think on it," he said. "I promise no more."

"I ask for no more," she said neutrally. They bowed slightly to each other and Tomar prodded his horse to catch up with Barys.

"How did it go?" his champion asked.

"She wants to fight."

"Then send her south so she may join the Great Army."

"She doesn't want to be part of any Great Army, I think."

Barys shrugged. "Understandable, perhaps. Neither do we."

"How are our forces stretched?"

"Tight along the border with Chandra, as you'd expect."

"You won't reinforce them?"

"For what purpose? We cannot hold the whole border against Lynan. Best to keep the bulk of our forces in reserve to strike where we have to, or to add to Areava's beast—assuming it ever moves north."

They rode on in silence. Eventually Barys said, "What are you thinking?"

"I am thinking of how to get Charion and the knights out of our hair."

"Order them to join the Great Army."

"I cannot order Charion to do anything of the sort. I'm not even sure I outrank Galen in the scheme of things. He is Areava's cousin, after all. I am nothing but a provincial ruler."

"You are king here," Barys said gravely.

"And why should I add to Areava's forces?"

Both rides stopped. Barys studied Tomar's face intently. "You *have* made up your mind, haven't you?"

"I think you can shorten your line on the border. Pull back the westernmost patrols. We can let Charion and the knights have that for their playground. That way they are out of the way, and will neither help nor hinder either side."

"When?"

"Send your orders out this afternoon. I will talk to Charion and Galen tonight, and they can leave tomorrow."

"Very well. And next?"

Tomar shook his head. "I have been praying for a way to avoid taking sides, but cannot see it yet. Still, every delay gives us more time to find a way."

"One way or another we'll be fighting before winter," Barys said grimly.

"I fear you are right. I cannot let Chandra become a battleground without doing something to help determine its fate."

Tomar escorted Charion and the knights to the edge of Sparro. While Tomar and Galen talked, Charion seemed distracted. Eventually the king asked her if something was wrong.

"It's the sea," she said.

Tomar looked quizzically at her.

"My capital is inland, yours is on the sea. I think I have grown used to the smell of it while I have been here. I will miss it going west."

Tomar felt absurdly flattered by that. It was not as if he had sited the capital. Still, it was *his* city.

"When this is over, perhaps I could visit again," she said.

"Chandra would be honored."

"Our two lands have always had much to talk about, after all."

Tomar laughed softly. "If only they had talked instead of drawn swords."

"Things would have been very different, I think." Her eyes seemed to see right through him, then, and he wondered if she saw deception or loyalty. He found himself wishing Charion had been old, male, and rude. People are easier to betray if you do not like them.

Enough, Tomar, he chided himself. *You have betrayed no one yet.*

They reined in at the ancient stone on the road west that marked the city's limits.

"Thank you for not sending me south," Charion said.

"I don't think Areava herself could force you to do something you had no mind to do," Tomar said.

Galen grinned at that, and offered his thanks as well.

"Do not thank me yet," Tomar told them. "When the war is over, we will meet again, I hope."

Galen saluted and rode to the head of the knights. Charion hesitated. "The world will never again be like it was, will it?"

Tomar shook his head. "Nothing you were certain of before can be counted on," he warned her.

"I always thought I wanted change when I was just queen of Hume and had nothing more exciting to do than negotiate trade agreements or make jokes about the king of Chandra. But I hate change. I hate what it does to us, and what it does to our people."

"It's not change you hate," Tomar said, but not unkindly. "It's losing."

Charion laughed out loud. It was the first time Tomar had ever heard her really let go. *God, if we both survive this, maybe I will woo her.*

"Farewell, King of Chandra," she said, turning her horse and galloping after the knights.

"Farewell, Queen of Hume," he replied to her back, and wondered if he would ever see her again.

Two nights after, Tomar was woken from sleep by one of his guards.

"What is it?"

"It is Barys Malayka, your Majesty. He waits for you in your chambers. He said it is urgent."

Tomar dressed quickly, his mind going through all the possible disasters that might induce Barys to rouse his king from his well-earned sleep. Barys was not one to panic, so whatever it was demanded his personal—and royal—attention and no one else's.

"It's Lynan," Barys said as soon as the king reached his chambers. Barys had been pacing up and down the room; Tomar could see his muddy prints everywhere.

"I wish you'd take your boots off," he said.

Barys looked down, his eyes following the twisting line of tracks that ended with him. "He's crossed the border," he added.

"How large is his army?"

Barys held up a single finger.

"What does that mean? One thousand? One division?"

"One man. Lynan. By himself."

Tomar looked stupidly at Barys.

"He was seen by two men at one of our posts not far from where the Barda River crosses our border with Hume."

"By himself?"

"Moving quickly on horse, with an extra mount. Two hours later, a group of Chetts also crossed the border; the guards were not sure how many, but they think around company strength."

"Troop," Tomar corrected him, absently. "They call them troops."

"One troop. About a hundred riders, give or take a handful."

"Their leader?"

"A woman. That's all they could tell."

"Korigan."

"Maybe."

Tomar raised his arms in exasperation. "What is going on?" His eyes opened wide. "He's coming here! That's it! He's coming to Sparro!"

"No," Barys said. "Lynan is heading southwest. So was the troop following."

Tomar found a seat and collapsed in it. "I don't understand. What does the boy think he is doing? Where does he think he is going?"

"I don't know the answer to either of those questions," Barys said, "but I can tell you what will happen if they don't change course."

Tomar did not like the sound of Barys' voice. "Tell me."

"Sooner or later, Lynan and his troop will run into Charion and the knights of the Twenty Houses."

"Oh." Tomar sat up straight. "Damn."

"I don't care how good a fighter the General's son is," Barys continued, "but I can tell you that he and a single troop of Chetts will not survive that encounter."

"Damn."

"My lord, you can no longer put it off. If you've already made a decision about which side you are going to support in this civil war, give me your instructions now. Before it's too late."

27

LYNAN rode both his mounts into the ground. The first fell when he was less than halfway to his destination, collapsing under him. He had tumbled over the ground and lay there dazed, for how long he did not know. When he finally got to his feet, he found the stricken mare trying to lift its head above the grass; one of its legs was broken.

"I'm sorry," Lynan muttered, and cut its throat. With some effort he took the saddle off the dead mare and put it on the survivor, cropping grass nearby.

He restrained his own impatience and forced himself to allow the second mare to take more frequent and longer breaks, sometimes even allowing himself to catch snatches of sleep, but by the end of the fourth day it was still too much for the animal. Within sight of the Forest of Silona it simply stopped. Lynan dismounted, and as if it was the signal for release it needed, it sank to its knees, lay down, and simply stopped breathing.

It was early evening. Clouds covered most of the sky and there was little light. The land seemed gray and empty. Ahead, perhaps fifteen leagues away, was the forest, the focus of all his fear and desire. He started walking.

Near midnight he stopped. He was near the center of a crest that ran along the western border of a broad valley. He looked eastward over the valley and saw the dark, undulating peace of it and was brought to tears. He wiped them away, surprised by the reaction, ashamed he could cry for himself like this, but despite everything that had happened to him he recognized at that moment a part of himself he had not touched since he had been given the vampire's blood, a part that was not interested in fighting or conquest or proving himself, a part of himself that yearned to be nothing more than alive and at rest.

Stop feeling sorry for yourself, he ordered, and used his eyesight to study the valley more carefully. Now he remembered it. The Arran Valley, where the mercenary Jes Prado had first caught him all those seasons ago. This was no place of peace. There was no such place anywhere on Theare anymore. He turned his back on it and resumed walking toward the forest.

He reached the first scattered stands of summer trees after dawn, their brown leaves already dropping. The clouds had gone overnight and sunlight scattered through the remaining canopy, warming his skin. He could hear the song of bird and insect. In the distance came the lowing of cows on one of the farms in the valley, now out of sight. As he continued walking, the summer trees were joined by wideoaks and then the headseeds, the largest of all the forest trees. The farther into the forest he went, the less effect autumn seemed to have on the land. Leaves were still green and supple, the ground still warm and moist. Strangely, despite all the evidence of burgeoning life, there was no longer any sound of bird or insect. High above a breeze stirred the tops of the trees, but the sound of it did not reach the ground.

There was just a great silence, a great stillness. Expectation.

Lynan breathed deeply, closed his eyes, and lay down on the ground.

He had arrived, and now only had to wait for Silona to find him.

Jenrosa did not know how far ahead Lynan was, but by using her magic to extend the endurance of their mounts she and her escort of Red Hands drove deep into Chandra, resting little, swallowing the leagues. When they finally stopped for the day, they all fell into a deep, recuperative sleep, again helped by Jenrosa's magic. Each morning, before light, they were off again, the land gliding by them as if they were at sea with nothing but waves to slow their progress.

Jenrosa, not a natural rider, had to concentrate all the time on staying on her horse, a relief for her, for otherwise her mind would dwell on was what would happen once she caught up with Lynan, or on the blank acceptance the Chetts seemed to have for her as their Truespeaker, something she knew with utter certainty she was not and never would be. *No Truespeaker would do what I am about to do,* she constantly told herself. The worst time was at night when they could not risk riding. Clouds scudded across the moon and stars, and every shape and every silhouette reminded Jenrosa of Silona. For all of that, she was far more afraid of Lynan.

Before sleep found her, in her mind's eye the universe seemed to fold and collapse onto one point in time, and each night that point came closer and closer. All her magic seemed to concentrate at that point. Beyond it, there was no Lynan at all.

At noon on the fifth day, exhausted and bedraggled, the party could see the outskirts of the forest halfway between them and the horizon. Very quickly Chett scouts found Lynan's dead mare, already partly devoured by scavengers.

"And it was his last mount," they told her. "There was only one set of horse tracks."

"And Lynan?"

"His foot tracks lead straight to the forest."

"Then we have to hurry!" she cried urgently, and the troop started its last mad dash. Even Jenrosa's magic could not save all the horses this time, and many of the riders dropped behind. By the time the rest of them reached the forest's edge, the sun was already down. They urged on their mounts, but they would go no farther, some of them even rearing and toppling their riders rather than go under the canopy.

"Make camp here," she told them. She dismounted, strapped on her sword and dagger, threw her saddlebags over her shoulder, and started walking deeper into the forest.

The Red Hands scrambled to catch up with her. "What do you think you're doing?" she asked them.

"You are going to find the White Wolf," said Sunatay, the troop commander, a middle-aged warrior who seemed to have more scar tissue than skin. "We will come with you."

"Your job was to escort me here, and will be to escort Lynan and me back to Daavis," she told her. "You cannot come into the forest."

"But you will be alone!"

"I have to be alone," Jenrosa said.

It was clear from the Chetts' faces that they did not understand.

"Do you know what lives in the forest?" she asked them.

"Something that wants to harm the White Wolf," Sunatay said.

"What on earth can harm Lynan?"

The Red Hands looked at one another. It was clear that they did not know.

"Only one thing can," she told them, "and her name is Silona."

The name passed among them like the lick of wind that comes before a storm. They recognized the name, and knew it was associated in some way with the White Wolf. Some of them took a step back from the forest. The fear that rose in them was atavistic, and even Jenrosa could feel it.

"She is so powerful that a thousand Chetts could not help Lynan. Only magic can defeat this creature. My magic. You must stay here, rest the horses. I will return with the White Wolf as soon as I can. Wait five nights for us. If we have not returned in that time, we will not be coming back at all. Do you understand?"

"Some of us should go with you," Sunatay persisted. "You might encounter something else in the forest besides Silona."

And let you stop me doing what I have to do? Jenrosa thought *I have come too far for that.*

"No beast lives in this forest. Stay here. You will only get in my way if you come with me."

Sunatay looked unhappy, but nodded gruffly. "Very well. Five nights. Then we come to find you."

"Rest," Jenrosa ordered them, and marched into the forest.

When she was out of sight, Sunatay beckoned to a man who looked as if he had seen as much combat as she.

"Rosof, you must take over the troop," she told him.

"Where are you going?"

Sunatay screwed up her face. "Where do you think?"

"You're going into the forest by yourself?"

"I will take two others. We will stay hidden from the Truespeaker. I do not want to disturb her magic."

"Then why go at all?"

"Because it is our duty to protect the White Wolf. Maybe the Truespeaker is right, and we will be useless against Silona, but maybe she is wrong in this. Remember, our ancestors once destroyed all the vampires who lived around the Oceans of Grass. And, Rosof, wait three nights, not five. If we are not all back by then, revenge us."

Lynan had expected her to come on the first night.

He waited with a mix of anticipation and dread, constantly fighting the urge to run away, to make for naked land and clear sky. He lay on his back, staring at the dark canopy, his sword drawn. He listened for any sound that might warn him of her approach, starting every time a branch creaked. On more than one occasion he thought he heard the soft padding of footsteps, but when he sat up and looked around, there was nothing.

When the first, fitful rays of dawn penetrated the canopy, he felt elation, but that evaporated with the realization he would have to endure a second night in the forest.

Or I could just leave, he told himself. *I have done my duty. I came to the forest to slay Silona, but I cannot spend the rest of my life looking for her.*

The argument did not work. He knew Silona would come to him eventually. She needed him even more than he desired her. Even if he ran to the farthest corner of Theare, he believed she would follow him, in his dreams and in his insanity. There was no escape from her now.

If he had a choice at all, anymore, it was to force the issue. He stood up, looked around him. There was one part of the surrounding forest that seemed darker and even more foreboding than the rest, and he knew instinctively the heart of Silona's kingdom lay that way. He started walking. His footsteps were the only sound. Several hours later when, as far as he could tell, the sun was at its highest, he stopped briefly. For less than a heartbeat the sound of footsteps did not. He pretended not to notice.

He resumed walking, keeping up a steady gait. At midafternoon he stopped suddenly. Again, a sound as if his footsteps had caused an echo. He knew it was not Silona, who could not come out in daylight. Someone had followed him all the way from Daavis after all. Ager? he wondered. No. The crookback was a wonderful rider, but his injuries meant he could not walk swiftly, and certainly not silently. Gudon, then. Perhaps. Korigan? No. She would stay with the army. Jenrosa?

Yes. It made sense. And yes, he realized then, it was she who had freed him from his insanity back in Daavis. Only Jenrosa would have had that kind of power, and the fact that it had been Jenrosa who first gave him Silona's blood gave her magic extra leverage. What had Silona said about Jenrosa? That she was the one he loved. He had denied it, and only now was beginning to understand how much of a lie that had been. He had told himself it was not true because she had chosen Kumul over him. Should he call out to her? Was she still afraid that he was mad? Or possessed, even? At the

same time, he realized Silona had still been wrong. The love he felt
for Jenrosa was not what he felt for Korigan, or even what he had
felt for the magicker at the start of their relationship. Jenrosa was
part of him now, part of what he had grown to become, one of his
true friends and companions. He owed her more than he could ever
say, and it said much about Silona that she had misinterpreted his
feelings for Jenrosa.

Yes, time to end this particular game.

He turned swiftly on his heel, smiling broadly.

And saw a man.

He stood thirty or forty paces away, between the gray trunks of
two headseeds, more silhouette than shape.

"I knew you heard my footsteps," the man said.

There was something vaguely familiar about the voice. For that
matter there was something vaguely familiar about the silhouette.
Lynan's smile disappeared.

"How long have you been following me?"

The man moved, not toward Lynan but around him, as if there
was an invisible wall between them.

"From the moment you entered the forest."

"You were with me last night," Lynan said, remembering the
soft padding.

"I was watching you." By now he was between Lynan and the
deeper forest, and Lynan could see the figure was dressed in a short
coat.

"Who are you?"

"I think you have come far enough, Lynan Rosetheme. Go back
to your people."

Lynan walked toward him. At first the figure retreated, but then
stopped, legs apart, as if he would physically bar his way. As he
drew closer, Lynan saw more detail. The man had long hair that rat-
tailed over his shoulders, and he was wearing a coat that was too
small for him; but the face was bowed slightly and he could not see
it from the shadows.

"You have come far enough," the man repeated. "Go back. I
would not hurt you."

Lynan continued advancing. "I have come this far to see a
queen, I would not go back now."

"The queen of the dead," the man laughed harshly. "She is the
one who does the visiting."

Lynan drew his sword. "Not anymore."

The man lifted his face, and Lynan stopped in his tracks.

"You knew me once," the man said.

It was the smell that first hit Lynan. It rose like a vapor from the background of rotting humus. The face was familiar, but there was still too much shadow.

And then he realized it was not shadow at all.

"I know you still," Lynan said, trying to keep his voice under control. He took a step backward.

The man spread his coat. "I still look after it for you."

"Roheth," he whispered pitiably. He remembered what the forester had been like when he had helped Lynan and his companions escape from Silona's grasp the first time they had met her: proud and strong and determined. By taking Lynan's coat, Roheth had wanted to throw the vampire off the traveler's scent.

"The ruse with the coat worked for two nights. Silona came back to my village, thinking you were still with us."

"I'm sorry . . ."

"But she was driven, you see. She had sensed the Key of Power hanging around your neck."

"I'm sorry . . ."

"And in the end nothing could save me." Roheth stepped forward. A beam of light struck what was left of his cheek, showed the bone underneath. "I paid the price of my hospitality."

"You have become one of her hounds."

Roheth laughed grimly. "Oh, yes. I herd her prey. I captured Belara once. Do you remember my wife?"

"Yes."

"She is no more." The voice was heavy with grief, but carried with it an obscene undercurrent of glee. "And Mira, little Mira. Gone, too. And Seabe . . ."

"Stop."

"But she still came after you, Lynan Rosetheme. Her mind had touched the Key and she wanted you."

"I can avenge your wife, Roheth, and your daughter. And Seabe, too. I can avenge all of those she has killed."

Roheth shook his head. His neck creaked. "I am her hound. I serve her completely."

"If that was so, you would have tried to kill me last night. You know what I intend."

"Now, but not then. Silona does not want you dead. Not yet, anyway. You only have two of the Keys. But I will not let you harm

her. She is all that is left in this world that I can love and I will not
let you hurt her. Turn back, Lynan Rosetheme, or I will kill you.
This is your last warning."

Lynan strengthened his grip on the sword. "Flee, Roheth. I
would not slay you."

"I am already slain, you fool."

Lynan swung with all his strength. The hound caught the blade
in its left hand, cutting out a wedge of bone and rotten flesh, and
yanked down. The sword was ripped out of Lynan's fingers. The
creature's right hand shot out and punched Lynan in the neck. He
fell back gasping, tripped over a root and landed heavily on his
back. Before he could recover, the hound was kneeling on his chest,
its hands scrabbling around his throat. Lynan twisted from one side
to the other. The hound rattled like a bag of bones but held on.

"I will eat you myself," Roheth hissed, and his fingers squeezed
harder.

Just as Lynan started blacking out, he felt something hold unconsciousness at bay, and then push it back. It was the rage returned, redoubled in strength, and it filled him with liquid fire. His
fingers found Roheth's head, felt the creature's skin slip loosely on
the skull, grasped even tighter, and he twisted with all his strength.
There was a crack and Roheth howled and fell back. Lynan kicked
himself to his feet and retrieved his sword. The hound was squirming on the ground like a cut snake, its head snapping from side to
side, its body jerking feebly.

Lynan roared and brought the sword down on the creature's
neck. The head rolled away, the jaws snapping open and shut, its
eyes rolling in their sockets. He brought the blade down again, and
again, and again, splitting open the skull. Shards of white bone flew
into the air, stung his cheeks. He struck until all the fire in him was
out, extinguished, purified, and he clambered away from the
slaughter he had made, stumbling deeper into the forest, the darkness closing about him.

Jenrosa tried to keep walking during the night, but she had
tripped over so many roots and rocks, banged her knees and head
against so many branches, that in the end, exhausted, she simply
gave up and slumped against a tree. She needed sleep, and knew
it, but her fear for Lynan made her heart-sick and would not let her
rest. She drew from the saddlebag a strip from one of Lynan's
shirts, burned it, kept aside half the ashes and threw the remainder

into the air. They drifted toward the center of the forest. Then she cleared a space among the leaf litter and asked questions of the earth. Lynan was ahead of her, and although Silona was not yet with him, something else was, a creature she did not recognize but which sent a shiver down her spine.

She closed her eyes and searched for the point beyond which there was no sign of Lynan, and it was imminent. Tonight, perhaps, tomorrow night at the latest. For a long time she had been afraid it meant Lynan's death, but now she was more afraid it meant something far worse: Lynan's complete surrender to Silona and his passing into that other existence.

She could not wait for dawn. She got to her feet again and started walking, keeping one arm above her head to ward her off any branches. She still fell many times, cutting her hands and face. She paused at first light to throw the remainder of the ashes and, following the direction they drifted, came across his tracks. He was still alive, and still apart from Silona.

Encouraged and renewed, she picked up her pace, not slowing until she found the remains of some horrific struggle. Whatever it was—whatever it had been—had almost certainly been the creature she saw revealed in the earth magic. She remembered stories told by Roheth and the other foresters who had given her and Lynan refuge the first time they had traveled through Silona's domain, stories about her hounds, the humans Silona changed to hunt down food for her.

This is what she will turn Lynan into. The thought drove her on, recklessly. She would do anything to stop that from happening.

Silona had saved his life again, Lynan knew. The anger that had filled him in his struggle against Roheth had been hers, a rage fueled by the knowledge that one of her creatures would try and harm Lynan. But now she knew where he was and would come after him. He also knew she must now understand she had no choice now but to kill him or change him forever, otherwise he would kill her. Why else, once free of her in Daavis, would he come to her domain?

"I will wait for you here," he said aloud, knowing the forest would hear him. It was not yet dark, but he would go no farther. He gathered together what dry leaves and wood he could find and started a fire. The warm flames raised his spirits somewhat, and the smoke disappearing through the canopy reminded him that there

was a world outside the forest. He shrugged off his poncho and put
it aside neatly. Then his sword belt and sheath, which he lay across
the poncho. He needed no unnecessary encumbrances for this fight.
He squatted in front of the fire, planted his sword in front of him,
and waited.

Night came too soon. Jenrosa cursed, wept. She could go no
faster. Exhaustion was dragging her limbs, making her eyes
cloudy, befuddling her mind. But she kept on, one foot after the
other, each step taking her closer to Lynan. A breeze. The first she
had felt since entering the forest. She stopped, one arm supporting
her against a tree. The breeze was cool but smelled of decay. Her
hair flurried around her face. A shadow passed overhead.

Laughter. The sound of it was like the point of a knife being
scraped under her heart.

Jenrosa shrank back against the tree, curling down with her arms
around her knees. She started saying prayers she had not uttered
since she was a little girl. Her skin felt as if it had been shrunk
around her face.

The shadow drifted north and west, and as soon as it had passed
over her, Jenrosa found she could stand again. She was ashamed of
her cowardice.

It is time, she told herself. *This is the only chance you have.*

She started running as hard as she could, chasing the shadow.

Lynan felt her sweep over him. It was like a dark sheet being
pulled over his mind. The light from the fire seemed to contract.
The trees on the other side of the fire swayed violently, then were
still.

"I know you're here," he said into the night.

"Where else would I be, my love?" she replied. He tried track-
ing the voice, but it seemed to come from all around him.

"I am not your love. I am your enemy. I have been from the first
time you touched me."

"You are harsh. Look what I gave you."

"You gave me madness."

"I made you invulnerable."

"You made me like you."

"I made you my lover," she said, and stepped forward into the
light.

Lynan could not believe how beautiful she was. His desire for her flooded him anew. He looked away from her face to the huge, dark shapes that grew from her back.

"You still want me," she said.

Yes, his mind said. "No. Never."

"You want to take me."

Yes. He curled his fingers around the hilt of his sword.

"You want me for your wife, your queen."

Yes. He stood slowly, as if held down by great weights.

"I have come to give myself to you. I surrender everything that I am to you. You can have my body, my heart. I will give you my soul."

"I will take your body," he said, lifting his sword, "and drive this blade through your heart."

Her wings came together in front of her with a mighty crack. A wall of air slammed into Lynan, throwing him to the ground and knocking the sword out of his hand; he scrabbled in the dirt for it. The light from the fire was blotted out and he looked up into the face of Silona. He screamed and kicked away from her.

"Here," she said. "Is this what you're looking for?" She kicked something on the ground, and his sword clattered next to him. He grabbed it and leaped to his feet, lunging forward. The blade sunk into her chest. Her mouth parted in surprise. He drove the blade in deeper. His face was only a hand's span away from hers. Her eyes caught his, and suddenly she smiled. She grasped the sword around the blade and without any effort pulled it out, shook it free from Lynan's grasp, and threw it over her shoulder. He heard it hit the fire, and sparks arced into the air.

"My heart is yours," she said in a singsong voice. "I will not let you cut it like that."

He drew his dagger and struck at her face, but her hand closed around his wrist and twisted, snapping the bones. He screamed in pain, dropped the weapon.

"I want you to make love to me, Lynan Rosetheme." Her other hand twisted around his hair and jerked his head toward hers. Her black tongue flickered between her lips. "I want you to kiss me."

She covered his mouth with her own. He pushed against her with his good hand, but it was like pushing against a tree. Her tongue, sharp, siphoned, pricked into the soft flesh at the back of his throat, and he gagged as his own blood gushed down into his gullet. His mind started slipping into a dark, spinning vortex, and there was no way out.

*   *   *

It was the fire that finally guided Jenrosa to Lynan. She edged to the limit of the light and saw him squatting with his sword ready before him, waiting for Silona. She wanted to cry out to him, tell him it would not be enough, but fate had decided the course for both of them, and she could only save Lynan's life at the risk of losing his soul, and she would not do that.

She put down her saddlebag and retrieved the makings she needed for the magic. She looked longingly at the fire near Lynan, but it was too far away for her to work it properly. With flint and steel she started smoke in a collection of dry grass and a second strip from Lynan's shirt, and when she started silently reciting the chant, a small flame curled into life. She could feel the power of the magic taking hold of her, but she had to restrain it until the right moment, when she could kill both Silona and Lynan at the same time. She did not imagine she could defend herself in time if she managed to slay only one and the other came after her.

Her concentration was destroyed by Silona's arrival. The forest itself seemed to move in welcome. The shock of it made Jenrosa forget her chant and her little fire started to wither. Desperately, she restarted the magic as she heard Lynan and the vampire talking. Inside she wanted to hurry, to get it over with and flee, but she forced herself to say each word in the chant properly. Again she felt the magic build up in her, and this time she would use it. She stood to make the final casting when suddenly Silona clapped her wings together and her fire was snuffed out as if it had been nothing more powerful than a candle flame. The magic in her evaporated and, suddenly empty, she fell to her knees. She heard Lynan's sword strike home and see looked up in time to see Silona take the weapon out of her chest and throw it away, then break his arm as he tried to stab the vampire with his dagger.

Jenrosa felt in the dark for the makings, but they were scattered. She glanced back at the fireplace. She would have to use that now. Then she saw Silona place her mouth over Lynan's.

Too late! She was too late!

"No!" she cried and rushed forward, drawing her sword. When she was within ten paces she raised the blade high and aimed for the back of Lynan's head. One of Silona's yellow eyes snapped open, focused immediately on Jenrosa. The vampire screamed, pushed out one arm just as the blade fell.

Jenrosa felt her whole body jar as the blade bit deep into what felt like wood. Her shoulder wrenched and she lost her grip on the sword. She screamed and drew her dagger, stabbing toward Lynan's throat, but this time Silona lunged forward and swiped at the magicker in turn, driving into her chest.

Jenrosa flew through the air and landed on her back. She felt as if every rib in her chest had been broken. She tried to cry in pain but could only whimper. Silona discarded Lynan, dropping him like a rag doll, and advanced on her. She tried to move, but nothing seemed to work.

Three dark shapes leaped over her. She heard the war cry of the White Wolf and saw firelight flash off sabers. The vampire grunted like a pig and jumped back, her wings swishing in the air. The Chetts moved apart and advanced on Silona from the front and both sides. They darted in, flicked with their swords, darted back again. Jenrosa could hear the wooden sound of their blades biting into Silona's flesh, and the vampire's growling in response. One of them dallied too long. Jenrosa saw a long arm ending in claws sweep out so quickly it was a blur. It struck one of the Chetts across the head, ripping it clean off. The body collapsed under a spray of hissing blood.

Again, Jenrosa tried to move. She managed to pull her feet under her. With the help of her hands she raised herself to a kneeling position. The pain in her chest felt like a dozen knives were impaling her. She moaned, stood up, looked around for a weapon. A scream. Another dead Chett.

Her sword was by the fire. She stooped to pick it up, found it almost impossible to stand again. The last Chett was dancing in and out of the vampire's range. It was Sunatay. *God, she's good,* Jenrosa thought, hope rising in her. If only she could get around behind the vampire.

She stopped herself. She was a magicker, not a warrior. She turned back to the fire. It was close enough. It was bright enough. She dropped to her knees in relief and started chanting.

Lynan coughed himself awake. He turned over and vomited blood. Fighting. He got himself to his haunches and looked up. Jenrosa! She was on her knees on the other side of the fire, chanting. Who was fighting? He looked around, saw Silona hopping like a deranged bird, pecking, swiping at a small, lithe figure who wielded a saber the way Kumul used to wield a long sword.

Sunatay, he remembered. *How did she get here? How did Jenrosa yet here?*

Then he saw the corpses of the two dead Chetts. His side was losing.

He pushed back with his hands, cried in sudden pain as his right wrist gave way. He used his left hand to sit back. He remembered now. Silona had broken his wrist, snapped the bones in two.

But no, the bones were knitted already.

He managed to raise himself to a crouch. He spat more blood out of his mouth as he looked around for his sword. He could not see it anywhere. There was a sword near Jenrosa. Hers, he assumed. That would have to do. He tried to stand up, but as he did Jenrosa's chant seemed to swell in volume and the sound of it was like a terrible weight on his shoulders. He could not move.

"Jenrosa!" he cried. "You're stopping me from moving!"

She did not answer, but she met his gaze and held it. He saw tears streaming down her cheeks.

Silona yowled. He looked around and saw that she was hardly moving. Sunatay was moving in closer, aiming her blows more carefully.

The rhythm of Jenrosa's chant picked up. Something stabbed him in the heart. The breath whooshed out of him; he tried to suck in air, but his lungs would not work. Again his heart spasmed in pain. He was back to his knees and he could see Silona was struggling, too, and Sunatay's blows were becoming heavier, deeper.

"Why?" he gasped at Jenrosa, turning back to her.

But still she did not reply. He tried to find an answer in her eyes, but all he saw there was pity. He collapsed, falling sideways onto the ground. The fire blazed in front of him and he saw in its flames two twisting figures which he recognized as himself and Silona. The flames moved to the rhythm of Jenrosa's chant. She was using her magic to kill both of them.

An inhuman roar behind him. The sound of Sunatay's blade sinking deep into the vampire's flesh, like an ax in wood, and sticking. Another inhuman roar. The sound of her wings sweeping through the air. Sunatay screaming.

The fire seemed to dim, the figures in it start to blur. Almost immediately he felt his lungs start to pump air back in and the pain in his chest disappeared. He pulled himself up. Jenrosa was mumbling, trying to recapture the chant.

But too late.

There was a beat of wings and Silona landed right behind the magicker, her face twisted in terrible fury, any semblance of beauty lost in the hatred and rage.

That was me, Lynan remembered. *Back in Daavis, that was me.*

"Jenrosa, move!" he cried, but his voice was nothing more than a croak. "Behind you!"

But too late.

Silona raised one clawed hand and brought it down against Jenrosa's back. Lynan watched, paralyzed, as Jenrosa jerked forward, her mouth gaping, her gray eyes wide open in astonishment. The vampire drew back, the hand covered in gore, and Jenrosa pitched forward on to her face.

Lynan screamed. He lifted himself to his feet but fell straight away. He could hear Silona panting, trying to get her own strength back. He moved forward on all fours to reach Jenrosa, saw the bloody mess that was her back. He started crying, could not stop it, tried to say her name. His right hand burned. He looked down and saw it was resting on the hilt of his sword, its blade deep into the fire.

And he remembered. In the middle of his insanity Silona had told him that all the others like her were slain by iron and fire.

He gripped the hilt, ignoring the pain, and used the sword to help him stand. Silona was already on her feet, her great wings stretching out behind her.

"So we start again," she said to him. She noticed the sword. "You learn your lessons very hard." She smiled cruelly at him, took a step forward, over the body of Jenrosa.

Lynan lunged, driving the blade deep, deep into her body, twisting the hilt as he did so.

Silona leaped into the air, screaming, taking the sword with her. Black blood sprayed into the fire, sending clouds of putrid steam into the night. She tried to beat her wings, but they would not work and she plummeted back to earth, landing on her back. She squirmed and grasped the blade with both hands. Smoke came from her fingers. She let go, wailing. Lynan went to her, took the hilt and twisted it again. Silona kicked away, crying, begging, her face that of a beautiful woman again.

"Lynan, my love, no, help me, Lynan, my love . . ."

He pulled out the sword and drove it into her neck. She jerked up on her shoulders, slumping. Her mouth opened one more time and said a word Lynan did not understand. The air around them funneled into the sky. Lynan felt his clothes and hair whip around him, and the vampire's wings flapped uselessly.

Then all was still.

Lynan ran to Jenrosa, gently turned her over. She was gasping for breath. Blood speckled her lips.

"I was wrong," she wheezed.

"Don't talk," he said.

She grabbed his arms. Her eyes were bulging, staring at his face. "I was wrong. I am the end point. Not you. I thought I had to kill you. I thought that was my destiny."

Lynan was crying again. "Please, Jenrosa, don't talk. Stay with me. Don't go."

"I'm sorry," she said. "I'm so sorry."

Lynan put her down gently, took her face in his hands and kissed her forehead. "Don't leave me, Jenrosa. I love you."

Her body arched in pain.

"What can I do?" he asked her, his voice pleading. "Can I help you do magic?"

"Nothing," she said. "I understand now. There is no Jenrosa after tonight. That is why it was all dark. I thought the blood was your cruelty, your madness, but it was my future. The whole time it was my blood."

"Blood," Lynan repeated. "God." He scrabbled over to the vampire's corpse and dipped his hand in the wound in her chest. He brought it out, his fingers dripping with her black gore. He returned to Jenrosa. "Here," he said, lifting her head.

"No!" she cried and slapped his hand away. "No!"

"It will save you!" Lynan cried. "You will be like me!"

She twisted pathetically away from him. When he tried to hold her, she grabbed his bloody hand and forced it down with all her strength and said into his face: "I would rather be dead than be like you!"

Lynan reeled back.

"Please," she whimpered. "Please."

He nodded, and she let him come to her again. He lifted her into his arms and cradled her, rocking back and forth.

"I love you," he told her again.

"I know," she said, then closed her eyes and died.

28

THIS must be the most peaceful corner of the whole continent," Galen said, not entirely happy.

Charion smiled to herself. A warm sun was climbing in a clear blue sky, a gentle breeze wafting up from the valley below brought with it the smell of baked bread; birds chirruped in trees. It was perfect. But Galen did not want perfect. *Neither do I,* she admitted to herself. *We both want battle. But just now it's almost possible to believe there is no war.*

Behind them snaked the column of knights, riders sitting easy in the saddle. Ahead of them a gentle crest eventually met higher land in the far northwest of Chandra. The valley east of them was quilted by fields and orchards. A couple of towns clustered around crossroads. To their west, the edge of a forest limned the horizon. Charion pulled out the map Barys had given them. Drawn on it were the geographical features marking their patrol area. The valley was called Arran; it marked the easternmost range. The Forest of Silona marked the southwest limit. The border with her own province marked the north limit, which is where they were heading now. To patrol the entire area would take five or six days, and then they would start again.

"We could cross the border," Galen mused aloud.

"We told Tomar we would take on this duty," Charion reminded him. "He could have told us to move south and join up with Areava's Great Army."

"He could have asked us," Galen said. "Nobody except Areava herself tells Galen Amptra what to do."

"Keep your airs to yourself, Kendran," Charion snorted. "This is Tomar's domain. We are his guests."

Galen shrugged self-consciously. "Yes, I know. At least we're not swinging our heels in some city, making polite conversation with boring minor nobles while our horses get fat on hay and grain." He looked sideways at Charion. "Still. A little cross-border ride wouldn't harm, would it? A day in, a day out. Might even gather some useful information about the Chett army and its whereabouts."

"We know where it is," Charion said crossly. "In Daavis. And we know where it's going when it does move. Sparro."

"Then what are we doing here?"

"Keeping out of the way," Charion said.

"Why would Tomar care where we are? We're all on the same side, after all."

Charion wondered if she should voice her doubts, but decided that was unfair of her. Tomar had shown them every courtesy and rendered them every assistance. But she could not forget some of the things the king had said, and the context in which he had said them; then they had not meant anything significant, but she had since had time to ponder them. He was a man of confused, perhaps even divided, loyalties. Tomar gave her the impression of being a very sad man trapped in very sad times.

"And that rubbish you said he'd given you about our force not being compatible with his army," Galen continued. "Well, all I can say is that if Barys was commander, it would be good enough for the knights. His reputation as soldier and general—"

Galen stopped when he saw one of their outriders galloping toward them from the west. He halted the column. The outrider arrived out of breath and sweating.

"Lord Amptra, Chetts! Here!"

"Where?"

"The forest! They are on its edge. A full company, at least."

"What were they doing?" Charion asked.

"Dismounted and resting, as far as I could see."

"Were you seen?"

In answer, the outrider pulled an arrow out of his saddlebag. "They got this into my pommel." He blushed. "Missed my prick by a finger's width."

"Then they'll ride for the border," Galen said.

Charion looked at the map again and jabbed with her finger at a point halfway between the forest and the valley, looking up to check the detail against the real landscape. "There. This crest flattens out. It's the only straight way between the forest and border."

"Northwest," Galen confirmed. He ordered two riders behind him to ride due west and see if they could locate the Chetts, and to let him know if they were mounted and riding. They galloped off.

"Will we catch them?" Charion asked.

"If we move now," he said brusquely and raised his clenched fist, the signal for the column to move to a trot. "What are they doing here?"

"Scouting party?" Charion suggested.

"This far west? Only if Lynan intends to move his army around Sparro and march directly on Kendra."

"But that would leave Sparro and Tomar's army directly behind him, and Areava's Great Army on his eastern flank. That doesn't make sense."

"Well, we'll find out from any Chetts we capture."

"We have to catch them first," Charion pointed out. She wanted to pick up the pace, but knew if they did that, they would blow the horses before meeting the enemy, and then nothing could stop them from escaping. "So much for this being the most peaceful corner of the whole continent."

After dismembering Silona's remains and disposing of them in the campfire, Lynan set about making a pyre for Jenrosa and the three Red Hands. He built a base from small branches and piled on it all the dry leaves and twigs he could scrounge. Then he placed Jenrosa's body in the middle, the Red Hands on either side, and placed more branches and leaves over them. When he set it alight, the flames took hold straight away. In moments the blaze was so intense he had to retreat several paces. By morning the pyre was reduced to little more than a pile of light gray ash. A breeze made its way from the outside world and blew the ashes around in an eddy that climbed up above the canopy and out into the world.

He needed to move, he knew that. He had to get back to Daavis. He was responsible for the fate of more than one companion. But his heart weighed so much the rest of him could not move. When Kumul had died, it had been as if Lynan's past had died as well; with Jenrosa's death, he felt he had lost his future.

Not so long ago there had been four of them. Refugees, exiles, outlaws. Now he was proclaimed king by his followers, he had a brave army behind him, but only he and Ager remained and he was not sure the cost had been worth it. Why struggle for a kingdom, for any birthright, if the price was everything you cared for?

He knew the answer and did not want to hear it, but inside his mind he heard it spoken in Kumul's voice. "Duty," Lynan said aloud. "I am Prince Lynan Rosetheme, son of Queen Usharna Rosetheme, son of General Elynd Chisal, and I will be king of Grenda Lear. I was born to duty. You showed me that, Kumul. And you, Jenrosa."

Saying their names made him want to cry again, but that would shame them. He took his sword and plunged it deep in the earth where the pyre had been. One day he would return to retrieve it, and to sit for a while by the place where Jenrosa had left this world and his life.

Rosof and the others had heard terrible things during the night, and in the morning he was left with the terrible problem of what to do. Sunatay had said he was not to come after her until three nights had passed, but what if she and the others needed help now? What he wanted to do was order his troop to mount and get away from this dark and evil forest, but they were Red Hands, and they had come to save the White Wolf. He could not leave, and as he thought about the problem, he realized he could not stay where he was and do nothing.

He made a decision to lead half the troop into the forest, leaving the other half behind as a reserve and to watch the horses, when two things happened that deepened his quandary. The first was a dark plume of smoke which the Chetts could see above the trees as soon as the southern sky was light enough; as far as Rosof could tell its source was many leagues deep within the forest. He did not know what it meant, but he was sure it had something to do with the sounds they had heard during the night. The second event was a sudden commotion to the east of their main camp. An outrider rushed back to tell him she had shot at a horseman but he had gotten away. Rosof groaned inside. The enemy had discovered their position, and they were several days' ride from any kind of sanctuary. He was left to make a decision that properly should have been Sunatay's, and he silently cursed her for leaving him in this mess. The other Red Hands, as skittish now as horses in the middle of a grass fire, were looking at him expectantly. Of all the choices facing him, his original decision still looked best to him, although he could not now take half his force with him.

"We cannot leave the White Wolf behind at the mercy of his enemies," he declared, trying hard to keep a quaver out of his voice. "We are the Red Hands, and we will not fail. I will go into the forest to find King Lynan and the Truespeaker, and our companions. I will take twenty with me. The rest of you will wait here. Prepare a barricade around the horses. The enemy will come, but if we are brave and strong they will not defeat us, and when I return with Lynan, we will cut them down like grass wolves attacking a herd of karaks."

Having been given a clear order, much of the riders' nervousness disappeared. Rosof got them started on the barricade, then chose twenty of the most fleet-footed of the troop and entered the forest. As the trees closed about them, Rosof did not feel any of the tension he had felt two days ago, the first time the Red Hands had tried to enter. He did not have time to wonder about it. He started a long, loping jog he hoped would get them to the source of the fire by the end of the day, and twenty warriors fell in behind him.

As they got deeper into the forest, the air became closer, harder to breathe, and they had to stop frequently for short rests. The forest felt like a great prison, and they found it hard not to be able to see the horizon or feel the wind on their faces. The only way to stop thinking about it was to run, to concentrate on every stride, every foot fall.

Then, about mid-morning, they found Lynan.

The meeting was eerily flat. For a long moment, surprised, Rosof could only stare at the prince, and in return Lynan seemed almost disinterested.

"We have come for you," Rosof said nervously. "We have a troop waiting at the edge of the forest."

"A whole troop?"

"Back there," Rosof said, pointing behind him. "Except for Sunatay, who went on ahead of us, and the Truespeaker, and two others."

"Sunatay is dead," Lynan said flatly. "So are her two companions."

"Dead?"

"As is the Truespeaker."

The Red Hands gasped in surprise. What could slay someone so

powerful as Jenrosa Alucar? She was a companion to the White
Wolf, and the first Truespeaker in a generation.

"Silona," Lynan said, as if reading their minds. "She killed them
all."

The Red Hands looked around them anxiously.

"No need to fear," Lynan told them. "She is dead, too. Our
friends died, but not in vain."

Rosof swallowed, not sure what to say, then remembered the
threat still to come. "Your Majesty, we must hurry to rejoin the others. An enemy scout found our location. We cannot have much time
before—"

"Yes, of course," Lynan interrupted. "Quickly, then, lead the
way."

"Where are they?" Galen demanded, standing in his saddle and
desperately searching the landscape for any sign of the enemy.
"Have we missed them?"

Charion, checking her map, shook her head. "I don't see how.
Either they moved farther west, which lengthens their journey
home and still gives us a chance to intercept them, or they are still
where the outrider first came across them."

Galen scratched his head. "But once discovered, what would be
the point of staying? They must know we would respond."

"Or they rode east," Charion suggested slowly, speaking as the
thought coalesced in her brain. "That way they are behind us, waiting for us to move out of the way before going for the border."

"Our force isn't large enough to cover all three options," he said
with some exasperation.

Charion said nothing. This was Galen's column. She was an
honorary member of the knights for the moment, but she was not
commanding.

"We head south," he said finally. "If they have not moved, we
will surprise them by coming from the north. If they rode east, then
we will come across their trail, and may still have a chance of
catching them. That's two out of three possibilities covered."

Their horses had already been going for three straight hours. It
was decided to rest them an hour before resuming. Galen ordered
some of his riders to scout south and east, however, to try and locate the enemy early.

Although the horses could rest, their riders found it impossible.
They strode up and down, they fidgeted with swords and gear, they

checked and rechecked harness and saddle and reins and buckles and straps. It was frustrating for them, and the tension inside them increased by the minute. When it was time to ride again, Galen made sure they still took it slowly, keeping the pace to an easy trot. Within an hour the first outriders were back from the south with the news that the enemy was still in place and had prepared barricades.

Galen, relieved the enemy had not escaped him, was still perplexed. "What could they be doing?" he asked Charion.

"I have no idea, but if they're putting up barricades, we're not going to be able to attack them by ourselves—at least not mounted, and I don't fancy going on foot up against Chett archers."

"We'll worry about that when we get there," Galen said. "If the position is too strong, we can send a message to Tomar to send some archers."

Galen slowed down the pace. It was midafternoon before they met more of their scouts, one with a superficial arrow wound to the thigh.

"How far from their lines were you?" Galen asked him.

"About a hundred paces," the scout said.

"They'd be effective at a hundred and fifty if the target was big enough, like a charging group of knights," Charion said. "God, I'd love to have a company of my archers with me just now."

"I'd risk a charge if we still had our armor," Galen confessed.

"Well, we don't, so you won't," Charion said. "We need reinforcements."

"My lord!" cried one of the knights, pointing toward the forest itself.

"More Chetts!" Galen said. "How many of them?"

"Twenty," Charion said. "If that's all of them, it makes it a troop in total. And look! Their leader! It can't be!"

Galen squinted to see as far as Charion, but there was no mistaking that white face. "I don't believe it." He glanced at Charion to make sure he was seeing what she was seeing. She nodded at him. "I don't believe it," he repeated numbly.

"We've got him!" she cried and kicked her horse's flanks. Galen lurched forward and grabbed her reins from her hands. "What are you doing!"

"Chett archers, remember!" he shouted at her. "What did you think you were going to do? Play pin cushion for the enemy?"

Charion flushed with anger. "How dare you—!" she started.

"I'm commander here, your Majesty," he reminded her, his voice suddenly cold. "And you are with us under my sufferance."

For a moment it looked as if Charion would explode. The other knights carefully edged away from the pair. Safer to be shot at by Chetts than cursed at by Charion or Galen.

"Bugger!" she screamed in frustration.

Galen's eyes widened with surprise. He had heard her lose her temper plenty of times, but never control of her tongue.

"Steady on," he said levelly.

She snorted through her nose like an angry bull. "Sorry," she said tightly. "But it's him, for God's sake! Lynan Rosetheme! We can end it now, Galen, we can end the whole bloody war here and now!"

"Not by ourselves," he said calmly. "They're not going anywhere. If they try to escape, we'll slaughter them. But we can't take them behind that barricade, not without armor. We'll send for reinforcements from Sparro." He signaled to one of the knights and said to him: "Take three horses. Ride them into the ground if you have to. Get to Sparro by tomorrow. Tell Tomar what's happened. Tell him we need archers and heavy infantry. Tell Tomar we have Lynan trapped."

"No need," another knight said.

Charion and Galen looked up together. Coming from the east was a new column of riders, at least five hundred strong, and flying above them the pennant of Chandra.

Lynan did not give much for their chances when he saw his Chetts were outnumbered by the enemy by three to one. For the moment, behind their earth and log barricades, they could hold them off, but eventually the enemy would bring up archers and heavy infantry, maybe even some heavy cavalry, and it would be all over. He thought of retreating into the forest, but the Chetts told him the horses would not enter it; he thought they might now that Silona was dead, but when he tried to lead one mare in under the canopy he almost got his head kicked in for his trouble. He guessed the evil Silona had wrought in that place would outlast her by some years. Certainly, the pain she had caused him would last the rest of his life.

Absurdly, because he was with them, the Red Hands did not seem to be remotely worried. He was the White Wolf returned, he was the invincible king; it was the enemy that needed to be pitied.

"We have to break out," he told Rosof. "We have no choice. The enemy will bring fresh troops soon, and we will be trapped. Now is our only chance."

Rosof nodded excitedly. "Better to go on horseback than stuck behind some wall like this."

"Order the troop to mount."

Rosof relayed the command. There was a flurry of activity and in moments the whole troop was ready to ride out.

"We ride due north," Lynan told them. "If any of us are wounded, or our horses killed from under us, the others must go on. Some of us will get through."

There was a spontaneous raggedy cheer from the Chetts, and Lynan felt his heart swell with pride that these rough riders from the Oceans of Grass would pin their future to his sorry ambitions.

"No," he said. "I was wrong. We leave no one behind. If anyone is wounded, the closest rider will take the reins. If anyone loses their horse, the next rider will take them up. We live or die together. I will not desert you again."

This time the cheer was raucous. Lynan thought they must have heard it all the way back to Sparro.

"Your Majesty," one of the Chetts said. "More cavalry."

The cheer died in all their throats. Lynan looked eastward, saw the Chandra pennant and knew it meant the end for all of them.

"I am sorry," he said, but so softly none of them would have heard him. There was no need for them to hear his despair. He looked down at his right hand. The broken wrist had healed completely. The burn from grasping the red hot hilt of his sword had not. It was a mess of blue-rimmed boils and bloody cuts. When Silona had died, he stopped healing like a vampire. He was again utterly, utterly human.

It could have happened at a more convenient time, he thought, but he could not help feeling relief he would die human and not something less, not something on its way to becoming like Silona.

All his Chetts were looking at him, wanting him to say something more. He could see in their eyes that it was not surrender they were expecting from him. "Well, my brave Red Hands," he called to them, "today you will prove yourself the fiercest warriors on Theare. I promise you, your descendants will sing songs about today and your part in it."

He turned back to the enemy. They could see what they were

doing now and were maneuvering to intercept them. "I don't suppose any one brought my banner?"

"Of course we bloody did," Rosof said, and drew one from his saddlebag. As the troop's second-in-command, when Sunatay was still alive as commander, the pennant was his responsibility. He jumped off his horse, found a long, thin branch, and tied the pennant to it, then remounted and wedged the makeshift standard into his right boot.

"Well and good," Lynan said, glancing over his shoulder to see the pennant catch the wind.

He raised his hand to give the signal to charge when something extraordinary happened. The fresh Chandra cavalry rode past the original unit, wheeled as if on parade to present their flanks to the Chetts, and continued on. One or two Chetts shot arrows, but for the most part they were too surprised to react. Finally, the column stopped between the Chetts and the rest of the enemy, right wheeled and lowered their spears—against their compatriots.

Rosof cleared his throat. "Your Majesty?"

To the unvoiced question, Lynan could only say: "I have no idea what is going on."

"What in the name of God are they doing?" Galen demanded as the Chandra column swept past them, then changed course to place themselves in front of the enemy. When they dropped their spears—in his direction—Galen did not know what to say. The rest of the knights started speaking all at once in sheer amazement. Charion said nothing, but she bowed her head, not wanting to believe what was happening. *Tomar tried to tell me,* she thought. *He tried to tell me.*

One rider broke ranks from the Chandran cavalry and rode toward them. He carried no weapon except for a long sword strapped to his back.

"That's Barys Malayka," Galen said.

Barys drew up in front of Galen and Charion. His expression was grim.

"What is the meaning of this, sir?" Galen demanded. "We have the enemy cornered here, and it is led by the traitor prince himself. Why do you hinder us instead of help us?"

Barys scratched his nose. "It isn't straightforward, I'm afraid, Galen Amptra. But the crux of the matter is that Tomar II, king of Chandra, has thrown his lot behind Prince Lynan."

Galen's draw dropped in surprise.

"Why, Barys?" Charion asked, her voice subdued.

"It was a question of loyalty, your Majesty," Barys replied.

Galen guffawed. "Loyalty? He swore an oath to Queen Areava to serve the crown of Grenda Lear—"

"He swore an oath to Queen Usharna," Barys interrupted. "And to serve the best interests of the kingdom. He believes he is best fulfilling that oath by supporting Lynan in his struggle against his sister."

Galen's mouth opened and shut like a fish gasping for air.

"What is to happen to us?" Charion asked.

"You are to head for Kendra immediately. You have safe passage for three days and three nights."

"And what happens to Prince Lynan?"

"He is now under my master's protection," Barys said.

"We could end it all now," Charion said urgently, leaning forward over her saddle toward Barys. "Kill Lynan and the war is over."

Barys shook his head. "Civil war is never resolved so simply." He retrieved a sealed letter from inside his coat and handed it to Galen. "For Areava, from Tomar, explaining his decision."

"No amount of explanation will rid him of his guilt," Galen said.

"King Tomar feels many things about this decision, but guilt is not one of them."

"This is tragedy, Barys," Charion said. "This is bloody tragedy."

"I won't disagree with her Majesty," Barys replied, "but the tragedy started in the royal palace in Kendra and with the Rosethemes, not in Sparro and not with Tomar."

"But—" Galen started, and again Barys spoke over him.

"You only have three days and three nights. I would make use of it, starting now."

29

IT was as if a god had marked the division between desert and pasture, between the land of the Saranah and the province of Aman, it was so clear. To the west of Makon, the ground was yellow with salt bush and sand, the blue sky as hard as diamond, while to the east the ground was plush with grass and the sky was cut by distant, snow-capped mountains. The Chett army moved quickly to the east, unburdened by loot or guilt, the ruin of a whole people behind them. Makon could not begin to calculate how many Saranah had been killed, but was sure it would be easier to count the survivors than the slain. The Saranah had paid for their attack on the Oceans of Grass with virtual extinction.

And now it was the turn of Aman.

Eynon reined up next to him. "No word from our scouts?"

Makon shook his head. "This border does not seem to be guarded."

"Why should they guard against the Saranah?" Eynon sneered. "You don't post spears against your pet."

"I think the way is clear to the first town."

"Cleybin, wasn't it?" He searched his memory for the information the Saranah merchant had revealed before he died.

"Market town for trade with the Saranah."

"Well, Aman will no longer need it, then."

"And after Cleybin?"

Eynon pointed to the mountains. "Straight to them. Pila is up there somewhere."

"It will be winter soon."

"Then we had better get a move on. Remember, Makon, mobility is the key. As long as we keep ahead of the news of our arrival, we will always have the advantage. Aman is not expecting an attack from the west, and many of their warriors will be in the east to fight Lynan. Once we take Pila, we can set down for winter, if need be." He nodded to the long and winding column passing them, Chetts from a dozen different clans now working together as a single force, proud of their achievements and determined to do more. Makon could see in every face the determination to see through to the end this expedition of revenge. "They will have earned a rest by then."

The scouts reached Cleybin just after dark, and carefully led the Chett column to it. For the last two leagues they dismounted, keeping one hand resting gently on their horses' noses, speaking to them softly, eyes and ears wide open for any hint of detection.

Like many small border towns, Cleybin comprised one main street ending in a market square, not much more than a cleared and leveled space, bordered by two-story houses and stores and behind them warehouses and sheds. At the other end of the main street was a small garrison with maybe twenty soldiers to keep the local peace and act as tax collectors. In total, Cleybin was made up of about a hundred dwellings and four or five hundred people. The Chetts flowed around the town like floodwaters around a levee, cutting it off completely. Most carried on in the dark, heading east, but Makon, his Red Hands and another five hundred stayed behind, resting until just before dawn.

At first light Makon and the Red Hands, starting from the market, galloped down the main street, shouting their war cry and throwing brands onto roofs and barns and animal pens. At the end of the street fifty of them dismounted and charged the garrison, overwhelming it before any of the soldiers could react. The residents of the town ran out of their homes screaming. Chett archers waited on the outskirts, shooting down anyone who tried to put out the fires, letting everyone else go. In an hour Cleybin was no more. Every structure was burned to the ground, and all its citizens scattered.

Almost a season had passed since Amemun's last message, and Lingdar was worried. Amemun knew how important knowledge was to the functioning of King Marin's secretariat; after all, he had established the office. For a while after the start of the Saranah incursion into the Oceans of Grass a report would come every ten days or so, delivered by a visiting merchant or courier on horseback from the border. The report might be nothing more than a short note, but often comprised detailed maps of the southern part of the plains, and precise records of numbers and clans of slain enemies. All good grist for the mill, all typical of Amemun's thoroughness and insatiable thirst for knowledge.

It was possible one or two of the reports could have been delayed, but not those for a whole season. Something was wrong. The trouble was, without information coming from the Saranah, Lingdar did not know *what* was wrong.

For the hundredth time she read the last letter she had received from Amemun. It was the usual summary of battles and skirmishes, but there was one sentence in the second paragraph which Lingdar came back to again and again. "The weather has been kind to us." This was Amemun's code that the Chetts had not yet taken the bait the Saranah offered. Marin's plan to draw the Chetts away from the eastern provinces was not working, a conclusion supported by the fact that the latest news from Kendra was about the fall of Daavis and the province of Hume. Indeed, Amemun's reports indicated that the Saranah were raiding deeper into the Oceans of Grass than Amemun or Marin ever believed they could without meeting any organized resistance.

So what changed, old teacher? Lingdar wondered to herself. *Why did your reports stop altogether?*

She feared the worst, but Marin refused to countenance that Amemun could come to harm. Amemun had been a constant in the king's life since he was only a boy, had been his family's closest adviser and confidant. Amemun was so tied up with Marin's dynasty and plans that the king could not conceive of a world without him.

But a whole season! Something *was* wrong.

And now her office was receiving no reports from the southern desert either, despite all her well-paid informants among Dekelon's people. It had been the information fed to her office from those informants that had allowed Amemun to approach Dekelon about the plan to raid the Oceans of Grass with any confidence of success. It had taken Amemun and Lingdar years to build up the nest of spies among the Saranah. Had they all been found out? Had Dekelon turned on Amemun?

She needed information. She needed knowledge. She was not getting either, and that worried her.

Just then a messenger came from the king, asking her to attend him immediately and to bring her maps of the west. Lingdar piled several scrolls into the arms of one of her clerks and hurried to Marin's chambers. There they found the king sitting stone-faced behind his large work desk.

"Maps of the southern desert," Marin said gruffly. "Now."

Lingdar nodded, selected the appropriate scrolls from among the bundle carried by the clerk, and laid them out on the desk. They were still incomplete, but Amemun's reports had filled in much that had previously been blank; the maps now revealed a strip of land from Aman's borders all the way to the Oceans of Grass, showing Saranah settlements and trade routes along the way. Marin stood, leaned over the map and scrutinized it carefully for a long while. Eventually he said: "You would have told me had any word come from Amemun?"

"Of course, your Majesty. Right away."

"Even if the news was bad?"

"Especially if the news was bad."

Marin grunted, turned back to studying the map.

Lingdar cleared her throat. "Your Majesty, what have you heard?"

"That's just it. Nothing." He pointed at a town called Cleybin. "I have a garrison there. It has not reported for five days." He pointed to a crossroads about a day's ride east of Cleybin. "I have another garrison here. The army office has not heard from it in four days."

"And I have heard nothing from my agents among the Saranah for even longer," Lingdar said slowly.

"So, nothing from Amemun for a season," Marin said, pointing to the Oceans of Grass. "Nothing from your contacts in the desert. Five days ago nothing from Cleybin. Four days ago nothing from the crossroads east of Cleybin."

"Have you asked someone from the army office to come?"

"They will be here presently."

Lingdar cleared her throat a second time. "Just so I know we are having similar thoughts on this, the evidence indicates something moving toward Pila."

"Rapidly moving toward Pila," Marin corrected.

"Something that has overwhelmed Dekelon's force operating on the plains."

"Something that has overwhelmed the entire Saranah nation."

"Chetts." Lingdar said the word like a curse.

"An army of Chetts."

At that moment a young clerk arrived form the army office. He apologized that none of his superiors could come, but they were currently engaged on urgent matters—

"To do with the lack of communication with their units west of the mountains," Marin finished for him.

The clerk's mouth dropped open.

"Don't worry, lad, I'm not a mindreader. Tell me what you can."

"The last message was from the garrison guarding the far side of the East Road Pass. That was two days ago. They have a cage of carrier pigeons only recently delivered. They do not reply to any requests for information. The garrison on this side of the pass has been alerted, and reinforcements are on their way."

"Reinforcements? What reinforcements?"

"The relieving garrison, your Majesty. The army office is letting them go five days earlier than they would normally."

"When were they going to tell me about this?" Marin demanded.

The clerk spread his arms. "Today, your Majesty. They just wanted to be certain of their facts, that's all."

"Lord of the Mountain! When it is too late to do anything, they will tell me!" Marin cried. "Go back to your office, boy, and tell them I said they have to send an army to reinforce the garrison on this side of the pass. Do you understand?"

The clerk nodded and ran off.

"Will they arrive in time?" Lingdar asked.

Marin suddenly looked exhausted. "It means we've lost Amemun, doesn't it?"

"I don't think we can say that yet, your Majesty."

"Speak honestly. You knew him almost as well as I. If there is any way he could have warned us, he would have found it."

Lingdar nodded. "I'm sorry."

"You tried to warn me half a season ago. It's my fault. I should have listened to you then." He straightened himself. "And to answer your question, I don't know if the army will arrive in time, but at least it will be heading in the right direction."

Lingdar was not sure what to say. Only a short while ago she had been worried about the lack of communication from Amemun and her agents in the desert, but the worry had been confined, abstracted. Now the consequences of whatever had happened west of the mountains were real and immediate. Pila itself was in danger, for the first time since its ancient war against Kendra before there was ever a Grenda Lear. It was still unimaginable, but the fear was real enough and threatened to paralyze her. She did not want to move, did not want time to start again.

"I'll need your most accurate maps of the province between Pila and the East Road Pass."

Lingdar roused herself from her lethargy. Instructions. She needed a goal, something to keep her mind occupied. "Yes, your Majesty," she said. "I will see to it personally."

It was their second night in the pass. Makon and Wennem huddled together under a blanket in a vain attempt to keep out the cold.

"At least it isn't snowing," Wennem said.

"I wish it was," Makon said. He looked up into the sky. "When the nights are this clear, all the heat in the land disappears."

"Well, we're halfway across if the scouts are to be believed," Wennem said comfortingly. "And then on to Pila."

Makon could see the whites of her eyes, and they seemed lit with an unnatural glee.

"Will taking Pila help revenge your family?"

"They were revenged when we destroyed the Saranah. Now I want revenge for my sake."

Her words made Makon shiver worse than the cold. "There has to be an end to it sooner or later," he said softly, and almost immediately felt Wennem stiffen beside him. "For *your* sake."

For a long moment she said nothing, but then she eased back against him. "I know that. But not yet, Makon. After we take Pila, I will be content to let go of my family's ghosts."

"And if we don't take Pila?"

"What are you saying?"

"I mean, what if—for whatever reason—we fail to take Pila. What will you do for revenge then?"

Wennem shrugged.

"I'm asking because a time will come, maybe sooner than you think, when you will have to decide what to do with your life. For the moment it is bent on revenge, but when there is nothing left to revenge yourself against, what will you do? Live in rage for the rest of your years?"

"No," she answered quickly, but even she heard the uncertainty in her voice. "Why do you ask these questions? Why do you want to upset me?"

Makon tried to find the words he wanted to say, but his mind refused to think. Inside, he groaned in frustration. "I don't want to upset you," was all that would come out, and it sounded like a declaration. And then, from nowhere, came, "I want to protect you."

$$\boxed{30}$$

THE autumn sun, still with some of its summer strength, was high in the sky. Kendra shimmered, golden, on its harbor. Pennants flew above towers and from ship masts. The effort needed for the war had slowed down business, but the markets still bustled with people.

Kendra persevered. So far.

Standing on the south gallery of the palace, Areava looked out over her royal city with pride and love, and terrible sadness. She shivered despite the heat of the sun on her skin. She could not help feeling both she and her city were in their last autumn, and that a cold and terrible winter was about to descend on them, a winter without end.

Orkid stood behind her, ashen-faced. The news from Chandra had been almost as great a blow as losing Sendarus and Areava's baby. It was a fundamental wrong, something so unnatural it was hard to believe let alone accept. It was as if the kingdom was being dismembered the way a calf is dismembered for a feast. Why had destiny turned against Grenda Lear? In all the years he had spent working with Grenda Lear, he had come to believe that the whole point of history had been the creations and growing power of the kingdom, that the kingdom had become as unassailable and unchangeable as history itself.

"Your Majesty, the council must meet urgently."

"Yes," she said, her voice distant.

"The Great Army is almost complete. It must march at the earliest opportunity, before Lynan can consolidate his position in Chandra."

"Yes."

"I will instruct Harnan to issue the summons immediately."

"And send Dejanus."

"Your Majesty?"

"Dejanus must leave for the army now. This morning. Order a pinnace from the navy to take him. That will get him to the hosting by tomorrow evening."

There was no answer from Orkid. She turned to face him. He looked like someone on the verge of making a terrible decision. "Is there a problem?"

He half-shrugged. "I'm not sure . . ."

Areava's eyes narrowed. "Do you think sending Dejanus to command the army is a mistake?"

The question seemed to resolve him.

"No," he said firmly.

"How long before my people know, do you think?"

"The message came from a carrier pigeon. Only you and I know about it, but as soon as the first merchant ship returning from Sparro arrives, word will spread like . . ." He stopped himself from finishing.

"Like fire, Orkid. Yes. And as destructive."

"I am sorry, your Majesty."

"Orkid, tell me, was there any reason for us to suspect that Tomar would forswear? Were there signs we missed? Hints or suggestions in his letters to our court?"

Orkid shook his head. "If so, none that I caught or understood."

She massaged her forehead with one hand. "I do not think Usharna would be in this position. I do not think she would have let things get so out of hand that one of her most trusted rulers would turn on her like this. What have I done wrong, Orkid?"

Orkid shook his head in protest. "Nothing, your Majesty! The guilt is not yours, but King Tomar's. He has betrayed you! He has betrayed Grenda Lear."

"Why?" Areava cried.

Orkid could not reply. He bowed his head in silence.

"Summon the council," she ordered, cold and angry. "And get Dejanus to his army."

Orkid left. Areava turned back to her city. She could imagine the despondency that would set in once the citizens learned of Chandra's desertion. Perhaps even panic. There was now nothing except the Great Army between Lynan and the capital.

Lynan. The name left a bitter taste in her mouth. He represented for her everything that was wrong with the world, a commoner above his station, a rebel and a revolutionary, a traitor and a warmonger. In his wake was nothing but despoliation, ruin, despair, the destruction of the traditions and laws that made Grenda Lear great. And all of this was reflected in his twisted mind, the maelstrom at the heart of her half-brother which the Key of the Scepter had let her see that night she lost control of her own dreaming. She had touched, tasted, smelled his insanity, and it made her feel unclean. In all her life she had never been afraid of any person, but now Lynan loomed in her dreams like the shadow of death.

Areava shivered, and wondered if she would ever feel warm again.

Dejanus was roused from his heavy sleep by a sergeant.

"I said I didn't want to be disturbed," he mumbled.

The sergeant grabbed him by his jerkin and forced him to sit upright.

Dejanus stared at the sergeant's face. "You!" he roared. It was the same man who had woken him so roughly the day after the city fire. He should have gutted him then, and would have been tempted to do so now if he was not feeling so damnably under the weather. "What do you think you're doing?"

"The chancellor is here to see you," the sergeant said.

"The chancellor? Hoot to the chancellor. Let him wait . . ."

"Under instruction of the queen," the sergeant interrupted.

Dejanus cleared his throat. "The queen?"

"Thank you, sergeant," said Orkid's voice. The sergeant backed away, and his place in Dejanus' limited line of vision was taken by the black-robed chancellor. "You are to get your fondest wish."

Dejanus sneered up at him. "My *fondest* wish? What would you know about my fondest wish?"

"You've talked about it often enough, complained to all and sundry that you have been deprived of it."

Dejanus stood up uncertainly. He did not like Orkid's tone one little bit. Uppity bloody Amanite. "What are you talking about?"

Orkid winced at the stale gust of breath that washed over him. The constable's clothes did not smell much better. "You had better get cleaned up."

"I'll get cleaned up when I'm good and ready."

"You can't greet your army smelling like a wine pot."

"My army?"

"You've got your orders. The queen wants you to take command of your army personally. Now."

"Now?" Dejanus supported his head with his hands; why was it feeling so impossibly heavy?

"As I said, you are to get your fondest wish. The army needs you."

"Why now, for God's sake? What's the hurry all of a sudden?"

"I'll explain to you on the way to your ship."

"Ship? I'll go bloody overland. I hate ships."

"You have to be in Chandra tomorrow. You'll go by ship. Order of the queen, I'm afraid."

Orkid's voice did not sound very apologetic to Dejanus. "How do I know all of this is really coming from the queen?"

"I'll take you to see Areava right away if you want proof, although I'm not sure she'll appreciate the interruption. It's been a busy morning so far—not that you'll have noticed here in your bed—and promises to get a lot busier yet."

"I need to pack—"

"Already done, thanks to Sergeant Arad. Good man, that. Might recommend him for promotion to constable." Dejanus' face flushed in anger. "After all, after being commander of the greatest army ever seen in Theare, you won't want to go back to being head door opener in the palace, will you?"

Dejanus did not know what to say. He had certainly never heard of the constable referred to as being "head door opener" before. He was damn sure no one ever called it that to Kumul Alarn's face when he was constable.

"Get cleaned up. I'll be back shortly to escort you down to the docks and explain to you the situation in Chandra."

Dejanus could feel panic building in him. It was too soon for him to take over real command of the army. He had not been given enough time to prepare. He needed to go over strategy with the queen and tactics with the marshal. He did not even have a general's ceremonial garb; at least, not the garb he thought someone in his position deserved.

"Can't someone go ahead of me and prepare the army for my arrival?" he asked, tying hard but unsuccessfully not to sound plaintive.

Orkid, who had always struck Dejanus as being so expressionless—so without normal human feelings—he might as well have been carved from stone, suddenly seemed to become even more inhuman. Dejanus thought he could feel *cold* radiating from the chancellor. He leaned forward so only Dejanus could hear him and said in a whisper that cut like a whip: "Listen to me, you oaf. Grenda Lear now faces the most dangerous days in its entire history. Through blackmail, fate, and sheer good fortune, you find yourself in command of the one thing that can restore stability and peace to the kingdom. If you fail, we will all go down under the heel of a conqueror who will have no mercy on you or me; if you succeed, you will become the greatest hero the kingdom has ever known, greater even than General Elynd Chisal. Not bad for someone who was once a slaver and mercenary without a coin of his own to spend on cheap wine or a diseased whore."

Before Dejanus could think of a reply, Orkid was gone. Sergeant Arad reappeared. "Right, sir," Arad said. "Best we get you cleaned up right smart."

"I have a headache," Dejanus said.

"Unfortunate," Arad said without sympathy, "and without remedy. You'll just have to put up with it, sir."

Powl tried to ignore the knocking on his door.

History, he thought. *It is all history.*

The knocking would not stop.

"What is it?" he shouted.

The door opened a crack and Father Rown's head appeared. He glanced at all the books and papers on the primate's desk. "Forgive me, your Grace, but you weren't at service yesterday, nor this morning, and I thought something might be wrong—"

"Nothing is wrong!" Powl yelled.

"Or something I might help you with."

Powl closed his eyes and breathed deeply to control his temper. "I need no one's help," he said between gritted teeth. "Just leave."

Rown swallowed. "Your Grace—"

"Leave! Now!"

"But the queen—" Rown said.

Powl looked glared at him. "The queen what?"

"There is an urgent council meeting this afternoon. We have been ordered to attend."

"Very well," Powl said tiredly. "Give me the agenda."

"There is none. It is an extraordinary council meeting. There will be no discussion of previous items."

Powl went to the door, opening it wide. Rown looked at him anxiously, obviously wishing he were somewhere else. "What do you mean no agenda? What's happened?"

Rown shrugged. "No one is saying."

"Something to do with the war." Powl said, more to himself than Rown.

"Almost certainly. Will I come by when it is time to attend?"

Powl nodded absently. "Yes. Do that. Thank you, Father." He withdrew and closed the door. What could have happened? And why was no one saying anything? That could only mean the queen alone, or perhaps the queen and Orkid, knew what was going on.

He shook his head in frustration. *It isn't important.* Compared to his new work, nothing else was important. He went back to his desk where his books and notes waited for him. *No one except me understands what it all means.* He ran his hand over one of the volumes from the tower of Colanus and laughed softly. The contents of the tower was a kind of joke played by Colanus on all his descendants; not intentionally, of course, but that innocence was the source for some of the irony.

Everyone assumed that because the volumes contained secret knowledge it must involve magic; that was certainly what the first great magickers themselves had assumed. It was also why they failed to translate the volumes: they could not see past their own desires. But Colanus had not gathered together ancient and arcane magickal practices, he had brought together all the myths and legends of ancient Theare to compile a history, a history that told where all the races came from, where the Keys of Power came from, why everything in Theare was the way it was.

So far he had only had enough time to translate small sections from each volume, enough to show him what the collections contained, how the history was organized, and one very special piece of information that intrigued and worried him: Theare, the name of the continent inhabited by all the known peoples from Haxus in the north to the Lurisians and desert Chetts in the south, was an ancient word for prison.

Orkid, late for the extraordinary council meeting, was hurrying back to the palace after delivering Dejanus to his pinnace. The constable had gabbled all the way to his boat, desperately trying to find some excuse that would allow him to stay in Kendra. At last Orkid had told him bluntly to shut up, and before Dejanus could

use that as an excuse to fuel his bad temper, the chancellor told him
about King Tomar's betrayal.

"Chandra is about to fall," Orkid explained carefully. "The only
thing preventing that, and preventing the way to Kendra being open
to Lynan and his army of barbarians, is the Great Army in southern
Chandra. Your Great Army."

The news about Tomar's defection was enough to shut up even
Dejanus, and the rest of the trip to the harbor passed without a single word of complaint, giving Orkid's conscience the space it
needed to agonize over his decision to support Dejanus for command of the Great Army in the first place. He knew in his bones it
was a disastrous choice, but desperately hoped the quality and size
of the army would be enough to overcome the failings of its general. Anyway, he consoled himself, he had no choice: Dejanus
could have brought them both down if Orkid had not supported
him.

When Orkid arrived at the main gate to the palace, he saw it was
blocked by a group of twenty or so ragtag riders who were arguing
with the Royal Guards on duty. He was about to push through and
leave it to the guards to sort out when he heard a voice he recognized. He pushed his way through the stamping crowd and grabbed
the reins of the horse closest to the gate. The rider twisted around,
his face suddenly angry, mouth open to curse or swear or shout, but
instead said in surprise, "Chancellor?"

"Galen Amptra? It is you!"

"Would you tell this fool of a guard who I am?"

Orkid hesitated—there was no love lost between him and any
member of the Twenty Houses—but in this time of emergency
petty rivalries were irrelevant. "It's all right, let them in," he said to
the guard. "This is the son of Duke Holo Amptra, and I will vouch
for him and his fellow knights."

"We are not all fellow knights," said a woman's voice. Orkid
glanced at the rider next to Galen, but did not recognize her under
the dirt and grime.

"I am sorry, madam, I meant no offense—"

"Not 'madam,' Chancellor," Galen said. "This is Queen Charion
of Hume."

Orkid swallowed. "My apologies, your Majesty. I had no
idea—"

"Understandable in my present condition."

Orkid waved them through but did not let go the reins of Galen's horse. "The last we heard you were still with Tomar," he said. "We assumed he imprisoned or ambushed you when he changed sides."

"Tomar gave us safe passage," Charion said. "We rode straight here."

"How many of you are there?"

"There are three hundred of us left," Galen said, despondent. "We have fought many battles."

"Did you speak to Tomar?"

"No. It was Barys Malayka who informed us of the changed political situation in Chandra. And he gave us a letter from Tomar to Queen Areava. If you could help us see her right away, I would appreciate it."

The mention of a letter made Orkid's heart miss a beat. "Do you know what the letter contains?"

Charion withdrew a piece of folded, brown parchment from her saddlebag and showed Orkid it was still sealed with Tomar's red crest.

"The queen is in emergency council right now," he said, his words tumbling over one another. "In fact, I was on my way to join her. Give me the letter and I will make sure she receives it."

Charion did not hesitate to hand it over. "Thank you. In that case, if you could assign us rooms to clean and change into other clothes . . ."

"My father will be proud to have you under his roof, Charion," Galen said.

Orkid noticed the sweet smiles that passed between the two. He was not sure whether or not that boded well for him and the court, but it warranted close attention. He never expected a member of the Twenty Houses to invite someone from the provinces to stay with them, even one as highborn as Charion. The arrogance of the Twenty Houses had long been one of the constants in Orkid's life at court.

"I think it better if I stay here in the palace," Charion said. "To do otherwise might offend Areava, and I would not willingly do that. And you forget that your father is of the old nobility, and they regard my status as not much better than a Kendran washerwoman."

Galen opened his mouth to protest, but honesty prevented him. Charion was right. "Very well, but I won't pretend I'm not disappointed. I will be back as soon as I can." He glanced at Orkid.

"After all, I am a member of the council that is meeting, unless Areava has replaced me."

"The queen would not do that," Orkid said. *No matter how much I might wish it.* "But the queen will not expect you to attend this afternoon after your long journey and all your travails. Report to her this evening."

"Until then," Galen said, this time to Charion. They kissed quickly, and Galen and the other knights quickly left the palace. Orkid called a passing servant across.

"Accommodation for her Majesty, Queen Charion of Hume. The royal guest wing. Make sure she has the clothes and toiletries she needs. And see to her horse."

The servant nodded, looked skeptically at the woman supposed to be a queen, and took the reins of her horse to lead her away.

"Thank you, Chancellor," she called over her shoulder. "I will not forget you came to my rescue at the gate."

"I'm sure," he said, not quite loudly enough for her to hear. He hurried to his office and carefully unsealed Tomar's letter. As he had been afraid, it detailed Tomar's reasons for siding with Lynan, including an account from Lynan of the events on the night of Berayma's murder. With one important exception—the conclusion that Areava must have been complicit in the plot that put her on the throne—the account was accurate. When he had finished reading it, he lit one corner over a candle and watched the parchment burn to a cinder on his desk.

It seemed to Olio that when Areava broke the news to her council that Tomar had declared for Lynan it was as if all the air had been sucked out of the room. Mouths gaped open, but no one could say a word.

Olio, who was the first to recover from the shock, asked: "What about the Great Army?"

"Still encamped in south Chandra," Areava said. "Dejanus is on his way there right now."

"So there is still a buffer between Lynan and Kendra?" asked an anxious Shant Tenor.

"Yes. There is a buffer in time, as well. It will take Lynan several days for his army to reach Sparro from Daavis, and several days after that for them to reach the south."

"But Tomar could attack first," one of the nobles said. "He need not wait for Lynan."

"Tomar would not dare attack the Great Army by himself," Orkid said derisively. "*He* is not stupid."

There was a shocked gasp from the members of the Twenty Houses; even Areava seemed surprised at the chancellor's uncharacteristic outburst.

"By the way, Duke Amptra," Orkid continued, nonchalantly, addressing another of the nobles, "your son is safe and waiting for you at home."

"Galen? He is returned?"

"What is this, Orkid?" Areava demanded.

"Galen and the survivors of the knights were given safe passage back to Kendra from Chandra. They arrived just before the meeting. They have brought Queen Charion with them."

"Why were they not invited here immediately?"

"I thought it best they have a chance to rest. They were exhausted, and had nothing except the clothes they arrived in."

"Did they bring anything else with them?" Areava asked. "A letter or proclamation from Tomar?"

"A letter," Orkid said carefully. "It contained nothing but slander and lies." His eyes flickered. "Against you, my queen. I burned it in anger."

"Orkid?"

"I am sorry, your Majesty. I know it was wrong—"

"Very wrong," she said. There was no anger in her voice, but that seemed to make the judgement worse for Orkid. "The letter would have ensured history noted the justness of our cause."

He bowed his head. "I realize that now, your Majesty, and apologize to you and the council for my lack of foresight."

Areava carefully regarded the chancellor. "We have other things to discuss now."

"City defenses, for example," the marshal said from the opposite end of the table. "Just in case the Great Army fails to stop Prince Lynan."

Olio saw a look of panic cross the faces of many members of the council.

"We can begin by diverting some of the Great Army's forces still on their way to Chandra to garrison duty here," the marshal continued.

"No," Areava said quickly. "The Great Army is still Kendra's best defense, and it makes no sense to weaken it. We have the Royal Guards, still the best soldiers in all of Theare. Kendra will be safe."

She caught each of the city representatives in her gaze. "And I count on all of you to get out that message."

There were subdued murmurs of agreement around the table, and a discussion started on how best to prepare Kendra for a possible siege. Olio contributed by suggesting he cooperate with Edaytor Fanhow and the primate to establish hospices and surgeries, an idea warmly received, but then found himself with little to add as the discussion moved to wall-building and troop deployment. He noticed that Orkid himself was contributing little; he seemed distracted and nervous, which was entirely out of character. The other surprise was the primate. It was not a matter of Powl being distracted—he gave the impression his mind was completely absent, and poor Father Rown sitting next to him was fidgety and seemed out of his depth. Could Powl have been so shocked by the news of Tomar's betrayal? Olio had thought Powl a man with deeper reserves than that; he saw Areava occasionally throw furtive glances toward the two clerics, obviously expecting the primate to speak up on several of the issues raised by others.

"Primate?" Areava eventually urged. "Have you anything to add to this discussion?"

Powl's eyes slowly focused on the queen. "No, your Majesty. At this point I have nothing to say." Then his eyes seemed to glaze over again.

"Ah, ah," Rown said, swallowing heavily, "I believe his Grace fully supports Prince Olio's suggestion of establishing hospices and other places to deal with any wounded the city might . . . umm . . . incur during the protraction of a . . . ah . . . siege."

Areava nodded slowly. "I see," she said, and continued with the meeting.

Areava held two audiences in her private chambers that evening. The first was with Orkid.

"I find it hard to believe you destroyed the letter from Tomar," she told him.

Orkid could not meet her gaze. "It was unforgivable, I know," he said, his head bobbing like some peasant supplicant from the country. "My only defense is that his intemperate language fired my devotion to you."

"So you fired the letter," she added dryly.

"Your Majesty."

"It is unlike Tomar to be intemperate about anything. He always struck me as a level-headed, reasonable person."

"What level-headed and reasonable person could betray his monarch?"

"I was hoping the letter would tell me."

"It was a rant, nothing more. Spiteful. Hateful."

"Nevertheless, it was *my* letter."

"I regret there is little I can do about it."

"Of course you can. We still have some of Tomar's pigeons?"

Orkid swallowed. He knew where this was going.

"Orkid?"

"I am not sure. I will have to check with the pigeon keeper."

Areava stared at the chancellor. "How could he not have at least one?"

Orkid shrugged. "I cannot speak for him, your Majesty—"

"I am not asking you to speak for him. At any rate, if there is a pigeon, we send a message to Tomar asking him to send us another copy of his letter."

"And if there is no pigeon?"

"We send a messenger under a sign of parley."

Orkid was astounded. "All this for a letter from a traitor?"

"All this so I can read what he said."

"I have already told you what he said."

Areava's voice rose. "I desire to read it for myself!"

Orkid knew he had gone too far with his argument. He bowed and retreated a step.

"And when I get the letter, I expect the seal to be unbroken," she added.

Orkid felt sweat start to bead his forehead. She was suspicious of his action in burning Tomar's letter, that much was certain, but was that all she was suspicious about?

He bowed again.

There was a knock on the door, and a guard entered. "Your Majesty, it is Queen Charion and Galen Amptra to see you, as you requested."

"Let them in, thank you. The chancellor was just leaving."

Orkid left, closing the door behind her two new guests.

Areava stood to greet Charion formerly. "We are honored to receive our sister from Hume."

Charion curtsied. It was not easily done, since Areava was the only person in the world she was obliged to curtsy to and she was out of practice, but there was no hesitation in the action. "Your Majesty," she said, and bowed her head as well.

Galen bowed even lower. "We are sorry to have been the bearer of such bad tidings, your Majesty."

"On that score do not fret yourself," Areava told them. "We had heard earlier in the morning. A private message had come by carrier pigeon."

"Ah, then the letter revealed nothing new."

"Alas, the letter never reached me. My chancellor, in his haste to defend my honor, destroyed it."

"Your honor?" Charion was puzzled.

"He tells me King Tomar's letter was scandalous and insulting to my person."

Charion and Galen exchanged surprised glances.

"Did you not find it so?" she asked them.

"We had not read it, your Majesty. It was still sealed when we handed it over to Orkid."

"I did not know." She waved them both into seats. "I have heard of the valiant actions your knights have taken part in, Galen. You will be pleased to know that in his last communication to me, Sendarus praised you and your companions most highly."

"Thank you. Sendarus had become a friend before he died, and had earned the respect of all who served under him."

"Including me," Charion said, "although we did not exactly get on at first."

Areava almost smiled then, but thought better of it. She was touched more deeply than they could know by their memories of her husband, but this was not the time for her to dwell on the past. "Thank you. Now tell me everything you can about Lynan and his army. Assume I know nothing."

From then until deep into the night, the three of them discussed only the war. Areava was disturbed, but not surprised, by stories of Lynan's changed nature. She was also disturbed by her guests' account of new Chett tactics and formations, such as the lancers and the Red Hands. It was soon apparent that the only real setback Lynan had suffered was the death of Kumul Alarn.

"Are you suggesting my brother cannot be beaten?" Areava asked with an undercurrent of anger.

"No, your Majesty," Charion said firmly. "His army, at least, can be beaten. We proved that in the first battle. As for defeating Lynan himself, well . . ." she nodded to the Key of the Scepter hanging from Areava's neck, ". . . you may be the only one who can deal with him."

"You think it will come to that? You think his army will reach Kendra?"

"I do not say to that," Charion said. "But one way or another, I believe he will reach Kendra."

Areava slapped the arms of her chair. "I should have taken command of the Great Army!"

"To what purpose? Are you a better general than this Dejanus I have been told has command?"

"We are both untried," she said.

"But he has seen combat."

"Yes," she admitted grudgingly.

"Then forgive me, your Majesty, for I do not doubt your courage, but Dejanus may prove to be the wiser choice after all. Defeating Lynan's army and defeating Lynan are two separate issues."

Areava slumped in her chair. The day had not been one of any cheer and a great deal of gloom. She was exhausted, and now was showing it. "Do you know," she said, subdued, "that I have not left the palace since my coronation?"

Charion and Galen exchanged glances, but it was not a question that invited response.

"Thank you both for coming tonight," Areava said, standing up. "We will talk again before long."

Charion and Galen stood up. "Your Majesty, one request?" Galen asked.

"If I can grant it."

"My knights and I can reequip ourselves with armor before another day has gone, and then it is only two days' hard ride to where the Great Army gathers. If you would—"

"I read your mind, Galen Amptra, but no. Your number now is so small that no matter how valiant you prove yourselves to be, you will not decide the day of battle one way or the other; yet if Lynan and his army should reach Kendra, your contribution here could be decisive."

Galen could not hide his disappointment, but he nodded. "As you wish."

As they were leaving, Areava said: "Galen, I find it hard to reconcile myself with the Twenty Houses, for long they were enemies of my mother and—I believed—myself, but obviously there are some in that group whom I would have as friends."

"You may have more friends in the Twenty Houses than you know, your Majesty," Galen replied.

It was dark and cold on the sea. The *Gentle Tide* was not big enough for Dejanus' liking, heaving low to the water and too easily rolled by any wave. Its crew of ten worked the single lateen sail and sheets with practiced ease but had little time for the constable as night voyages were never completely safe, no matter how well the captain might pretend to know the coast.

Left largely to his own devices Dejanus sat for the whole journey behind the wheel house which protected him from the worst of the spray, standing up only to relieve himself over the side; the first time he went for a piss he almost slipped over the wale, resulting in him emptying his stomach as well as his bladder into the churning waves.

By the time the *Gentle Tide* was easing against the dock of a small fishing village in south Chandra, the sun was still an hour from rising and he could see there was no one to greet him. As soon as the pinnace was secured, he got off, leaving no thanks for the captain and her crew for the safe and quick journey. They silently cursed him and then set about unloading the rest of their cargo.

Dejanus walked into the village, heading for the building that most looked like it might be the local equivalent of an inn. The door was locked. He banged on it until some old, sleep-encrusted man opened it a crack and demanded to know who was banging away at this hour. Dejanus used his strength to shove the door wide open, sending the man sprawling on the floor. He stepped in and saw the long drinking bench that showed he had guessed right. In the wall opposite the bench a large fire still burned.

"My name is General Dejanus," he said. "Are any of my officers staying here?"

"One, your Mightiness," the man groveled. "He arrived late last night—"

Dejanus picked up the man by his the collar of his night shirt. "You are going to do three things. First, get me a warm wine. Second, wake the officer and tell him to report to me immediately. Third, make me breakfast. I'm *very* hungry."

"Yes, your Mightiness!" the man said and disappeared, his feet pattering away into the darkness behind the bench.

Dejanus chose a seat near the fire, put his legs up on one of the tables, and waited. Before he was warm, the old man returned with a wooden cup full to the brim with mulled wine and cinnamon. Half a cup later a skinny, nervous ensign appeared, helmet under one arm and a sheaf of papers under the other.

"Why weren't you at the dock to greet me?" Dejanus demanded.

"Sir, you weren't due until this morning."

Dejanus considered humiliating him, but he was tired after the voyage and there was no audience to learn the lesson. Instead, he harrumphed and pointed to the papers. "What are those?"

"The General's papers, sir."

"I don't have any papers, Ensign."

"Begging your pardon, General, sir, but Chancellor Orkid Gravespear says you do." With that the ensign held them out. Dejanus, automatically flushing with the mention of Orkid's name, took them with little grace.

"Is there anything else the General wants, sir?"

"Hoping to get back to bed, Ensign?"

"Yes, sir."

"Well, sit down. You can wait until I've gone through each and every one of these papers. Before you do, though, see what's holding up my breakfast and get me a proper lantern."

Dejanus turned over the first paper. It had something to do with supplies, but he was not sure if it was supplies that had arrived or supplies still to come or supplies awaiting distribution. Under items were listed shoes, belts, pots. Then there were three other columns, and he had no idea what they represented. The second paper was an invoice from a local farmer, but Dejanus could not tell if it had been paid or not. The third paper was a series of squares linked by lines, and each square had the name of a Lurisian infantry unit in it. What was this supposed to represent? He scrabbled through the papers for something useful, for something he could understand and act on. One of the last papers had his name on the top, and the names of other officers underneath, one or two of which he recognized. These were the commanders of the units in his army. Probably cocky long-servers all of them, thinking they were going to have it all over him because he had been "head door opener" in the palace. Well, he would show them, he would show them all.

The ensign and old man returned, the latter carrying a large tray with bacon and eggs and ham and another cup of mulled wine.

"I'll just go and get the young officer some," he said as he scurried away.

"You'll do no such thing!" Dejanus roared after him, and then to the ensign: "You can wait until bloody morning when everyone else gets fed."

"Sir," the ensign said dejectedly.

Dejanus put the papers aside. He would put them all on the spike at the shit hole when he got to the army camp. He wondered if generals in the field got their own shit hole.

He turned to the food and wolfed it down. The voyage had made him hungry. Must have been all that sea air. And jittery. He could not sit still.

"So much to do," he mumbled around a mouthful of ham.

"Sorry, sir?"

Dejanus glared at him. "I was talking over my breakfast. But since you asked . . . how far to the camp?"

"About an hour's ride, General. I've got two horses ready for us."

"Good. Get packed. Now. We leave as soon as I finish here."

The ensign sighed resignedly and left to pack.

"I'll show you all," Dejanus said to his back.

The ensign pretended not to hear.

31

IT was an excited scout, riding hard and raising a small cloud of dust, that told Lynan his army was approaching. He could not help tensing. He had dreaded this day since sending a message to Daavis for Korigan to bring the Chetts south to Sparro, and asking her to let Ager, Gudon, and Lasthear, her Chett teacher, know that Jenrosa had died fighting Silona. He would soon have to face his friends and prove to them that not only he was free at last from Silona's influence, but also Lynan Rosetheme again in every sense and ready to lead his army to victory against Queen Areava.

Duty, he reminded himself. *Sometimes it is due to individuals, and not just groups.*

The scout rode up to Lynan and Tomar. "The Chett army is an hour behind me," he said, his eyes wide with wonder. Then, almost as an afterthought, he added: "A small group rides ahead of them."

"That will be your friends," Tomar said.

"Would you mind if I went ahead and met them by myself?"

"I understand. I will wait for you here with the . . . ah . . . official delegation."

Lynan smiled. The official delegation consisted of Tomar, Barys Malayka and a nervous mayor of Sparro decked out in his official robes and chains.

"I won't be long," Lynan said, and spurred his horse. A short while later he saw three people dressed in Chett ponchos and wearing the wide-brimmed Chett hat coming in his direction. He reined in and waited. Although he no longer had the excellent vision he possessed while Silona was alive, he could tell well enough by the way they rode that it was Korigan, Ager, and Gudon. The Chett queen was the best rider he knew—it was like watching some creature that was half-human, half-horse. Gudon rode with the slight sway he learned as a barge pilot on the Barda River, and Ager, although only a tornado could take him off his saddle if he was determined to stay on it, rode as if he was designed for walking, although with his crookback he was not actually designed for either.

Lynan tried to calm his beating heart, tried not to shout out in joy at seeing them again. He watched them slow from a trot to a walk, and they approached him slowly, almost cautiously. Ager was the first to reach him, then Gudon, and finally Korigan. He could see the uncertainty in their faces, the vestige of fear. He drew in a deep shuddering breath.

"It's me," he said.

Ager reached out and touched his face. "Your skin has changed. It's almost normal."

Lynan did not hide his surprise. "I have been too afraid to see myself in a mirror. But look." He held out his right hand, still blistered and raw from grasping the red-hot sword from the fire.

"Why hasn't your hand healed?" Ager asked.

"Silona died," he said simply. He had no other explanation.

Korigan maneuvered her horse so she was sitting right beside him. She took Lynan's head in her hands and forced him to meet her gaze. He did not flinch from her. "Your eyes are brown," she said in wonder. "Like a Chett's. I was never able to tell before." She leaned across and kissed his forehead.

Gudon looked on, a knowing smile tugging at his lips. "Truth, little master, I knew you never really left us."

Lynan felt his eyes sting. "Truth, Gudon, I did for a while."

"But you came back," Ager said, and Lynan could see tears stinging his eyes, too.

"Because of Jenrosa," he said, the words tumbling out.

Ager and Gudon swallowed hard then.

"News of her death sent your army into grieving," Korigan said carefully. The other three knew the two women had not been friends. "Especially Lasthear and the other magickers. They cannot believe they have lost their Truespeaker so soon and in this way."

"I don't think she ever accepted she was a Truespeaker," Lynan said. "She just wanted to be Jenrosa Alucar." He blinked away his tears. "Whoever that was to be."

"If she lived," Korigan said, "I think she would have accepted her fate." She smiled unexpectedly. "As you know, we did not get on; that is always the way between a monarch and a Truespeaker."

"Truth," Gudon said. "It was like that between my mother and Korigan's father, your namesake."

"And between me and Jenrosa, toward the end," Lynan said glumly.

Korigan gently touched Lynan's hand. "I am sorry for the pain her death must be causing you, and so soon after the death of Kumul Alarn. At least they will be together now in whatever peace death may bring."

Lynan nodded his thanks for her words. "When the war is finally over, we will have time to grieve properly for both of them, as well as all our friends and supporters who sacrificed their lives for my cause." He glanced at all three of his companions and felt a surge of great love for them. "Until then, let us use our grief to drive our anger and fury against the enemy."

"Tell me, my lord," Barys said to Tomar, "what do you think of having several thousand Chetts on your doorstep?"

"I think, my champion, that I prefer it to having several thousand Kendrans, Amanites, Lurisian, and Storians on my doorstep."

They spoke in a low voice so the mayor could not hear them. The mayor was a nice enough fellow, likable and hard working in his office, but the kind of man who thought everyone should always get on, even in time of war. He was sitting on a placid, bow-backed hack, and looked as uncomfortable as it was possible to be done up in mayoral finery and with nothing witty to say in the company of a king and his champion.

"You still have those, I'm afraid," Barys continued. "The Great Army will not leave now you have declared war on its queen."

"I have done no such thing."

"Semantics, my lord."

"Politics, my champion. And never forget that Lynan may have won his victories with his army, but he won his army—and won over the entire Chett nation—with his mother's knack for diplomacy. In the end, when all the fighting and dying are done, it is politics that will determine the shape of the future, and Lynan has proven to me he understands that."

"Do you think you can win this war?"

"I believe Lynan can. You've spent time with him the last few days. What do you think?"

"I think he is like his father in some ways."

"He has a softer tongue."

"He has the same hard head, which bodes well for all of us. Sometimes, when I look at him, I think he is the General reincarnated, but then he'll say something or do something that reminds me Lynan is his own man." He glanced quickly at Tomar. "Unfortunately, however, the only thing I am not sure about is this army of his."

"They've done well so far."

"They lost to the first Grenda Lear army they met."

Tomar shrugged. "Not much of a loss, really. The Chett army remained largely intact while the Grenda Lear army was reduced to not much more than a rump of its former strength, and then within two seasons the Chett army recovered well enough to capture Haxus—something never achieved by a Grenda Lear army, I might point out—and then Hume."

"Some would say they have captured Chandra as well."

"Some would be wrong, then, although I have no doubt Chandra would have fallen to Lynan had I had not joined with him."

"I'm curious, my lord. When *did* you make up your mind to join him?"

"I think a part of me must have decided as soon as I read his letter. A great wrong was done in Kendra when Berayma was murdered, and if it isn't revenged, the heart of the kingdom will rot away."

"I did not think you cared so much for Grenda Lear."

"I am not foolish enough to believe that little Chandra can survive by itself in this age of giants. If—when—Lynan wins his throne, Theare will hold only one kingdom. I'd rather be a part of that than opposed to it."

"Well, then," Barys said, pointing up the road where Lynan and his three companions had just appeared, "here comes the future."

The king smiled at the mayor and waved him forward. "How are you feeling, Lord Mayor?"

The mayor smiled nervously. "F–f–fine, thank you, your Majesty."

Tomar patted his shoulder. "You'll be fine. Just remember not to insult the Chetts accidentally; they hold a grudge better than any other people on the continent."

The mayor stared wide-eyed at Tomar.

"Cruelly done," Barys said under his breath.

"Just want to keep him on his toes."

"He won't sleep for a week now, afraid some barbarian assassin is after him."

Tomar cleared his throat and said to the mayor: "It is very difficult to insult a Chett, by the way."

"W–w–wonderful," the mayor said, unconvinced.

Sparro's docks were almost empty. All the ships belonging to the great merchant fleets from Lurisia and Kendra had fled to their home ports when Chandra changed sides in the civil war. Tomar's soldiers had been able to seize eight before the others made their escape, but that had only been a small proportion of the traffic in the harbor at the time bringing supplies for the Great Army as well as the normal run of trade goods. There were still ships belonging to Chandran merchants tied up at the docks, as well as increasing numbers of ships from Haxus, but, in a way, they made the vacant berths even more obvious.

"Did you ever go to sea during your time in the east?" Korigan asked Gudon. They were walking along the harbor's edge, a little behind Lynan and Ager. It was late afternoon, and the sun made the water ripple with flames. Korigan had never seen anything quite like the sea, and for the first time in her life felt the pull of something as grand and limitless as the Oceans of Grass.

Gudon shook his head. "Never tempted, I must admit. It took me a long time to get used to being a barge pilot on the Barda, what with all that water underneath me. On an ocean-going ship, it would be infinitely worse."

"I believe Ager spent a good part of his life working on merchant ships."

"Yes."

"I wonder if he misses it."

"I wonder, cousin, why you are talking about the sea instead of Lynan."

Korigan laughed bitterly. "Because I am afraid of what you and I might discover between us." She glanced at Gudon, almost shyly. "Do you know he did not come to our bed last night? Tomar gave us a sumptuous room. I waited for him. I wanted to tell him how glad I was to be with him again. I fell asleep eventually."

"How much do you love him?"

Korigan's gaze dropped to her feet. "I don't know. What can I compare it too?"

"You've had lovers before."

"Yes, and never loved them. I don't know if it is possible to love someone more than I love Lynan."

"And?"

"But I think it is possible for Lynan to love me more than he does."

"Ah."

"In a way I am glad he did not come to bed last night. I am afraid to be alone with him again."

"But he is no longer under the influence of Silona."

"I have only known him since the vampire's blood flowed through his veins. Will I know him now?"

"Truth, cousin, you already know him. The Lynan I knew before Jenrosa gave him Silona's blood was the same man afterward. Until his last, great fever, he only changed in battle. If he loved you then, he still loves you now."

"If he loved me then," she said quietly. She stopped, looked north out over the ocean, and tried to imagine what lay beyond the horizon. She had heard of the Far Kingdom, a legendary place on the other side of the Sea Between, a land peopled with strange and monstrous beings. Was it possible to travel so far you could leave all your fears and doubts behind? And what would life be like without those fears and doubts? Was there someone at this very moment in the Far Kingdom looking south and wondering the very same thing?

"When I received Lynan's message that Jenrosa had died destroying Silona and saving his life," she said, "my first reaction was to wish it had been me that had died for him. In that moment I forgot that I was a queen, that my life is never truly my own. Lynan has that power over me, you see."

Gudon did not know what to say. He had never before heard love professed so earnestly, so honestly, and it made him feel ashamed.

"How up to date is Tomar's information on the Great Army?" Ager asked Lynan.

"Very. Largely heavy infantry; some archers, but not as many as they would have had if Chandra had contributed. Some cavalry, most light, a few medium regiments. Nothing like the knights, though."

"So our lancers are the heaviest horse?"

"So far as Tomar knows."

"That's good. And what exactly will Tomar contribute to our army?"

"I've asked mainly for infantry, especially the Arran Valley regiments. Otherwise mainly supply—food, wagons, ambulance carts, and surgeons."

"None of his cavalry or archers? They are very good."

"They will be needed to hold Sparro and the surrounding countryside. If Areava has any military advisers worth their salt, she'll try to take the province by the sea. She has the only fleet left in Theare after we burned most of the Haxan navy at their docks."

"What chance have we of stopping that?"

"None, but if we are forewarned, then Tomar can prepare a warm welcome for any invasion."

"And who will forewarn us?"

"I have an idea about that," Lynan said.

"I assume that's why we're walking along the harbor."

In answer, Lynan pointed to a ship tied to a dock about forty paces away. Ager squinted at it with his single eye. "She looks trim. Whose is it?"

"Do you not recognize it?"

Ager shook his head. "Should I? Is it one of my old berths?"

"You could say that."

By now they were close enough for Ager to read the name on the bow. He laughed softly. "The *Dry Land*?"

"Turn it around."

"The *Land Dry*?" he asked, and Lynan groaned. "Oh, I see. Dry for wet. Land for sea." Something clicked in his brain and he laughed softly. "Dry for spray. The *Seaspray*, of course!"

"If you look on the foredeck you'll see its owner waiting for us."

"Grapnel! Grapnel Moorice!"

The man on the foredeck waved at the pair. When they reached the ship, he gave them each a hand-up. After quickly embracing, Ager stepped back to take a good look at the man. He was tall, with closely cropped brown hair; huge gold earrings hung from each lobe and a white scar on each cheek that joined with the corners of his mouth made him look as if he was grinning sardonically at them.

"You haven't changed at all!" Ager said, smiling broadly.

"It's only been a year and a half since we last met," Grapnel said.

Ager was surprised. "God, it seems like ten years have passed.

So much has happened." His smile disappeared. "I suppose Lynan's told you about Kumul and Jenrosa."

Grapnel nodded grimly. "I was sorry to hear it. I did not think anything could kill Kumul. I expected him to outlive us all. And though I only met Jenrosa the once, she seemed a brave lass. I am sorry for your loss."

"What are you doing here?" Ager asked, quickly changing the subject. "And what have you been doing?"

Grapnel shrugged. "What else can a merchant do except play at trade? I lost my business in Kendra, of course, and knew I had to lie low. After I helped you lot make your escape from Kendra, I headed out to sea as far as I dared. It was a long, hazardous journey, the telling of which I'll bore you with one night. Eventually, we made Kolbee. I stayed there for half a year, changed the name of the ship, and started plying the coastal waters between Haxus and here. When word got around that Tomar had sided with Lynan, I went to the palace."

"And was immediately conscripted for scouting duty," Lynan finished. "Ager, meet the admiral in charge of my fleet."

"Admiral Moorice? And how many ships do you have at your disposal, Admiral?" Ager asked.

"One," Grapnel said. "But she's a beauty."

Ager could not help grinning. "Wonderful. Lynan's Royal Navy has one ship, and it's called the *Dry Land*."

"*Dry Land* for not much longer," Grapnel said gruffly. "She'll be *Seaspray* again by this time tomorrow."

"Grapnel will take *Seaspray* and stand out to sea; no other ship and crew in Theare has their experience on the wide ocean. Tomar will have plenty of warning should Areava's navy be ordered to attack Chandra."

"Before that happens, there's much to be done here," Grapnel said. "So if you will excuse me, my crew and I have work to do. When this is all over, we can spend a few nights telling each other tall tales about our adventures."

Lynan and Ager said good-bye to Grapnel and disembarked. "It's strange how close I feel to that man," Ager said. "I had not met him before that night we fled the palace, and talked with him only briefly for the short time we stayed in his home. And yet I feel about him the way I might feel about a brother I had not seen for many years."

"We are bonded by our misfortune," Lynan said sadly.

Ager put a hand on his shoulder. "I cannot stop thinking about her either."

"She should be here with us. If I had fought Silona's control with greater determination and courage, she might still be alive."

"Taking that line, if you had commanded the army better in our first battle against Grenda Lear, Kumul would still be alive."

Lynan looked up sharply at Ager, his face crestfallen.

"And if you take that line," Ager continued, his voice angry, "Berayma met his end when he did because you were too self-absorbed to see what Orkid and Dejanus were planning to do."

"That isn't fair!" Lynan cried.

Ager jabbed him hard in the chest with a finger. "And blaming yourself for Jenrosa's death is?"

Lynan blushed. "I . . . I'm sorry. I shouldn't have said what I did."

Ager's anger bled out of him. "No, but grief can make us say and do things we don't mean to."

Ager wanted to say more, wanted to talk to Lynan about Kumul and Jenrosa, but Korigan and Gudon caught up with them and the moment to do so passed.

"What have you two been talking about so earnestly?" Gudon asked lightly.

Ager waved at the *Dry Land*. "Our navy," he said.

Gudon looked impressed. "A beautiful ship. A good start."

"Yes," Ager agreed. "A small start but a good one. Well, Lynan, that takes care of the seaward threat. How about the threat from the Great Army? How are you going to deal with that?"

"I'm going to attack, of course."

"What numbers are we talking about?"

"With Tomar's contribution, our force will reach about twenty thousand."

"And Areava's?"

Lynan shrugged. "About forty thousand."

The other three gaped at him.

"Give or take one or two thousand," Lynan added. "Some may have joined since Tomar's break from the Areava." He started walking back to Tomar's palace. "Come on. We have a great deal of work to do."

"What's the hurry?" Ager asked. "We just got here."

"I want to attack the Great Army before it grows any larger. If we can destroy it, I think we can end the war before winter."

32

MAKON kept his breathing as shallow as possible to keep out the stink of the burning bodies. He was crouching behind a low stone wall, and dangling in front of his eyes was the charred arm of an Amanite soldier, the fingers curled into claws. He glanced over his shoulder to find Eynon. The clan chief was still directing fire arrows into the palace to make sure Amanite archers could not see properly to shoot at Makon and his three troops of Red Hands when they made their charge. He risked peeping over the wall. There was an expanse of nearly sixty paces between him and the palace itself; the space was covered in bodies, draped like strange sculptures over hedges and fountains and garden beds. Impossible for cavalry to cross that distance across all the obstructions, which left the only Chett units trained to fight on foot—his command. Smoke drifted in front of the palace like low cloud. Some smoke poured from the palace itself.

If only Ager Parmer could see his Red Hands now, Makon thought. *He'd be proud.* An enemy arrow thudded into the wall near his head and he ducked down again. *And shit scared.*

He and his Red Hands had been fighting now for three days, from the end of the pass across the mountains where they defeated the army sent to stop them, and then down to the capital, and then through Pila's streets to the palace itself. And now, after a long and bloody campaign, they had finally reached the end of vengeance. For what must have been the hundredth time, Makon again checked with Eynon. He saw that the archers had switched to normal arrows. Eynon looked at him and gave him the signal. No more waiting.

Makon stood up, raised his short sword above his head, and screamed the cry of the White Wolf. He did not wait to see if the other Red Hands were with him, but jumped over the wall and ran as fast as his legs could carry him toward the palace. An Amanite soldier with a spear appeared from behind a hedge. Makon fell on him, plunging his sword into his chest as they hit the ground. He stood up, tugging his sword free, and started running again. Red Hands surged around him. Arrows whistled by his head. He heard screams, choking gurgles, cries, and ignored them, barged through a fire-eaten wooden door shoulder-first. He fell onto a stone floor and the wind was slammed out of him. Gasping, he turned onto his back. A spear point clanged on to the floor between his legs. He swiped at the shaft with his sword and scuttled away, still on his back. The spear drove down again, snagged his poncho. He rolled, snapping the shaft under his weight and kicked out. His foot connected with something soft and his head hit a wall. He shouted in pain and anger, sat up in time to see his opponent doubled up and holding his balls. Makon swiped at the man's head, slicing through an ear and hitting the skull. The enemy screamed, jumped back into the sword of a Red Hand, and collapsed. Makon scrambled to his feet, looked around. He was in a narrow corridor with archways at either end. Red Hands poured through the exits. He heard weapons clashing, men grunting and wailing, bodies falling. He chose the exit on his right and charged through. A large room with bench seats on two sides. Ten of his men were pushing against as many Amanite spearmen, getting under the points of the enemy weapons and using their swords up close. The spearmen died. Two archers behind them fired one arrow each, dropped their bows, and ran through another archway. One of the Red Hands fell with an arrow in his chest.

"Come on!" Makon cried and led the way through the second archway. They found themselves in a large hall. Light from windows high in the wall crisscrossed smoke from a fire consuming a wooden staircase that led to a second-floor gallery. Archers were lining the gallery. Makon swore under his breath and made for the staircase, hopping over flames, coughing and choking on the smoke, leaping three stairs at a time. He heard someone give orders to the archers, and they swung their bows around, but too quickly and tangled with each other. Some arrows were loosed from half-drawn strings and looped into the air to fall harmlessly below. Two archers fell with arrows in their backs. The remainder could not see through the smoke clearly to aim but loosed their arrows anyway. They whirred through the air. Then Makon and six Red Hands were upon them. The archers retreated on each other, pushed to get out of the way, fell screaming as they were stabbed in the back and then thrown over the gallery into the fire below.

More Red Hands were pouring into the hall now. "Put out that fire!" Makon screamed at them, then led his band off the gallery into a corridor. Tapestries hung from stone walls. Diffused light from clerestories showed off their colours. Makon wanted to stop and wonder at them, and could not help thinking that Gudon would love this place, but he pushed on. There were doorways ahead; each was opened, each room checked for enemies. They started discovering servants and peasants, old people and children; one or two put up a fight and were quickly slain, the rest cowered and pleaded for mercy. Most of the time they got it. The corridor twisted and turned. More rooms, antechambers, libraries, and offices. Makon felt he was getting closer to the most important section of the palace, the royal quarters and throne room, something confirmed when enemy soldiers appeared at the other end of the corridor and charged with the cry of the great bear. The Red Hands replied with their own war cry and met them with a bang of steel against steel. The enemy was armed with swords and bucklers and proved as good at fencing as the Red Hands. The battle in the corridor swung one way and then the next as advantage was won in the confined space and then lost again. There was room for only three to fight shoulder to shoulder in the corridor, and as warriors tired or died, they were replaced by those waiting behind them. Eventually, it came to push and shove, and the greater number of Red Hands started to tell. The enemy soldiers tripped or fell from sheer exhaustion and were trampled underfoot, row after row. Red Hands bringing up the rear used their daggers to cut throats and stab through eyes. The floor was slick with blood, and the stink of it was stronger than the smell of smoke. When the last enemy fell, the Red Hands could do nothing for a while except lean against the wall and regain their breath. They all looked like bloody wraiths, and they grinned at the sight of each other, their teeth white against the gore.

"They were good," one of them said, pointing his sword at the train of Amanite corpses behind them.

"Now they're just dead," said another.

"Enough rest," Makon gasped, struggling to stand upright. "We haven't taken the palace yet."

At the end of the corridor they came to another gallery, this time overlooking another great space. Makon looked down and saw it was the throne room, and that the throne room had become a battle field. Chetts—Red Hands and clan warriors—led by Eynon, were hacking their way through the last of the Amanite defenders. At the rear, sitting on a great, basalt throne, sat a large, bearded warrior Makon assumed was King Marin himself, a large man with a thick, dark beard and shoulders as broad as Eynon's. Resting under his two huge hands was the biggest battle ax the Chett had ever seen. As he watched, Marin stood up and roared a command. His warriors retreated from the Chetts and rested their weapons. One or two were cut down by overeager Chetts before Eynon commanded them to halt, then took a step forward.

"Do not ask for mercy, lord of Aman," Eynon said fiercely. "For what you have done against my people, I will grant you none."

All eyes settled on Marin. "You are the leader of these barbarian worms?" he demanded.

"Eynon, clan chief of the Horse clan, deputy of King Lynan Rosetheme." Eynon smiled then. "The same King Lynan who split open your son."

Marin's face clouded and he roared his defiance. "Single combat, Chett! You against me!"

"If you win?"

"My warriors live."

Eynon considered this for a moment. "And you?"

Marin shrugged. "What's it matter anymore?"

Eynon shrugged in turn. "Truth. Very well."

Warriors on both sides fell back to make room for the two leaders. Marin took a step down from the throne, turned to a pale clerk standing by who gamely held a sword that was too big for her, and said: "Lingdar, whatever happens to me, please record how I gut this Chett."

The clerk looked at her lord with big eyes and nodded.

For a moment the two leaders studied each other, and they in turn were studied by the troops around them. Makon thought they were evenly matched in size, and where Marin's face and beard made him look dark and ominous, Eynon's golden skin and scarred, battered face made him look somewhat demonic.

Suddenly, Marin leaped toward Eynon, his ax swinging above his head. Eynon dodged to his left and the ax crashed into the granite floor, gouging out chips, sending sparks into the air. Eynon's saber slashed in reply, but for all its size, Marin could wield the ax as easily as Eynon wielded his sword, and he brought it up in time to block the blow. The weapons clanged, the sound echoing in the throne room. Warriors from both sides cheered.

Marin twisted his wrist and the ax blade turned, jamming Eynon's saber, then punched with his left fist, catching Eynon just under the ribs. Eynon gasped, turned to his left to free his saber, but Marin kept up with him, spinning on his heel. He punched again, a glancing blow against the Chett's ear. Eynon shouted, let go of his saber, jumped forward, and used his elbow to land a blow on the king's nose. It was Marin's turn to cry out and he stumbled back, bringing his ax up defensively. The saber dropped and Eynon caught it in midair, twisted on his heel, and slashed toward the king's midriff. Marin saw the move and blocked it with the ax handle, changed his grip and let the ax swing down and then up. Eynon danced out of the way, but not quickly enough. The ax blade sliced across his chest.

Makon, with every other Chett in the hall, gasped in horror. For a moment, no one moved, not even Marin. Eynon looked down; blood seeped through the jerkin. He looked up at Marin and said: "Not deep enough." He lunged forward with the saber before Marin could react, and the king's body seemed to swallow half the blade. Marin gasped, doubled over, took Eynon's sword with him. Eynon bent over to pick up Marin's ax, brought it up over his head and swung it down so hard it sheared clean through Marin's bull-like neck and bounced off the stone floor. Blood fountained into the air. Eynon dropped the ax and rolled over the king's body, placed a foot on his chest, and tugged free his saber. He then strode over to Lingdar, casually knocked aside her sword and breathed into her terrified face: "Whatever happens, please record how I cut off your master's head."

Eynon stood up straight, turned to his Chetts. "If Marin's warriors surrender now, they will be spared."

Immediately, there was the sound of spears, swords, bows and daggers dropping to the floor.

Eynon grinned down at all of them. "So much for that," he said. He swayed on his feet, seemed to tip over to one side, and collapsed.

There was light first, and then shade. The light hurt Eynon's eyes, and the shade confused him. And his whole body hurt as if it had been split in two. Then he remembered. He had been split in two, or near enough and still survive the experience. He tried to take a deep breath. The spasm of pain made him moan out loud.

"How do you feel?" asked a voice he recognized.

Eynon licked his lips. He tried a word experimentally, but it came out as a croak.

"If you were going to ask 'How long?'—the answer is five days."

The shade solidified into Makon's face. Eynon tried speaking again. "No."

Makon grinned at him. "'No' you don't believe it's been five days, or 'no' that wasn't what you were going to ask?"

"Water?"

Makon took a cup from a nearby table, gently eased Eynon's head up, and let him take a sip. It was cold and good and made his mouth feel less like a rat's nest. "I was going to say . . ." he started, but his mouth gummed up again. He took more water. "I was going to say that was the most stupid question I have ever heard."

Makon grunted. "Well, however you feel, you're confined to bed for some time to come."

"Bed?" Eynon realized then where he was. He had never laid down on anything quite as comfortable as this before. And the room had real windows, with glass. Sun was pouring in. The air was warm. He glanced down at his body. A long ridge ran from the tip of his rib cage down to his navel, crisscrossed by stitches. The skin around the ridge was yellow and purple, and dried blood encrusted each stitch. "Beautiful," he said.

"Wennem did it," Makon said. "No one else was game. She said you saved her, and she wasn't going to let you die."

"It's only a cut."

"She had to stitch part of your stomach, too."

"Oh." He frowned. "I remember being sliced. Not much after."

"You beheaded King Marin. Aman has fallen. The province is yours."

"Mine?" Eynon shook his head. "No. I am a Chett. I don't need a province. It belongs to Lynan, if anyone."

Makon looked seriously at laim. "You wanted to be king once, did you not?"

"What do you mean?"

"When you opposed Korigan. I thought you were the enemy of my people back then."

"And what do you think now?"

"Did you want to be king?" Makon persisted.

"Never. I just didn't think we Chetts needed a monarch at all. I admit I was probably wrong, but now we have tied ourselves to Lynan the issue is irrelevant. So tell me, Makon, you have been by my side now for a long time. We have fought together. We have shared food. Did Lynan ask you to watch me?"

"Of course."

"Did he ask you to kill me?"

Makon pursed his lips.

"You can kill me now and no one would be the wiser," Eynon said carefully. "You could just say I never recovered from the wound."

"I was to use my discretion," Makon said. "I have used it. You live."

"Help me sit up."

Makon did, with some difficulty. It was hard finding a position for Eynon that did not put too much pressure on the stitches, but he refused to lie down again.

"More water."

Makon helped him drink more water from the cup.

"What does Lynan really think of me?"

"At first he thought you were a thorn in his side. Then when you came to join him after all, he was not sure what to think of you. Then you helped win Daavis for him, and he thought very highly of you. He likes you."

"But he still wanted to make sure of my loyalty."

"He is king. You and Korigan are the keys that determine Lynan's hold over the Chetts. He has Korigan's support. He had to have yours as well."

"Or be rid of me entirely."

Makon nodded.

"What will you report to Lynan now?"

"That his loyal servant Eynon has taken Aman for him."

"And what will you do next, oh, faithful servant?"

Makon smiled. "Return to my clan." He glanced outside. "Eventually. The clear sky and shining sun are deceptive. Winter is setting in around the mountains. We are trapped here until spring." He bounced on the bed, making Eynon groan. "Still, the palace will make it a warm and comfortable winter."

"And Wennem? What will you do with her?"

"Take her with me, if I can."

"Does she know that?"

"I think so," Makon said, but Eynon heard the uncertainty in his voice.

"There is another way," Eynon said.

"Oh?"

"It is not unusual for a man to join the clan of his wife."

Makon's jaw dropped.

Eynon started laughing, but it hurt too much. "Close your mouth. You look like a fish."

Makon closed his mouth.

"It isn't something you considered?"

"I am from the White Wolf clan. We have been enemies of the Horse clan for . . . a long time."

"Only thirty years," Eynon said.

"Since before I was born."

"But our clans are not enemies anymore." Eynon looked grim. "My clan is too small now to threaten anyone."

"I know. But . . . to change clans . . . to leave Gudon and Korigan . . ."

"You would not be leaving them," Eynon said. "Korigan will still be your queen, and joining the Horse clan does not stop you from seeing your brother."

"No," Makon admitted.

"And it would help strengthen the ties between our two clans. Heal the wounds. Convince other clans that were once in opposition to Korigan and her father before her that it is time to put those differences behind us."

"Truth," Makon admitted again. Still, his reluctance was obvious.

"There is another reason," Eynon said. "In fact, two reasons."

"Go on."

"First, Wennem, I think, does not want to leave the clan. She would think it a betrayal of her husband and child. Second . . ." Eynon waved at the cup, and Makon helped him have another drink. "And second, I need an heir."

Makon heard Eynon's words, but for a long moment they did not mean anything. "Yes, I can see that," he started to say, then stopped. He looked at Eynon, saw nothing in his expression that showed he was playing a joke on him. "Ah," he said.

"Ah? Is that all you can say?"

Makon stood up, changed his mind and sat down again. "Ah."

"It would mean adopting you as my son. But since I have already adopted Wennem as my daughter that would present no problem if you were to marry her."

"Marry her."

"You see," Eynon said, putting a hand on Makon's shoulder, "because I have adopted her, I could not let her go to the White Wolf clan."

"Of course."

"So you joining the Horse clan is the best solution all round."

"Yes."

"And, as I said, I need an heir. I want you to lead my clan after I am gone." Eynon ran one hand down his ridge of stitches. "And for some reason, the need has become more urgent than it once was."

DEJANUS stood outside his tent drinking red Storian wine from the biggest cup he could find. From his vantage point on a slight rise he could look out over the Great Army. His Great Army. He had to remind himself of that every now and then, seeing as everyone else in the kingdom seemed to want to tell him what to do with it.

"You promised me those supplies, General," one of his captains was saying. "My company is eating porridge three times a day because we no longer have any bread or meat."

"At least your soldiers have porridge," another captain cut in. "General Dejanus, my warriors have to take food from nearby towns because we've received no supplies at all since arriving from Lurisia."

Dejanus took another gulp of the wine. Down below he could see Amanite light infantry marching up and down, looking splendid. That was his doing. The first thing he had noticed on his arrival at the camp was the loose, slovenly way some of the regiments seemed to deport themselves. Well, he had fixed that. But did anyone thank him?

"General, my soldiers haven't eaten properly in ten days, and we don't have any steel and wood to replace weapons we've lost or broken in training."

Not far from the Amanite light infantry, some Storian cavalry were charging at targets and hurling their javelins, sounding terribly fierce.

Dejanus' aide, a polite and deferential Lurisian named Savis, coughed politely to get his attention.

"What is it?"

"A messenger from Captain Urling, General."

"Urling? Who's Captain Urling again?"

"In charge of the Amanite light infantry, sir."

Dejanus pointed to the regiment marching in the camp below. "That's our Amanite infantry."

"Half of the contingent, sir. The other half you posted several leagues north to run the pickets and carry out scouting duty."

"Scouting duty? Infantry? Why not our cavalry?"

Savis timidly pointed to the cavalry practicing with targets. "Otherwise occupied, sir."

"What about the medium cavalry? Those units from . . . you know . . ."

"Also from Storia, sir."

"Where are they?"

"You ordered them to set camp about five leagues south of here."

"Did I?"

"They are your reserve, I seem to remember."

"Ah, yes." Now he remembered. When he had arrived, another thing he had noticed was that no one thought about matters like a reserve. He had fixed that, too. Apparently.

"What does this . . . Captain . . . ?"

"Urling, sir."

"What does Captain Urling want?"

"He reports that he is seeing increased activity to the north, sir." Dejanus blinked. "Enemy soldiers?"

"Not as such, General. Increased dust in the air, birds, some wild karak fleeing south, that sort of thing."

Dejanus grunted. "Urling would be scared by his own shadow. Are you sure he doesn't mention any sign of enemy soldiers?"

"Positive, sir."

"Well, bloody not likely to, eh? Who in their right mind would take on the Great Army of Grenda Lear?"

"No one in their *right* mind, sir," Savis said cautiously, remembering some of the tales about mad Prince Lynan that were circulating currently in the camp.

"There is also a message from Chancellor Orkid Gravespear."

Dejanus cursed. "What does that interfering bastard want? Same as always?"

"I'm afraid so, General. He insists you advance on Sparro as soon as you are able."

Dejanus spread his arms in appeal to the captains around him. "God spare us from idiot civilians! Doesn't he understand the problems of a Great Army like this? I can't solve all of them overnight. The army isn't ready yet. It needs more supplies. It needs more training." He turned on Savis. "I thought I asked you to send a message to him about our supplies?"

"I did. He says in his reply . . ." Savis took out a crumpled note from a vest pocket. ". . . that we have enough supplies to feed a city twice the size of Kendra for a year."

Dejanus grabbed the note from Savis' hands. He read it quickly, scrunched it in his fist and threw it away.

"In a separate message," Savis said, pulling out another note, "the chancellor stresses that since winter is almost upon us, it may soon be too late to do anything at all with the Great Army and it may have to disperse."

Dejanus grabbed that note, too, and threw it away without reading it. He put his face close to Savis' and said: "This army will not disperse because by winter it *will* occupy Sparro. There's time yet!" He swallowed another mouthful of wine. "By the way, what happened to those supplies that arrived last night?"

"You ordered me to send them to the cavalry reserve." Dejanus frowned at him. "The one five leagues south, sir."

"I thought we were going to use them for the Amanite pickets?"

"We were, sir, originally. But you changed your mind."

Dejanus frowned. Last night he must have forgotten about the pickets between the Great Army and Sparro. He had trouble remembering all the units under his command and where they were and what supplies they already had and what they still needed.

"Sir?" Savis said. "Captain Urling?"

"Tell him to stop worrying," Dejanus said curtly. "When the enemy moves, he'll see more than dust and birds in the air."

"Yes, sir," Savis said, and went to tell Urling's messenger.

Lynan was pulled back into the woods by the scout. "There, on the rise," the scout said.

Lynan had to squint, something he was not used to doing. Having Silona's blood coursing through his veins had had some advantages. He could just make out two spear-carrying infantry squatting on top of the rise. They were very still, not talking to each other.

They seemed very alert, but their position was too low to see over the woods.

"How many?" he asked.

The scout pointed to a second rise about fifty paces south of the first and no higher. "Two more on that one," the scout said. "Between them is their camp. Maybe two or three hundred light infantry besides the fifty or so we ran across pretending to be scouts."

Lynan nodded. "I've seen enough."

The two slowly retreated back through the woods. Fifty paces west they came across a clearing. Waiting for them were Korigan and Gudon with the horses. Beside them was gray-haired Akota, one of the oldest chiefs and now in command of a banner made up of Chetts from different clans. Lynan had seen her in combat using a bow he would have trouble even pulling.

"Well?" she asked impatiently.

Lynan took the reins of his horse from Gudon. "It's time," he said.

Akota grinned at him, wheeled her horse around and trotted off.

"We had better get to the Red Hands," Lynan told the others. "Akota is so excited she is likely to start without us."

They carefully followed Akota along a trail that wound its way through the woods for another two leagues, eventually emerging on to farmland, now churned up under the hooves of hundreds of horses. Akota's banner was already on the move, and the Red Hands were looking on anxiously. Then they saw Lynan and knew they were not going to be left out of the coming battle.

Captain Urling scowled at the messenger. "Dejanus said what?"

"That you should stop worrying about nothing. When the enemy moves, you'll see more than dust and birds in the air."

Urling shook his head. He could not believe his ears. He had fought for Grenda Lear in the Slaver War as a lowly Amanite recruit and worked his way up to commanding his own battalion of light infantry. He *knew* the signs of an approaching army. He *knew* the enemy was on the march.

"So the Great Army is still in camp?"

"It was when I left, Captain."

"The idiot," he said under his breath, not wanting anyone to hear his opinion. Morale was low enough without subverting the authority of the commanding general. He thanked the messenger and turned to his second-in-command, another veteran of the Slaver

War named Ordt. "Dejanus is going to need hard proof. We need a prisoner."

"Our patrols just ain't seeing anyone, Captain. They're seeing plenty of signs, but no enemy as such."

"A night patrol might have better luck. Send one out this evening, heading northwest where we saw all the dust this morning. They should be able to cover five or six leagues and still get back before daylight."

Ordt nodded. "That's fine, sir, but what if they don't find anything either?"

"Then we pull back to the main camp," Urling said. "The Chetts are out there. I can feel it in my bones. I'm not going to let them cut us off."

"The General won't like that."

"He'll like it a lot more if we bring a prisoner back with us."

"I'll see to it, sir."

Ordt turned to go, but Urling grabbed his arm. "Listen."

Ordt did, but heard nothing above the normal sound of the camp. There were birds nearby, a flock of them scattering into the sky . . .

"Something's coming," he said.

Urling dropped to the ground and put his ear against it. He shot straight back to his feet. "Form up!" he shouted. "To your flags! First and second companies north of the camp, third and fourth companies south! Quickly!" He pushed Ordt to the south. "It's cavalry! Put a company on either side of the road. I'll take the north!"

"What happened to our lookouts? And where are our scouts?"

Urling glances at both the rises. There were no lookouts there now. "Gone. All gone. Hurry! Take the south!"

There was sudden confusion in the camp, but the Amanites were professionals and soon gathered around their company flags. Urling and Ordt had started setting up an ambush when the first riders burst into the valley from the north. Chett horse archers, riding full pelt, their bows already drawn. Ordt quickly ordered his companies to join Urling, but it was too late. The first volley of arrows fell among the Amanites like a hail storm, followed quickly by a second and then a third. The Chetts galloped through the camp and scattered Ordt's force, firing arrows into the fleeing soldiers. When they reached the end of the camp the Chetts dismounted and set up a line running oblique to the road. Ordt managed to gather some of his soldiers together and meet up with the survivors from Urling's group; the captain was not among the living, however.

"The enemy's dismounted," Ordt told the survivors. "This is our only chance. We have to charge them. We have spears and shields to their bows; at close quarters we'll slaughter 'em. Keep two paces apart, two lines, one directly behind the other, shields up, and run. Got it?" Those who heard nodded, terrified. "Once we're past them, get to the forest and make as best you can for the Great Army. All right, up now! Companies one and two form the first line, three and four the second."

Despite the swarm of arrows now falling on them, they managed to form some semblance of two lines, their raised shields protecting them most of the time. A handful fell with arrows in their legs and feet. Ordt raised his spear for the order to charge when he heard more horses behind him. He swore, looked over his shoulder, and saw Chetts not armed with bows but with the saber, and each hand with a sword was dyed red past the wrist. He knew what that meant, and despite all his years in the army and the all the combat he had seen, he still pissed himself.

Lynan was coming.

It was almost sunset. Terin's long shadow, and those of the lancers who lined up either side of him, darkened the ground before them as if they were stretching for the enemy camp. A single rider galloped along the line until she reached Terin, reined in hard.

"Ager Parmer is ready," the rider said. "The Ocean clan has barred the road north."

Terin nodded and the messenger maneuvered her horse behind the line. Terin looked left and right. The lancers were calm, sitting well back in their saddles, their weapons held vertically. Then he looked down on the enemy, who was so confident and so completely unaware.

A shout came from below them. Someone in the camp had finally noticed the cavalry on the rise to their west. Terin saw people stop and look up at him. They would see the lances, assume they were more cavalry come to join them in the reserve. Then they would wonder why they were line abreast, and why they were sitting on the hill and not moving. Then doubt would set in.

Right about now, Terin told himself. He nudged his mount forward a few paces and drew his saber out of his saddle sheath. He heard the riders behind him sit straighter in the saddle, gather their reins, change their grip on their lances. He smiled, raised his saber high enough for the sun's last rays to catch its blade, then dropped his arm and spurred his horse into a walk. The line started moving behind him. He watched the enemy below and could imagine their doubt turning to panic as they recognized the beginning of a charge.

Terin wished he could move to the gallop straight away, but it was too far for the horses to run and still have the strength and wind they would need for the battle; more, they were going downslope, and experienced riders never forced their horses to gallop downslope.

The enemy were starting to run to and fro, some scrambling to fit saddles on their horses, others disappearing into their tents to get weapons, still others jumping bareback on horses and running away as fast as they could. Most of those fleeing headed south, and they were of no concern to Terin or the Chetts, but many ran north in the direction of the Great Army camp—and, Terin knew, Ager's waiting Ocean clan; none of them would be allowed to get through.

The lancers were off the slope now and Terin eased his mount to the trot and then the gallop. He held his saber out as Lynan had shown him, with the elbow bent slightly. His blood raced with the sound of his banner charging behind him. Some came abreast as the line started to break, their lances couched low.

A short fence, easily cleared, and then the first of the defenders, some on horseback. Terin swiped at a head, missed, the impetus of his charge carrying him on. Someone with a sword appeared from behind a tent. He swung underarm, catching the side of the man's head. Still at the gallop. An officer on a horse, armed with a straight sword. Terin brought his arm up again, shouted his war cry. His saber punched through the officer's arm and through to his chest. The impact tore the saber from Terin's grasp as his horse slammed into the officer's mount and went down. Terin tumbled on the ground, sprung to his feet. His horse tried to scramble up, but its back was broken and it collapsed onto the enemy officer, killing him outright. Terin waited until the horse squirmed aside and retrieved his saber, finished off the wounded animal, grabbed the reins of the officer's stallion and remounted. His lancers were all around the camp, finishing off the scattered groups of defenders. The enemy that could escape had done so; it was too late for the rest.

Dejanus woke with a thumping headache that seemed ready to punch out his eyeballs. He managed to swing his feet out of his cot, then had to stop. Savis came into his tent, looked down at his general with his head in his hands.

"I heard you get up," he said cautiously, wishing now he had stayed out.

"What is it?" he said testily.

"Some of your captains are begging to see you."

"Whining, are they?"

"They have concerns—"

"Concerns!" Dejanus shouted, and immediately moaned as pain seemed to grip his whole skull and shake it.

Savis blanched and retreated a step. "About supplies, sir. Some regiments have been without food for several days now. And Captain Harden from Kendra died in his sleep two nights ago and his regiment wants to know which officer is to replace him. And there are representatives from three nearby towns who are here to complain about the army's use of their wells, and to report the theft of several cattle and sheep and several bales of hay—"

"Enough, Savis, enough. Why is everything happening at once?"

Savis did not remind Dejanus that most of the problems had come up over the last several days. He did not relish a tongue-lashing this early in the morning. "Will you be up and about soon, sir? I can tell those waiting to come back, if you like."

"Yes," Dejanus said. "Later. Tell them to come back later. And get me some wine."

Savis nodded and left. Dejanus slowly, cautiously, stood up. He had slept in his uniform and it stank of stale wine. He ran his fingers through his hair to straighten it, strapped on his sword, and stood there. What now? How could he organize this army to besiege Sparro when its captains could not even solve their own supply problems? Orkid had not given him an army, he decided; he had given him a rabble commanded by petty officers without initiative. He deserved better than this.

There was an argument outside. He heard Savis' voice try to rise above the hubbub. Another voice rose above Savis'. Then, suddenly, it all went quiet. After a moment Savis reappeared.

"You had better come out, sir."

With a low growl Dejanus burst out of the tent. The sudden brightness blinded him and he put a hand over his eyes.

"What's going on?" Dejanus demanded. He looked down and saw a young man in the uniform of the Amanite light infantry. Several captains, pale-faced, hovered around him. "Don't tell me, another bloody message from Captain Urling. Well?"

"We are attacked, sir!" the Amanite called out.

The words hit Dejanus like physical blows. He actually reeled back. "No," he said.

"Yesterday afternoon, General," the Amanite continued. "At least a thousand Chetts. We heard them coming and were able to prepare an ambush. We killed many hundreds and drove them off."

Dejanus did not know what to say. The one thing he truly believed would never happen was that anyone would dare attack the Great Army. The messenger's last sentence sank in. "You killed hundreds of them?"

The messenger nodded.

"And you drove them off?" There was a note of hysteria in Dejanus' voice.

The messenger nodded again. "But my captain is afraid they will try again today."

Dejanus swallowed. "I see."

"He suggests this is a wonderful opportunity."

"He does?"

"He thinks the Chetts will come in even greater numbers, but still only expect to find four companies of light infantry. If you could reinforce us with the other companies of light infantry, and maybe some cavalry, the captain says your victory will be even sweeter."

"My . . . victory?"

"As general of the Great Army, of course it would be your victory," the messenger said, surprised Dejanus should doubt it. "As last night's victory belongs to you. After all, it was you who placed our infantry so far forward."

"Yes, of course."

"So you will send the reinforcements?" the messenger asked hopefully.

Dejanus did not answer right away. His mind had grasped the opportunity offered and run away with it. *If I defeat the Chetts today, I can claim* two *victories. That will shut up Orkid and all my whining captains. Maybe even terrify that fat fool Tomar into surrendering Sparro to me.*

"I will do more than send reinforcements," Dejanus said. "I will bring up the whole army, and I will lead it personally."

The messenger seemed overjoyed. "This is better than even my captain expected."

"Go back to Captain Urling. Tell him we're on our way. Tell him we'll be there by midday."

The messenger bowed and left. Dejanus turned to all the captains who had come that morning to complain. "Well? What are you standing there for? Get your companies ready to march!"

The captains scattered. Dejanus turned to Savis. "Get word to all the other units whose captains were not present. We march in one hour. We march to victory."

"Here they come," Korigan said, watching the dark line of the enemy snake its way north from its camp.

"And all in marching order," Gudon said, shaking his head in amazement. "This Dejanus is a fool."

"He is a kingslayer," Lynan said flatly. "Can you tell their order?"

Korigan nodded. "Some medium cavalry in the van and light cavalry on either flank; not much of either, though. The rest of the Amanite light infantry comes next, then archers, then heavy infantry, the general and an escort of more cavalry, supply wagons, and the last of the heavy infantry bringing up the rear."

"We need to lure the cavalry away from its infantry support, especially the archers," Lynan said.

"What we need is bait," Korigan said.

Akota said: "I can take care of that." She stood in her stirrups and pointed north. "The road bends around the copse there. That's where I'll set it up."

"Fine," Lynan said. "Take whatever you need to do the task, but make sure none of the enemy horse get away."

Akota grinned. "That will be a pleasure."

Captain Mylor of Storia was enjoying the morning jaunt. The sun was pleasantly warm without being too hot, something she had found easy to take after the cooler climes of her native province in the south of the continent. There was a light breeze brushing across the landscape. She and her company were in the van, so avoiding all the dust kicked up by the footsloggers. And best of all they were on their way to severely punish the army of this renegade Rosetheme.

She found Kendrans a peculiar bunch at the best of times, but the Rosethemes seemed to concentrate all the strangeness in a few individuals, throwing up the best and the worst of their kind. The sooner this civil war was over, the sooner she could resign her commission and get back to her father's vineyards.

There was a picturesque little copse to her right, around which the road bent. She tried to remember the map she had studied that morning in the General's tent, but only had a vague recollection of a small wood. She had no real idea how much farther they had to go before reaching the picket camp established by the Amanites. Perhaps it was even around this bend? Time to give the horses a bit of a run, she decided, and urged her horse into a trot. Her company followed her example and they drew ahead of the column. As she rounded the bend, she saw about one hundred paces ahead of her twenty or so mounted Chetts, relaxing as their horses cropped at the grass by the side of the road. She glanced quickly over her shoulder to make doubly sure her company was behind her, gave the signal to charge and kicked her horse to the gallop. The Chetts looked up in shock and whipped their mounts with their reins. They moved quickly back onto the road, but Mylor knew she had them. The distance between them closed to sixty paces, then forty. Mylor could feel her surprise turn to excitement; it was like being on a hunt back home. Thirty paces. She aimed the tip of her spear at the back of the nearest Chett rider, right where his kidney would be.

Then, from the copse running along the right side of the road, came a sound like the furious whirring of bees but a hundred times louder. She was stopped from dwelling on it when the Chetts she had been pursuing peeled off the road and wheeled around in a maneuver that would have been impossible on her big charger. She overshot them, caught a glimpse of them loading their bows. She reined in and desperately pulled her horse around. The road behind her was covered in the dead and dying, and all of them belonged to her company. She stopped, her mouth dropped open in shock, and she realized what the sound must have been. Hundreds and hundreds of arrows. She had never heard nor seen such a thing before. Some of her riders were turning and turning again, looking for someone to fight, and then from the copse came a shower of arrows as thick as a cloud. The last thing she saw was the last of her company fall to the ground with an arrow in the throat, then she felt herself pitch back over the saddle with the force of several shafts plunging into her chest and stomach at the same time. She was dead before she hit the ground.

*   *   *

The ensign leading the remnants of the Amanite infantry, a grizzled old campaigner who had worked his way up from the ranks, recognized the sound coming from the copse ahead. He immediately halted the column and ordered his infantry to form a line across the road, and signaled to the officer leading the archers behind his infantry to copy him. As the two units started to spread out, a regiment of heavy infantry ran into the rear ranks of the archers and an argument started. The officer in charge of the archers raced back to sort things out. His own soldiers stopped forming their line, not sure what was happening or who was in charge. Some of the more enterprising actually strung their bows, nocked a flight arrow and put a handful of the heavier barbless arrows in the ground before them, but they were on level ground and could see little ahead of them because of the Amanite infantry, now neatly organized in three lines across the road. The argument behind them was getting fiercer when a commotion started in front of them as well. They looked up as one and saw it was no argument, but the curses of the Amanites watching their doom ride down upon them.

As soon as the enemy cavalry had been cleared away, Akota reformed her banner. She waited until she saw Lynan and his Red Hands appear at the northern end of the road and gave the signal to charge. They stormed around the copse and found the Amanite light infantry had formed a defensive line across their path. Without hesitation the column split in two, one heading east around the Amanites, the other heading west. As they passed the enemy, the Chetts, directing their horses with their knees, loosed a salvo, reloaded, loosed again, and by then were parallel with the foot archers, still disorganized, and shot another two salvos. The foot archers scattered, causing chaos among the Amanites in front of them and the heavy infantry, still entangled with their lines, behind them. Amid the panic, the Chetts dropped more and more arrows, and to the enemy it was like a dark rain of death.

Then the Chett horse archers had passed on, continuing down either side of the road, shooting salvos into the regiments behind, and those in the van thought that for the moment it was over and they could reorganize their lines and perhaps even counterattack, but before their officers could rally them the Red Hands appeared, led by a screaming, pale-faced madman who could only be Prince Lynan.

At first the surviving Amanites thought the banner would course around them and shoot their arrows, but then they noticed these Chetts were holding sabers, not bows. Before they could tighten their lines and raise their spears, the Red Hands ploughed into them like a pike slashing into a school of fish.

Lynan would not let any rider pass him. He came around the bend at full gallop, his saber ready, chose his target, and dug the spurs into his mare's flank. The horse seemed to leap into the enemy. Lynan's saber swung down to his right, slicing open a head, then caught another skull on the upswing. He brought the sword down on the other side, cutting off an ear, brought it up and down again on the right. He tore through the first line, then the second, slashing in wide arcs, scattering the enemy before him, and then was upon the archers. Here he went for arms and hands and eyes, and instead of charging through, he wheeled around to ride along the line the archers had tried to form, then pulled back and wheeled around again. To the archers, it was like being attacked by a windmill with a steel blade instead of sails, and they dropped their weapons and fled. But by then the rest of the Red Hands were among them, and no matter which way they ran, there seemed to be Chetts waiting for them, their terrible swords lopping off heads and limbs. The air around them was wet with a bloody mist and they gagged on the smell of it.

By now the more experienced officers among the enemy had organized some of the heavy infantry companies well enough to offer some resistance. Chett arrows had little effect on their armor and shields, and when their lines were properly formed there was little the Red Hands could do to get at them.

Lynan saw it was time to go. He ordered the retreat, and as the order was passed along, the Chetts broke contact with the enemy and rode hard for the north, back the way they had come. Behind them they left most of the enemy milling in confusion, their vanguard utterly destroyed.

Dejanus was ready to flee south and desert his Great Army, but Savis pointed out that meant they would have only their small escort of cavalry; he controlled his fear and decided to stay with the column.

"We march south immediately," he ordered. "Everyone about face. Back to the camp. At least there we can defend ourselves properly. And I can demand Chancellor Gravespear send us more regiments. We are outnumbered already!"

The rest of the army did not need much convincing. Although still largely intact, word had spread through the column about what had happened to the van, and no one wanted to share its fate. The light cavalry that had been protecting the army's flank now took the new vanguard and led the way back south, followed by the regiments in reverse order from their march north. By early afternoon they were in sight of the camp, and were heartened to see their reserve of Storian cavalry riding up the road to greet them. Then, with horror, they watched as the Storians lowered their lances and charged.

Lynan had waited patiently for this moment. So far he had used only a handful of his banners, but now it was time to unleash his whole force. The Great Army was demoralized, unsure of who was friend or foe. Lynan gave the signal and, led again by Akota, the horse archers poured over crest and out of forest to bear down on the enemy column, but this time she led fifteen banners instead of just her own. Like a dark tide they flooded around the column, shooting salvo after salvo of arrows into the densely packed infantry. Fire arrows slammed into the supply wagons, sending black plumes of smoke into the air. As if that was not enough, Terin's lancers, dressed as Storians, had swept away the Great Army's last vestiges of cavalry and then driven into the heavy infantry before they could set their lines. The lancers drove through the center of the column like a chisel through a block of mealy wood, splitting it into two. The final blow came when the Red Hands charged from the east, hacking and slashing their way through all opposition, and from the west charged Ager's Ocean clan, doing the same on the other side of the road.

As before, Lynan led the charge of the Red Hands. His saber was red to the hilt with gore and the enemy reeled back from him, terrified. One soldier managed to stick a spear into his horse before being ridden down, and the mare sank to the ground. Lynan loosed his feet from the stirrups and jumped off. Within seconds, Red Hands had surrounded him, one offering him her horse. He mounted and charged into the enemy again, his saber whistling through the air.

It took the Red Hands a long time to hack their way from one end of the column to the other. No one asked for mercy, and no mercy was given. Eventually, Lynan had to stop, overtaken by exhaustion. His sword arm refused to lift anymore and his borrowed horse could go no farther. He slid out of the saddle, put the point of his saber in the ground and rested on the hilt. A short while later he was joined by Gudon and Ager. The three embraced quickly. Before them, the Chett horse archers were still sending their short black shafts into the enemy, but then had to dismount and scrounge among the dead for more arrows. To the west the sun was only a hand's breadth from the horizon, making the whole world look as bloody as the battlefield.

They were joined by Korigan.

"What remains of the enemy is mainly heavy infantry," she told them. "They have gathered together and formed a square, showing little except their shields and helmets. Our arrows find a mark occasionally, but we are running out and the enemy is not inclined to return them, and Terin's lancers cannot charge their wall of spears. Should we let them go? Wait until they drop from thirst and hunger? Or ask them to surrender?"

Lynan shook his head. "We can't spare the time to wait for thirst and hunger to do our work for us. Who looks after them if they surrender? And if we let them go, they will reinforce Kendra."

"Then what can we do?" Korigan asked.

Lynan and Ager exchanged weary glances. "Only one thing to do," Ager said.

"And there are only two banners who can do it. Your clan and my Red Hands."

Korigan looked at them, puzzled. "What are you planning?"

Lynan stood straight, leaving his saber in the ground, and drew his short sword from its sheath. "Find Terin for me."

"What now?" one officer asked, voicing the question in everyone else's head. There were three of them in the center of the square, the last officers left alive. "We can't stay here. They'll just surround us, continue to pepper us with arrows, and wait until we are dying of thirst."

"We can try moving," another officer said. "If we do it slowly, we should be able to maintain the square."

"And go where?"

The officer shrugged. "Well, Kendra."

"It'd take us a year!"

"There's only one thing for it," the third said. "We wait for nightfall and make a run for it."

"They'll be waiting for that."

"Didn't say they wouldn't be, but there ain't nothing else to do, and some of us will make it."

"Something's happening to the north," someone from the square said.

All three officers looked that way.

"I don't believe it. I thought Chetts never fought on foot."

"And what's that they're holding?"

"Fuck, they're carrying short swords. Who'd have thought, eh?"

"What are we gonna do now?" asked the first officer, his voice rising with panic.

"Stay calm, first off."

"Charge them?" suggested the second officer.

"Look west, against the sun," the third officer said. "There's the bloody Chett lancers. We deploy to charge their foot, they attack our flank and roll us up all the way to the Sea Between."

"There must be something we can do."

"Fight and die," the third officer said, leaving to join his company. "Fight and die."

Lynan let Ager plan and lead the attack. He deployed his clan and the Red Hands into troops, and set the troops along an oblique line. When he was happy with the deployment, he raised and lowered his sword. The line started to move. At first they kept good formation, but unused to walking for any distance, let alone marching, the line soon became ragged, but the oblique angle largely remained. Ager was in the lead troop, Lynan in the middle one and Gudon in the last, and their commands and firmness helped stop the attack from degenerating into a wild charge. When he was only thirty paces from the enemy square, Ager raised his sword again and picked up the pace. It was impossible for him with his crookback to actually run, but by the time his troop was ten paces from the enemy he could let them go and they slammed into the shield wall, ducking under spears, tearing away shields and jabbing at faces with their short swords. The second line of spearmen jabbed at the Chetts, finding unprotected heads and necks, but not quickly enough to stop the wall from shuddering under the assault. More spearmen joined the press, too far back to use their weapons effectively, but able to lend their actual weight to the line in front.

Then the second troop of Chetts hit. As with the first troop, the wall actually seemed to ripple with the impact and started to give way, but extra spearmen rushed to give their support and the square held.

Then the third troop threw themselves against the enemy, and the fourth and the fifth. The wall was starting to buckle, and the Chetts were clambering over the dead, grabbing spears by their shafts, pulling them out of the hands of the enemy and stabbing and cutting with their swords. Spearmen fell back moaning, hands over their faces, blinded, mutilated, bloody, and dying. More Chetts hit the square, and then it was Lynan's turn with the first troop of Red Hands. They rent the air with the war cry of the White Wolf and leaped between the spears of the enemy, falling on the shields that blocked their way. Lynan thrust at any face under a helmet, and used his free hand to grab at spear shafts and shields. The swaying line of heavy infantry would start to buckle and then straighten as fresh soldiers joined the ranks.

A spearman jabbed at Lynan's face. Lynan ducked and stabbed in return but hit only air. The spearnan jabbed again and Lynan automatically ducked a second time; but the spearman let the spear slide through his hand so it became unbalanced; the spear's head dipped and the soldier tightened his grip and thrust down with all his strength.

Lynan screamed with sudden pain as the spear top lanced through his right side just above his hip. Two Red Hands grabbed him by his arms and pulled him out of the way. Warriors rushed around him to fill the gap, but many stopped fighting to watch Lynan; they had never seen their invincible leader bleed.

He shifted his sword to his left hand and with his right covered the wound. He stepped back into the line. "It is nothing!" he shouted. "Are the Red Hands afraid of a little blood?"

The Red Hands grinned at one another. Lynan was all right. Victory would still be theirs.

The spearmen forming the other three sides of the square, who could not clearly see what was happening but could hear the terrible sounds of battle and the screams of the dying and wounded, involuntarily started to pull closer together. The square started to lose its cohesion, and then came the inevitable. One of the last Chett troops to attack found a gap and charged through to assault the spearmen from inside their own formation.

Lynan knew the moment the square collapsed. It happened so quickly, so unexpectedly, that one moment he seemed to be surrounded by enemies, and the next he was standing alone, surrounded by nothing but discarded shields and spears. He told himself to join the pursuit, but he knew Korigan and Terin had been waiting for this moment, and he could feel through the ground the lancers and horse archers moving in for the final kill. He told his feet to move, but his body rebelled. The wound in his side was throbbing and blood had trickled down his leg and into his right boot so his toes squelched in the stuff. He was too exhausted to do anything, even sit. All around him rang the cries of the victorious Chetts and the wailing of the enemy who knew they were about to die.

The Great Army is destroyed, he told himself, and wondered why he felt nothing but shame.

"There was nothing I could do," Dejanus mumbled to himself. "I was told it was a Great Army, but it was a hollow gourd, an empty promise."

He sat on the end of the dock, apart from his fellows, the few members of his escort that had managed to escape with him in the first few terrifying moments of the Chett ambush. Now he was back at the small fishing village in southern Chandra where he had arrived what seemed only days before, and was waiting for a boat of any description that might take him back to Kendra. He dare not go overland. The Chetts were everywhere. The only thing Dejanus knew for sure was that the Chetts did not have a navy.

He studied the flagon of cheap red wine the local inn had given him. It was crude stuff, but it was having an effect, so he took another mouthful. Some of the wine dribbled from the corners of his mouth

Dejanus frowned. He would get back to Kendra and have a few words with Orkid about his so called Great Army. And maybe he would have a few words with that bitch of a queen, too. They tried to set him up. They set him up to die with their Great Army.

He hiccuped.

They will have to make me constable again. Head door opener. Yes, no Chetts are interested in ambushing head door openers.

In the darkness he saw the phosphorescent bow wave that meant a ship was coming. He stood up and waited. As the ship got closer he realized it was a small sloop, probably a local trader. That would get him back to Kendra by tomorrow night. If the captain was going that way. He waved to his escort. He would make sure the captain was going that way.

He decided to sit down again. For some reason, his legs did not want him to stand up.

Yes, tomorrow he would be in Kendra, and he would have a word with Orkid Gravespear. In fact, he would have lots of words with him. Maybe the chancellor would give him a new army. A real one with real soldiers and real supply.

That would be fair. And with a real army behind him, he would never be afraid again.

Korigan herself bandaged Lynan. She would let no one else near him. Lynan did his best to stifle his cries, but he had never felt so much pain before. He felt ashamed and apologized to Korigan.

"You do not have to prove yourself to me, Lynan Rosetheme," she said quietly.

Lynan looked at her, realizing he had not properly done so since Jenrosa's death. She was truly the most beautiful woman he had ever met, and he felt desire stirring inside him again, a feeling perverted by Silona and one he had since tried to repress. He had avoided Korigan whenever he could. He had treated her cruelly.

"Still," he said, "I am sorry. You, at least, deserve more from me."

She glanced up from her work with the bandage, briefly met his gaze. "You are my king," she said. "I have no right to expect any more than—"

"Stop it," he said. "We both know you are more than subject to me."

"Am I?"

He touched her face, and ignoring the spasm of pain it caused in his side bent over to kiss her. "Silona told me it was Jenrosa I loved—"

"Don't," she interrupted. "I don't have to know this—"

"Yes, you do," he said, interrupting her in turn. "And I did love her. She was my friend and Kumul's beloved. But Silona lied to me, and I am only now starting to learn just how much. You mean more to me than any simple comfort. You are not just my companion. You are not just my lover."

Korigan met his gaze again, and this time held it. "You *love* me?" she asked.

Lynan understood her meaning.

"Yes," he said.

< 34 >

OLIO and Edaytor were on their way back to the palace after inspecting the first of the new clinics established with the co-operation of the theurgia and the church. They were deep in conver-sation, not really aware of the other people on the street and alleys they walked along. In front and behind them walked a small escort of guards, bored and thinking of the beer they would be drinking when off duty. When the rock struck the wall above Olio's head, the party stopped, startled by the noise. Edaytor bend over to pick up the rock.

He looked up at Olio in surprise. "I think someone *threw* this at you."

The guards, suddenly alert, surrounded their royal charge, look-ing fiercely for any sign among the milling crowd for the assailant but seeing no one particularly suspicious.

Olio was blushing. He found it hard to believe that anyone would dislike him enough to want to hurt him. He was embarrassed to realize his feelings were hurt, "Maybe it was thrown at *you*," he said to Edaytor, only half-joking.

Edaytor did not even bother replying. He was eyeing two young men chatting under the entrance to an inn across the way. They were intent on looking only at each other, not glancing away now and then like people do when they are normally conversing. Then Olio noticed the guards appeared anxious. They did not like being out of their environment in an uncertain situation and wanted to take their prince safely behind the palace wall. "You go on," he told the prince.

"What are you going to do?" Olio asked, not liking the idea of the prelate being left behind. "What if the rock was meant for you? I'll leave you a guard."

"No," Edaytor said firmly. "Go home, your Highness. I'll come and see you this afternoon."

He nodded to the constable in charge of the guards, who fell behind the prince and started marching, forcing Olio to move along.

"Edaytor!" Olio cried.

"This afternoon!" Edaytor called after him.

He waited until the royal entourage had disappeared among the crowd and then made his way to the two youths he has spotted before. They pretended he was not there, so Edaytor cleared his throat.

"Can we help you?" one of the youths asked, feigning boredom.

Calmly, he said: "Why did you throw this rock at Prince Olio?"

The youth looked indignant. "I didn't throw no rock!"

"One of you did."

"You can't prove that!" the second youth declared angrily.

"I don't have to," Edaytor replied. "All I have to do is suggest to the Royal Guards that you attacked their prince and they would not hesitate to cut you down where you stand."

The pair paled, but they did not seem intimidated. The first one said, "You're here by yourself, now, Prelate Fanhow. There ain't no guards nearby to help *you*."

Edaytor leaned closer so his face was less than a hand's span from the youth's. "I'm a magicker, you fool. I don't need a guard to smite you."

The youth blanched, looked down at his boots to avoid Edaytor's gaze. The man he had thought nothing more than a rich, fat courtier suddenly seemed far more dangerous than any guard. The second youth wore an expression that suggested he would rather be anywhere else than here with his friend.

"I want to ask you some questions."

"About what?"

"I don't pretend to think you're the smartest lad in Kendra," Edaytor said casually, "but I certainly don't think you're *that* stupid. What are your names?"

"Leandeon," said the first.

"Wheremer," said the second.

"Now, Leandeon and Wheremer, I don't know which one of you threw that rock at Prince Olio, and at this point I don't care. But I do want to know why."

The two youths looked at him with disbelief. "You're not serious," Wheremer said. Edaytor simply raised his eyebrows. "I mean, everyone knows who Olio is—"

"Prince Olio," Edaytor corrected him. "Or 'his Highness.'"

"And everyone knows his Highness is a witch, just like his sister!"

Edaytor was so astounded he did not know what to say.

"And that they sacrifice children to make their magic!" Leandeon added.

"I resisted my natural inclination to turn you over to the guards," Edaytor said seriously, "but now I wonder—"

"But everyone knows it's true!" Wheremer said, his voice half-pleading. Leandeon nodded frantically. "Isn't it true that Areava—"

"Her Majesty!" Edaytor declared. "Or 'Queen Areava'!"

Wheremer shook his head. "Damn, Prelate, don't tell me how to speak of these people." He jabbed in the air with a finger. "Isn't it true that she murdered her own daughter to make magic! And that same night the fire started in the old city? And Olio was in the old city at the same time to help her!"

"This is ridiculous!" Edaytor cried.

"No, not ridiculous!" Leandeon said. "These are facts!"

"Facts!" Edaytor sputtered. "You two have no idea—"

"But that isn't all," Wheremer said, talking over him. "She murdered her own brother to win the throne, and blamed poor, bloody Lynan for the crime."

Edaytor stood back, horrified. "Who told you all of this?"

"Why, it's common knowledge," Wheremer said. "Everyone in the city knows."

"Then everyone in the city knows nothing," he said. "Queen Areava loved Berayma. She would never have harmed him. And she desperately wanted a child. Like every ruler, she wants an heir. And why would she want the old city to catch fire? None of it makes sense."

The two youths glanced at each other. "Well, I'm just telling you what everyone knows," Wheremer insisted.

"Since when have they known this?"

"Ever since God's been punishin' Grenda Lear for Areava's crimes," Leandeon said. "The Chetts have turned against us, we who saved 'em from the slavers. And we've lost Hume and Chandra, and at least one army, they say."

"What crimes?"

"What we've been tellin' you about," Leandeon said. "And she sleeps with her poor dead husband's uncle."

"The chancellor!" Edaytor exclaimed.

"It's all common knowledge. God's punishin' us for her crimes, hers and her brother's."

Edaytor looked at their faces, their expressions angry and so certain, and did not know what to say. They had showed him a glimpse of a world he had never suspected existed. He found it difficult to comprehend how anyone could believe the lies and fantasies he had just been told, but if Leandeon and Wheremer were being honest, the common population did believe it.

"You are all fools," Edaytor said flatly, and left.

Tomlin was cleaning out the pigeon house, as he did most of every day. He had just finished shoveling the guano from the second level into fertilizer sacks when there was a flurry of wings and the rattling of coops from above. He hurried to the third level and saw that all eight coops reserved for the Great Army's pigeons were now full. He went to each coop and took the message from the leg of each pigeon. He knew this was mighty strange, and he hurried to the chancellor's office. When the secretary saw him rush in, he did not hesitate, and went to get Orkid. The chancellor appeared almost straight away and put out his hand for the message. Tomlin gave him the whole batch.

"Eight messages?"

Tomlin nodded. "And all eight pigeons came from the Great Army."

Orkid sat on the edge of his secretary's desk and opened and read one of the messages. Tomlin and the secretary saw him pale. He opened and read a second message, then a third and then all the rest. He breathed out slowly and said to his secretary. "Tell the queen I must see her immediately."

The secretary bustled off.

"I'll be goin', then?" Tomlin said.

The chancellor nodded and Tomlin, feeling more uneasy than he could ever remember, returned to the pigeon house.

Left alone, Orkid picked up one of the messages. It did not matter which one he read. They were all the same.

"To the pretender, Areava Rosetheme, and Chancellor Orkid Gravespear. Your army is dispersed like chaff. I am coming. King Lynan Rosetheme."

*   *   *

The *Waveskipper* made it into Kendra harbor just before noon.
As soon as he disembarked, Dejanus, hung over and befuddled
from the all the red wine he had drunk on the short voyage, headed
straight for the Lost Sailor Tavern. He stumbled into the main
room, sat at the first table he came to. Other patrons stared at him,
knowing who he was and where he should be. He growled at them
and they looked away. A scared waiter came to him and he ordered
the best house red and paid a whole gold coin for it.

"But, sir, I cannot change this!"

"Don't worry about it," Dejanus said. "Money won't be worth
anything this time next week." The thought struck him as funny and
he burst out laughing. The waiter scurried away. While Dejanus
waited, the patrons left, one by one, until he was the only guest left
in the whole tavern. The waiter returned with a large flagon of wine
and a mug, then scurried away again.

Dejanus set to with serious intent. He quaffed one mug in three
long swallows, waited only long enough for his insides to warm up,
then started on the second. By the time he was on his third, he was
feeling braver than he had since he led the Great Army to relieve
Captain Urling.

"What did happen to that man?" he wondered aloud. Probably
butchered by the Chetts, just like all the other poor bloody soldiers
under his command. "Not my fault!" he shouted. They were brave
but untrained. Nothing he could have done. He did his best under
the circumstances.

"Orkid's circumstances," he grumbled. "Conspiring against me.
I'll gut the bastard." But first he would have more wine.

"Yes. Today. Do what I should have done a long time ago. I'll
cut him, I'll cut him from bow to stern. I'll spill his guts all over his
bloody, bloody papers and all over his bloody, bloody signatures."
But what of Orkid's friend, the queen? "I'll cut her, too. Slice her
open like Orkid. Then I'll be king." He burped. "And kings don't
have to be afraid of anything."

Powl could read no more. Some secrets should never be known.
He closed the volume he had been translating and pushed it away
from him. It felt like he was pushing away temptation. History was
more than knowledge, he decided; it was incendiary, it was anath-
ema to stability and order. With this understanding, which had
been growing slowly now for several days, came something else,

something he referred to as his conscience even when he knew it was not that simple nor that sacred. He had forgotten what it meant to be a priest, which was to honor God.

I have done everything but honor him, he told himself. But it was not too late. He was still primate, and from now on he would shoulder those responsibilities as best he could. *And one day I will confess. When the war is over, when the kingdom is at peace . . . when I am at peace with myself . . . then I will confess my crime against Giros Northam and against the church, and accept whatever punishment is my due.*

Having made his decision, he gathered together all the notes and translations he had made on the volumes together with the volume he had been working from, left his office, and went straight to the tower of Colanus. He put the volume in its correct place. He considered, for the briefest of moments, destroying the books, but he had no authority to do such a thing, not even as primate. After he left the tower, he went to the church library. Six novices were gathered around the fireplace, reading from texts and parchments. When he entered, they quickly stood up, but he waved them down and, ignoring their looks of amazement, threw his papers onto the fire. He watched to make sure none of his work escaped the flames, smiled at the novices, and started back to his office. On the way he passed the Book of Days. It was open, as always, to its last entry.

He stopped and carefully tore out the pages he had despoiled. Again his novices regarded his actions with amazement, and again, he smiled genially at them. Before leaving, he read again Northam's last entry, the one he wrote the day Powl had murdered him.

I pray for guidance and for the souls of all my people; I pray for peace and a future for all my children; I pray for answers and I pray for more questions. I am one man, alone and yet not lonely. I am one man who knows too many secrets. I pray for salvation.

"I pray for salvation," Powl repeated to himself, and then, for the first time in his life and without hesitation and meaning every single word, he prayed for salvation, and the novices still watching him were farther amazed to see tears roll down his cheeks.

*   *   *

When Orkid arrived at Areava's chambers she was with Harnan Beresard and, he was surprised to see, another Amanite, a tall, thin woman of middle years with the saddest face he had ever seen. Then he noticed that Areava, too, looked grief-stricken. Had the queen already heard about the destruction of the Great Army?

"Orkid, I have terrible news," Areava said.

"I know," he said. "I have just come to tell you."

"I am sorry. It must be dreadful for you."

Orkid blinked. Of course it was dreadful, but why particularly for him? And who was this Amanite woman? He understood then that Areava was not talking about the Great Army's defeat. Which could only mean . . .

"My brother," he said. He turned to the woman. "Who are you?"

"Lingdar. I am . . . was . . . head of King Marin's secretariat."

"Was?"

"I am sorry, Chancellor Gravespear, but your brother is dead."

"I see," he said, his voice barely more than a whisper. His body suddenly felt incredibly heavy. He put a hand on the back of a chair to support himself. "How?"

"Pila has fallen," Areava said.

"Fallen?" He did not understand. Fallen to whom?

"The Chetts have taken Aman," Areava said, and had to stop. She nodded to Lingdar.

"A Chett army invaded the southern deserts, wiping out the Saranah, and then invaded Aman. They were upon us before we realized what was happening. No one believed the Chetts were organized enough to send an army to the east and send another south as well."

"This army, where is it now?" Orkid asked slowly.

"They are making preparations to winter in Aman. I do not know what they will do in spring."

"They let you go?"

"They let anyone go who did not want to stay in Pila."

"Amemun?" he asked, remembering his old friend. "Did he escape?"

"I am not sure, but I think he fell with the Saranah. He was with them when the invasion took place. He may still be alive, but it seems unlikely to me."

Areava came to Orkid and put her arms around him. "The new is almost more than I can bear," she said, "but how much more ter rible it must be for you. Together we have lost almost everything we care for in this world."

He tried to speak, but could not. *I am chancellor,* he told himself, and pushed away the grief that threatened to overwhelm him.

"There is worse news," he said roughly.

Areava let him go and stepped back. "What news is that?"

He held out one of the messages sent by Lynan. She took it from him hesitantly and did not read it right away. He watched as her skin went gray. She knew; she could see it in his eyes.

"How many were killed?" she asked.

"I do not know."

"Lynan will be here soon."

He heard Harnan's sharp intake of breath.

"Yes, I fear so."

"I have lost the north and the west," she said. "I fear that I have lost the whole kingdom because of it."

"I fear that, as well."

She shook her head then straightened, brushed down her clothes as if cleaning away dust and dirt. "No. I will not accept that. I am queen of Grenda Lear, daughter of Usharna Rosetheme. I will not surrender to this rebel and outlaw." She turned to Harnan. "Let the new constable know the situation. What is his name?"

"Arad," Orkid said. He could feel himself take strength from her. He stood up straight, too, and no longer needed to rest against the chair.

"Yes, Arad. Tell him to prepare the palace for a siege. He must get whatever supplies he can from the city. Get whatever warships are in harbor to set sail immediately. They are to go to Lurisia and Storia to pick up reinforcements. Send urgent messages by pigeon to all the provinces still under my authority; they are to raise new regiments forthwith and train them over the winter. Send messages to each of the Twenty Houses; I want every able-bodied noble armed and in the palace to help defend it. Find Olio and tell him to come to me immediately, and his friend the prelate."

Harnan nodded and left, and she turned back to Orkid.

"I know you want to learn as much as possible about the fall of Pila and your brother's death, but I cannot spare you for long—I need you now as I have never needed you before. For the moment, return to your office with Lingdar; she will tell you what she had told me. I will come to see you later this afternoon."

"I am always at your service."

Areava surprised him by smiling then. She patted his hand. "I know, old bear. I know."

Dejanus was in a brave mood, fueled by red wine, defeat, and despair. He tramped his way up to the palace. The guards stared at him as he passed through the main gate, not daring to question him. He went straight to Orkid's office. When the secretary saw him, he almost fainted. He tried to stop Dejanus, but was carelessly brushed aside. He entered the office, and there he was, the architect of all his ills, sitting behind his desk as if he had not a care in the world.

The chancellor himself.

Orkid stared at him for a long moment, then said almost casually, "I have a guest."

For the first time Dejanus noticed the tall woman. She was obviously an Amanite. "Get rid of her," he said.

Orkid said to her, "It's all right. I will talk with you later."

The woman nodded and left, walking sideways around Dejanus to get through the door.

"I thought you would have had the decency to die with your army," Orkid said.

"Oh, you would have liked that."

"You have destroyed us all. Areava is preparing to fight, but we both know she cannot win against Lynan. Not now. He is driven by more than revenge."

"I have come to kill you," Dejanus said plainly, and was surprised how easily he said the words.

"For what reason? Not being a fool and a coward like you?"

"Be quiet!" Dejanus growled.

"Why? You are going to kill me, apparently. What else can you threaten me with?"

"I will tell the queen—"

"What? And how will that affect me if I am dead at your hand? You don't scare me, Dejanus. You never have." He stood up and came around his desk to stand only a hand's span from the general. "You are the weakest, most stupid, most lazy, most terrified man I have ever met."

Dejanus could do nothing. The insults were like blows inside his skull, and his mind reeled from them. But he could do nothing.

Orkid walked around him to leave his office. "I am going to see the queen," he said to his secretary. "Call Constable Arad. General

Dejanus is to be arrested." He walked into the hallway, stopped and came back, tapping his lips with a finger. "In fact, tell Arad that he is unwell; the defeat at Lynan's hand has dislodged his mind. He is not to talk to anyone."

Orkid turned to leave again when Areava herself appeared, her face twisted in fury. "I have been told Dejanus was seen coming here. Where is he?"

Dejanus heard her voice, heard the anger and the hate underneath it. It was not fair. He did not deserve this. He did not deserve to be hated. It was *Orkid's* fault.

"And he will pay," Dejanus whispered. His hand seemed to fall of its own accord on the hilt of his dagger. He looked down, slowly lifted his hand, then rested it again, but this time on the hilt of his sword.

"He is unbalanced, your Majesty," Orkid said quickly. "And dangerous. I would not advise—"

"I'm not asking for your advice, Chancellor," Areava said darkly. "I want to ask the General what he has done with my army . . ." Her voice faded when Dejanus appeared from Orkid's office. The first thing she noticed was the hollowness of his eyes, as if they had sunk into his skull. The second thing was the sword he carried in his right hand.

Orkid saw her gaze shift from him, and he turned quickly on his heel. "Now, man," he said to his secretary. "Get Constable Arad."

"Stop there," Dejanus ordered, and there was enough authority in his voice to make the secretary hesitate. "*I* am constable. I have returned, your Majesty, to take up my proper duties."

"My . . . army . . ." she said hesitantly.

Dejanus shrugged. "Badly trained, your Majesty. Badly equipped. Badly supplied." He smiled. "Brilliantly led. But what was that against so much?"

"There is none left of it?"

"You still have me," he said. He absently scratched his beard with his free hand. "Oh, and my escort. Thirty medium cavalry. Stoians all; alas, not very good cavalry as it turns out."

"I will have your head, Dejanus," she said evenly. "Insane or not, I will have your head."

It was then, for the first time in his whole life, that Dejanus realized he was no longer afraid. "If you are going to take my head, your Majesty, it should be for a greater cause than the loss of your straw army."

"Your Majesty," Orkid said quickly, his voice rising, "you should leave now. Dejanus is insane. There is no telling what he might do." Again he turned to his secretary. "For God's sake, man, get Arad!"

The man scurried off, terrified Dejanus would try and stop him, but the General, still smiling, simply watched him go.

Areava stood her ground.

"Well, here we are, the three of us," Dejanus said. "Fitting. Will you tell her, Orkid, or will I?"

Areava looked at Orkid. "What's he talking about?"

Orkid, keeping his gaze locked on Dejanus, said, "I tell you, your Majesty, he is not himself. I have no idea what he is talking about—"

"I am talking about the murder of Berayma. I am talking about a plot to put you on the throne, Areava, and to blame your brother for the crime of regicide."

"Olio?" Areava asked. "Why Olio . . ." Then she realized what Dejanus meant. "No."

"But yes!" Dejanus said. "And it worked so well! You hated Lynan so much you would believe anything about him so long as it was bad."

"No, that isn't true," she said. "I didn't hate him—"

"Of course you hated him!" Dejanus roared. Orkid moved forward toward Dejanus, but the General raised his sword to keep him away. "Everyone in Kendra knew how much you hated Lynan, no matter how much you protested otherwise. You detested him because his father was a commoner. He sullied your precious Rosetheme bloodline. If it hadn't been for your pride and hate, none of Orkid's plan would have been possible."

Areava saw Orkid's shoulders slump. Her heart felt like ice. "Orkid?"

"It is not true," the chancellor said, but his voice was weak. "None of this is true."

Dejanus rolled his eyes. "Such protestation! That will convince her!" His smile slipped away, replaced by a sneer. "Of course it is true! He and his brother had it planned ten years before your mother died. Berayma could not be allowed to live because he was too close to the Twenty Houses, and everyone knew how much the Twenty Houses hated anyone from the provinces. How could Aman increase its influence if Berayma was king? More importantly since Marin had only one child, and that a son, how could Aman marry into imperial power if Berayma was king?"

"Sendarus?" Areava's hands gripped the Key of the Scepter hanging from her neck. "He married me because of a *plan?*"

Orkid spun around to face her. "No! No, never! Sendarus never knew! He wasn't a part of it . . ." Orkid stopped when he realized what he had said, what he had admitted. "God, Areava, I'm sorry . . ."

"Too late, Amanite," Dejanus said, his voice filled with scorn. "Now tell her the whole truth, how you pinned down Berayma's hands while I drove my dagger straight through his royal neck."

Orkid was still looking at Areava, but his gaze was focused on something else, on a distant point in time when everyone he cared for was still alive, when the plan had seemed to go right, and his life's work had come to fruition. All gone now, all destroyed, and no hope of ever getting it back.

Yet there was one more task to perform, one more duty to fulfill. Orkid swung around, knocking aside the blade still pointing at his chest, and reached for the dagger in Dejanus' belt. Dejanus automatically stepped back before the chancellor could reach him, and tried to bring the sword back into play, but the wine coursing through his body and brain befuddled his and instead all he managed to do was slam the flat of the blade against Orkid's shoulder, driving the Amanite closer toward him. Orkid shouted in pain but had the presence of mind to steal the dagger from the belt before Dejanus could move out of the way again. At the same time he kicked out, connecting with Dejanus' knee, and as the man collapsed, Orkid used all his strength to thrust the blade into his neck.

Dejanus opened his mouth to scream but could only cough on the red tide pouring out of his mouth. Orkid pulled out the dagger and stepped back, and Dejanus went down like a hammered calf, his blood spurting high into the air.

Orkid looked down, and instead of seeing Dejanus' face, he saw Berayma's. All the bile and all the guilt he had been carrying since that terrible night he had slain the king welled up inside him. He gagged, vomited, could not stop it. When the retching finally passed, he hung his head back and cried: "Oh, Lord of the Mountain, what have I done?"

But it was Areava, not his god, who answered. "You have betrayed me," she said.

He turned to face her, wiping his mouth and beard on his

sleeves. "No, Areava, no. I *love* you." He held out the bloody hand still holding the dagger. "All of this was for Grenda Lear. For your mother. For *you*."

Areava went to him quickly. At that moment he thought, crazily, she was coming into his arms, and could not resist when she took the dagger from his hand and plunged it deep into his chest. He folded over her like a broken tree, his arms flopping on her shoulders, his head resting against her cheek. "I loved you," he said with his last breath, his blood frothing in his beard, as Areava twisted the knife and screamed her hate for him.

That night she dressed in her armor and swore not to take it off until her brother Lynan was dead at her feet. She told no one what she had learned about his innocence regarding Berayma's death; that was no longer important. After all, it was Lynan who had invaded his own home with barbarians from the Oceans of Grass, Lynan who had slaughtered Grenda Lear's finest regiments, Lynan who had so cruelly slain her husband and—by that action—slain her birthing daughter. Lynan was the greatest enemy of all, and, if only he could be cut down, the kingdom might yet be made whole.

That night she also ordered a huge pyre to be made in the courtyard, and on that she had thrown the bodies of Orkid and Dejanus. No priest was asked to say a prayer over them. That night she also ordered Lingdar to leave Kendra; she did not care where Lingdar went, so long as it was not to remain within the borders of her kingdom. That night she also was among the first to see above Ebrius Ridge the long line of torches that she knew was the advance troops of Lynan's invading army. Within a day, two at the most, Kendra would be under siege.

"Come, my brother," she said into the night, tightly grasping her Key of Power. "Come to me so we can finish this."

Later she noticed her hands were all bloody. She stared at them, mystified, for she had bathed her whole body after killing Orkid; then she noticed the marks were in the shape of the Key. It was the amulet that was stained, but it was old blood, wine red and brittle, as if it had been on the Key for a year or more.

"It is Berayma's," she said aloud, and found she could finally cry.

35

L YNAN arrived on the outskirts of Kendra at midmorning. From his vantage point on the Ebrius Ridge, it seemed absurdly at peace. The city lay like a complex quilt on the gentle slope from the foot of the ridge down to the sea. The sun sparkled on the harbor and above the waters wheeled kestrels and seagulls. Then he noticed how empty the place looked. Except for one or two fishing vessels and a trader in dry dock, there were no ships, and all the streets were virtually empty. Here and there figures scurried along, ducking from one doorway to another. It was as if the whole city had been depopulated by some terrible plague.

That would be me, he said to himself. *Lynan the plague, never Lynan the conqueror. And never Lynan the king.*

"They will learn," he said aloud. He turned to Ager. "When we left, my friend, did you ever think we would return with an army at our back?"

Ager shrugged. "At the time, I thought the exile was permanent; I did not think we would ever return, with or without an army."

"This city is not built for a siege."

"No. Only the foot of the ridge is fortified. Once past that, even the palace is open to us. Kendra always relied on the provinces to buffer it from any attack, and the strength of its navy."

"I will change that," Lynan said. "I will make this city impregnable."

Ager glanced sideways at Lynan. "Impregnable against what? Once you take Kendra, you will have the whole kingdom. Those provinces in the north most likely to oppose you—Hume and Chandra—you now control, and we learned from Eynon's messenger last night that Aman—the only province in the south that could oppose you—is held for you. Even the kingdom's traditional enemy, Haxus, is in your hands."

"If I can do all of this, someone else can as well," Lynan said. He sat straighter in the saddle, and put a hand over his side. The wound had been cleaned and bandaged tightly, but it still throbbed with pain. The Chetts had draughts that could ease the pain, but they also dulled the senses, and he could not afford that today. He nodded to the wall immediately below them; along its length were finely garbed soldiers, their armor flashing in the sun. "Royal Guards. The best troops in Theare."

Ager snorted. "I once thought so. Before our exile, I trained them for a while. But now I have fought with the Chetts, and seen what they can do with some close order discipline and a short sword in their hands. The Royal Guards will not stop us."

"I would not see the city too damaged," Lynan said.

Ager did not answer.

"I do not want its citizens to hate me."

"As soon as you attack their city, they will hate you," Ager said. "Don't spoil it for the Chetts, your Majesty. They have come a long way for this. Give them a day. After that you can call them off. But give them a day."

Lynan swallowed. "I wonder if the people in Kendra have any idea what is about to happen to them?"

"They think they do, but except for veterans from the Slaver War, no one in this city has seen a battle up close."

They were joined by Korigan. "Your army is in place, your Majesty," she said formally.

"Then start the attack."

Areava stood on the south gallery. From here she could not see Ebrius Ridge and the fluttering pennants of her brother's army. She thought it obscene that his flag carried the Key of Union as its symbol. Before her spread her beautiful city, sacred Kendra, capital of a kingdom that turned out to be more dream than reality. She tried to imprint what she could see on her mind so that whatever happened in the next few hours she would never forget what it was she was fighting for.

It is not between me and Lynan. It is between order and chaos, between civilization and barbarity, between the natural order and usurpation by ambition. With a terrible sadness she realized that whether or not Berayma had been murdered, Lynan inevitably would have become the enemy of Grenda Lear. She wondered if her mother had seen that, and perhaps had given him the Key of Union in the vain hope it would show him what would be lost in a civil war.

There was a polite cough behind her.

"Olio."

"Sister. You look more than formidable in your armor."

She turned to face him. He was dressed in armor, too. "You look strange kitted up for war."

"I feel strange. I think I am too small for the breastplate—"

"No, I mean you are destined for other things. Usharna showed great prescience in giving you the Key of the Heart. Where is it, by the way?"

Olio tapped the breastplate. "Underneath. It did not seem right, resting on armor."

She left the south gallery, hooking one arm through his. As they walked, they listened for a moment to the strange sound of their armor clanking in the empty hallways.

"I'm sorry about Orkid," Olio said, and felt his sister's grip tighten. "I know how close you two were. Imagine Dejanus killing him like that. I knew they were rivals, but I was sure they had been friends once. And then for you to have to save your own life by killing Dejanus! The whole world seems to be upside down."

"Are the hospices ready?" she asked, changing the subject. "I fear we'll be needing them soon."

"We have two ready and fully equipped."

They emerged into the courtyard. Waiting for them there were the knights of the Twenty Houses; some were mounted, but most were on foot. There would be little use for cavalry in a street-by-street fight for the city, the one fact that gave them hope against the Chetts, who traditionally fought on horseback. Among the knights were Duke Holo Amptra, his son Galen, and Queen Charion. Areava felt a pang of jealousy that their armor was so obviously dull and battle scarred and hers was as shiny as a new coin.

"Your Majesty," Duke Amptra greeted her, bowing deeply.

"Dear uncle, the Twenty Houses have outdone themselves."

"We are always ready to serve the throne," he said.

Aye, but not necessarily the monarch, she said to herself, understanding the distinction. *But what of that now?* she asked herself, and thought of the army about to attack them. *Nothing,* she answered herself. *Nothing at all.*

Edaytor Fanhow came through the main gate, carrying his weight well despite his puffing. He bowed to Areava, gave a nod and half a smile to Olio.

"How go the theurgia on the city's behalf, Prelate?" she asked him.

He looked despondent. "Pitifully, your Majesty. Every spell they make is easily defeated by a counterspell from whatever magickers Lynan's army has employed."

"They must be Chetts," Charion said.

"How can they be?" Edaytor asked. The question was rhetorical and no one answered. "They have no formal structure to control and employ magic. I can only think they are using magickers from Haxus, although none of us had any idea they were this far advanced."

"Then we will rely on our strength and courage," Duke Amptra said, but in a subdued voice that almost suggested strength and courage would not be enough.

"I will need your knights as a reserve," Areava told the duke. "Keep some mounted as a flying column."

She made for the gate.

"Where are you going, sister?" Olio asked.

She looked at him in surprise. "To the wall, of course. My place is by my people."

"Your Majesty, you cannot do that!" Galen said, shocked.

"And why not?" Areava demanded frostily.

"You are our leader," he explained. "You cannot afford the luxury of risking your life on the front line. You must stay here and command."

"Command what? What order would you have me give? We hold the enemy at the wall or we lose the city."

Against that there was no argument. Galen and Charion glanced at each other and nodded simultaneously. "Then we will come with you," Charion said. "If the wall is good enough for one queen, it can bear the honor of supporting two."

"And where Charion goes, so go I," Galen said.

Areava smiled at them. "Very well."

"And me!" Olio cried. "Don't leave me out of this!"

"You are the holder of the Healing Key, brother," Areava said.

"And if I fall you must take over. Your place *is* here where you can do the most good."

"But—!"

"No, Olio!" Areava said sharply. "That is a command." She went to him then and held him to her, and whispered in his ear: "Please, sweet brother, obey me in this."

Olio swallowed. When Areava let him go, he stood straight and nodded. "I will obey you in all things, your Majesty."

"You have always been my strength," she said. "Knowing you are here will make what comes easier to bear."

Constable Arad had almost finished inspecting the wall. Everything he had seen of the Royal Guards showed him they were determined to do their duty. They looked splendid in their blue uniforms, although the braid and cloaks and fancy helmets had all been discarded, replaced by good, strong pot helmets, round shields, and breastplates. They were ready with spear and javelin and sword for anything the outlaw Prince Lynan could throw against them. For a while now they had watched the Chett cavalry slowly and cautiously wind its way down the escarpment. Arad had resisted the temptation to carry out a raid against them when they were so vulnerable because he knew there would be archers on top of the ridge ready for just such a sortie, and he had no archers of his own to counter their volleys. By midmorning there seemed to be the equivalent of six or seven regiments in the short space between the wall and the foot of the ridge. Arad could not help wishing Areava or one of her ancestors had fortified the top of the ridge instead of the city itself.

Still, he kept on telling himself, they were horse archers, not infantry, and they would not know the first thing about scaling walls. Then he remembered that the inhabitants of Daavis had probably thought exactly the same thing.

He had just under a thousand Royal Guards at his disposal for the wall, a structure half a league in length. Instead of putting them all on the walkway he kept three companies in reserve in the center, not far from the wall's only gate. He knew Queen Areava was arranging other reserves, but did not know what she intended doing with them.

With luck, he was telling himself, *we will hold long enough for reinforcements to arrive from the southern provinces.* It would take two or three days for the fleet to reach Storia and Lurisia, and then a day to load up with infantry and another two or three days to return. About six days in all. With a lot of luck, yes, he could hold. After all, he was in command of the Royal Guards, the best soldiers on the continent—

The air was suddenly filled with the sound of several thousand bowstrings being loosed at the same time. He jerked his head to the right and saw a dark cloud lifting from the enemy regiments, reach high into the blue sky, stay suspended there for an instant, and then plunge back to earth, straight toward him and his guards. He, like all the others on the wall, watched hypnotized, but something in Arad shook loose and he shouted: "Down!" and brought his shield up over his head as he squatted against the parapets. He could not help squeezing shut his eyes. Arrows clattered against his shield, on the stone work. He peeped out from underneath his shield. He saw two guards down, one dead with an arrow in the neck, the other wriggling on the parapet with an arrow in his stomach.

"Hold that man!" he cried, but too late. The guard was squirming so violently he tipped over the edge. His scream was cut off by the ground below.

Cursing, Arad risked standing up and looking over the parapet, just in time to see another volley loosed. "Down!" he cried again, and this time all on the wall hunkered down beneath their shields.

He wondered how long this would go on for. The Chetts would have to run out of arrows eventually, but the effect on the morale of his guards would be dreadful.

"They are all hiding like turtles," Gudon said happily to Lynan, pointing to the wall.

"Good," Lynan said. He put a hand on Ager's crooked back and Gudon's good one. "Now, my friends."

The two men grinned. They dismounted, an action copied by every Red Hand and every warrior in the Ocean clan, waited for the third volley and then rushed forward twenty paces. They stopped, and when the fourth volley was loosed covered another twenty paces. In this way, the sound of their approach covered by the storm of arrows, they made it to the base of the wall undetected. Another volley and their ladders went up. That was the signal for the archers to lower their bows, and for the assault proper to begin.

"It's stopped!" one of the guards called out, the relief clear in his voice.

Arad was not so sure. He waited a while longer before risking standing up again. He looked over the parapet and found himself face-to-face with a Chett. He screamed involuntarily and whacked down on the face with his spear shaft. The Chett countered it with a short sword and then was over and on the walkway. Arad had time to retreat a step and lower his spear before another Chett appeared. He lunged at the first, impaling him, then desperately tugged at his sword. The second Chett was now over the wall and advancing, but another guard had seen the danger and thrown a javelin. The Chett gasped and fell forward, the javelin wobbling in his spine.

"Up!" Arad yelled. "Up! The enemy is on the wall! The enemy is on the wall!"

The guards still hiding under their shields stood as one just as a tide of Chetts washed over the parapets. Arad flung himself at the closest, knowing something desperate would have to be done or the guards would not be able to hold the wall for the next hour let alone six days. He slashed down with his sword, slicing through a Chett shoulder, tugged the blade free, cut to his right and felt his whole arm jar as the sword missed its soft target and bit into stone. A short sword scraped off his breastplate. He lashed out with his shield, felt it connect with something more yielding than the wall, then jabbed underneath the rim with the sword point. There was a squeal, and a dark figure disappeared off the edge.

Arad knew he was just reacting, and forced himself to think calmly even as part of his brain took over the function of defending himself. He quickly scanned the walkway. The Chetts outnumbered the guards, but the guards were better protected and better armed, and he told himself it was all right after all—his side could deal with this assault. Then he noticed that the greatest concentration of Chetts was near the wall's only gate, the same gate he remembered Sendarus and the kingdom's first army marching through last spring on its way to save Hume from Haxus. If the enemy got control of that and let in the main force of Chetts, nothing would save Kendra. He descended to the ground by the nearest stairway and ran as fast as he could in his armor to the three companies kept in reserve. They were watching the battle on the wall, desperate to join in, but knowing that if they moved now and were needed somewhere else later on, they could lose the city. The company captains received the constable's arrival with huge sighs of relief.

Arad ordered two companies to go directly to the gate and hold it at all costs. The other he led up the walkway he had come down and threw them against the enemy. The fighting was fierce, and the guards used every weapon at their disposal: spears, swords, the edges of their shield, their mailed fists, and their booted feet. The Chetts resisted fiercely, but the Royal Guards were better protected and took greater risks than their foe. Step by step the Chetts were being sandwiched between Arad's force and the two companies that had now reinforced the gate.

We're going to do it, Arad told himself. *We're going to hold the wall.*

Ager realised the Chetts were going to be thrown off the wall soon. Unless the gate was opened and reinforcements let through, then they would have to start all over again, and this time at much greater cost. He managed to fight his way to the gate, arriving at the same time as two companies of Royal Guards. The tide was definitely turning against the Chetts now, and Ager looked around desperately for some way to regain the initiative. He noticed the guards on the walkway above the gate were being led by a short, wide-shouldered man who never lost a fight. He caught a glimpse of the man's face.

Sergeant Arad, he recognized with a shock. A good man. A very good soldier.

Ager managed to retreat from the battle in front of the gate itself and climb back up the walkway. He used all his skill with a short sword to force his way over the gate to the other side. Guards kept on trying to slice and skewer and slash him, but he dealt with each attack coolly, dispassionately, not looking at their faces because he knew some of them had been his friends. There was a sudden break in the fighting, and Ager found himself directly facing Arad himself.

"Sergeant!" he called out.

Arad looked at the crookback with surprise, and then with something like disdain. "Not sergeant, Ager Parner, but constable!"

"Better you than Dejanus who, I'll bet, won the office for murdering Berayma!"

"Don't twist history to justify your betrayal of Grenda Lear!" Arad shouted back. He raised his long sword and advanced on Ager.

Ager waited until Arad was close enough to take a swipe at him and leaped forward, putting himself well inside Arad's reach. He lunged with his own weapon, but found it blocked with the guard's shield.

"I remember your tricks with the short sword," Arad said, and drove down with the pommel. Ager dodged aside, but caught the blow on his right shoulder. He roared in pain. Arad quickly drew his sword arm back to stab Ager, but the crookback leaped forward again and at the same time threw his short sword from his right hand to his left and thrust at the guard's midriff. Arad retreated a step, slashing down with the shield. Ager sidestepped, slipped, and fell on to his knees; Arad's sword whistled above his head. He slashed at the guard's legs, his blade biting deep into the right calf muscle.

Arad shouted, fell back again, but his right leg gave way and he fell forward. Ager's lifted his short sword and drove it up with all his strength. It sank to the hilt into Arad's stomach. The guard gasped, toppled sideways. Ager pulled out his sword and placed it against Arad's throat. "I'm sorry, Sergeant," he said, and pulled the blade across. Blood sprayed across Ager's face as Arad's breath hissed out of the wound.

"The constable is dead!" Ager shouted. "The constable is dead!"

The Royal Guards did not know who had shouted the words, but the effect was immediate. Each guard felt their heart grow heavy and their courage diminish. None retreated, none turned their back to the enemy, but it was enough. Ager charged into them, his sword seeming to take a life with every thrust, and behind him his Chetts redoubled their efforts. The guards started to fall back.

Areava, Galen, and Charion were halfway to the wall when they heard fighting break out. They ran the rest of the way, reaching the battle out of breath and with pools of sweat settling in their boots and gloves. All three quickly assessed the situation and realized how desperate it was. Areava drew her sword, shouted "To me! To me! Kendrans to me!" and charged toward the knot of warriors struggling around the bar to the bronze gate. Galen and Charion drew their weapons, shouted their war cries, and flanked the queen as she drove into a knot of Chetts trying to get their hands on the bar to slip it out of its bracket. Areava hewed right and left, not waiting to finish off those she wounded and maimed but pushing on to free the gate of every enemy. She could hear the muffled sounds of swearing and screaming warriors all around her and above her on the walkway. The guards, aware the queen herself was now among them, regained their courage and morale and started fighting back as if they were suddenly possessed by demons. The Chetts could not hold out against them, and started losing ground.

Areava finally reached the bar. She had to stop to regain her breath and loosen her muscles, especially in her sword arm which felt as heavy as lead. Galen and Charion, still flanking her, had no such trouble and the queen looked at them in envy. A guard saw she had stopped and hurried to her, bowing deeply. "Your Majesty, are you all right? You are not wounded?"

Areava surprised herself by laughing. "No. Just tired. I'm not used to personally smiting my enemies."

The guard flashed a smile in return. "It is joyous work!" he cried, and left to rejoin it.

"That's the spirit," she said, more to herself than anyone else. She shook her right arm one more time, slightly changed the grip on her sword, and stood away from the gate so she could see up to the walkway. Heavy fighting was still going on up there, and it seemed to her that the Royal Guards were getting the worst of it. Then she saw Ager.

"Captain Parmer," she said, and watched in admiration as the crookback moved almost magically to dismay his enemies.

"I remember him from Daavis," Charion said.

"I remember him from long before then," Galen added with distaste. "Let us finish him here and now."

Lynan and Korigan watched the progress of the Red Hands and the Ocean clan on the walls. Their hearts rose and fell with the sway of battle, and Lynan found it almost impossible to bear.

"They must open the gate soon," he said.

"They will," Korigan said, her voice unreasonably calm.

"Look! More guards! That little one leading them is a demon!"

"He fights very well." She considered asking for her best archers to shoot at him, but the distance was just a little too far, and the chance of hitting one of their own just a little too great.

Lynan heard tramping behind him and turned to see that a regiment of Chandran infantry had arrived, tired from their long descent from the ridge.

"Infantry?" he thought aloud. He wheeled his horse around and approached one of their officers. "It's a hard climb down," he said.

The officer nodded, not really sure what to say to this formidable looking man.

"Good training, however," Lynan continued.

"Training, your Majesty?"

"For climbing up," Lynan said. "Tell your men to get ready." He pointed to the wall. "They're going up there. Leave your spears behind. Just swords."

The officer saluted. "Yes, your Majesty."

A short while later the regiment was ready, dressed in a long line. As Lynan dismounted Korigan said, "What do you think you're doing?"

"I'm going to lead an assault on the walls of Kendra."

"You're wounded."

"I'm king," he replied. "My place is up there with my warriors."

"Your place is here, with your army. Ager and Gudon know what they are doing."

"No doubt. So do I."

"Then I'm coming with you," she said and dismounted to be by his side.

He frowned in thought. "Good idea, but I think you should bring your own warriors."

"There are no other infantry here."

"No, but there are several thousand archers. If we get them on top of the wall, imagine what they could do to the enemy on the other side. We might not need to open the gate then."

Korigan did not even reply, but hurried off to order two banners of horse archers to dismount and line up behind the Chandran infantry. When Korigan was by his side again, Lynan started walking forward, and three thousand warriors followed him. Halfway to the wall he started to trot, ignoring the pain in his side, and by the time he reached one of the ladders he had enough momentum to leap past the first five rungs. He did not wait to see how close behind the others were, but quickly climbed to the wall, leaped over, drew his sword, and ran along the walkway to the gate.

Gudon finally reached Ager, something he had been trying to do ever since he and his Red Hands had climbed the wall. The resistance from the guards had been fierce, and it seemed to Gudon that he was losing two warriors for every guard that went down, but when the cry went up that their constable had fallen, the odds shifted in favor of the Chetts. At last, Gudon and the Red Hands broke through the last knot of resistance on the eastern part of the walkway; he ordered half of them down the nearest stairway to secure the gate itself and then led the other half to reinforce Ager. When he finally managed to find a place in the line next to his friend he said, "You're a hard man to find."

"It's my size," Ager said, and grunted as he used the flat of his sword to knock out a guard, then used his feet to kick him over the side. "It makes me hard to find in a crowd."

"Truth," Gudon said. "Duck."

Ager ducked and Gudon stabbed a guard in the face; as the man fell back, Ager stood erect and stabbed him in the stomach.

The fighting seemed to become more intense then and neither had any breath to talk. When their sword arms were too sore and tired to move anymore, they fell back and let others take their place. They found a place against the parapet to rest for a moment. They flexed their fingers to rid them of cramp. There was a commotion below and they leaned over to see what was happening, but the walkway stopped them seeing anything.

Then Ager heard a too-familiar voice, one from his not-too-distant past. "To me! To me! Kendrans to me!"

"Fuck," he swore under his breath.

Gudon looked at him with concern. "What is wrong, my friend?"

"Areava! She's here!"

He tried to lean over farther and Gudon had to pull him back.

"We've run out of time," Ager told him. "We have to win up here—now!"

He drew his sword, pushed his way back to the front of the battle on the walkway, Gudon by his side, and redoubled his efforts. The Royal Guards fell back or were killed where they stood. For a moment, Ager thought they just might do it, just might clear the walkway completely before she could make a difference. Then he heard the victory cries of the guards below and knew they had just lost their chance of capturing the gate. A short while later he watched her coming up the stairway, flanked by two other fighters, both of whom he recognized. She did not rush but moved with the calm determination he remembered she always used. *Just like her mother,* he said to himself, and the thought made him uncomfortable. The surviving guards rallied around Areava, and more guards were coming up the walkway from down below now that the gate had been secured. Ager readied himself for the onslaught, exchanged a quick glance with Gudon and could see he was thinking the same thing. Neither of them were going to get out of this alive.

Areava could not believe her eyes. Instead of retreating before obviously superior numbers, Ager and his determined friend charged them, the remaining Chetts crowding close behind. Royal Guards rushed to stand in front of her, but the enemy assault was so desperate that most of them were cut down. More guards pushed their way forward, and in the end their numbers started to tell. The fighting became such a close affair that swords no longer had room to swing, and soldiers had to stab to strike their opponents. Then some of Royal Guards behind the front line used spears to jab at the faces of the Chetts. The enemy took a step back, then another, and Areava knew she had them.

Suddenly, the air was rent by the most horrific war cry, more animal than human in its ferocity. Areava could not help twisting around to see what had caused it, but there were ten or more guards in her way. She pushed her way through them and saw, running toward her, her brother. The face was different, terribly scarred, but it was Lynan. She snarled like a great bear and charged forward herself before anyone could stop her.

Their swords struck and the sound rang across the battlefield. The expert training they had received all their lives from childhood automatically took over their actions. For those who watched it was like a dance, formalized, ornate, but also a dazzling display of violence. The swords moved in a blur, thrust and parry, slash and counterslash, slid along each other in a metallic hiss, whirred and clanged. White sparks flew off their swords, and blue sparks flew off the Keys of Power around their necks.

For a long while no one dared intervene. Galen and Charion were the first to come to their senses and rushed to help Areava; but Korigan reached Lynan's side and with her a handful of Chandran infantry, fresh and eager to prove their mettle. Over the gate, Ager and Gudon renewed their attack on the Royal Guards. Now the battle swung back in the invaders' favor. Wherever there was a clear space on the walkway, a Chett archer would take position and start shooting arrows into the guards below still trying to reach the battle on the walkway. This close, the archers did not miss, and the guards fell by the dozen, pierced two or three times by short black arrows.

Then Lynan, more experienced in combat, saw a chance against

Areava. In parrying one of his blows she raised her sword arm a fraction too high, and before she could lower her arm he had moved his blade underneath hers and then lunged. She saw the danger and twisted aside, but his short sword slid under her breastplate and stabbed her near the pelvis. She yelled in pain and fell back. Lynan pulled his arm back to deliver a killing blow, but Galen and Charion hauled her back out of the way as guards took their place in the line.

"Let me go!" Areava cried. "I'll kill him! I'll kill him!"

"No, your Majesty," Galen said. "He will kill you." He lifted her breastplate to inspect the wound. The cut was deep, but the blood was bright red and seeped out. He looked up at Charion. "She will live. Get her back to the palace."

"What are you going to do?" Charion asked.

"Give you time to get away."

"No!" Areava cried. "Don't take me away! Let it end here one way or the other!" She tried to fight them but, between her exhaustion and the wound, could not push them away.

Charion looked at the queen and then at Galen. "I don't want to lose you," she said.

"I know," Galen replied.

"If you die, I will be queen of nothing."

Galen shook his head. "You will always be queen of Hume; nothing can ever change that."

He leaned forward quickly to kiss her, then stood up. "Get Areava out," he said and rejoined the fight.

Charion put Areava's arm around her shoulder and started moving her back to the closest stairway. A guard with a bloody head wound saw what was happening and took Areava's other arm. Between them, they managed to get Areava off the wall. They rested a moment and then started moving away from the battle and back toward the palace.

Lynan was furious. Areava was escaping him and this bloody nobleman was stopping him from getting to her. No matter what he did, Galen Amptra seemed able to read his mind and block him. Feeding the fury was the pain his wound was causing him, but there was simply nothing Lynan could do about it. In the end it was a common foot soldier who did the deed; a Chandran swordsman, finding his opposite dropping from sheer exhaustion, saw an opening to his right. He was not aware the enemy thus exposed was

Galen Amptra, one of the great nobles and soldiers of Grenda Lear, he only knew that there was a raised arm, a loose breastplate and an instant to make a decision. The Chandran thrust sideways with all his strength, and his sword pierced skin and muscle, slipping between two ribs to rip open blood vessels and one of Galen's lungs. Galen dropped to his knees and Lynan saw his chance. He slashed at his enemy's neck and sheared right through. The head leaped back and was lost, the body slumped down and slid in its own blood off the walkway, and fell to the ground below.

Galen's loss finished the demoralization of the guards started by Areava's wounding. They threw down their weapons and fled, and the Chetts and Chandrans fell on them like grass wolves until there were none left alive on the wall. Before reinforcements could arrive from elsewhere in the city, Lynan ordered the gate open, and the rest of his banners rode through. They turned left and right until all the ground behind the wall was filled with them.

They waited.

"My lord?" Korigan asked Lynan.

Lynan nodded

Korigan grinned mirthlessly, and gave the order to take the city.

The priests were trying to save the library. They had formed two chains, the first passing buckets of water from a well to the inferno—started by fire arrows—raging inside the church wing of the palace, the second passing books and parchments in the other direction to an ancient wine cellar.

Powl and Father Rown were in the library choosing the most precious volumes to be saved first. There was so much to move and so little time that they knew many would be lost. They could hear the fire not far away, crackling and whooshing as it moved like a live thing closer and closer to the library.

Powl had almost reached the Books of Days and had made the decision to pass them by. What use the daily thoughts of primates past when all the knowledge of the continent was at risk? The thought made him stop. He paused in the action of passing on the atlas and almanac of Agostin, a book he knew was one of Queen Areava's favorites.

Not just the daily thoughts, he told himself. In a way they represented the distilled knowledge of all the learning represented by the library, especially as it applied to their lives as priests and not simply men. He skipped the intervening books and went straight to the Books of Days, and quickly, urgently, started passing them out.

A new sound was added to the fire, a strange whistling. Arrows broke through the library windows, sending glass in every direction. Some of the priests left the line and Powl had to order them back.

"Not long, Fathers, not long! Hold on to your courage and pray to God!"

More arrows, appearing from nowhere as if they were cast by God himself. One priest fell with an arrow in his leg, and two of his fellows had to carry him out. There was an explosion from the hallway and smoke belched into the library. Now even Powl knew it was time to go. They had saved what they could.

"Flee!" he shouted. "All leave the library!"

There was an ordered rush for the exit. Powl was joined by Father Rown and together they made sure all the priests got out safely.

"Now you, Father," Powl said to Rown. He spied the last Book of Days, the one that should have held his contributions. He went to collect it.

"Your Grace?" Rown called out.

"I'll be with you in a moment." He picked up the book and put it under his arm, then suddenly lurched forward, a moan escaping from between his lips. He fell against Rown.

"Your Grace?" Rown asked, catching the primate in his arms. "What is wrong?" Then he felt the arrow in the primate's back. He looked at it and almost fainted.

"I need help!" he cried out, but there was no one left in the library. There was a terrible sigh and fire took hold of the farthest shelves.

Rown lifted Powl in his arms and staggered out of the library. Powl was unconscious, limp in his arms like a sack of grain, but somehow Rown found the strength to reach the courtyard. There, other priests realized what must have happened and rushed to Rown's aid. They carried him out of the church wing to the great hall where other wounded and may of the dying had been brought, and laid Powl down on his side. The primate was still breathing when a healing priest and a magicker came to inspect the wound. They looked grim, and shook their heads at Father Rown.

"Oh, God, no." He held the primate's hand in his own and prayed for a miracle. Other priests gathered around and bowed their heads in prayer.

Powl's eyes flittered open. Rown could see them trying to focus on his face. "Father Rown?" His voice was barely more than a whisper.

"I'm here, your Grace."

"Have to tell you. Have to tell you about Colanus."

"Colanus? I don't understand . . ."

Suddenly the primate's eyes focused clearly on Rown's face. "No," he said, his voice stronger in the last flush of life. "I want to tell you about Primate Northam."

"Northam?"

Powl grabbed the sleeves of Rown's cloak and tried to lift himself off the ground. "Father, I *killed* him."

"No," Rown said, smiling sadly. "You've been hurt, your Grace; you don't know what you're saying."

"I suffocated him because he wanted you to succeed him instead of me."

Rown felt his heart skip a beat. "Me?"

Powl let go of Rown's cloak and slumped back against the floor. A thin line of blood trickled from the corner of his mouth.

"You have to know that Northam never told . . ." Powl stopped and frowned.

"Told you what?" Even as he asked the question, he knew what Powl meant. If Northam did not want Powl to succeed him, then he never passed on the name of God. He looked at Powl in horror. "You don't know, do you?"

Powl laughed, which made him cough. More blood seeped from his mouth. "I'm a fool. It was there all the time. Old Giros *did* write it down."

"Wrote what down?" Rown urged.

"Listen, Father," Powl said, his voice fading again. "God has a name, and the name is everything that God can be." He coughed again. His eyes closed and the skin around his cheeks seemed to pull back. "A single word reveals all there is to know about God."

"What is it?" Rown asked. "Your Grace, do you know the name of God?"

Powl whispered a word, but Rown did not hear it.

"Please, your Grace, can you tell me?" He leaned over so his ear was right next to Powl's mouth when the primate whispered the word a second time.

Rown sat back heavily. "Of course," he said, astounded. *How could it have been anything else?*

Powl's chest stopped moving. Rown reached out and closed the primate's eyes. He said a prayer for Powl's soul, but knew with certainty he would not need it. In the end, God had given him what he had obviously wanted more than anything else. Forgiveness.

The healing priest returned and, when he saw that Powl had passed away said a quick prayer as well. When he finished he looked up in horror. "Father! Father! The name of God! Did he pass on the name of God?"

Rown smiled and gently placed a hand on the priest's shoulder. "Indeed," he said, and then to himself: *Salvation*.

The most bitter fighting took place in the palace courtyard. Duke Holo Amptra and the knights repelled every assault at great cost to the enemy.

Areava refused to be taken inside the palace. She would go no farther than the steps that led to the great hall from where she could watch fighting in the courtyard. Olio was called for to heal her, but Areava would not let him.

"The wound is not fatal," she told him. "And I would be ashamed for this wound to be healed when so many of my people must suffer without any hope at all."

"Sister, I cannot heal every wound; you know what happened to me last time I did that. But you are the queen. The people need you to be whole—"

"No, brother. They need Grenda Lear to be whole."

She would not discuss it any farther, even when Edaytor Fanhow pleaded Olio's case, promising to make sure Olio did not harm himself.

Areava kept Charion by her side at all times. Charion shed no tears for the death of Galen, and did not pretend that he could somehow have survived the battle for the wall, but Areava could see she was grieving deeply. During a lull in the fighting they told old Duke Amptra what had happened. He nodded grimly and returned to his knights, but he seemed to age another ten years.

"What will happen now?" Olio asked Areava.

"Now we wait for Lynan," Areava said. "I do not know what his plans are, but I do know we cannot resist him." She looked at her brother and said sadly, "I have lost the kingdom."

Lynan stayed near the wall until it was almost sunset. His wound had been so aggravated by the fighting that he found it al-

most impossible to walk. Korigan reported to him that except for
the palace, the city was now entirely under his control.

"Do we know who is in the palace?" he asked.

"We know that Areava was taken there," Korigan replied, "and
that some knights still defend it. Parts of the palace have burned
down. We do not know who is alive and who is not. Perhaps Areava
was slain in the fighting."

"Let us finish this," Lynan said. "Get me a horse."

A mare was brought to him and he was helped into the saddle.
With Korigan, Ager, and Gudon by his side, he rode down from the
wall to the palace. On the way he saw what his Chetts had done to
many of the houses, and what they had done to those who resisted
them, and it filled him with a great sadness. He saw Kendrans looking out at him as he passed, fear on their faces, and that made him
feel sad as well. Yet when he finally reached the palace he had fled
from the night Berayma was murdered, he found he felt nothing at
all. It was almost as if everything that had happened since then had
happened to someone else. There was no sense of victory, just exhaustion. Chett archers blocked the way to the courtyard, letting no
one in or out. When they saw Lynan approach, one of them came to
report.

"There are a few knights left, your Majesty, and Areava directs
them. We can finish them off with one more attack, I am sure of it."

Lynan carefully dismounted and approached the entrance, his
Red Hands bustling around him. He could see the top of the palace
over the wall that surrounded it. Black smoke billowed into the sky
from the west wing. That would be the church library, he thought
sadly. The bodies of guards and knights littered the streets outside
the wall. Any dead Chetts had been carried away by their comrades.
He could hear the buzzing of flies, and seagulls fought over carrion.
Above them all hovered kestrels, sometimes diving down to take
the tastiest morsels.

"That is what we have become," he said aloud.

Korigan rode next to him and dismounted to stand by his side.
"Lynan, your army is ready to finish it," she said, "Just as you
wish."

"I do not think I need to finish it with my army," he said slowly.
"The enemy . . . my sister . . . must know it is over."

"But she is queen on your throne!" Korigan said, surprised by
Lynan's change of heart. "You cannot be king while she lives!"

And that is what I want, isn't it? he asked himself. Had not

Kumul and Jenrosa and hundreds of Chetts died for his cause? And had he not decided when he crossed back to the east from the Oceans of Grass that his cause was winning the throne of Grenda Lear? Or had all those people, all those he cared for, died for nothing?

But still he hesitated. Korigan stood in front of him and held his head between her hands. "As I love you, and as I know you love me, I tell you with all my heart that I wish there was some other way for this to end. But I do not believe the future can bear the weight of both Areava and yourself. It will tear the continent apart."

He nodded, and the breath shuddered out of his lungs. "It is time." He walked back to his horse and mounted. He unsheathed his saber and held it in his right hand, tightened the reins in his left. Korigan, Ager, and Gudon took their places on either side of him.

Ager cleared his throat. "Lynan, before the first battle we fought in the east, I asked you if you were prepared for what comes after. I am asking you again."

This time Lynan answered truthfully. "I don't know," he said.

Ager shrugged. "That's what I thought." He looked at his friends and was filled with a sudden grief he could not at first understand, but then realized it was because Kumul and Jenrosa were not here as well, here at very end as they should have been. "Oh, fuck it," he said. "Give the order, Lynan."

Lynan raised his saber. The Red Hands drew their weapons, the archers before the entrance to the courtyard drew their bows.

"Now!" he shouted, and kicked his horse into a gallop.

For Olio it started with a rain of arrows, black darts that rose over the wall and landed, clattering, on stone and armor.

"Help me up," Areava ordered, and Olio and Charion put her arms around their necks and lifted her to her feet. She grunted in pain, then brought her arms by her side. "I am fine now," she said. "Look out for yourselves."

All three drew their swords. Before them the knights readied their own weapons, the sound of their clanking armor echoing around the courtyard.

Another volley of arrows, and then came the cavalry led by the youngest of the Rosethemes, pale and slight and filled with a terrible fury.

Olio, seeing him, remembered him, and the shock of it was paralyzing.

*   *   *

Lynan was crying before his horse entered the courtyard. Tears blurred his eyes, and rage filled his heart. He smashed into the first line of knights, sending several tumbling to the ground, and brought down his saber so hard onto a helmet that the metal buckled underneath and the head within was crushed. Almost immediately his horse was struck and it fell to its knees, already dead. Lynan struggled to loose his feet from the stirrups. A poor knight, dressed in nothing but a coat of chain mail and a pot helmet, came at him with an ax. Lynan deflected the first swing, got his right foot loose, ducked under the second swing, got his left foot loose, blocked the third swing and kicked the knight between the legs, and as he went down Lynan's saber sliced open the back of his unprotected thighs. The knight squealed and rolled in pain. Lynan ignored him and threw himself at a better-armed opponent wielding a long sword with practiced strokes; three dead Red Hands already lay before him. But Gudon was there before Lynan, ducking under the longer reach of the enemy and thrusting the point of his short sword straight into the man's face. The knight swallowed the point and collapsed in a fountain of blood.

Another ax-wielding knight attacked Lynan, but before he could deliver a stroke, two Red Hands were on top of him, cutting, slicing, slaying. Lynan moved on as if he was part of an irresistible tide, his Red Hands overwhelming the few defenders left. The courtyard became slippery with blood as the knights retreated to the steps in front of the great hall to protect their queen. Areava and her two companions did not wait for the onslaught, but charged down the steps and into the fray. Lynan tried to reach her, but knights threw themselves in the way, lashing out with swords and mailed fists. Lynan started to wonder if the battle would ever end. He could not breathe without sucking in air misted with blood, and his nostrils were filled with the scent of hot metal as blades and armor sparked. His foot slipped, and he instinctively put out his hands to arrest his fall, his fingers landing in the face of a dead knight. He struggled back to his feet, feeling nauseous, feeling the fighting had stopped.

It's all over, he thought, and then realized that was not the case. Both sides had just pulled back from each other to rest. Chett warriors stood resting on their weapons, panting like dogs, trying to get one clean lungful of air. The surviving knights, panting even more heavily, pulled back to the steps, Areava behind them.

Afterward, Lynan was never sure what made him do it, but he lifted his head back and shouted at his sister: "Surrender!"

The courtyard fell silent; even the panting stopped.

Lynan stepped forward, heedless of his own safety. "Areava, surrender to me!"

All eyes rested on the queen, all ears waited for her answer.

Olio had fought without knowing how he did it. He recognized the moves he had been taught in training, but he had no real control over it. While he blocked attacks and parried, while he sidestepped as he needed to and struck where he could, he could not rid his mind of the memories that flooded in, of Lynan when he was a child and then as a young man. After waking from his insanity, he had not remembered anything about Lynan, had felt nothing for him except a kind of abstract repulsion because of his assault on Grenda Lear; but on seeing Lynan in the flesh his real feelings had returned, and he remembered he loved this man, this pale demon who was trying to kill their sister.

Then he found himself on the steps to the great hall, his sister behind him, and there was an unexpected lull in the fighting. Knights crowded before him. Charion jostled to his right.

"Surrender!"

His brother stepped forward from among the red-handed Chetts. "Areava, surrender to me!"

He looked over his shoulder, saw the indecision in his sister's face. Then she said: "I am queen of Grenda Lear! I am sworn to defend the throne!"

"You have defended it, sister, but you can do nothing more. Surrender to me, acknowledge me as king, and all of you will be spared. I swear it."

Olio found himself hoping she would accept it. He did not want her to die. He did not want to have to try and kill Lynan. He wanted it all to end. He glanced between Lynan and Areava, and he saw the expression change on his sister's face, saw the determination change to exhaustion, and saw the hope in Lynan's eyes. And then he saw the Chett female, tall and regal. She was moving to the back of the crowd and the Chetts parted for her, bowing. Her walk was determined, stiff. He felt the Key of the Heart warm against his skin and saw a blue light emanating from the top of his breastplate. He noticed his sister and brother's Keys were glowing, as if in anticipation of being finally joined together once more. The Chett female said something to one of the archers, and the archer raised his bow, an arrow already nocked.

"No," Olio said, and then louder: "No!"

All eyes turned to him and he pointed to the archer, but too late.

Ager could not believe his ears. *Why now, Lynan?* he wondered. *Too much has happened. There are too many ghosts between you and your sister for peace between you to mean anything.*

Yet he found himself hoping Areava *would* surrender, that the slaughter could stop. Then he heard a figure in front of the queen cry out "No!" and he recognized Olio. The prince was pointing toward the back of the Chetts and Ager looked over his shoulder, but he was too short to see over the crowd. He heard a shocked cry from those in front of him and he turned back. At first he did not know what had happened. Areava took a step forward and stopped. That was when he saw the arrow in her chest. It had pierced the Key of the Scepter and her heart. Her eyes were wide open in shock. Her sword dropped from her hand, clattering on the steps.

Olio and a short woman in armor grabbed for her, but she fell backward landing heavily.

For a moment nothing happened, and then, as one, the knights roared in fury and hatred and charged.

Ager barely had time to react. He jumped forward to help protect Lynan, but Gudon and several Red Hands beat him to it.

The Chetts were pushed back by the ferocity of the attack, but they were as skilled as the knights and far more numerous, and slowly, inevitably, the defenders were cut down where they stood. A gap appeared between Ager and the steps. He saw Olio and the short woman he now recognized as Queen Charion bent over Areava. He ran forward. Charion heard him coming and raised her sword, but he knocked it aside and then slammed his fist into her jaw. She fell back, unconscious. Olio turned to him and his eyes widened with recognition. "Captain Parmer, I can heal her!" He pulled the Key of the Heart from beneath his armor and held it up to Ager. "I can heal my sister just as my mother healed you! Please, let me save her!"

Ager hesitated, his one good eye drawn to the glowing Key, and in that moment could see a future where Areava was alive, where the three surviving children of Usharna found a way to overcome their past; then the illusion evaporated and he saw only the blood on the steps.

"Please, Ager!" Olio begged.

Ager shook his head. "Forgive me," he said, and brought the hilt of his sword down on Olio's skull.

The prince crumpled; Ager knelt and felt for a pulse in his neck. He found one and sighed in relief. Then, reluctantly, he looked down at Areava.

Her eyes moved, focused on Ager's face. He put his hand on the arrow still protruding from her chest. Her lips parted and she said in a sigh, "End it."

He nodded, put his other hand over her eyes, and pushed the arrow through.

LYNAN gave Kendra to his Chetts for one day. He left the city and rode to the top of Ebrius Ridge. Korigan, Gudon, and a small escort of Red Hands came with him. He had wanted Ager to come, too, but the crookback was nowhere to be found. The last anyone had seen of him, he was by the bedside of Prince Olio.

From the ridge, Lynan looked down and could see a dozen fires burning in the city. Even this high up he could hear the screams of the dying as the Chetts slew those who tried to stop their looting. He wanted to turn the horse around and ride away, and not stop until he came to the Oceans of Grass and the kind of freedom he knew he would never experience again. He had not understood when he crossed back to the east what he was going to lose, that more than the lives of his friends would be sacrificed to secure the throne.

But Lynan could not turn away. All of this was his doing. He could no longer blame Orkid and Dejanus for all the suffering now experienced by the people of Kendra.

He stayed on the ridge until the sun set. For a moment the dying light blazed off the four Keys of Power hanging around his neck. Kestrel Bay shimmered. When night came, the stars were blotted out by smoke rising from the city.

Korigan dismounted and took the reins of his horse. "Your Red Hands have made a camp for you. Let me take you there."

Lynan looked out over Kendra, aglow with fire, and said in a voice so quiet that only Korigan could hear, "What have I done?"

"Why my lord," Korigan replied, as Gudon led his horse away from the ridge, "you have destroyed a kingdom. And now . . ." she sighed deeply, ". . . and now you must build another."

John Marco

The Eyes of God

"THE EYES OF GOD isn't just about warfare, magic, and monsters, although it's got all of those: it's about the terrible burden of making choices, and the way the seeds of victory are in every failure, and tragedy's beginnings are in every triumph."
—Tad Williams

Akeela, the king of Liiria, determined to bring peace to his kingdom, and Lukien, the Bronze Knight of Liiria, peerless with a sword, and who had earned his reputation the hard way, loved each other as brothers, but no two souls could be more different. And both were in love with the beautiful Queen Cassandra. But unknown to anyone, Cassandra hid a terrible secret: a disease that threatened her life and caused unimaginable strife for all who loved her. For Akeela and Lukien, the quest for Cassandra's salvation would overwhelm every bond of loyalty, every point of honor, because only the magical amulets known as the Eyes of God could halt the progress of Cassandra's illness. But the Eyes could also open the way to a magical stronghold that will tear their world apart and redefine the very nature of their reality.

0-7564-0096-1

To Order Call: 1-800-788-6262